The Divine Apprentice
By Allen J Johnston

ISBN 978-0-9912664-0-1

Cover created by: Amber Johnston
Editor: Ken Poff
Editor: Holly Schaffer

Acknowledgements:

I would like to acknowledge the many people in my life that took the time to help with this dream of bringing you this book. First, I would like to thank my mother, Judy, who warned me that this is not her genre. When she finally decided to read it, she could not put it down. I cannot thank Ken Poff and Holly Schaffer enough for their efforts. They spent much of 2013 reading the first, second and third book in this series. Their insight and comments definitely helped make this book what it is. I want to thank my amazing wife, Amber, for putting so much time into this I would almost consider her a co-author. However, she insists that this is my work and she just helped. She was part of this every step of the way. I cannot say thank you enough to my daughter, Kendra. This amazing angel sent down in the form of my daughter is the reason this book is finally seeing the light of day. She is one of my biggest supporters and makes me see life for the beauty it is.

Prologue

Judeen glided into the room silently and froze as she watched the Blue Flame of the Divine dance across her father's hands. The Divine Power made her uncomfortable, and when her father used it, she got knots in her stomach. The way his eyes changed, appearing as though they were large, black marbles while he was using his special gift unnerved her more than she could say.

"Must I extinguish this life?" Zayle asked of no one as he let the flames drift away. He picked up the child and held him at arm's length while studying him.

"But Father, he is just a baby," Judeen said as she looked at her child in worry. Zayle startled at her voice.

"Daughter," Zayle said with a heavy heart, "I understand, but you know how my gift works. You know how the Divine works. If I could change it, I would, but I can't. I have explained his future to you many times. Do we dare take this chance?" he asked as he agonized over what he must do. "The Divine gift he receives makes him the most powerful among our kind. Judeen, he can draw on unlimited amounts of the Divine, and this makes him too dangerous."

"You said your gift is not always accurate," Judeen said as she struggled not to plead.

"What I said was, the future it shows me is not necessarily the one that will come to be. There are many possibilities. The one I see is the one that is most likely, but I have seen others."

"Others?" Judeen asked hopefully.

"I have seen a future where Kade is not corrupted by the

power. Daughter, as much as you dislike the Divine, your son has the potential to be the strongest of us and save our kind, or...." Zayle stopped, not willing to finish for fear of crushing her heart. "Those with great power struggle greatly. He may be too powerful, but he also may be our only hope," he said as he let out a long sigh and slowly lowered the baby back into the crib. "I have seen futures where he cannot even wield the Divine."

"Father, are you not able to vanquish this evil yourself?" Judeen asked as she wrapped her arms around herself. For something to be too powerful for her father, one of the most talented Chosen in existence, did not bode well.

"It hides from my gift. It makes no sense," Zayle said as he spun through the moves for the Divine Fire and studied it closely once again. After a moment, he snapped his hands closed and the blue fire drifted away. The black in his eyes receded like a liquid sliding to the center of his eye and then the normal brown shown through. Zayle ground his teeth hard and his hands were balled into tight fists of anger. "I have to make a choice, and the future I need to see is hidden from me."

"Father," Judeen said as she laid a gentle hand on his forearm, "you will do the right thing. I have faith in you," she said, knowing how much having a grandson meant to him.

She leaned over the crib, kissed her boy on the forehead and then turned to leave her father to his decision. She knew Zayle suffered greatly over this dilemma, but she trusted his judgment...no matter what he decided. She did her best to keep from crying as she walked from the room and turned to the right to walk down the hall. Had she turned left, she would have seen her husband, Garig, standing as still as a statue, taking in everything that was going on.

Zayle studied the child for a long time as he struggled to do what he must. Just when he was certain on the course of action to be taken, he would hesitate with his hands over the crib while looking into those innocent eyes. He hated his gift for showing him what was to come.

He brought the Divine Fire to life again and studied it for several long seconds. He snapped his hands shut and made up his mind. He had his doubts, but if they were to discover the danger that approached, Kade was to be their best chance. Zayle reached for the boy and lifted him once again as he looked deep into his eyes. If he had known Garig was standing in the hall, he would not have spoken, but believing he was alone, he uttered five words that would haunt Garig for the rest of his life.

Five years later...

"Father, it has been too long since your last visit. Why can you not come more often?" Judeen asked as she sat next to Zayle on a bench while the two of them watched Kade play.

"The more contact I have with you, the more I put you in danger. After this visit, the next time I return, it will be for the boy. I have my reasons, but it is imperative that I am very careful. I must be or everything I have worked for will be for naught."

It was a cruel joke the Divine played on him, giving him a gift that was more like a curse. It tortured him with visions that he did not dare alter. It showed him his daughter suffering terribly while being brutally beaten and he could not change it...not if he wanted her to live. The powerful Master Chosen wished with all his heart that he could keep her safe, but he knew if he altered her future and his grandson's, they would all suffer a terrible fate. He could not see what the evil was, but he knew his daughter crossed paths with it, and when she did, Kade would be the one to learn of it. For now, he knew he had to trust his gift. He clenched his jaw against the vision of his daughter hanging bruised and beaten at the top of a wooden structure and stood to walk out into the yard.

"How would you like to see something?" Zayle asked.

"What is it?" Kade asked as he looked on in wonder at the man in the long, flowing cloak that brushed the ground as he walked. With a gleam in his eye, Zayle brought the Blue Flame of the Divine to life. Kade's eyes grew as big as saucers.

"Whoa," Kade said as he stared in wonder. "Can you do more?"

"I can," Zayle said, and with that, he gracefully flowed through thirteen moves and threw his hands into the air. There was a bright flash and a deafening thunder as a bolt of Divine Lightning raced skyward.

Kade fell on his backside and stared, wide-eyed. Zayle studied Kade closely. After a moment, a smile slowly crept across his face as he looked lovingly upon his grandson. Kade was like the son he never had. The boy was breathing deeply as his eyes glanced from Zayle's hand up to the heavens. It only took a moment for the child to grin from ear to ear.

"Can you do it again?" Kade asked excitedly. "Please," he pleaded. Zayle was more than happy to oblige. For a moment, Zayle reached up and gripped a medallion hanging around his neck. After just a second, he smiled again and then let the lightning fly one after the other. He spun through several more moves and he and the boy vanished from sight.

"He makes me uncomfortable," Garig said as he slid up to his wife. The image of Zayle holding the baby five years prior sprang into his mind. He pressed his lips together in frustration as he searched the yard for his unseen son and father-in-law.

"Garig, he is my father. He cares for our son. He does. There is more going on than you are aware. You must trust him," Judeen said as she looked him in the eyes. Garig softened ever so slightly.

"I will trust you. But I do not think I can ever be comfortable with him."

Judeen stopped as she listened to her father and her son play. It made her heart feel good to hear her father laugh. It rarely happened since mastering his gift. She focused on the sound of her son and her father and a smile spread across her face. Yes, her son would be in good hands. Grandfather and grandson popped into view, startling Garig and Judeen.

"Mother, can I do that?" Kade asked excitedly while pointing to the stranger. Before she could respond, Zayle spoke first.

"Maybe someday I can take you away and train you to be even more powerful than myself," he said as he knelt down and looked the boy in the eyes. Kade lit up as he turned to plead with his mother. Just as she was about to respond, she froze, seeing a look of sadness in her father's eyes. Zayle saw his daughter watching him and the sadness vanished to be replaced by a huge smile. "He is a fine young boy."

"Kade, go play while I talk with Zayle," Judeen said while giving Kade an affectionate swat on the bottom.

"But mother…," Kade started to protest until she gave him a look. He shrugged in defeat and turned to go but not before beaming at the stranger and saying, "I want to learn." And then he was off.

"I will give you two time to talk," Garig said and turned to leave without waiting for a reply from either.

"Father, why must we keep your identity a secret from him?"

"Judeen," Zayle said with compassion in his voice. "Daughter, he will make decisions based on that knowledge that will lead to disaster. He must never know. Not until the right time."

"When is that?"

"I cannot say, but if he were to learn my true identity, it would be a disaster for us all. He must only know me as a master who has agreed to teach him…if he can even learn. The next time I come for him will be on his tenth birthday."

"You are leaving again? So soon?" Judeen asked, trying hard to hide her sadness. "You have only been here a day. Can't you stay at least a little longer?"

"I must go. I have no choice. Please," Zayle said, almost pleading, feeling a hand gripping his heart. He wrapped his arms around her and pulled his daughter into an embrace, holding her while she wept, cursing the Divine with all his being.

Five years later…

Judeen paced for hours the night before Kade's tenth birthday. She knew her son never forgot the promise given to him by the stranger and that promise was to be fulfilled tomorrow. For different reasons, both mother and child found sleep elusive.

As the sun rose above the trees, there was a knock on the door. Judeen jumped, and without even opening the door, knew who it had to be. Kade raced for the door and flung it open, grinning widely as he looked upon the stranger who had returned as promised. He spun toward his mother with a smile that reached his eyes. Judeen swallowed and put on her bravest face.

"I am glad to see you again," Judeen said, as she indicated for him to enter. His face showed signs of stress with the sunken cheeks and the haunted look in his eyes. But, when he smiled, it all seemed to melt away.

"I am happy to be back. I made a promise to this young one and I intend on keeping it," Zayle said as he leaned over to look Kade in the eye. He held his fingers in the shape of a bowl. Soon, there was light glowing in the palm of his hands. Kade's eyes went wide as his thirst for knowledge kindled a fire in his heart that would never be quenched.

Zayle stayed for most of the day, knowing it would be a long time before he saw his daughter again…if ever. Kade was eager to be on his new adventure as he urged his newfound friend to take him away. Garig was quiet, when he was around.

Against his better judgment, Zayle stayed until the sun was starting to set. Kade never strayed far from the Master Chosen's side. There was no chance this man was going to get out of the young boy's sight. Finally, the time came for grandfather and grandson to be on their way. Kade danced from foot to foot as he stood by the front door, eager to be underway.

"Wait for me outside," Zayle said to the boy, who eagerly shot out the door. Zayle turned to Judeen and wiped a tear off her cheek. He wrapped her in a hug and closed his eyes as he fought his own sadness. He could not bear to tell her it would be their last embrace. Zayle cursed the Divine again and stepped back. He looked into his daughter's eyes and she shivered as she saw her father melt away to be replaced by a powerful Master Chosen. He reached into his long cloak and pulled an envelope from a hidden pouch, holding it tightly as he spoke.

"There will come a time in the future when Kade will come to see you. You must give this to him. It is imperative or all we have done will be for nothing. You must keep this safe no matter how long it takes. Our future depends on this. Promise me," Zayle said so intensely that Judeen had to fight the urge to step back.

"I promise," she said as she gingerly took the envelope as if it might bite.

Garig turned and stormed from the room. This was all he could take. All this man did was bring sadness and suffering to this family. To make matters worse, he was now taking Kade away to study the ways of the Divine. If Zayle had not been so adamant that the boy had very little chance of learning the Divine, he would have flat out refused to allow it at all. But, Judeen was very convincing when she had to be. If he had his way, there would be no such thing as the Divine.

Two years later...

"So this is the boy that saves us?" Jorell asked as she watched Kade work in the field.

"Yes," Zayle lied. Well, it was only half a lie. He hated that he could not tell her the whole truth but too much depended on things going as planned. He closed his eyes and the image of her broken body lying in a clearing with a young girl crying over her haunted him. For the hundredth time he cursed the Divine, and he cursed his gift.

"Darcienna would love it here," Jorell said casually as she looked off in the distance to see Zayle's protection barrier shimmer.

"No," Zayle said almost too quickly. Jorell flinched at his response. "I am sorry. It is complicated but she can't." Jorell shrugged her shoulders at her old friend's eccentric ways. It was getting late and she knew she needed to return to her hidden garden. She had her own student to attend to.

Kade looked up to see who his master was talking with but she turned away just as he tried to focus on her. He shrugged his shoulders and went back to raking the garden. This chore was supposed to help Kade find inner peace and allow him to sense the Divine as it flowed through all life, but all Kade found were sore muscles.

So far, the Divine Power was as elusive as the sun during night. Kade found himself becoming frustrated as he struggled to even sense the ancient power let alone wield it. But, with a steady flow of encouragement from his teacher, Kade continued day after day, trying to coax the power to respond to his will.

CH1

"Try! For the love of the Divine, put at least a little effort into this!" Zayle yelled. "If that is the best you can do, then we are all doomed!" he continued to scream. "You ask for the more powerful callings, and yet, you cannot do a simple Drift Calling? Come on Kade, try harder! You should have been able to cause your awareness to drift on the first try! NOW CONCENTRATE!" Zayle roared with more force than he intended, turning red in the face. He brought his fist crashing down on the table, causing his apprentice to jump. Kade could feel the disappointment coming off Zayle in waves. As much as the Master Chosen wanted to hide his frustration, he no longer could. Kade saw it as plain as if Zayle had outright called him a failure. It stung. Kade felt the swirl of emotions as his anger boiled over.

"This is the most useless calling in all the green lands!" he shouted as he stormed out of the cabin.

This was all Kade could take. For weeks and months, Zayle

had become more and more intense to the point of every session turning into Zayle screaming until he was hoarse. Whenever Kade tried to talk with him, the Master Chosen would only wave him away and tell him, "Later." That was all he ever got from his master no matter the reason. This was too much. For the first time ever, Kade stormed out in the middle of a lesson. Zayle screamed after him but that only spurred him into running.

"Why?" Kade asked himself in exasperation, as he entered the woods. "Why is he acting as if I need to know everything this very day?" he asked out loud.

The path was well worn from his many walks he had taken recently in an attempt to relieve his frustrations. As he stormed on, he dwelled on his recent arguments that he had with his master, Zayle the Chosen. Over and over again he asked himself why he had to learn such useless callings instead of the more important ones.

"Why should I study callings like Awareness Drift when I could be learning exciting callings like how to fly like the swiftest bird or run as fast as the fiercest animal?" he asked himself for the hundredth time as he threw his hands up in the air dramatically. "Every time I ask about any other calling, he always tells me that I must focus on the basics. Bah. Focus on the basics my arse. I want to learn something important! I want to send lightning to the heavens!" he shouted as he threw his hands up to the sky and visualized a blast racing toward the stars.

I have all the discipline I need no matter what Zayle says. I don't know how he thinks that learning the simpler callings is going to help me master the more difficult ones. If I just focus on the better callings, I will be able to master them all just fine. It is just an excuse to keep me from learning what I want. It's all just an excuse. Maybe…maybe he can't because he has lost his touch. Maybe…oh, I don't know, Kade thought to himself as he continued walking.

Taking a deep breath, he started going over his most recent

lesson as he wandered. Thinking back, he recalled his failure to perform the Awareness Drift Calling. He had relaxed his body, as the calling demanded, and recited the ancient word as required. It was only one word. Float. *Simple enough*, he thought to himself. He had felt…something.

*Was my body feeling lighter, or am I just thinking it was because I want it to work? h*e asked himself, but it was useless. He had had enough of the ridicule and ranting from his master, and he needed to leave before he said or did something that would really get himself in trouble.

This was the first time in all his years of training Kade had lost his temper with his master, much less stormed out right in the middle of a lesson. The knot in his stomach grew as he contemplated how fast he was going to be told to pack and get out when he returned. It had been nine years of agonizing failure after failure as Kade struggled to develop his abilities. Finally, in the tenth year, he was starting to show real ability, and now he had blown his chances to become the greatest Master Chosen ever.

Have I just thrown everything away that I have worked for?

He continued to walk, not paying attention to where he was going as his thoughts raced. He knew he was lucky to even be taken as an apprentice at the age of ten, but appreciation only went so far. Most apprentices were taken at ages as young as five or even younger. Ten was unheard of and he knew it.

For that matter, he thought, *why was I taken as an apprentice at all?*

Not being able to answer his own questions, his thoughts continued on as if unable to slow. *I want to be famous like Zayle*, Kade thought. This had been Kade's desire since the first day of his training. It was slow going and it was difficult to be patient. Patience was the one area that he knew he struggled with, and that was being generous.

He thought back to ten years ago when Zayle had given demonstrations of his abilities. Kade was in awe of the raw power. He was eager to go with Zayle, excited to wield the Divine.

Kade marched deep into the woods, losing all track of time. It had been nearly an hour when he started to notice that his surroundings were not as familiar as they should have been. This was the furthest from the cabin he had ever walked, with the exception of his one trip to Corbin. He kicked a rock absentmindedly and stumbled. It was right then he heard a deep, reverberating growl followed by a hiss that sounded like a massive snake.

Kade felt his pulse race wildly as he realized he had wandered from the protected area. Zayle had warned him countless times that extremely dangerous animals had been seen outside the barrier, but it never really struck home since he had not observed them himself. Now, every warning came racing back as he forced his eyes to focus on the massive beast that stood just several long strides in front of him. Fear lanced through his body, causing him to become paralyzed. He knew he should run, but at the moment he could not get his muscles to respond.

The dragon launched itself at him and Kade knew this was the end. More out of chance than skill, and a slight bit of reflex, he fell to the side, dodging the dragon's deadly claws. At first, Kade believed he was lucky to have avoided the quick death that was certain to come, but then, he felt a warm trickle of blood running down his forehead.

The dragon landed clumsily and emitted what almost sounded like a yelp. By this time, the adrenalin had kicked in, and Kade was on his feet as the dragon struggled to stand. He worked the only calling Zayle was willing to teach him that was combat-worthy. The words and motions came to his mind quickly as he called for the Blue Fire of the Divine. The flow of the power reminded him of standing in the middle of a river while the current swirled around him. The power was euphoric. The flames flared to life, dancing several feet above his hands as its mesmerizing, brilliant, blue energy eagerly awaited its target. Zayle had made it clear it was only for self-defense. If defending himself from a creature that could eat him in one or two bites did not qualify, then nothing did. Kade's heart was pounding as the thrill of finally using the Divine made his head buzz.

The dragon turned and re-oriented on him, but this time, Kade was ready. For anyone watching, they would have seen his arm coated with blue fire, even though Kade felt nothing but a surging power coursing through his muscles. In an instant, Kade sensed that he was missing something important. Something nagged at him, but he pushed it out of his mind, eager to let fly his deadly calling. He pulled back his arm, as though to throw but hesitated. Out of the corner of his eye he saw a large puddle of red liquid. Ignoring it, he refocused on the dragon. He clenched his jaw in determination as he stepped forward to hurl the blue fire of death. Everything was a blur and then…he perceived things as though they were in slow motion. It was surrealistic as his mind captured every little detail of his surroundings. He could feel a breeze on his arm and the warm trickle of blood as it dripped over his eyelash, causing him to blink. He noticed the way the dragon fearfully eyed the flames dancing on his hand. The area smelled of fresh rain and a drop of water dripped off a leaf. And then…he was extending his arm, launching the blazing inferno of heat directly at the dragon's head. Or at least…that was what he was planning, but at the very last second, for reasons he could not understand, he turned his hand slightly. It was enough so that the flame shot past the dragon, exploding loudly against a boulder. He flinched as he felt the blast of heat blow back at him.

Without taking his eye off the dragon, Kade slowly turned to study the red liquid and recognized it for what it was. The crimson fluid was the dragon's blood. It was not trying to attack him, but was instead, only trying to defend itself. Kade knew he should have been

5

an easy kill for the dragon, but its feeble attack was far from what it should have been. He was seeing more clues by the second. The dragon was hunched in an odd position. Even if he did not know what a dragon should look like, he knew this was wrong. It was also dragging its left wing on the ground. However, Kade knew what really made him throw the Fire Calling wide at the last second, and it was not seeing the three horrible slashes along its neck, either. It was seeing a look of fear and despair in the dragon's eyes, as though it had been beaten. Pity and compassion welled up in Kade, and his anger dwindled.

The dragon's head came up with renewed determination as it realized the blow had missed. Kade turned pale as his colossal mistake struck home. Throwing away his only means of defense was foolish. It was nothing more than an animal that could not appreciate the compassion Kade had shown it. It may be hurt and it may be stumbling, but it was still more than a match for him. Panic, again, seized him as the dragon had taken in a breath and was about to incinerate him. Now, the dragon had the upper hand. He considered the Fire Calling, but even before he began, he knew he would be dead before he could release it.

Kade was not sure why, but something told him that the dragon was considering not attacking. There was a feather light touch in his mind, and then it was gone. He quickly dropped his hands to his side and very slowly moved back a step. Moments took eons to pass, and yet, no fire. He slowly, and as non-threatening as possible, locked eyes with the dragon. It was still ready to blast him with its fire. Was that intelligence he was seeing? Maybe not at a human level, but it was there.

Kade continued to work his way backward as the dragon watched him closely. His heart was pounding so hard he was sure it was going to burst at any moment. To his amazement, the dragon let out its breath, along with flecks of blood, and with that, the fire went out. It wanted no more fight. Kade backed a little more as the dragon eyed him wearily. It appeared to be slowly backing away itself…or trying to back away. He turned to go, but just then, the dragon slumped to the ground heavily. Its breathing turned into a wheeze. It struggled to stand again but gave up. Kade got a sick feeling in his stomach as he watched.

"Kade," he said to himself, "get out of here. Just put one foot in front of the other and start walking. No, not walk, run!"

Inside, Kade knew what he was going to do, even if he did not want to acknowledge it. It was stupid and foolish, but that was who he was. He knew he could not just leave something that was helpless. And besides, it was the first dragon he had ever seen.

He took a deep breath and let it out, taking a step toward the dragon. Its head came up slowly, and Kade could see it was struggling to breathe. He cautiously approached the dragon and put his hands up in what he hoped would appear to be a sign of non-aggression. The dragon flinched and desperately struggled to its feet. Kade knew it was using every last little bit of health and energy to make this one last stand. Cursing himself for a fool, he quickly lowered his hands. The dragon tried to pull in a breath of air but failed, and instead, coughed up flecks of blood. Kade moved even closer. Just out of the dragon's reach, he lifted his right hand and made the simple move that would bring the Healing Calling to life. His hand glowed with a soft, amber light.

It was now or never, he thought to himself. He slowly moved into range of the dragon's deadly teeth and reached out for the three deep slashes on its neck. The dragon's lips quivered and a deep menacing rumble made it clear that the dragon meant business. But, its legs wobbled dangerously and Kade could see the dragon's eyes losing focus quickly. At any moment it was going to fall to the ground.

The Divine Power leapt into the wound. The dragon jumped,

and to Kade's surprise, it was able to draw in enough air to ignite its dragon's breath. Kade put his hand up slowly and completed the calling for a second time. Again, it shot into the dragon, but this time, it sank deep into the wing. The dragon flinched and let out a puff of air that singed Kade's hand. He swallowed hard. That was too close.

The dragon's eyes appeared to clear just a little. It flexed its neck slightly and even tested its wing. Although mended to a great degree, Kade knew the calling had its limits. He slowly backed away with his hands out to the side. When he was about two strides away, he, again, considered leaving. Something was nagging at him, but he could not quite put his finger on what it was. He was missing something else, but what?

The dragon seemed to let some of its tension go as it watched him curiously. Kade could see that it was also trying to consider what to do. It looked at him, back at its wounds and then back to him.

Was it actually going to realize that I posed it no threat? Kade asked himself incredulously. *Is there a chance that it is really intelligent enough to know I mean it no harm? It must be. It just has to be!*

Kade felt his heart start to pound as the depth of what was happening hit him. He was here with a real, live dragon, and it was not going to eat him. It was actually interacting with him…in a sort of way. It slowly moved forward as best as it could on its injured leg. It looked at its leg and then back to Kade. It gave a sort of huff and looked at its leg again. Flecks of blood formed on its lips

"How could you have survived with all those injuries?" Kade whispered out loud. The dragon's ears swiveled at the sound of his voice. "You are listening to me?" he asked in awe. The dragon's ears twitched, then it edged closer and again looked at its leg and then back to him. Kade's eyes widened in understanding. "Okay, let me see if I can do something with that," he said as he approached the wounded leg. The dragon was fighting its internal instinct to kill as its lips parted. Kade was waiting for the guttural sounds of a verbal threat, but it never came. The twitching of its lips, however, continued.

Ignoring the dragon's teeth that were flashing in and out of view, Kade moved closer. Not really knowing why, he was certain it was not going to attack. There was a feather light caress on his mind again for just a moment, and then it was gone. Finding it hard to ignore the whites of its teeth that kept flashing into view, he edged even closer. Although Kade was certain the dragon knew he was no threat, he could not ignore the fact that it might just decide to eat him when he was done. He hoped with all his heart the giant, magnificent beast was no danger to him, but all he could do was hope there was, indeed, intelligence in there.

He slid up to the dragon, in awe of its size and marveled at what a killing machine it was. The smell of blood and sweat assaulted him the closer he got. His fear start to well up as he approached, but he forced himself to continue. His stomach felt as though it were full of bats fluttering wildly. He tried to stay wide of the dragon's head, but every time he went to pass, the dragon would shift, causing him to approach from the direction of those deadly teeth. Kade steeled himself the best he could, and holding his breath, slowly edged by those massive jaws. He could feel its hot breath on his arm every time it breathed. Its big, golden eyes watched him closely as he reached toward the badly damaged leg. The Divine Calling leapt from his hand and melted into the dragon's hide. Again, the dragon flinched and its lips shot up, revealing dangerously sharp, dagger-like teeth that were made for rending.

Kade held his breath and felt his head start to swim. His life depended on his instincts, and he knew it. At least, he hoped his instincts were right, but it was more like a guess. But, that was not right either. Something was telling him the dragon would not attack.

It breathed into his face and inhaled several times to get his scent. Kade's hair fluffed every time the dragon exhaled. He almost gagged as he struggled to breathe. He backed away slightly and stopped as he noticed the sleek back, the supple neck and the graceful way the dragon moved. It was an absolutely beautiful work of nature, and he was right here next to it. It was exhilarating, and he was scared to death. He then looked down at its ten-inch long claws and realized he was crazy not to have run for his life.

The dragon's large, golden eyes continued to study him as he studied it. Its breathing was still a little ragged, and there were flecks of blood on its lips. Kade tilted his head to the side and narrowed his eyes as if to listen to a far off sound. His eyes lost focus as he realized what he was listening for was inside his head. Kade threw all caution to the wind and confidently walked back to the dragon. He placed his hand on its neck. The dragon's neck muscles turned rock hard at that touch but it still held. The rough skin felt strong and soft at the same time. He called on the healing, and placed his hand on the dragon's chest, letting the Divine Power flow into this wondrous creation.

The dragon seemed to ease under his touch. It took several deep breaths as it drank in clean air. It flexed its muscles and shifted its wings as though it were preparing for flight. Then, without warning, its wings shot out and it leaped into the air. It pumped hard one time before bellowing in pain and then came crashing, very ungracefully, back to the ground. The wing had snapped. Kade dove to the side to avoid being crushed under the massive weight. He rolled several times and came to a stop, panting. When he looked up, the dragon was just regaining its feet.

"No, you cannot fly yet," Kade called out to the dragon, throwing his hands up in an attempt to signal it to stop.

Calming himself from what he thought was his end by a falling dragon, he tried to see how much it had re-injured itself. It opened its wings again and winced in pain as it flexed them. It gave out a pathetic yearning sound as it looked up to the sky. Kade's heart went out to it. Suddenly, that nagging feeling that he was missing something returned, causing him to stop. He cast a casual glance around and then, once again, pushed it from his mind.

The dragon folded one wing back while the other dragged on the ground. As it struggled to use its damaged wing, it made sure to keep Kade where it could see him. It might realize that Kade was no threat, but its years of instinct and survival would not allow it to completely turn its back on something unfamiliar to it, especially when it knew he had power.

Kade slowly edged up to the dragon. Placing his hands on its wing, he sent the healing power to do its work once more. The dragon eased a little. Kade was pleased with the results, even if it was still going to take a while to completely mend.

Maybe a few months, or maybe weeks, if the dragon was lucky, he thought as he considered the injury. The more he thought about it, the more he began to realize how lucky he was he had stumbled upon an injured dragon instead of a healthy one. He always considered dragons to be monsters and for good reason; they eat people and animals…or so the stories say.

The nagging feeling returned, but this time it was so strong that he was unable to ignore it. Kade looked around as his chest started to tighten. "What?" he asked himself, unsure why he was feeling tension. He narrowed his eyes and scanned the area; for what, he was not sure.

Kade found himself looking into the dragon's eyes as if the reason for his unease could be found there. Its giant, golden discs the size of a dinner plate definitely held a level of intelligence as it regarded him. Its eyes appeared to shine as though they were made of pure gold.

Giving a short, quick laugh, he realized that the dragon was doing the exact same thing he was doing and chided himself for being paranoid. His discomfort had to be coming from standing so close to such a massive killing machine. It was examining him, looking at his dark brown hair, his medium build, his dark brown eyes and his light skin. He was athletic and stood just short of six feet tall. He was not full of muscles, but he was very fit. He had good posture, for the most part. His hair was cut short, making it easy to keep clean. His eyes had a seductive quality that women found almost irresistible. He was even told once that he had bedroom eyes.

Kade knew he was a good challenge for any man with his two hundred pounds. He was stronger than he looked, but even at ten times his strength, he would not have been a challenge for the dragon, even with it being injured. He knew this was one fight he would have lost and there would be no seeing a town healer or anyone ever again, for that matter. He swallowed and wondered what it was thinking of him.

The dragon snorted uncomfortably. Kade realized he was daydreaming again. He mentally told himself he would have to do less of that since it's what got him into this trouble in the first place. Had he just stayed on the protected path, nothing could have threatened him. No animal was able to pass the barrier unless Zayle allowed it.

Kade dismissed his thoughts and regarded the dragon. It was looking at him while tilting its head back and forth. He realized the dragon was waiting for him to do something. But, what? Zayle had never thought to teach him what to do with a dragon. Why would he? No one has ever encountered one and lived to tell or brag about it. At least, not like this. It was said in the days of old that dragons were more abundant, but that was a long time ago when the Ancients still walked the land.

Without warning, the dragon flexed its mighty haunches and launched itself directly at Kade with a deafening roar. The look in its eyes was of killing as it came at him. The fear lanced through Kade's body as he threw himself down, waiting for the crushing weight to drive him into the ground. The dragon sailed just over his head. And then the nagging feeling exploded in his mind as he heard the dragon collide with something just behind him.

Kade mentally kicked himself for not realizing whatever had caused the injuries on the dragon could still be in the area. As he was regaining his feet, he heard a shriek so loud and penetrating that it stood the hairs up on the back of his neck, setting every nerve in his body on fire. There came a second crash as the dragon, and whatever it was fighting, landed just behind him. The ground shook, causing Kade to stumble before catching his balance. He forced himself to run, but after just a few steps, he turned, hoping he would not regret his decision.

What could really threaten a dragon? he thought, but he knew, after seeing the injuries on the dragon, it had to be at least as large.

His heart leapt into his throat as he focused on the two combatants. He was very wrong. The beast was not only as large as the dragon but larger by quite a bit. Kade considered turning and running again but quickly felt shame for the thought. That thing must have been in mid-leap, coming directly at him when the dragon had intercepted it. He could not live with himself if he left the dragon to die when it had just risked its life to save him. Maybe it was not specifically for him, but if it had not intercepted the creature, the outcome would have been the same.

Looking on in horror at one of the few fabled beasts reported to actually be able to kill a dragon, Kade fought to control his panic. Here, standing directly in front of him was a grimalkin. It was not as he had seen in the books he used to read. This thing looked wrong. It was not the cat-like image he would expect. No. It was a grotesquely twisted form of what looked to have been feline at one time but now was something completely different. It had wings with feathers that

13

looked dirty and decaying. It had a hooked beak that was brown and jagged with chips broken out of it. Its eyes were sunken and shallow. But one thing was certain; this creature was meant for killing, and it meant to kill the dragon. At half again as large, it was clear that the grimalkin had the advantage.

The dragon was fighting furiously and even caused a deep gouge in the monsters chest, causing blood to flow. However, it was not slowing the massive animal, and Kade knew the dragon was not going to win this fight. It only had a few new wounds, but it was obvious which one was going to perish and which one was going to survive.

His indecision was tearing him apart. He knew if he tried to help the dragon, he would draw the monster's attention, and that would mean death. He also knew if the dragon lost, he was most likely the next target. One thing he was certain of; if he attacked the grimalkin, he was next, if he did nothing, the dragon was doomed.

He considered turning and running again but immediately felt shame for the second time. Anger flared in him so strong that he shook. Nothing else mattered now. All he could see was the deadly battle being waged in front of him. All concern for his own life evaporated and was instantly replaced with fury. He accepted that he was going to die, and now he was going to do it fighting. Kade felt his heart pound hard as adrenalin raged through his system.

The dragon tried several times to leap back and draw on its dragon's breath only to have the grimalkin close the distance rapidly. The dragon tried over and over to get distance to use its fire, but the grimalkin always charged in, giving the dragon no chance to use its natural weapon. They were tangled once more in their deadly embrace. The dragon was taking injuries quickly. It staggered and barely dodged a killing snap of the grimalkin's beak. The creature was going for the dragon's neck with almost every lunge now. Again, it launched, and this time, it nicked the dragon, drawing a small amount of blood. If not for its lightning quick reflexes, the dragon would already be dead. Time was running out.

That last attack was too close. This was all Kade could stand. His anger consumed him completely.

How dare this thing attack such a magnificent creature that I had just healed! Kade thought as he felt his pulse racing. As valiantly as the dragon fought, it was going to die, and that would just not do. The grimalkin had the dragon in its claws, trying savagely to get its hooked-beak into the dragon's throat. Seeing this was the very last thing Kade needed to launch into action.

"Not today!" he screamed as he charged forward "NOT TODAY!"

Kade opened himself up to the Divine Power and its full might, calling on the seething, blue fire and hurled it with all his anger. His words may not have caused the creature to hesitate, but when the Divine Fire exploded on the beast's hide, he knew he had its attention. Fear tried to force its way back into his heart. The grimalkin looked directly at him and paused, but…only for a moment. Kade felt fury more intense than ever as he gritted his teeth so hard in such fierce determination that he could have bit through brick. His hands balled into fists so tightly that he was shaking. He curled his lip in a snarl and hissed, "You intend on dismissing me that easily? Then ignore this!" Kade yelled as he lit the cat up with another blast of the blue fire. The flames were getting larger with each calling, but Kade did not notice. Unknown to him, his Divine gift had come alive. Kade's gift of unlimited Divine Power had him pulsing with power.

The dragon took advantage of the distraction and sank its teeth deeply into the grimalkin's flesh, tearing out a large chunk. The creature roared and attempted to renew its attack. Kade unleashed another Fire Calling just as the cat-like creature tried for a killing blow. Fear of watching the dragon die, along with rage at this beast, brought on a desire to destroy another living creature stronger than Kade had ever felt in his life. He willed death into every Fire Calling he threw, and each time it was just enough to throw the beast off before it found its mark.

Kade continued to yell as he threw blue fire over and over, doing everything he could to draw its attention. He had no idea what he was going to do if it turned on him, but right then, he did not care. He only knew he absolutely must save the dragon.

The grimalkin decided the man had caused it enough problems. With a mighty screech, it came off the badly injured dragon and leapt toward Kade with death in its eyes. His arm back with yet another Fire Calling, Kade froze in terror as the massive beast bore down on him. It was only when he was staring death directly in the eye that his anger faltered, and he became paralyzed with fear.

Without warning, when the beast was just several strides from him, it came down hard on its chin with enough force to cause Kade to stumble. Not knowing what had happened, he let loose the Divine Power directly into the grimalkin's face. It screeched in pain and anger as it attempted to rise. It was then that Kade saw the dragon had fastened its teeth into the grimalkin's right, hind leg and was holding on for all it was worth. The cat-like creature kicked out with its left, hind leg, knocking the dragon back, causing even more wounds.

Kade darted around the beast to get to the dragon. The grimalkin screeched again and made a swipe with its massive paws directly in front of itself where, seconds before, Kade had stood. It dawned on the Apprentice Chosen that the grimalkin's vision had been affected by the Divine Fire. Hope flooded through him. The grimalkin tried again and again to find the man that had caused it so much pain and confusion. With every passing moment, the beast's actions became more violent as it screamed in rage in its desperate attempt to crush the man that had taken its sight.

Kade slid to a stop next to the dragon that was lying on its side and started the Healing Calling. He focused on the vital areas first, making sure its life was not going to wink out right before his eyes. Too much blood was gushing out, and the dragon was having a hard time breathing, but not for long. Kade fired calling after calling into the dragon. The breathing quickly eased and the dragon stabilized. Working as fast as he could, Kade healed the broken leg, then the wing, and finally two other deep gashes that were oozing too much life. He did his best to ignore the thrashing, wild beast, but he was afraid at any moment, through sheer luck, it would stumble upon him and the dragon. His heart beat wildly as he continued to focus on the dragon without so much as a glance at the deadly grimalkin.

With the dragon's life once again brought back from the brink of no return, Kade raced to its head. Its eyes were rolled back, and its tongue was hanging out in the dirt. He willed the Divine Power into the dragon and the healing took hold. He held his breath, hoping the dragon would recover before the grimalkin found it. He forced himself to ignore the deadly creature, even though he could feel the cat-like being getting closer through the pounding on the ground. Another healing and the dragon's eyes cleared. It shook its head and then locked its huge, golden eyes with Kade's. His eyes lost focus for just an instant as something caressed his mind. It was only a moment and then he was brought back as the grimalkin let out an ear-splitting screech.

Now we have a chance, Kade thought as exhilaration raced through his body. *Kill*, he thought…or…were those his thoughts?

Determination flooded through him in a rush as he stood and turned to face the grimalkin. The cautious side of him knew he should coax the dragon into turning and running. He knew they should flee so they both could live, but he discarded the more prudent plan and let his anger explode as he filled himself to overflowing with the Divine Power. He danced through the moves for the Fire Calling and lit up as blue fire sprang into existence. Working faster and faster, he blasted the creature over and over, causing it to howl in pain. A malicious smile crept across his face, and with every cry from the creature, it grew. He let out a yell of blind fury at the evil beast as he attacked, showing it no mercy. The dragon followed with its own deafening, violent roar that was so fierce it shook. It renewed its attack, leaping at the grimalkin with a vengeance.

The Fire Callings were definitely having their effect. The area smelled of burnt flesh and hair, but Kade barely noticed. The dragon tore over and over with its claws and rent with its teeth in a mad fury. It leapt back, spun in the air, and before it landed, took a deep breath and blasted the creature with such a torrent of flame that Kade could feel the heat wash over him, causing him to cough and stagger back. The grimalkin howled in pain, and then renewed its attack, desperation controlling its moves. It fought like an animal that was cornered, knowing its life was in peril. With a lucky strike, it knocked the dragon to the ground.

Kade was amazed at the amount of damage the beast had taken but was still coming. He knew it was far from over, but if he and the dragon could just keep working together, he was more than certain that they would prevail. Twice, the cat had knocked the dragon down, and once, even got a hold of it, but with the help of the Fire Calling, the dragon was able to get loose.

The dragon saw its opening, and with amazing ferocity, launched at the evil beast, sinking its teeth into the grimalkin's neck as deep and hard as it could while latching on with its claws. The time for darting in and out was past. The creature tried desperately to dislodge the dragon that was attached to its side but failed. It tried repeatedly to crane its neck and get its hooked-beak into its attacker, but the dragon was wrapped too close to its hide. It wailed loudly, sensing its end was closing in and fought with desperation that shook the ground dangerously. It flipped onto its side and kicked furiously but the dragon was not coming loose. Kade continued to deal blow after blow, showing no mercy. The dragon bit down hard with its teeth that were still fastened in the grimalkin's neck. Every muscle in its body bulged as it strained to bring its jaws together. And then…something snapped. The grimalkin twitched hard, and then its eyes half closed as the breath hissed out of it. The thrashing slowed moment by moment, as its life force quickly waned. Finally, it lay motionless on the ground, twitching slightly as the spirit of nature reclaimed its essence.

When the grimalkin was finally still, the dragon did something that shocked Kade; it started to feed. He looked on in awe. His mind started to whirl and the ground seemed to move, even though he was standing still. He was soaked with sweat and breathing heavily but he hardly noticed.

Kade sank to his knees, finally able to give in to his fatigue. Sweat dripped off his arms as he wiped the blood from his face. He looked at his hands and was surprised to see them shaking terribly. He tried to steady them but to no avail. An uncomfortable warmth crept up his back, and his stomach started to feel queasy. He tried to calm himself when he noticed how strange the grass felt on his face. That was the last thought he had before he passed out.

CH2

With a mouth full of grimalkin, the dragon looked over and saw Kade lying on the ground. It stopped chewing and raised its head slightly to focus on the prone body. With a huff, it abandoned its feast and bounded over to the man. Becoming agitated, the dragon nudged Kade several times. It sniffed rapidly in Kade's face and relaxed when it sensed breathing. Relieved that he was still alive, it protectively laid down next to him, nudging him every so often.

Over the next few hours, many animals had come for the feast. The dragon just looked on as it lay next to the unconscious form. Only once during their rest was an animal careless enough not to notice the deadly dragon as it prepared to feed on the helpless man. It was the last mistake the animal ever made. Every other creature was wise enough to give the dragon a wide birth.

As Kade slowly started to awaken, he noticed an extremely unpleasant smell and wondered what Zayle was concocting. He heard the odd sounds of some type of animal but tried to ignore it and return to the world of dreams. All of a sudden the stench increased along with a warm blast of air. He opened his eyes and blinked as the puff hit him in the face again. His eyes burned instantly, causing him to squeeze them shut, as he gagged and coughed roughly. He moved back and opened his eyes to find a large golden disc not more than two feet away.

It only took another moment and then panic hit him as the memories of a giant cat-like beast slashing at him formed in his mind. The dragon, sensing his panic, leapt to its feet and spun around looking for the danger. Its body was tense as it looked for whatever had caused the man fear. It spun to the right, then the left, then spun completely around, expecting an attack from behind only to find nothing. The dragon huffed several times from the tension of getting ready for battle.

After a few more moments, all the memories came back and Kade looked around, noticing the beasts feeding on the large, toasted carcass. His eyes then fell on the one unfortunate animal that had come too close to him, and he was certain that the dragon must have torn it apart defending him. He dizzied at the thought of being so helpless. The animal could have easily killed him while he was passed out. He got that feeling of stopping at the edge of a cliff just before falling off.

"You did this," Kade said as he rose shakily. "You kept me safe while I was out," he said with awe in his voice.

Kade was staring at the dragon in fascination for a lot of reasons. The first was that this was a real, live dragon and it was not eating him. He felt gratitude and smiled. He walked up to the dragon and ran his hand over the supple, strong hide in amazement and noticed fresh wounds that were still unhealed. The dragon flinched several times but then relaxed quickly. It did not take Kade long to put the Divine Power to use once again.

The dragon showed its appreciation for the healing by giving

Kade an affectionate nudge with its muzzle. This was hard enough to set Kade down a little roughly on his backside. He looked at the dragon and laughed for the first time that day. Its mouth hung open casually as it breathed, but those teeth gave Kade pause. He got to his feet and patted the dragon on the neck. He marveled at the power and strength he felt rippling through its muscles.

Suddenly, a different kind of panic raced through his body as he noticed the position of the sun. *I have been out here for hours,* Kade thought as his pulse quickened. *Zayle is absolutely going to flail me when I get back if he does not flat out send me on my way.* He felt the urge to race back to the cabin. In all the years of training, he had never missed more than one session, not to mention leaving and staying gone for hours.

Kade frantically looked around the clearing, trying to find the way he had come and spotted the rock his first Fire Calling had hit. Before he could start to move, he felt the dragon nudge him from behind, causing him to stumble a step or two. He turned to see his new found friend staring at him, as if to ask, "What?" The dragon made a short growl that might have seemed like a threat, if you had just met it, but Kade knew better. He understood it was the dragon's way of asking what was wrong. He was not sure how he knew, but he was certain beyond a shadow of a doubt that he was correct.

"I have to get back," Kade said in a rush but of course the dragon only tilted its head as its ears swiveled back and forth. "I have to...ah you don't understand," he said in frustration. "What should I do with you?" he asked out loud as he raked his hands through his hair.

The dragon spread its wings as if to fly. Kade grabbed it in an attempt to hold it on the ground, hoping it would get his meaning. He could feel the muscles bunching and relaxing as if the dragon was on the verge of taking flight. It flexed its wings but then winced in pain. It looked to the sky, flexed its wings again, and again, winced in pain.

It gave a low, mournful cry as it slowly folded its wings back to its sides. It looked up at the sky again and then at Kade, as if pleading with him to help. Kade felt sad for the miracle of nature and wished he could heal its wing completely, but he could not. It just did not work that way. His Divine Power could heal back to generally what was meant to be, but the body always had to do the final touches.

Kade moved to the wing and patted the dragon as if to say, "I understand," but he knew the dragon was expecting him to use his healing again. It was watching him intently, waiting. All he knew to do was show it he had done all he could by healing and letting the dragon see on its own that it was not enough. After several times, he gently grabbed hold of the wing and slowly pushed it back to the dragon's body as if to say, "No, you cannot fly." It was enough. With a deep, mournful cry that touched Kade right down to his very soul, the dragon accepted its fate. It gave its injured wing one last look and then slumped to the ground.

"I am sorry, my friend," Kade said with compassion. "I wish I could heal you completely, but it does not work that way. That is as good as I can do," he said regretfully, as he stroked its neck.

Kade moved to the front of the dragon, taking its sagging head in his hands and looked it in the eye. He did not know how to convey that it would fly someday, but he knew he could at least try to comfort it.

"Don't worry my friend. You will fly again. Just not today," Kade said.

The dragon lifted its head one more time and looked at the sky with a yearning. Kade could see its wings shift only momentarily before they settled back to its side. Its head lowered as it gave a halfhearted roar, and then its head sank down, looking at him. Kade felt his heart breaking for this wondrous creature. The dragon searched the clearing with what appeared to be a lost look, as if to say, "Where do I go from here?" or "What do I do now?"

Something in Kade's chest started to ache, and he developed a lump in his throat. He couldn't take it. He had to do something, but what? He thought about it for just another moment before coming to the obvious conclusion. It was really the only solution he knew he would come to, anyway.

"Hey dragon," Kade said, looking it in the eye. It did not seem to hear. "Hey," Kade said as he gave it a slight shake to get its attention. "How would you like to come home with me?"

There was no response. Kade pointed to the dragon, then to himself, and then back the way he had come. It paused a moment, not understanding but not really caring. Kade pulled on the dragon's head and said, "Come with me." It just sat there not showing any signs of moving. Kade walked back the way he had come and beckoned for the dragon to follow. Although it was not getting up, he did have its attention now. It tilted its head from side to side as it watched.

"Come with me," Kade said again as he approached the dragon and tried to pull at it. "Come on. I know you are smart so figure it out. Come with me."

Kade went back and forth a few more times, tugging at the dragon. He would go a little further down the path each time, and then come back to tug at the dragon once again. Its head lifted a little further, realization dawning on it. The dragon climbed to its feet and lumbered toward him, showing none of the grace it had displayed in battle. Kade took one last look around the clearing and then turned for his home, hoping his master would show mercy. At least, he hoped he still had a master.

Kade noticed the dragon was alert once again, watching the animals that Kade now realized were watching him. He looked around at all the wildlife and was grateful for this mountain sized watchdog. He thumbed his nose at some of the larger, more savage looking ones that would have eaten him without a moment's hesitation. Some of the animals flinched at every step the dragon took. A few even scurried away, unable to control their fear.

It took Kade longer than he hoped to find the protected path. Once on it, he began to think about what Zayle was going to say and how he was going to explain why he was gone so long. He looked back over his shoulder at the massive, docile animal lumbering closely behind and chuckled to himself.

Well, I am sure he will forgive everything when he sees what I have brought back, he thought.

Kade continued walking, lost in thought as his mind flitted from one thing to the next. Another half hour passed as he continued to imagine his teacher's reaction. He even laughed one time, as he pictured how he was going to make a grand showing of his dragon and watch as Zayle's eyes popped out of his head. Eager to see his master's reaction, his pace quickened. As soon as he finished that thought, he instantly felt something was missing. It was quiet. Too quiet. Then, when he heard a distant roaring, it hit him; his dragon was on the other side of the protective calling that he had so casually walked through. He was lucky to have heard the call at all as the barrier had a way of reducing sound. He raced back to find the dragon clawing at an unseen force. It even appeared that it slid backwards with its claws digging into the ground. Kade ran up to the dragon and stroked it on the shoulder, calming it.

"It's okay. I did not mean to leave you," he said as he patted the side of its head affectionately. The dragon visibly relaxed.

"I need to leave you for just a short time, but I will be back," Kade reassured the dragon. "Just stay here," he said, pointing to the ground. It tilted its head in that fashion it did when it was trying to understand. "I forgot about the Barrier Calling."

The dragon gave a pathetic whimper. It was very much unlike what Kade would have expected, but then he really did not know what he should have expected. He racked his brains, trying to figure out a way to communicate with the dragon.

"You can't come any further," Kade tried to explain, knowing it was futile. "Well, I am just going to have to try to get you to understand I am going to come back." And with that, Kade came up with an idea.

He walked several steps in the direction of the cabin, while watching the dragon. When it started to become agitated, he would return and sooth it until it was calm. After several times of doing this, the dragon seemed to stay calm longer between each trip, allowing him to go further each time. On the seventh time, Kade was able to get just out of sight before the dragon would sound its mournful cry. After several more times of this, Kade decided it was time to make a break for the cabin.

"I will be back. Wait," Kade said as he pointed to the ground. He was shocked to see the dragon actually sit. It reminded him very much of a dog.

Kade walked calmly until he was out of sight of the magnificent creature. He stopped for a moment and listened, hoping he would not hear that mournful cry. After several long, tense moments, there was nothing. He turned and ran for all he was worth. He burst through the front door to the cabin, yelling excitedly for his master.

"Zayle. You must come!" he shouted over and over, but there was no response. Anxiety filled his heart as his thoughts returned to the dragon. He pictured it pacing and trying to call to him. His heart raced as he ran from room to room.

"Since when have we become such good friends that we are on a first name basis, Apprentice?" Zayle asked in a scalding tone, as he laid heavy emphasis on the last word. There was danger in his tone. Anger rippled off him in waves. He walked out of his study, which Kade was sure had been empty just moments before.

Zayle was well into his seventies but he appeared to be in his mid-forties. Kade was certain that his master had found a calling that slowed aging and hoped he would share that knowledge with him someday. The Master Chosen was strong of body and sharp of mind. He was the most gifted Master Chosen living. To be around him made you feel as if you were in the presence of power. When he spoke, it was with authority.

"I am sorry, Master. Please forgive me. I forget myself," Kade said with his head down, feeling embarrassed for addressing his master in such an informal way. He could feel his face burning from embarrassment. His pulse raced as he yearned to explain that he had a dragon for him to see. He opened his mouth several times but closed it when his master would raise a threatening eyebrow. Zayle could pontificate to great lengths, and Kade was afraid this was going to be one of those times as he scolded Kade hotly.

"I want to know where you have been for the last four hours. You know I do not allow you to leave in the middle of a lesson!" Zayle said heatedly, his face tight from controlled anger. For a moment, Kade wished he were back facing the cat-like creature instead of this verbal attack. The grimalkin could only kill him, where Zayle intimidated him to the very core of his being, making him squirm uncomfortably.

When Zayle paused to formulate his next assault, Kade seized on his chance and inhaled so quickly to tell of his dragon that the Master Chosen actually flinched. Before he could start to speak, doubt crept into his heart as he thought back on a time when he used to tell stories about monsters coming for him. It was more that he was telling of dreams he had that seemed so incredibly real, but Zayle always claimed he was making things up. He let out his breath and drew another just as quickly.

"I don't know if you will believe me, but I swear what I am going to tell you is the truth," Kade said, cringing inside because he knew he had used the exact same words in the past.

Zayle turned his full attention on Kade, his eyes boring holes in him with obvious doubt, as if to say, "You dare treat me like I am stupid!" Kade felt a rush of panic and exasperation flood over him, but he forced himself to continue.

"No, no! Please give me a chance!" Kade pleaded desperately.

"Well?" Zayle asked with patience that was quickly slipping. "Go on already with this…story. It better be good or I just might not have an apprentice any longer," Zayle said, not really meaning it. Whether he wanted to admit it or not, he was deeply fond of Kade, but his impatience and temper made him say things at times that he did not mean.

"Well, first, I ran into this dragon that tried to kill me while I was walking," Kade said, noticing the blank look on his master's face. He was confused at the lack of any response or reaction. Master Zayle should have given some sign of believing or not believing but silence definitely was not normal. Kade rushed on. "After we started fighting, I noticed it was injured and tried to help it by using the Healing Calling you taught me, and it became my dragon," Kade said all in one breath, afraid when he was done talking his master was going to chastise him harshly. He could see his chance to convince his teacher evaporating as the story even sounded unbelievable in his own ears.

"Go on," Zayle said a bit ominously. Kade was shocked at the encouragement to continue.

"Well, right after I healed the dragon, it saved my life from a grimalkin," Kade said unsteadily, getting a bad feeling in his gut that things were not going well. He could not see what he was missing, but he was sure it was not good. Before he could continue, his hopes were crushed as Zayle interrupted.

"A grimalkin?" Zayle yelled incredulously.

"Yes! A grimalkin almost as big as this cabin and it had

28

wings and a beak," Kade said as he waived his arms around in the air. "And it was trying to attack me when the dragon intercepted it and almost got killed," Kade said. He paused a moment as he saw a look pass through Zayle's eyes so quickly he was not sure he saw it at all.

"So you say it almost got killed? What happened? Did you use your grand powers to fend it off and save the dragon?" Zayle asked sarcastically as he waved his hands over his head, clearly deciding that this all was an elaborate story to cover up for leaving in the middle of a lesson.

"Well, sort of. I used the Fire Calling to try to kill the creature and help the dragon, since it saved my life," Kade said hesitantly.

"And I suppose this all happened just outside the protective barrier? Hmmm?" Zayle asked, sounding as though he did not believe what he was being told, but Kade sensed something was out of place.

Was it fear? he thought to himself as he contemplated his master's expression.

"Do not analyze me!" Zayle roared.

It was something Kade would do at times when he and his master were in one of their debates. It infuriated Zayle, but it was also part of what the Master Chosen liked about Kade. It showed a sign of thoughtfulness and intelligence, and that is what kept those that used the Divine Power alive. The number of Chosen with the talent to use the Divine was almost nonexistent as it was.

"Well, actually it was far from the shield. I lost track of the distance," Kade said, believing he was losing the fight to convince his master. Desperation made it hard to think logically. He suppressed the urge to yell as he fought to organize his thoughts.

"And, of course, you are going to tell me that the dragon and grimalkin were able to get through my Barrier Calling?" Zayle asked skeptically. "And I bet you stopped them from smashing this cabin, and I bet you're even going to tell me you saved me. That must mean

I owe my life to you," he added, gaining just a little control but tossing in a fair share of sarcasm. "Come on, Kade. You don't really expect me to believe anything you just told me, do you?" Kade hesitated, believing that his master actually meant the question…almost. "Why don't you try telling me the truth instead of making up this wild story?" Zayle continued, exasperated. Kade sensed there was more to this conversation than he was aware of, but he was unable to grasp why.

"But, it is the truth!" Kade pleaded desperately. "Look," he said, pointing to his forehead where the dried blood had smeared. Zayle glanced up and for a second, Kade thought his master was convinced.

"Okay, Kade. If you can't tell me the truth, then you can expect no lessons in the use of the Divine Power for at least one month, and you will be splitting all the wood and plowing the field for the garden without my help. When you feel like telling me the truth, come find me. I am very disappointed with you," Zayle said as he turned to go into the den. But, Kade could swear that Zayle was acting…odd. Kade shook his head roughly, desperate to convince his master. But, the more Kade thought about it, the more he got the feeling that Zayle was hoping to hear Kade say that this was all made up.

"Master, no!" Kade said as he grabbed Zayle by the arm. He felt his teacher go as rigid as iron. When Zayle turned back to face his pupil, his face was ash-white. Kade pulled his hand back quickly, as though he had reached into a fire and grabbed the hottest coal. Zayle's eyes slowly slid down from his student's eyes to linger over where Kade had just grabbed him. The apprentice could feel the whirl of emotions, causing his head to spin. He froze, waiting for the verbal barrage he knew was coming.

"This had better be good. What would ever make you think it was okay for an apprentice to touch his master?" Zayle asked in a hiss that was barely audible.

"The dragon! It's waiting for me back by the path," Kade said with excitement as he felt like the biggest fool for not bringing it up sooner.

"Of course. This is the dragon that was able to break through my calling, right?" Zayle asked, the anger causing him to shake, but again, Kade was sure there was more going on than he could see.

There was a look in his master's eyes that Kade could not understand. He ignored it as he knew he had better do this quickly or he was going to lose his chance to convince his master, and he would find himself a beggar in the streets of Espren. He took a precious moment to calm himself as he breathed deeply, forcing himself to think.

"I stake my training that what I say is true," Kade said in more of a rush than he wanted. "Please come see the dragon. If everything I have said is not true, then I will leave immediately," he said, almost instantly regretting risking his way of life.

What if the dragon is gone when I return to the path? Kade asked himself, as he dried his palms on his pants. Even though there was a strict understanding of apprentice to master, Kade had come to care about Zayle as he would his own father. He fought down a sense of panic at taking this risk, but he knew this would get Zayle's attention.

The Master Chosen seemed to lose all his anger as he studied his student, taking in the disheveled hair and the torn clothes. Kade saw Zayle's eyes flit to his forehead and then they were distant, as though he were considering something, or possibly...replaying a memory in his head. Kade misunderstood, believing his master was losing interest and panicked. "I promise, Master! Please, just this once, trust me! I give you my word!" Kade begged as he tried to make his voice more firm, but it ended up sounding closer to pleading which, of course, he was.

31

Color returned to his face as he looked at Kade, considering his offer. Sadness flashed in his eyes for just a moment and then disappeared. He knew that Kade lived for the day when he could command the Divine Power, and for him to make this offer could not have been easy.

"I know how important your training is to you, so I am going to give you this chance. If you can't produce the dragon, then you leave today," Zayle said, hoping the threat of accepting Kade's terms would cause him to change his story. Seeing that his apprentice wasn't going to give a different accounting, he continued. "Now, show me this dragon," he said, fearing he would find no such creature. Kade ran out the door quickly, urging his master to follow. Even though he had his failings, Kade was the cherished son that Zayle never had.

"Well, he could not get past the calling, as you said, so I have to take you to him," Kade explained. He could see his master's resolve firm as his face tightened into anger combined with what Kade thought might be uncertainty.

"This had better be real or you will regret wasting my time," Zayle vowed.

"The dragon is right outside the barrier. Right along the path," Kade said as he pointed animatedly. He found himself trying to, once again, analyze his master's reaction.

"I did feel a slight pushing in that vicinity," Zayle said more to himself. "Could be anything from fluctuation in the Divine Power to a large animal, but we shall see. Okay," Zayle said resolutely, "show me your dragon. I will come to see if it exists. We leave after I get my walking cloak. Be ready."

Kade breathed a sigh of relief but even five minutes was torture. Every second that ticked by brought thoughts of disaster. *What if the dragon is gone?* he thought as he felt panic well up again. *Why would a dragon wait for me when it barely knows me? How would it know how long it was supposed to stay?*

Fear of losing his apprenticeship worked its way back into his heart. He was deep in thought with all the possible things that could go wrong when he flinched at the sound of Zayle's voice. Kade went in and saw his master standing just inside the door to the den. He had his red walking cloak on, but was not moving. Kade froze as he watched Zayle standing very still, staring into the Blue Flame of the Divine while it danced in his hands. His eyes were the blackest of black, with no whites showing. He was studying the flames as if watching a scene unfolding before him. His eyes looked this way and that way, taking in what he was seeing. Zayle frowned deeply, and then he looked up to see Kade watching him. The flame faded out and the frown disappeared as though it had never been. The black faded and the Master Chosen's eyes returned to normal. Kade had only seen his master do this one other time, and it unsettled him just as deeply now as it had then.

"Alright Kade, I shall go see this dragon," Zayle said as he brushed past his apprentice.

Kade found it hard not to push as he fought to stay behind his master, as was appropriate. He found he was breathing in huffs of frustration as he struggled to control the urge to race ahead, or prompt his master to pick up the pace. Every time he opened his mouth to compel Zayle to a greater speed, he would close it again, knowing that his teacher would only stop and lecture him on proper behavior. An apprentice is not to tell a master what to do.

Besides, he kept telling himself, *at least he is going to see the dragon and know that I have spoken the truth.*

Kade looked at his beloved teacher several times and could have sworn that it was a look of worry he was seeing. It was clear he was contemplating something, but what? They continued on like this the entire walk. He was considering asking what would worry his master when he realized they were approaching the spot where his dragon should have been. He tried to swallow and could not. His throat seized up as his fears about the dragon leaving became a reality. That feeling of just about falling off a cliff and barely catching himself at the last moment was back, but this time it was different; this time he was going over the edge. Everything was falling apart. He found it difficult to think as he raced past his master and stared at the empty spot where his dragon had been.

"He was right here! I swear he was!" Kade said in rushed words, as desperation started to crush any hope he had of proving that he had spoken the truth.

Kade was afraid to look his master in the eyes. His mind was still racing when he started yelling for the dragon at the top of his lungs. He yelled over and over, but there was nothing. The only thing that answered him was the sound of the wind. Kade did not see that Zayle was watching him intently, studying him.

"Dragon, where are you?" Kade screamed, frustration and anger gripping his heart. Still, the area was quiet. Zayle seemed to breathe a sigh of relief and glared at Kade with a look that said, "I knew this was going to happen."

"I swear on my life, Master! He was right here!" Kade said as he stabbed his figure toward the ground. "Look," he said as he noticed the scrape marks where the dragon had clawed at the dirt.

Without even a glance, Zayle started to turn and walk away, saying, "I'll expect you to pack your things tonight. I will give you a day to figure out what you are going to do," he said, knowing that he was only doing this to force the truth out of Kade. At least, he thought he would not force his beloved apprentice to leave. Maybe it would be for the best, but that was to be decided later when things settled down. For now, Zayle would let his apprentice believe he was to leave.

Kade, now angrier than his master had ever seen him, screamed until he was hoarse. Over and over, he called out to the silent forest. He listened hard for any sound, but the area was quiet. Kade took a deep breath and put everything into his next call, turning red in the face.

"Dragon, where are you?" Kade screamed.

Surprised by this last attempt, Zayle slowly regarded his apprentice with narrowed eyes. Kade yelled several more times, every yell becoming weaker and weaker until he stopped and hung his head. Grief overwhelmed him at the thought of leaving the one place he truly felt like he belonged. His place was here with Zayle, studying to be the greatest Master Chosen there ever was. Now, his dreams were fading right before his eyes. He told himself he would not break down, but instead, he would be a man about it. He could feel the start of a tear form in his eye.

"I am sorry," Kade said with as much control as he could muster. "I guess he left," he added but already regretting saying it, knowing his master did not believe the truth. Persisting when Zayle had made up his mind never worked out in his favor.

Kade walked past his mentor on his way toward the cabin. He could not even bring himself to look at the Chosen for fear of seeing disappointment in his eyes. But, he still glanced back, and before he could look away, noticed a strange look on the Master Chosen's face. Zayle was turning his head as if listening. He slowly raised his hand over the ground, as though feeling heat rise from a fire. After several movements with his hand, and a few unrecognizable words, a shimmer shot forth to hit the ground.

Kade started to get a bad feeling in his gut. Zayle seemed tense and it worried him. It worried him deeply. He took a couple of steps toward his master and asked, "What?"

"Hush," Zayle commanded. "Something," he said slowly. "Something comes. And, it's large."

Zayle slowly looked up and regarded the woods, but it was worry that Kade saw in the man's eyes. *Why?* he thought to himself.

Why would Master appear to be so worried and even...afraid? Kade pondered as he saw a look in his master's eyes that he could not ever recall seeing. It was then that he felt the vibrations of something hitting the ground hard and coming fast. The vibrations were getting stronger by the second. His heart leapt as his hopes started to soar.

Could it be my dragon? Kade considered, fearing to hope too much. He paused for a moment, liking the thought of having a dragon once again. He liked it more and more, considering no one else had a dragon. Well, no one that he had ever heard of that was alive. There were stories of Ancient Chosen having dragons, but that had been millennia ago. Any moment his dragon was going to burst out of the woods, proving to his master that everything he had been saying was true.

His hopes were rising until his analytical mind took over, forcing thoughts into his head that were not as promising. *What if it is another animal? What if it's another grimalkin?* He fought the panic as he watched the woods intently. *It has to be the dragon,* Kade thought as the shaking of the ground increased. The thought of a cat-like creature charging at them had him on edge. He relaxed just a little but only a little as the protective barrier shimmered.

Kade noticed his master watching him, reading all his facial expressions. He wondered what his master saw and what conclusion he drew. But, the look of worry on Zayle's face did not sit well with him. Kade was certain his master was keeping something from him. He was considering asking what was wrong, but the sound in the forest was getting louder, and closer. When it seemed as if it was almost upon them, there was a deafening roar that made both men's hearts jump. The sense of shear power in that sound made Kade swallow hard. The dragon burst into the opening and slammed into the barrier. It bounced off so violently that Kade thought it might have broken its neck. After a few moments, it quickly regained its feet, and its eyes locked onto Kade. The dragon reoriented and

36

pushed against the barrier, trying to get to the man it had known only a few short hours, but was attached to, nonetheless. The stories he had heard about the Chosen having dragons briefly flashed through his mind, and then he was focused on this one.

Kade felt as if his heart might explode with joy as he raced toward his dragon and threw his arms as far around its neck as he could. He never felt a more sweet sensation on his face than the supple, leathery feeling of his dragon's scales. Zayle looked on in horror, expecting this beast to snap up his apprentice with those dangerous teeth.

"I thought you had left," Kade said in a rush. "I cannot begin to tell you how happy I am to see you," he said, not wanting to take his hands off the dragon, as if doing so might cause it to flee and never come back.

Kade turned with pride and overflowing joy to introduce his new dragon but froze with the words stuck in his throat. The look of horror and dismay on Zayle's face mixed with fear on the edge of panic caused Kade's pulse to quicken. Overwhelming confusion filled him as he looked upon his master, whose eyes appeared to be coming out of his head. This was very much not in Zayle's behavior, and it had Kade scared to the very core of his being.

"Master, what is it? What is wrong?" Kade pleaded.

"This can't be!" Zayle said as he quickly spun through the moves that would bring the Blue Flame of the Divine to life. The Master Chosen's eyes turned pitch black, as if made of marble. Kade winced at the image. This was twice in one day and it was more eerie than Kade cared for. The fire danced in Zayle's bare hands. He moved his head back and forth, watching…something. He quickly snapped his hands shut and the flame drifted away. "Is the part about the grimalkin also true? Is it really out there?" Zayle said, regaining his composure.

"Yes," Kade said, an uneasy feeling spreading through his

body.

"How?" Zayle asked himself, as his mind worked furiously. He spun on Kade, and with eyes more intense than the apprentice had ever seen, demanded, "Quickly, take me to it! Hurry! I must see this!"

"I am not sure if I can. I was deep in thought as I was walking and not really paying attention where I was going," Kade said, hesitantly.

"I must see this creature," Zayle said with so much force that Kade flinched and took a step back.

"I will do what I can," Kade replied as an idea came to him. He turned to the dragon. "Can you take me to the grimalkin?" Kade asked. The dragon looked at him in confusion. Chastising himself for being a fool for thinking the dragon would understand, he got down on all fours and pretended to take a swipe at the dragon where it was previously injured. He was at a complete loss as to how to communicate what he needed, but he had no other ideas so he repeated the action. The dragon gave a huff and took a step backward.

"So, you know I am talking about the grimalkin. Well, that is good. Now, how to get you to take me to it?" he asked to himself as much as the dragon. It was tilting its head back and forth, watching Kade closely. "Where?" Kade asked as he stood and walked in the general direction he knew it had to be. "Where?" he asked again, as he indicated the woods with a sweep of his arm while looking at the dragon. Kade felt something brush his mind, and then it was gone.

"OK, well I will do what I can, Master, but I only recall the general direction," Kade said, giving up on communicating with the dragon. He turned and started down the path. Suddenly, the dragon gave a grunt and lumbered by. Both men watched it with curiosity as it stopped and turned to look at them. Kade got the feather-light touch on his mind again and looked deep into the dragon's eyes. He could almost swear he was connecting with it in some way, but that was crazy thinking. It had to be.

"Master?" Kade asked, surprised at the dragon's action.

"I say we follow. I must see, and if this is the only way, then we try."

Kade and Zayle worked their way through the heavy brush, trying to stay with the dragon, but it did not want to stay on the path, so it was not easy going. It only made sense. The dragon had to be following the scent of the grimalkin, leading them directly to it.

The dragon had to stop several times to wait for the two men. After having to call the dragon back constantly, it did a curious thing; it came over next to the two men and knelt down. Kade and Zayle looked at each other in amazement.

"Master, do you suppose he...wants us to ride?" Kade asked in disbelief.

"It would appear that way," Zayle said as he narrowed his eyes, studying the fearsome creature. "There is only one way to find out, and that is to try mounting," he said in awe.

Kade had never seen his master in awe of anything. As a matter of fact, he could not recall ever seeing his master show much emotion of any kind, aside from anger and frustration. Kade cleared his head and focused on the task at hand.

"Here goes," Kade said as put his foot on the dragon's leg. He reached up, grabbed ahold of the ridges on the dragon's neck and struggled to pull himself onto its back.

Now, it was Zayle's turn. He approached the dragon cautiously from the left side. As he closed the distance, the dragon swung its head around to follow his movements. Zayle hesitated, noticing those sharp teeth. The dragon's lips were twitching slightly.

"Are you sure this dragon of yours will not try to make a meal out of me? I don't like the look in its eyes," Zayle said as he matched the dragon stare for stare.

And, to make the point even more so, the dragon gave out a low rumble, as more of its razor-sharp teeth showed. Clearly, it was not accepting of all people. It was then Kade realized Zayle was drawing on the Divine.

"Master, I think it senses your use of the power and does not like it."

"And I am to completely put my life in its hands?" Zayle asked, incredulously.

"Master, would I be sitting on its back if it planned on killing us?"

"Apprentice," Zayle said, "you had better be right." And with that, Zayle let the Divine Power melt away.

"Dragon, it's okay," Kade said as he stroked its neck. "He is not going to hurt you," he said in a soothing tone.

The dragon craned its neck just a little more to look at Kade. After a moment, it seemed to accept his urgings and allowed the Master Chosen to approach. Zayle held his breath as he reached up to grab Kade by the forearm and smoothly swung up to land behind his apprentice. The dragon tensed at the new touch, but to their relief, did nothing more.

"Your new pet is very solid," Zayle said. He looked over at the wings, readying himself for flight. It took a moment for Kade to realize what his master was expecting. He chuckled but only briefly as his master glared at him hard enough to freeze him solid. Even if Kade was turned away, he could have felt that glare right through the back of his head.

"He cannot fly, Master. He was injured in the fight and needs time to heal," Kade said humbly. Zayle relaxed slightly, but only slightly.

"Well, it will still be much faster than walking, so let's get your new pet moving," Zayle said as he looked the creature over in amazement.

The dragon was regarding the pair as they talked. It appeared to be very curious as to what was going on. Kade and Zayle were both surprised to see it holding perfectly still as it analyzed them. They looked at each other and then shrugged. Zayle, again, became impatient but sat still, waiting.

"Okay, dragon, let's get moving," Kade said as he pointed the way they had been going. "Let's go find that grimalkin."

The dragon let out an ear shattering roar that shook both men to the bone and left their teeth rattling. With that, it leapt with amazing power that almost unseated them both. After a few uncomfortable moments of getting situated, the dragon settled into a comfortable lope. But, even at this, it was not easy to stay seated.

"Why does he do that?" Kade asked, expecting his master to always have the answers.

"I believe they do it to warn any predator to stay out of the way, or it could be some kind of dominance or territorial issue," Zayle said as he rubbed his ears.

"Well, if I heard a sound like that, I would definitely stay out of his territory."

After running for almost fifteen minutes, the dragon came to a stop just fifteen feet from the charred remains of the grimalkin, or what left of it. There were considerably more animals in the area now and they were all of the predatory variety.

The dragon flexed its shoulders while sticking its neck out and glared at the animals in the clearing. Several moved but many more continued to feast on the cooked meat. The dragon let out a deadly hiss, causing a few more to scamper out of harm's way. The dragon, feeling its warning was not being taken serious enough, stood up and opened its wings to their full size. Kade was amazed with the splendor of this magnificent beast as he slid down to the ground. Zayle also quickly slid down, sensing it was going to attack at any moment.

The dragon obviously took offence that not every living creature had run for its life and launched into the remaining animals with another one of those ear-splitting roars. It proceeded to rend everything it could get its jaws and claws into. It was not a pretty sight at all. It made Kade slightly queasy to think back on what would have happened to him had the dragon not been so badly injured when he first blindly stumbled onto it. Ironically, it occurred to him that he probably owed his life to the grimalkin.

Kade shook his head and watched his dragon do what it did best; hunt, tear flesh and feed. He glanced at Zayle and saw his master deep in thought. The feeling that something serious going through the Chosen's mind returned, and the more Kade thought about it, the more he knew he needed to know what it was.

Later, he told himself, but it was getting more and more difficult to keep saying later.

The dragon charged around the carcass in search of something on the other side to fight. Kade looked around the head of the cat-like monster and saw a grizzly bear hit the ground for the last time. The dragon looked up, sensing something coming and took a step toward Kade, hissing as it got ready to pounce for its next attack. It stumbled slightly as it caught itself, just barely recognizing Kade before it leapt. It lowered its head and took a slow, shuffling step backward as its head swayed from side to side. It was a pitiful sight.

The half leap toward him was enough to put a lump the size of a grapefruit in his throat and cause his heart to pump several times very hard. Kade quickly approached the dragon, giving it a pat on the shoulder, letting it know everything was ok. He felt a strong, growing admiration for this dragon that could be so fierce, and yet, was so gentle with him.

As he stepped back, Kade noticed a small superficial cut and quickly healed it, as a show of affection. This was his dragon, and he enjoyed taking care of it. He patted it on its side to let it know the healing was done. Its head came up and it looked Kade over, analyzing his face closely. After a few long moments of looking directly into his eyes and seeing no displeasure, the dragon perked up.

Kade returned to his master with the dragon on his heels. He thought Zayle was looking at him in wonder and amazement. He could not have been more wrong. Zayle went back and forth between the dragon and the grimalkin several times. The look of concern crossed his face and just as quickly, it was concealed.

Without much thought, Kade blurted out, "Master, why do you look as though you are…?" Kade said and then hesitated, not finishing the question. He never knew Zayle to be afraid of anything. The powerful Chosen had immense control of the Divine Power and there was not much that could threaten him. Kade was afraid of insulting his teacher but he had to know. "Master?" Kade persisted.

"It is not the grimalkin that I fear but what is meant by the creature being here," Zayle said as he furrowed his brow, returning his gaze to the hulking mass of flesh. "It is what is meant by the monster being here," he repeated to himself. He quickly called on the Blue Flame of the Divine. Zayle stared intently at the scene only he could see for several long, tense moments and then snapped his hands closed.

"Master, I don't understand," Kade said, ignoring the knot that was pulling tighter and tighter in his gut. He had had enough of his nerves being frayed for a lifetime, but it would appear that it was not going to end anytime soon. "What does it mean?" he asked as forceful as he dared, the image of those deep, black eyes still haunting him.

Zayle quickly held up his hand in a gesture that commanded silence. Kade knew this command well as his master would use it when the Apprentice Chosen was asking too many questions or when he just wanted a moment of silence. He did that curious thing where he tilted his head and seemed to be listening again. Then, his hand came up and the Divine Power shot forth to hit the ground once more. Zayle's eyes widened as he stood perfectly still for several long seconds.

"We must leave now!" Zayle almost yelled. It was definitely a command that was not to be ignored. "Now, Kade, now!" he said again more forcefully.

"Okay," Kade said in a rush.

The dragon had started to chase the other animals that it thought had strayed too close to its new companion. It started to make a game out of this until Kade called to it. The dragon was more than eager to answer his new friends call.

"Dragon, come over here. We have to leave right away!" Kade said in a rush. "We have to leave now! The master says there is still danger here," he said as he gestured around the clearing. The dragon sensed his panic, but did not move. It had no idea what was being said nor did it understand what was happening.

"Kade, now!" Zayle bellowed, fraying the apprentice's nerves even more.

"We need to go back," Kade said as he pointed to himself, then Zayle and then back the way they had come. The dragon looked in the direction he was pointing, but clearly nothing was making sense. Zayle pushed Kade toward his dragon, eager to be racing for the protective barrier. The dragon flinched hard as it swung its head around, almost knocking the two men off their feet. Kade moved closer again and placed his hands on the dragon as though to pull himself onto its back. There was that odd, slight brushing in his mind, and then the dragon knelt down. Kade stepped onto the dragon's leg to help boost himself up and then reached down, grabbing Zayle by the wrist, pulling him onto the dragon's back.

As soon as Zayle was seated, the dragon's head came up sharply and it sniffed the air several times in rapid succession. Kade could feel its body go rigid. The dragon's muscles became as hard as a rock. It bounded to its feet as it made a quick survey of the area and then bolted off the way they had come. Even though they were ready for it, they almost lost their seating.

Kade saw what looked almost like terror on his master's face. He tried to tell himself that everything was going to be fine, but the fear wrapping itself around his mind was paralyzing. As much as he tried to convince himself that they were in no danger while in the presence of the mighty Zayle, deep down inside he knew better. Zayle was no longer able to conceal his fear and it scared Kade to the core.

"We will be back behind the barrier in no time, Master," Kade said, trying to reassure himself as much as his beloved teacher. He was met with silence. Before he could say another word, he heard what had Zayle so concerned. At first, he was hoping it was his imagination, but in the pit of his stomach, he knew he was about to find out what his master was afraid of and why the dragon had reacted so intensely.

The sound was starting to get closer but that could not be. The dragon was racing through the forest as swift as the wind. Trees and brush alike passed by in a blur.

What in the world could match the speed of a dragon, much less catch it? Kade thought in despair.

"Master, do you hear it?" Kade yelled over the wind. Again, he was only met with silence. "It sounds like something is following us."

"Kade, you must get the dragon to move as fast as it can. We are in grave danger outside the Barrier Calling," Zayle said with so much conviction that Kade felt his throat constrict. He swallowed hard to loosen his chest and took a deep breath, ready to scream his panic.

"Dragon, run! Run for all you're worth!" Kade yelled. The dragon understood the urging as its huge muscles bunched and exploded with a burst of speed that left Kade speechless. He felt a rush of adrenalin as the wind raced by. This was sheer power and grace. The dragon twisted and turned better than any cat could, as it dodged in and out of trees on its headlong race for its life.

By his guess, Kade surmised that they were halfway to the barrier, but it was about that time that he could feel the vibrations of something heavy hitting the ground behind them. He looked back and saw the tops of the trees moving as something easily shoved them out of the way. He knew something massive was coming after them at speeds even greater than the dragon's. Kade rubbed his eyes, not believing what he was seeing. The trees were falling and moving, but there was nothing there. He rubbed his eyes again and looked as hard as he could but still…nothing.

It was then that a childhood story came rushing back to him about cats and invisible giant creatures made of the Divine, and he knew, in an instant, that it was no story. These were facts that Zayle had told him, and when Kade would refer to them as stories, Zayle would never say different.

"Master, I think we are being followed by…something," Kade forced out past the fear that threatened to choke off his voice.

"I know, and I know what it is," Zayle said with certainty.

The dragon sensed their urgency and added yet even another burst of speed. Kade was almost speechless as the ground blurred by. Each stride covered a great distance, and yet, Kade was pushing for more.

"Use your Divine Fire Calling. We need to slow it down so we can make it to the barrier!" Zayle yelled over the wind.

"But, I can't even see it. How am I supposed to fight it?" Kade asked in desperation.

"Just start throwing your Divine Fire where you think it is! Try! You must!"

Kade was thankful for the dragon's smooth ride as he turned

as far as he could and started throwing Divine Fire over Zayle's head. Performing the moves for the calling was a challenge and was dangerous beyond understanding. For Zayle to ask him to do so on the back of a dragon that was racing wildly through the forest could only mean the worst.

Kade was rewarded as his first Fire Calling exploded against something unseen. It was massive and it scared Kade to death. Whatever it was hesitated only momentarily when the blue fire erupted against it, but then it was back at full speed with a roar of hatred and anger. The hairs on the back of Kade's neck stood up, but he forced himself to continue throwing the Fire Callings as fast as possible. To his dismay, each calling was swatted aside. The being was determined to catch them, and Kade knew with complete certainty that if it did, they were done. Because of the smoke trail coming off the invisible giant, they had something to aim for.

Kade almost lost his balance when Zayle sent his own calling arcing back at the creature. It had been a very long time since he had seen his master display such deft movement. Zayle's hands flew at blinding speeds to send the bolt of lightning racing at the creature. The explosion alone made Kade's ears ring furiously, not to mention the flash of light that almost blinded him. The lightning was a direct hit but it was not going to stop the beast. Although it bellowed in pain, it was just too powerful, and both men knew it. This was something made from the Divine but used for evil, and it was going to take much more time than they had to figure out how to defeat it. The creature was gaining on them, and it was becoming all too obvious they weren't going to make it to the barrier unless they could get some distance between themselves and it. He shook his head in disbelief and yelled to his master.

"It is going to catch us!"

"I know," Zayle said with desperation filling his voice. "I have an idea. Do you recall that Transparency Calling I taught you?"

"Yes...I do," Kade said hesitantly. "Yes," he said a second time, trying to sound more confident. He knew Zayle could hear the doubt in his voice but continued on regardless. "I will do my best," he added.

"You can't just try this time, you have to do it!"

"Just tell me when," Kade said, forcing confidence in his voice. Anger started to fill him. The same kind of anger he felt when he turned on the grimalkin. The kind of anger that makes a man take up a fight that he knows he should run from.

"Now!" Zayle ordered.

Kade did his best to clear his mind. The creature roared as it anticipated catching its prey, causing him to lose his concentration. Kade could hear the dragon's labored breathing and told himself to focus. Right now was not the time to add more things for him to concern himself with. The calling took a lot of motions and thought at the same time, making it almost impossible while trying to stay astride. If the thought and moves were not perfectly timed, the calling would not work and could produce disastrous results.

"Now Kade!" Zayle yelled and Kade knew there was no more time for preparation. It was now or never. He was vaguely aware of Zayle preparing his own calling as the Divine flowed into both men.

Here goes, Kade thought as he closed his eyes and went through the motions. The danger of performing such a calling in this situation was causing his heart to pound like mad. Upon completion of the last move, he was more than eager to cast the calling, desperately hoping he performed it correctly. He let the Divine flow and it left him to do his bidding. He opened his eyes and instantly clenched every muscle in his body, expecting to hit the ground with a bone-crushing impact as his dragon veered off to the right. Confusion racked his brain as he watched his dragon shoot off into the woods with its two passengers. With his teeth clenched and his breath locked in his chest, realization slowly dawned on him of what must have happened. An Illusion Calling. He gave a shuddering heave of his chest as his muscles unclenched and hope flooded anew.

"Well done, Kade," Zayle whispered as the malevolent creature thundered past them after the illusion, its footsteps pounding the ground. "Another few seconds and it would have had us. Look ahead. I can see the barrier. We shall survive," Zayle said, boosting Kade's hopes.

With a jolt of adrenaline, it occurred to Kade that they might make it to the safety of the barrier, but the dragon would be kept out, meaning certain death for it. With forced quiet, Kade whispered, "We cannot leave the dragon outside the barrier. It will not survive if that thing finds it."

As if to emphasize this, the creature roared and was quickly coming back. Kade looked up and saw the smoke coming straight toward them. They had moments at best.

"Kade, we must go," Zayle hissed.

"I will not leave the dragon to die," Kade insisted.

"Get your dragon ready then, because this is going to be close," Zayle said as he refocused on the calling.

The dragon slowed and then came to a stop as it pushed against the barrier. It huffed several times and grunted with the effort. Kade patted it gently in an effort to calm it. *Patience*, Kade thought as strongly as he could. *Patience*.

Kade could feel his master working with the Divine Power as he started to do whatever it was he was going to do. The creature stopped for several moments and then started in their direction once again. Kade held his breath, waiting, hoping.

"Master, hurry!" Kade said in as much of a hushed voice as he could muster.

"Silence!" Zayle hissed. "If this is done wrong, we won't need to worry about that thing. This will destroy us instantly."

Kade forced himself to stay quiet. He tried to keep the dragon calm by patting it on the neck and whispering to it. To his amazement, it stopped pushing against the barrier and stood completely still. But, its muscles were rock-hard, and it was ready to shoot off in any direction.

The creature was getting closer to them by the second. Kade knew it was tracking them, and he knew it was going to find them if they did not get through the barrier soon, but what he could not understand was how. The creature took several long strides in their direction, covering almost half the distance. Just then, Kade heard the creature take several long, deep breaths and realization came crashing down on him.

"It smells us," Kade whispered before he could help himself, on the verge of shrieking.

The creature jerked in the direction of the sound and snorted as if startled. This close, Kade was able to just make out the creature through whatever calling was hiding it. It was massive and muscles bulged on its huge arms. It had a head like a hog with horns coming off the side where ears should have been. But, what Kade saw that really caused his throat to constrict were the claws coming off of the end of each hand that had to be close to four feet long. One swipe of those deadly weapons and they were done. The creature roared in anticipation as it moved in for the kill, taking several more steps in their direction. It stopped and smelled the air again. It knew.

Kade could feel the dragon quivering, on the verge exploding into action. The creature grunted and took a swipe in the clearing where the dragon had previously tried to get through the barrier. The ground erupted as four deep gouges tore it apart only feet away. The dragon was shaking as it fought its instinct for fight or flight.

I can't believe I am going to die after surviving all that has happened, Kade thought in despair. He clenched his teeth and decided he was not going to go out without a fight. He wished he had his master's skill but at least he had something. He could feel the dragon crouch slowly as if sensing Kade's intent. He was not sure if the dragon was getting ready to fight or run, but right then, he knew he had to focus. He felt for the Divine and started to draw it into himself, binding it to his will.

The creature took several more deep breaths as it tried to find the man it was sent to kill. Kade could swear he heard a grunt of satisfaction, and he was sure it was looking directly into his eyes. At least he would go out fighting, but before he could mold the Divine into his desires, his master's voice crashed into his nerves with a shout of, "Now Kade! Get this dragon moving!"

"Run!" Kade yelled as he urged the dragon forward frantically.

The dragon's muscles exploded as it lunged through the barrier to safety. Kade's hopes soared. He was ready to thank the Divine when he felt Zayle slam into his back with a force that sent him sprawling through the air. The dragon cried out in pain as it, too, was sent tumbling. The creature roared in anger and hatred. Kade hit the ground hard, knocking the wind out of him. After a moment, he dragged himself to his feet and took several steps away from the edge of the barrier. The creature tried over and over to reach the man just barely out of its grasp, roaring in hatred louder and louder each time. When Kade was satisfied the creature was indeed kept out, he turned his attention to his beloved teacher.

"Master Zayle, we made it," Kade said as he stumbled around, trying to find his cherished teacher. He ignored the blood dripping down his face from the gash on his forehead. He staggered a little as he left the rock with his blood smeared on it. It was hard for him to think as the world spun. "Master, didn't you hear me? We made it. Master?" Kade asked again, forcing his vision to clear as best as he could. "Master?" he asked, trying to ignore the rocking motion of the ground. "Master!" Kade yelled but was met with only the sound of his dragon's labored breathing. He knew this should matter, but

51

thoughts were hard for him to form. A faint sound reached his ears.

"Kade."

"Master, is that you?" Kade asked, confused.

"Kade," Zayle said as the breath hissed out of his body.

"Master, NO!" Kade screamed as he heard the life slipping from his cherished teacher. "Hold on! Master, HOLD ON!" Kade screamed in panic.

CH3

A jolt of adrenalin forced Kade's mind to clear. "I will remove the Transparency Calling. You will be fine," he said with urgency as he drew the Divine Power out of the calling. Both the dragon and Zayle faded into view. Kade saw the two long, deep gashes that ran from the tail of the dragon to between its wings, where just moments before, they had been sitting. He panicked as his mind processed what he was seeing. Then, Kade spotted his cherished master, lying in a pool of blood.

"Zayle!" Kade yelled as he ran up to his mentor and quickly dropped to his knees. "NO! This can't happen," he said as he brought the Divine Healing to life. "No!" Kade said with determination. The power flowed into his master over and over but seemed to sink right back out.

"Master, get up. We need to get back to the cabin," Kade said, not accepting what his eyes were showing him.

Kade felt exhaustion threaten to overwhelm him as he tried to concentrate on performing the calling without stopping. It was hard to focus on his beloved master's face as the unbidden tears blurred his vision. Desperation turned to despair as he cradled his teacher's head in his lap and wept with uncontrollable sobs that racked his body. He knew he could not heal a body that had no spark of life left. With no spirit in the body, there was nothing for the healing to attach to. He threw his head back and howled in pain, his heart threatening to burst.

Several long moments later, he slumped slightly and held his master as if to not let him go. "No," he said weakly, as he looked down at his teacher and gently stroked a piece of hair out of his face.

He tried to pull Zayle to a sitting position and saw the deep slash marks on his back that had brutally ripped the life out of him. He slowly lowered Zayle to the ground and slumped over the body, feeling himself start to fade from the intense mental fatigue. It was then that he heard a sound that caused him to stop and listen.

With a start, he remembered his new found friend. He sat bolt upright, and his head whipped around as his eyes locked onto the dragon. His body was numb, but he forced his legs to move. He stumbled over to his wounded companion and started the Healing Calling just as the dragon shuddered, taking an uneven breath. He panicked as he realized the dragon was on the brink of death.

"No. I will not let you die, too!" Kade said with conviction as he worked the Healing Calling over and over, ignoring the exhaustion that threatened to overwhelm him. Sweat ran down his back, and he could feel his muscles start to shake and twitch from the exertion. "Live! By the great Divine, LIVE!" Kade yelled. "I know you are still alive! I can sense it in you!" he said, despair starting to work its way into his heart. He felt that he was in a war with death itself, and the fear that he was losing lanced through his body.

Spots started to dance in his vision as he focused on completing the calling over and over. The dragon was still not breathing. Kade started working the calling as fast as he could, putting his hands on the wound and letting the Divine Power sink in. Fatigue was starting to cause his hands to falter slightly, but he concentrated even harder and forced his protesting muscles to work.

New tears started to form, his motions slowing and then came to a stop, as he slumped to his knees in defeat. The world spun and Kade put a hand on the ground to catch himself from falling. His labored breaths came in rasps as he cried out, "No! Not you, too! You cannot die when you trusted your life to me and saved mine! You cannot die, too!" Kade said as grief assaulted him anew.

He hung his head as the tears flowed unhindered, not noticing when the dragon took in a slow, very shallow breath. Nor did he notice when the dragon let it out again. Kade felt something drift through his thoughts but the thoughts were not his. He stopped and tried to focus on the dragon. He blinked the tears from his eyes and wiped them with the back of his hands, holding his breath as he waited. He forced his shaking hands to perform the healing calling one last time and then watched…praying with all his might.

He looked at the dragon, and his breath caught in his throat. *Could it be?* he thought, afraid to hope. The wounds did not appear to be as bad as he remembered. He shook his head and focused hard. *The injuries definitely looked as if they have closed up slightly,* he thought again, as he moved closer.

Now, filled with determination, he completed the calling several more times, ignoring his protesting muscles. His lungs were burning furiously and spots were dancing in front of his eyes. With every move, he willed the dragon to heal. He was sure he could sense life now. He was rewarded with his next calling, as the wounds smoothly closed. He looked at the gash running down the dragon's back and knew if the claws had been just a hairs-breath either way, it would have ripped a wing right off.

The dragon took another breath and let it out. Then it took a deeper breath that was closer to normal. It relaxed its body as its breathing came more freely. It opened its eyes, and with a look as though it were trying to drag itself from sleep, focused on Kade. The dragon slowly labored to get to its feet but failed, falling back to the ground. From where it lay, it nudged Kade with its muzzle. The apprentice gave a weak smile through his exhaustion and patted the dragon on the side of its face.

Kade got an uneasy feeling and looked around the clearing. Something still did not feel right. Something was making him uncomfortable. Then, his eyes fell on the spot where the creature had torn at the ground with its claws. With a rush, he realized why he was feeling uncomfortable. They were being watched.

Kade's eyes slowly traveled up to where the creature's face should be. If he looked closely, he could just barely make out the monster. He felt cold anger grow in his heart, and his lips curled into a snarl. He looked the creature in the eye and felt a raging hate filling him. He made a vow to himself that he would kill this evil thing, or give his life trying. Kade felt true hate for the first time in his life. Blackness covered his heart. Vengeance!

"You may have won for now, but this is not over!" Kade yelled. He heard what sounded like a low chuckle. His anger flared as he conjured the Blue Fire of the Divine and threw it in the direction of the giant. This effort was almost too much as it threatened to topple him, his legs wobbling horribly. To Kade's disappointment, the creature swatted it aside like it was nothing and taunted him with another laugh. Kade's hatred pulsed in him with every beat of his heart. Never before had he ever wanted to take a life as he did right then.

His fists clenched so tightly his hands ached. All he could do was watch as he saw the brush move, and he knew the creature was leaving. But, he knew it was not gone for good. He yelled one last time and then gathered his precious master in his arms and carried him to the cabin.

It had been two days since Kade buried his teacher by his favorite garden. He performed the last rights, which if what he was told was true, allowed a Chosen to transition over to the other side smoothly with their abilities. It was said that there were many hazards encountered when a Chosen died, and if one did not have the Divine Power, their chances of suffering were great. Zayle had just recently taught this to him. Kade pondered the timing of this many times as the days slipped by.

After a week, the crushing pain that gripped his heart eased just a little. Once more at his teacher's graveside, he tried to puzzle out what was happening. The image of his mentor's scared eyes flashed through his mind.

Unable to answer his own question, he left the grave and headed for the cabin while his mind continued to whirl as if it were out of control. The events of the last several days made it virtually impossible to think clearly...until this moment. As he was walking, an odd thought occurred to him. He stopped and considered what Zayle had said just days before. He was on the verge of recalling something important about death and crossing over, but he just could not bring it to the surface. He shook his head and continued to walk and then abruptly stopped as it came to him.

"Master," he said as he turned and looked back at the grave. "When you talked about finding a way to cross over from the other side, were you expecting...?" Kade let the sentence trail off. He looked at the ground and his eyes narrowed as his thoughts went around and around with his small revelation. This was just too much to contemplate this soon after Zayle's death. He shook his head and turned for the cabin once more.

Kade's mind kept pulling up images of Zayle sitting at his desk with thick tomes laid out before him. Every time he saw his master reading during the past year, Zayle would be deep in a book on the afterlife. The more he thought about it, the more questions he had.

There had to be meaning to all this, Kade thought. *It was as though Zayle knew, but at the same time, he was surprised,* he thought as he came to a stop in front of the cabin. His mind was whirling with questions as he stood for many long minutes, not moving.

He did know, Kade thought suddenly. *He taught me that ritual, knowing this might happen.* "What did you not tell me? What do I need to know?" Kade asked out loud as he looked at the freshly dug grave. He realized that he was actually waiting for an answer, as though at any moment Zayle would speak to him. But, the only sound that came was the wind and the rustle of the trees off in the distance. He used to think this was the most serene, peaceful place in the world. Now, it only held pain for him.

"What was so bad that you, the most powerful Chosen of the Divine, were afraid?" Kade asked as he began to pace. His analytical mind was starting to fire as his eyes narrowed.

Kade thought back on a time when he had walked in on his master while Zayle had been in the den, studying. He was pouring over his books about the dead when he said out loud, "You will not win! I will find out who you are," Zayle said vehemently.

"Who?" Kade had asked his master, startling him.

"Nothing you need to know right now," was Zayle's response as he violently slammed the book closed.

Suddenly, he felt a touch on the back of his neck, causing him to jump and yelp. He spun, expecting to find Zayle, but instead, found his dragon watching him quizzically. Kade felt like a fool and smiled with genuine affection at the dragon, grateful for the mental distraction. He ignored his pounding heart and reached up to scratch right under its jaw. It loved this, as was evident by the quiet rumble of pleasure that came from deep within the dragon. Kade chuckled to himself.

"Don't worry. It will be okay. I have a feeling that my master knew this was going to happen and was preparing for it," Kade said, feeling his heart rate return to a normal rhythm.

Kade paused as he recalled Zayle telling him that exact same thing. Every time he would inquire what his master was studying, Zayle's response was, "You will understand in time, the Divine willing." Just when his mind started to work again, the dragon huffed, drawing him back to the present. Kade shrugged his shoulders and decided to let it go for the time being.

"I need to go back into the cabin. I have a lot of work to do," Kade said as he turned for the door.

Kade walked into the empty home and felt as though he were walking into it for the first time. He noticed the worn wooden floor and wondered why his master never lived in anything nicer. He knew with the power Zayle commanded, he could have had almost anything he wanted. It was as if he wanted to keep it simple so as not to be noticed.

Kade turned to his right and walked the three steps it took to the entrance of Zayle's study, where all the books of knowledge were kept. He made the passes through the air, drawing the Divine up through his body and then out his hands to deactivate the hidden trap. Kade stopped again as another thought came to him. It had been only three weeks since Zayle had taught him how to disarm the calling and gain access to the study. Another thing to ponder.

The room was ten feet wide by fifteen feet long. There was a table in the middle with an old high back chair made of wood. The back and seat had black leather padding. The leather was well worn and cracked from years of use. The table was centuries old and had a lot of meaning to Zayle. For the life of him, Kade could not place the type of wood. This is where Zayle did almost all of his studying. There was a bookshelf to the left as soon as he walked into the room. Kade could feel a surge of excitement with the thought of all that knowledge at his fingertips for the taking, and then a pang of guilt stabbed at him.

"I did not want power this way, master," he said out loud. "I would give all this away to have you back," Kade said as he took a step back to emphasize the point. He sighed, taking a step closer to the bookshelf and then another to stand right in front of it.

The bookshelf appeared as old as Zayle. There were many books on the two lower shelves and just a scattering of books on the upper two levels. Kade slowly perused the labels as he ran a finger across each one. HOW TO USE THE JUNG TREE TO RELIEVE TENSION.

Bah, he thought and moved on, hoping for something that had more substance to it. He pulled book after book off the shelves, trying to find one that would give him some kind of information that he could use; either a useful manipulation of the Divine Power, or knowledge of what was happening and why. Unfortunately, every book was just like the first, so he discarded them all.

There was a slight rattle of the wind at the far wall, drawing his attention. He turned and walked the three steps to stand in front of the window. It was two feet wide and two feet tall with a cross made of wood, meeting in the middle to hold glass, if they were to use glass. Kade marveled at the simple calling that kept everything out, to include rain or bugs, but allowed the breeze in. Zayle had a way to alter the calling to keep the wind out, if needed, but on nice days, Kade could always feel the breeze wafting out of the study and through the cabin.

The wall to his right had a large board with all kinds of scribbles covering it. None of it meant anything to Kade. He tried his best to decipher it, but Zayle had never taught him the key. Tight lipped from frustration, he turned again and surveyed the room. Just as he was considering leaving, his eyes caught what looked like a small scrape mark in the wooden floor at the very edge of the rug that lay in front of the bookshelf. He walked over and stood there, looking at the floor. He slowly bent down and pulled the carpet back.

"Now what do we have here?" he mumbled to himself, expecting to find a trap door. "Nothing?" he questioned in surprise as he slid the carpet out and away from the bookshelf.

Taking a step back, he noticed the way the scrapes arced toward the bookshelf and stopped right at the edge. His eyes widened slightly, and the corners of his mouth barely twitched, as though he was on the verge of a smile. He moved closer and examined the sides of the bookcase.

"These look like they were made by the bookshelf," Kade said as he bent down and ran his fingers in the grooves. He stood and proceeded to examine every spot on the bookcase for a secret lever or handle. No matter what he pulled or pushed, there was no other indication at all that there was a lever of any sort. He even tried to pry the bookshelf away from the wall, but it was firmly stuck and gave no indication that it would open. He might as well have been trying to move a boulder.

If the master had trusted me enough to show me his secrets, this would not be that difficult, Kade thought as he moved to the other side of the bookcase. Just as he started to turn away, he caught a glimpse of metal. He peered closer and was rewarded with a discovery of what looked like a hinge.

"I knew it!" Kade exclaimed excitedly.

His excitement quickly turned to frustration as the bookcase stubbornly held onto its secrets. No matter how hard he pushed or pulled, it would not budge. It felt like wood and looked like wood, but clearly there was more at work here than could be seen by the eye. Kade shook his head slightly as he looked on in frustration.

"Master, did you not want me to find this?" Kade asked out loud, as an image of Zayle standing in front of the bookcase formed in his mind. He felt a twinge of sadness as he closed his eyes, picturing his teacher moving about the study and sitting in the chair behind him.

He opened his eyes and glanced over his shoulder at the chair. It was empty. He swallowed and refocused on the bookshelf.

The Divine Power, he thought to himself, realizing what must be at work here. He closed his eyes and recited the words in his mind that meant reveal. The calling was so simple it was almost impossible to make a mistake. As a matter of fact, it was one of the simplest callings to perform. But, without knowing of it and knowing the words to speak in your mind, it would still be out of reach for any chosen, even a master.

Kade looked through his closed eyes and saw a faint, pulsing, green glow surround the bookshelf. He smiled to himself, knowing he was finally getting somewhere. "What about going through the middle?" he asked out loud as he started pulling all the books off the shelf and piling them on the table. Something in him knew it was not going to be this simple, but he had to try. He pounded on the back panel, hoping to hear a hollow sound. Kade frowned, hearing nothing but a solid knock.

Okay, one last thing to try, he thought as he walked out of the room.

Kade turned and went outside, searching the ground for what he needed for his next attempt. Finally, his eyes landed on a fairly large rock. He picked it up and carried it back into the cabin. He turned to the right and almost walked into the study. He caught himself at the last moment, dropping the rock and even coming up on his toes before rocking back on his heels. He was just a hairs-breath away from forgetting about the protection calling. It automatically reset when the room was empty. He knew it would have paralyzed him, and with no Zayle to find him, he would have surely died on the floor. An ugly shiver ran down his back as a dozen bats flapped around in his stomach. He chastised himself for being careless.

Kade thought back on the time he found out about the trap the hard way. His master had not found him until two hours later, paralyzed on the floor. It was the most uncomfortable two hours he had ever spent.

"That was just too close," he said out loud. He swallowed hard and tried to loosen the knot in his shoulders.

Kade calmed his nerves as he prepared to deactivate the calling. He said the words in his head to allow access to the den while moving his arms in the required way. This time, he closed his eyes and used his Divine Sight to make sure it was disarmed. He was pleased to see the faint yellow outline around the doorframe, indicating that the calling was no longer active.

Kade picked up the rock and went to the bookcase. He hesitated for a moment, feeling guilty as though he were violating his master's den. It was one thing to move books around but quite another thing to destroy his master's possessions. Kade reminded himself that this all belonged to him now, certain that Zayle would want him to have whatever was hidden behind the bookshelf.

He held the rock against his right shoulder with his right hand supporting most of the weight. His left hand was on the bolder to help steady it. He took a step with his right leg, while at the same time, putting all his weight and strength into throwing. Kade waited for the splinters of wood. He flinched and almost missed seeing it bounce off without even leaving so much as a scratch. He tried to dodge the rock as it bounced to the floor and then straight into his shin, sending him into a cursing rage as he limped around the table, afraid he had broken his leg. He looked down and saw a rip in his pants where blood was just starting to seep through.

"By the mighty Divine!" Kade cursed, grateful his leg was not broke but angry, nonetheless, for being unsuccessful yet again.

Kade stopped in front of the table and brought his fist down hard as his master had done a week prior. Frustrated, he considered blasting the bookshelf with the Divine Fire. He quickly rejected the idea, certain if it worked, he would burn down the bookshelf and whatever was behind it instead, not to mention the cabin, also.

Or possibly, he thought with sarcasm, *the calling would bounce right back at me.*

"Why could you not have taught me about this?" Kade asked in frustration as he gestured toward the bookshelf while staring at the imaginary Zayle sitting in the leather bound chair.

He gritted his teeth against the pain and limped around the table to sit. Studying the bookcase, he waited for the answer to jump out at him. He racked his brain and tried his best to recall anything Zayle may have said that would help him with this riddle, but there was nothing. He calmed himself as he analyzed the bookcase carefully. Studying each shelf, he looked for anything that was different.

"Why can't it be something simple?" Kade asked out loud as he leaned back in the chair and covered his face with his hands. He paused as he thought back on something Zayle had said. "What was it you used to say about the simple way?" Kade questioned as he rose from the chair. "Something about, not always looking for the hard way, but instead, look for the easy way, especially when the situation seems hopeless."

But that does not make sense, he thought as he stood in front of the bookcase.

Really? Kade thought, sure he had it. His eyes went to the entrance to the room and then to the bookshelf. "You always did say that getting in here was simple. So, was that your way of getting in behind the bookcase, also?"

Kade took a deep breath, closed his eyes and went through the motions of the Disarm Calling. He smiled to himself as he sent the Divine into the bookcase. He let out his breath and used the Reveal Calling.

"What? Why?" Kade asked, baffled that he was wrong. "But, I was so sure that was it," he said slowly, looking up and down at the bookcase through closed eyes, searching for something that would indicate that he had deactivated a calling.

Kade tried once more to see the Divine around the bookshelf but to no avail. There was no calling holding it in place. Kade sat there for several moments with his eyes closed, trying to figure out what he was missing. He examined every shelf closely as he slid his hands along the wood. His fingers touched a knot that was slightly raised. Kade stopped and his eyes popped over. He studied the lump that was just a bit more worn than the wood around it. Putting his thumb squarely on the knot, he took a deep breath and then pressed. To his amazement, the bookcase swung effortlessly open without a sound. Kade felt his heart pound as he eagerly waited to see what secrets were now being revealed.

Was it a secret room or maybe even a secret doorway to a tunnel? Kade asked himself in excitement. He stared in amazement as the light fell across the open space. Finding only a small cubby large enough for just a few books was very anticlimactic.

"Okay. Well, not quite what I pictured, but at least we are getting somewhere. These must be important to be this well hidden," he said as he looked over five books that appeared to be incredibly old and one that appeared fairly new. Two of them he recognized, but the others, he had never seen before.

Reaching out very slowly, Kade picked up one of the books and brought it back to the table, holding it very carefully as if it might break. He closed his eyes and performed the Reveal Calling. As he expected, there was a blue aura surrounding the book. He opened his eyes and looked on the tome in amazement.

"Such a powerful calling," Kade said to himself. He knew that different colors meant more of the Divine was at use, and blue was a very high level. The more of the Divine Power that one handled, the more dangerous it was.

Kade recalled that Zayle always had his lessons laid out for him on the table whenever he entered the study. He was never allowed in the room prior to a session. He glanced up at the bookcase and now understood why.

Kade thought back on the thief that attempted to steal one of the books several years back and shuddered. The thief never even had a chance to scream as he turned to stone. His body was sent back to the man who had hired him. Zayle had mentioned that Doren, whoever that was, was going to like that delivery. The message was clearly understood, as the books were never threatened again.

Turning the book over in his hands, feeling the aged leather, Kade's curiosity built as he craved to learn the secrets at his fingertips. He ran his hands over the cover and could feel the knowledge calling to him. He looked at the book longingly, eager to know what was hidden within.

As long as nothing goes wrong, maybe I will try this book Kade thought. The image of the stone thief flitted through his mind, but he forcibly ignored it. He did not want the more cautious side of him making him wait.

After the feeling of awe at the thought of new and powerful callings passed, he performed the Disarm Calling. Kade put his hand on the cover and felt a giddy sense of adventure as the excitement built. He opened the book slowly, anticipating the great and awesome knowledge that was about to be his. He looked at the first page and frowned. It was a calling for making it rain.

"Bah. What is this? I would care if I was a farmer, but this is useless unless I want to get wet," Kade said with disappointment. He turned the page, afraid he would not find anything more exciting. "Now this is more like it," Kade said in excitement as he read, LIGHTNING CALLING. As tempted as he was to learn this, he decided to continue searching for anything that would help him understand what had caused Zayle to be so afraid. He mentally marked it as the first calling he was going to return to, when he had time. He quickly flipped through the book but soon realized that it was not going to give him the information he needed.

"Later," he said as he set the book down and patted it as if to say, "Stay right there until I get back to you." He returned to the bookshelf and glanced back at the table, feeling the desire to learn the great and powerful callings. He shook his head and mentally chastised himself.

Pulling another book off the shelf, he shivered slightly when his eyes landed on the cover and the symbol that he instantly recognized. He swallowed hard and handled the book as though he were holding something so delicate that a whisper would damage it. He desperately did not want to set off this calling.

"Wow, when you protect your books, you take no chances," he said, keeping his hands clear of the symbol.

This calling was deadly because the demon on the front actually came to life when the book was opened by the wrong person with the wrong calling. The creature was only two inches tall, but Kade knew it wasn't the size of the demon that was mattered but the deadly venom dripping from the demon's claws that was to be feared. He knew if the demon scratched him ever so slightly, it would cause agonizing pain beyond anything he had ever experienced and his death would be long and torturous.

Kade had only seen the demon one time and that was when it had first been summoned. He was allowed to watch the incredible conjuring shortly after he became an apprentice so he would know what could be called if someone had manipulated the Divine Power incorrectly. Zayle explained what the demon could do so Kade would never be foolish enough to try and mess around with it. Until now, he never knew what his master had done with it.

While holding the book, he got the feeling that he was being watched. He looked out the window, remembering the invisible creature, but saw nothing that would indicate there was a presence there.

It does not feel like it is outside, he thought, getting a very sick feeling in his stomach.

Kade looked around cautiously, worried that he had tripped one of his master's traps. He could sense the Divine Power moving ever so minutely, but it was there. He proceeded to set the book on the table when his eyes caught a slight movement from the cover. He stopped, staring at it for several long moments and was relieved to see no change. He let out the breath he was not aware he was holding and proceeded to set the book down once more. As he was placing the it on the table, the demon's head moved ever so slightly, keeping its eyes on him. Kade's hand pulled back reflexively, as if it had been stung.

He froze. He got a knot in his stomach and a sick feeling that caused his skin to prickle. He stared at the demon, and again, saw no movement. But, he could not shake the uncomfortable feeling that the hideous, little creature was looking him right in the eye. He leaned down, getting just inches from the demon and stood perfectly still for several long seconds, looking directly into its eyes, when all of a sudden…it blinked. Kade jumped and stumbled backward, slamming into the bookshelf.

"No! You can't! You cannot come out unless the book is opened. I know you can't!" he said defiantly. He looked at the book and noticed that the old, worn pages caused the book to spring open slightly. It was almost as if the pages had become wet and then dried, causing them to not be flat. "No!" he screamed as he realized what was about to happen. He recalled the book had been wedged between two others, keeping it closed. "NO, I did not open you! NO!" Kade said vehemently, hopelessly.

He knew the calling was starting to activate and felt panic well up in him. He quickly closed his eyes and used the Reveal Calling. He flinched. The angry, red pulsing coming off the book was almost too bright to look at with the Divine Sight. The calling was going to snap at any moment. His mind started to reel as he frantically tried to think. He considered making a run for it but then hesitated, and instead, leapt for the book, slamming it shut. By this time, the demons head was actually sticking up out of the book. It was eerie and odd looking. Afraid of being bit, Kade kept his hands on the edges. It was actually sneering at him.

"NO!" he screamed at it in defiance. The creature seemed to enjoy this as its grin deepened. Kade could sense the mind of the demon as it started to materialize more and more. He knew it was only seconds before this creature was free, and he also knew, without any doubt, that it was coming after him with a vengeance. If he did not do something quickly, he was going to die an agonizing death.

Don't panic, he told himself.

Kade looked back at the book and saw that the demon had one of its wings loose. It was flapping furiously, trying to free the rest of its body. For a moment, Kade thought it looked like a bat that was stuck against the book. He grabbed one of the other books and slammed it with all his might into the demon. This only caused it to work harder.

"How could I be so stupid?" Kade howled as his attention snapped back to the creature. He considered smashing the demon again, but he knew that it would only annoy it. Kade froze as an idea flashed into his mind.

If I can just complete it before that thing gets free, Kade thought as he rushed to put his plan into action. Making sure to keep his hands clear of the demon, he picked up the book and hurled it across the room as hard as he could. It came open as it fluttered away

He knew he had no time left, and if this was to work, it had to work now. He jumped back away from the book and called on the Divine Power, just as the sound of the demon's wings hitting the cover stopped. He sent the Divine Power to do his bidding and threw himself back against the wall.

A high-pitched shriek pierced every last nerve in his body, causing him to clench his muscles hard. It was like a dagger being driven right into his mind, instantly scrambling his thoughts. He felt a slight feather-light touch at the end of his nose, and then…nothing. He pried his eyes open with effort and looked at the book. Seeing nothing, he gasped in relief and fell against the wall. He closed his eyes and looked with his sight. There was a faint, yellow outline, indicating that the trap had been neutralized.

Kade stumbled to the table and fell heavily into the chair, wiping sweat from his forehead. His muscles ached painfully from the tension. He took a deep breath, let it out and slumped forward in the chair, dropping his head against the table with a thud. After taking several long, deep breaths in an attempt to calm himself, he sat up. He looked at the book, lying on the floor in the corner while he listened to his heart pound.

"Master, I am sure to parish without you," Kade said as he glanced in the direction of the grave.

Kade took a deep breath to draw strength into his body as he put his hands firmly on the armrest, preparing to lift himself out of the chair. He hesitated only slightly and then heaved himself up. His legs felt weak, but he forced himself to walk over to the book with the image of the demon. He knew it should be safe, but he was still in no rush to touch it. Bending over, he picked it up very carefully. Turning it over in his hands, he half expected the demon to leap out at him. When he looked, all he saw was its image flat on the cover.

"All I had to do from the start was deactivate the calling," Kade said, feeling very stupid for not thinking of it from the beginning. He shook his head at his own ignorance and returned to the table.

"It's a good thing Master taught me that calling, or I would be with him right now. And, lucky for me it was a simple calling," Kade said to himself as he wiped sweat from his forehead again. He stopped for a second, recalling his master's words. "You always said it would be the simple callings that will make the difference. Maybe there is wisdom in your ways after all," Kade said.

The Healing Calling is also pretty simple, Kade thought.

Kade handled the book with care, even though he knew it was no longer a threat. He placed it on the table and opened it slowly, still afraid of the demon. He could feel his nerves starting to twitch and tried to relax by shrugging his shoulders and rolling his head around. It helped very little.

He watched the book with his Divine Sight to make sure the aura surrounding it did not waiver from safe yellow. It took him several long seconds to even open just the first page. After watching intently for what felt like hours, he finally accepted that it was safe.

Kade looked at the first page, shocked at what he was seeing. There were many pictures of demons. Surprisingly, there was even one that looked identical to the image on the cover of this very book. Kade flipped to the cover and then back to the page as he studied the creature. Yes, it was identical to what he was seeing. The writing on the top of the page read, HOW TO BIND A DEMON TO YOUR SERVICE.

"I am sure I am not ready to try something like this," Kade said, pulling his hand away from the book, as though it were full of thorns. "I am certain I would just get myself killed," he said as he flipped to the next page.

Surprised again, he froze as he stared at the page. The world as he knew it was shifting right before his eyes. Things were not as he always believed them to be.

How this must have been a heavy burden on you, Kade thought as he read, NEEDED TO SEE INTO THE WORLD OF THE DEAD. He glanced at a drawing on the page and saw that it was some sort of arch. He was not sure if this was important, but by the looks of it, it was. Kade read further down the page and became lightheaded as he immediately recognized the calling on the page. It was the Drift Calling. His head started to spin. He studied every page but nothing seemed to make sense. He returned to the page with the Drift Calling and studied it, hoping something would come to mind.

Why did this matter so much? Kade asked himself. Unable to answer his own question, he closed the book and placed it back in the cubby.

Next, Kade pulled a red, leather book off the shelf and carefully set it on the table, making sure that he did not open it accidentally. He chose this book because it looked like the oldest one on the shelf, and maybe the most important. Hopefully it held the information he was looking for. The cover was old, worn leather with many symbols etched into it. At least, he hoped it was leather. It had an oily feel to it, and it made his skin crawl to touch it. He shook his head, realizing he did not want to know what it was. The cracks in the cover also indicated it was very old.

Kade closed his eyes and activated the Reveal Calling. He looked closely at the book and saw a combination of red, green and a faint blue. His eyes came open and went wide at the amount of protection this book had. He moved his hands slowly away from the book and regarded it for several long seconds.

"You placed three on this one alone?" Kade questioned incredulously as he shook his head in wonder. "You must really want this book protected. Okay then, maybe this has the answers I need," he said as he prepared to disarm the callings.

Kade made the motions to deactivate the traps while saying the ancient words in his head. He reached for the book but froze, chastising himself for being careless so soon after his recent disaster. He closed his eye, performed the Reveal Calling and was shocked to see both the blue and green outline still on the book. He tried to disarm them again, but the two callings were still present.

"Why?" Kade wondered aloud.

He sat back in the chair and regarded it through half-lidded eyes. He leaned forward, put his fists under his chin and stared at the book, waiting for something to come to mind. He tried to recall anything Zayle had said that would help but came up blank. Finally, he knew he was either going to take a chance and open the book or put it back on the shelf. The demon so fresh in his mind made the choice easy. He gently picked up the book and returned it to the shelf.

He reached for another book and pulled it out carefully. This one was made from some kind of metal. Kade placed it on the table and sat down in front of it. He performed the Reveal Calling but saw nothing. He placed his hand gently on the cover and hesitated, turning his head slightly as though listening with his mind. He closed his eyes to help him focus better. It was so faint he barely felt it, but he was certain he could feel the Divine. He pulled his hand back and performed the Reveal Calling again. He looked closely, and just when he was about to open his eyes, he saw it; a shimmer, as though heat were ever so slightly coming off the book.

"I almost did not see that," Kade said as he swallowed the lump in his throat. "I remember what you said about this one," he said, feeling confident.

Kade completed the Disarm Calling, but this time, he used a slight variation. Closing his eyes, he looked with his inner sight and was pleased to see that the shimmer was gone. He opened his eyes and placed his hand on the cover. He felt for the Divine Power as he held his breath and found nothing. Steeling his nerves, he smoothly opened the book, alert for any signs of danger. As the cover hit the table, a loud roar filled the room, causing him to jump back from the book in full panic. As he pushed away from the table, he tipped over in the chair, slamming into the floor. His heart was pounding so hard he thought it was going to burst through his chest.

Kade scrambled to his feet, preparing to meet this new danger. His eyes scanned the room, and stopped at the window. Slowly, his jaw unlocked as he huffed in exasperation.

"You," Kade growled as he made eye contact with his dragon. "Blood and ash! You almost stopped my heart!" he said as he took in a deep breath and let it out. The dragon slowly backed away from the window but did not take its eyes off him. "What?" Kade asked as he shook his head, still trying to recover. "You want me to come out?" The dragon gave a grunt which Kade took for a yes. "Okay, Okay. I could use a break," Kade said, eager to get some fresh air and steady his shaking hands.

He picked up the book and placed it back on the table. He was very careful not to close it for fear of resetting the calling. He backed away slowly, taking another deep breath and was actually grateful for the distraction. Glancing once at the bookshelf, he turned for the door. As he left the room, Kade could feel the familiar tingle on his skin as the protective barrier activated.

While exiting the cabin, Kade almost tripped over the dead animal that was lying on the ground. He looked at the dragon, preparing to ask it why and found it watching him with ears perked up. Kade chuckled lightly, realizing that his friend was proudly displaying its catch and offering it to Kade. The apprentice looked at the animal and felt his stomach rumble. The dragon moved closer and nudged it toward Kade as if to say, "Here, take a bite."

"Oh no. I don't eat raw meat," Kade said as he patted the dragon on the muzzle. He went into the cabin and quickly came out with some wood, a large, sharp knife and a long metal spear about five feet long. He grabbed ahold of the animal and brought the knife down with several hard swings, severing one of the legs off. He grimaced as the fresh, hot blood splashed on his arm. The sight of blood always made his stomach turn, and lately, there was more stomach turning than he cared for. He forced himself to ignore it.

Kade speared the piece of meat and set it by the fire pit. He dropped some wood into the ring of rocks as he prepared to cook. He stood for a few moments, considering how he was going to make the fire. Zayle had always been the one to start the fires so Kade did not feel confident that this was going to go as smoothly as he wanted. If he used the Divine Fire Calling, he was certain he was just going to blast the wood right out of the pit.

"I just need to figure out how you were able to light the fire without the big explosion," Kade said as he felt the Divine swirling in him. "Maybe…I can control how much Divine Power goes into the calling," he said as he closed his eyes and followed the subtle current of the power. It was peaceful, calling him to follow it and forget the world. Kade opened his eyes to break the trance so he could focus on his train of thought.

Turning toward the open field, he performed the Fire Calling. He held it in his hands, the blue flame dancing off his fingertips. Kade closed his eyes and felt for the Divine as it fed the fire. There…he could feel a way to lessen how much flowed through him if he focused. He choked off the flow of the Divine, feeling it slowly dwindle and then it vanished before he could attempt his idea. He completed the calling again and watched as the flames completely engulfed his hand. He closed his eyes and felt for the flow once more. Slowly, he squeezed it off and opened his eyes, preparing to throw, but before he could send out the blue flame, it melted into the air. Kade took a deep breath to calm his frustrations and performed the calling again. As he did before, he felt for the Divine and slowly choked off the flow. As it dwindled, he opened his eyes and threw. It hit the ground, setting an area twice that of the pit on fire. He walked over and stomped out the flames in exasperation.

"No wonder why you were always so angry with me," Kade called over his shoulder toward Zayle's burial plot. "I struggle with everything."

Once again, Kade performed the Fire Calling and closed his eyes, trying to stay calm as he focused. He choked off the Divine, and when he thought it was just about right, quickly opened his eyes and tossed the fire toward the field. It died out before it got halfway to its target. Kade felt himself wanting to scream in frustration as he balled his fists. He took a deep breath, and after holding to the count of ten, let it out, forcing the stress from his body at the same time.

"I can do this," Kade said as he closed his eyes and performed the calling again.

He relaxed his mind and forced everything out except the Divine. He felt the way the power moved through him as he fed the flame. He studied it as he applied a little pressure, squeezing it off slowly. At the point where it started to collapse, he opened his eyes and threw. It hit the ground, setting it on fire. He smiled as he looked at the results. Not perfect but easily sufficient.

Kade practiced the technique one more time and then moved to stand in front of the ring of rocks. He planted his feet and closed his eyes, but before he could perform the calling, a hot puff of bad breath hit him in the face. His eyelids flew open and he coughed several times, stumbling back while covering his mouth. He gagged and fought the urge to get sick.

"Light and ash! Don't do that!" Kade said in muffled words as he pressed his sleeve tightly to his mouth. He put one hand on the dragon's chest and pushed. At first, it leaned forward to resist, but after a tap from Kade on its shoulder, it moved back. "Now stay here," Kade said, pointing at the ground.

He uncovered his mouth and returned to the fire pit. He closed his eyes again but then quickly opened them to make sure the dragon had not followed. Satisfied, he closed his eyes and reached for the Divine Power. He started the Fire Calling, and with as little of the power as possible, opened his eyes, readying to toss the fire into the pit. Unfortunately, he was forced to let the fire go. There, with its nose on the wood, was his dragon.

"You need to stay where I put you," Kade said, leaning into the dragon's chest again, trying to push him back. The dragon stared at him with a quizzical look but gave no sign that it was going to move. It tilted its head back and forth several times and then sniffed at the meat. Kade thumped the dragon on the chest and it, grudgingly, moved back. "Now, stay here," Kade said, stabbing his finger at the ground. "Stay," he said with emphasis. "I am trying to start a fire."

Clearly, this was making no sense to the dragon as it, again, tilted its head from side to side. Kade could not stifle his laugh as he considered how silly this massive killing machine looked. He shook his head and turned away, trying to focus on his task.

He returned to the fire pit once more and readied himself for the calling. He glanced at the wood and then the dragon, making sure everything was where it needed to be. Satisfied, he started again.

"This is going to work," Kade said to the dragon. It misunderstood and started to come to him. Kade quickly ran to it and put his hands on its chest. It stopped. "Stay," he said again, pointing to the ground.

Back at the pit once more, Kade prayed there would be no more interruptions. His stomach was starting to protest at the lack of food. The thought of cooked meat made his mouth water slightly. Closing his eyes, he felt for the Divine Power and performed the Fire Calling. He did not need to close his eyes for this, but he found it easier to concentrate and feel how much of the Divine Power he was channeling. When he felt he had it just right, he opened his eyes and let the fire shoot into the pit. Kade felt a backlash of heat when the flame hit the wood. He retreated quickly, shielding his eyes.

"Well, it worked," Kade said to his dragon. Again, it was tilting its head back and forth. "Just watch and you will see," Kade said as he picked up the speared piece of meat and laid it across the fire. "I am cooking it," he said over his shoulder. "Give it a while."

The dragon lay down with its head on its front legs while it eyed the meat hungrily. Kade smiled to himself at the thought of this fearsome beast being his...pet? Companion? Well, he was not sure, but for now, he would just consider this his dragon and leave it at that.

Ten minutes went by when the dragon's ears came up and its nose started to twitch wildly. Kade noticed its peeked awareness and laughed. He found it very amusing to see the dragon start to drool and smiled to himself.

Soon, my friend, soon, he thought as his stomach growled loudly.

The dragon looked at him while licking its lips. An uneasy feeling spread over him as the dragon's teeth shown. He knew there was no threat to himself, but it still unnerved him to a small degree. Kade looked past the dragon's teeth and into its eyes. There was a question in those eyes and Kade knew it was as simple as, "Can I have some?" He could not help but to laugh.

Kade went over and dragged the rest of the fresh meat to the fire pit. The dragon was watching intently now. After another thirty slow minutes, Kade took the cooked meat off the spit and laid it on a rock, doing his best to keep it out of the dirt. He then turned back to the rest of the meat and started working to put it on the spit. He started the food cooking and turned back to the piece on the rock.

"Smells pretty good eh, my friend?" Kade asked as he picked up the very hot food. He took a huge bite and exhaled with his lips pulled back, trying to cool it. After shaking his head slightly, he swallowed his tasty bite and smiled at the dragon. "Here ya go," he said as he tossed the food into the air toward his friend. He flinched as the dragon lunged, catching it in a crash of teeth before it even got a chance to get close to the ground. The only thing Kade heard were the dragon's teeth coming together in a crash. Kade marveled at the deadly prowess.

"Not too bad, eh?" Kade asked as he rotated the animal on the spit.

He smiled to himself, knowing the dragon would spend the next hour watching the meal closely. He decided he would put the time to good use and went back into the cabin, already picturing the ominous, strange, metal book. He used to look forward to going into this room, but now, he felt a sense of dread.

Kade went into the cabin and made the right turn, stopping at the door. After the appropriate motions, the trap was disarmed and he proceeded into the room. He glanced out the window to see the dragon settle down close to the fire. Kade smiled to himself as he watched it stretch out its neck and smell the food.

Turning his attention back to the book, Kade sat down and forced himself to think critically once more. He examined the cover as he placed his hand on it, getting ready to flip it open. Just as he was curling his fingers under the edge of the cover, he paused. Something was not right. He sat there for several long moments, and then it hit him.

"I left you open," Kade said, peering intently at the book. He drew his hands away and closed his eyes. It took only a second for the shimmer to reveal itself once again. "So, you reset just like the door. Why does that not surprise me?" Kade asked rhetorically, as he glanced at the entrance to the study.

Completing the Disarm Calling once more, Kade checked for the shimmer and was pleased to see it gone. While holding his breath, he smoothly opened the book and was rewarded with nothing but calm. There was nothing at all. No reaction and nothing on the page. He turned to the next page and found another blank sheet. He looked closely for anything, sure he was missing something. He could feel power coursing through the book, so what was this? Closing his eyes, he studied the page, hoping to see a glimmer or a clue that would help solve this mystery. Still, there was nothing.

Turning another page produced the same results. Kade started flipping through the book faster and faster but found nothing written anywhere. There had to be more. He waited patiently, giving his mind a chance to figure out this mystery. He studied the book, but after ten long minutes of staring, willing it to reveal its secrets, he sat back in his chair and let out a sigh.

Maybe today was not the day to learn this book's secrets, he thought to himself as he closed it and placed it back in its hiding place. He decided to sleep on this one and perused the remaining books. This time, he chose a small, black book. It was about four inches tall and three inches wide. The cover looked like bark, but when Kade grasped it, all he felt was thin leather. He held up the book, turning it over and over, careful not to open it. He returned to the table and sat.

Kade closed his eyes and used his sight and saw the Divine Power pulsing around it. Another faint, blue light. Kade went through the motions to disarm the trap, but when he looked again, he saw that the trap was still active. He shook his head and decided he had had enough of difficult, dangerous books.

Maybe later, he thought to himself as he got up and put the book back into the cubby.

"That should have worked," Kade grumbled to himself as he looked at the last book still untouched. This one was lying flat on its side. He slowly put his hand on it and slid it out, trying to be as delicate as possible. The cover felt like cloth. Or maybe it was more like silk. Kade tried to decide, but then in the next moment, he was sure it was closer to course burlap. He had a suspicion that he was not going to be able to pin down what it felt like. With both hands holding the book closed, he moved to the table and gently set it down.

"Master, how do you keep from setting these off yourself?" Kade asked out loud. He knew that if Zayle were here, his response would be, "With years of practice."

Closing his eyes once more, he looked for the familiar shimmer of Divine Power and found nothing. He opened his eyes and leaned closely, looking over every inch of the book. Again, he closed his eyes and performed the ritual. Nothing. Fearing the cleverest trap yet, he carefully placed his hand on the book and felt for the faint vibration that was present when a calling is placed on an object.

"Is this another one that is going to keep its secrets from me?" Kade asked of no one in particular. He narrowed his eyes as he studied the tome hard. His gut told him that nothing was out of the ordinary here, but it just did not make sense. His gut might be saying there was no danger but his head screamed, "Be careful." He turned the book over and tried to see with his inner sight once more but again, there was nothing.

"No protection at all? None?" Kade asked of the book. "Well," he said as he placed his hand on the cover, "master always said to trust my gut instinct, and right now, it says nothing is here, so…" and with that, he flipped the book open and jumped back behind the chair, waiting for lightning to strike. Nothing. With the exception of the pounding in his ears, the room was dead silent.

Slowly, he sat down in the chair without taking his eyes off the book. The tension faded from his body as he felt his weight sink into the worn leather. He focused on the first page and froze as he took in what he was reading. CREATURES FROM MY VISIONS. This book was written in a heavy hand. Kade recognized it instantly as his master's writing. A sense of sadness moved through him along with a sense of discovery. With anticipation, he turned the next page and saw an image of the grimalkin.

"What?" Kade asked out loud in surprise. "So, that was why you were so concerned. You knew if what I was telling you was the truth, it meant…well, what did it mean?" he asked, his anger growing as he looked upon the image of the cat-like creature. He did not realize it, but he was gripping the table so hard with his left hand that his knuckles were turning white. He was gnashing his teeth, and the muscles in his neck were taught. Second by second, the hatred in his heart grew.

"So, you were sent to kill my master," Kade said in a growl. He almost did not recognize his own voice.

Kade felt the rage explode in him. He brought his fist down hard on the page as if to smash the creature like a bug. Kade thought back on his master and put considerable effort into suppressing his fury and failed miserably, as one lonely tear worked its way down his cheek. Wiping it away angrily, he refocused on the book.

He forced himself to calmly turn the page. It had one simple word as the title. It read, TARGOTH. Kade looked at the page, surprised to see no picture at all. It explained about the fearsome creature being forty feet tall and walking upright with long arms that could almost drag on the ground. It was said the creature had long claws at the end of its fingers but this could not be verified. The targoth was made of the Divine Power and had a natural ability to blend in with its surroundings.

"Targoth," Kade said to himself as he looked out the window, remembering the invisible creature that had taken his master's life. "Yes, we will meet again," he said. Kade could have sworn that he heard a mocking laugh way off in the distance, but when he listened closely, all he could hear was the slight rustle of the wind.

Flipping through the pages, Kade turned white. Every picture was of something that he had believed to be a myth. These were his nightmares. But, here they were in this book as real as he himself.

As real as my dragon, he thought. He turned his attention back to the book and continued reading, trying to find anything that would give him more information. After turning to the last page, he closed the book and sat staring at it.

Kade took a long, deep breath and let it out slowly to calm himself. Knowing he could not do anything about it now, he got up and slowly crossed the room to the hiding place and put the book back. He moved to the window, considering what to do next. Kade inhaled sharply as he remembered the cooking meat.

Running out of the house at full speed, he skidded to a stop next to the fire. The dragon was still next to the fire pit, doing its fair share of drooling. Kade avoided stepping in the slime as he worked his way around the fire. He reached out and took ahold of the spit, and then jerked his hand back instantly from the heat. The spear dropped back into the "Y" shaped brackets, almost bouncing out and into the fire.

Kade blew on his hands and started looking around for something to grab the spit with. Seeing nothing, he raced back into the cabin and returned shortly with towels wrapped around each hand. He grabbed for the spear and maneuvered it off the fire. The smell of the fresh meat, as the grease dripped into the fire, was almost enough to make him take a bite before it cooled.

The dragon was on its feet, watching him intently. Kade could feel the heat from the spit start to come through the towels. He quickly leaned the spit against a boulder and shook the towels off his hands. A part of the meat dragged on the ground. Kade was certain that the dragon would not hesitate to devour it, even with a little dirt seasoning. He looked at the dragon, and once again, it had that questioning look that said, "Can I have some?" as more drool hit the ground.

"You can have some when it cools down," Kade said and then paused as he laughed at what he had said. "You must think I'm pretty strange, huh? Why would a fire breathing dragon need his food to cool?" Kade asked and chuckled. The dragon looked at Kade and then back to the meat.

Picking up the knife, Kade quickly carved out a large chunk for himself. Next, using the towels once more, he picked up the spit and dragged it over to the dragon. He put his foot against one side and pulled the spit out. The dragon sniffed the sizzling food and quickly eyed Kade as if to ask permission to tear into it.

"Go on," Kade said, indicating the meat. "Eat," he prompted as he pointed to the food with the knife. The dragon sniffed the savory food as the succulent smell of the meat made its stomach growl loudly. It smelled the food several more times and then tore into it hungrily. For reasons Kade could not put into words, he felt affection well up in his chest for this creature that could be so incredibly fearsome, but at the same time, be so gentle. He smiled as he enjoyed watching the dragon devour its food. It was uncooked in the center, but the dragon did not appear to notice or care.

Kade returned to his food and took a huge bite. He closed his eyes and savored the flavor as he felt the juices run down into his stomach. Right then, he could not recall anything ever tasting so good. He ate until he felt like he was going to burst. He prepared to toss his unfinished meat away when he got the feeling of being watched. He slowly looked up to meet the dragon's gaze.

"How would you like to finish mine?"

The dragon gave a grunt that Kade took for a yes so Kade, not thinking, held the meat out to his friend. The dragon lunged, fastening its teeth into the meat with a crash but did nothing more. Kade jumped back, quickly checking to see if he was missing a hand. Seeing as everything was still there, he relaxed and looked back at the dragon.

"What's the matter? Go ahead, eat," Kade said, swallowing hard, waving the dragon away with his still attached hand. It paused momentarily and then lay down, chewing eagerly.

Starting to feel tired, Kade moved over to the dragon and slid down its side while leaning back. It finished its food in no time and then curled around him slightly. It craned its neck to look at him and then rolled just a little so its feet were not under it but not going over onto its side, either.

Kade found himself staring up at the sky, watching the clouds drift.. He reflected on the first meeting with his new friend and smiled. He felt the dragon twitch, waking him from his daydream. He tried to ignore the movement but the dragon continued to swing its head around, trying to reach its back. Kade looked over his shoulder and watched as the dragon tried several more times. He got to his feet and watched the dragon with curiosity.

"What are you doing?" Kade asked as he moved around to the dragon's other side. It swung its head around again, but it was clear that its neck was not meant to be that flexible. It tried and tried to reach the spot right between its wings but to no avail. Kade walked up, pushed the dragon's head out of the way and stood on his toes. If the dragon was not already lying half on its side, he would not have been able to reach. But, as it was, he was able to hit the spot, which was evident when the dragon's eyes rolled back slightly and its eyelids half closed.

Kade could not help but to chuckle at how silly the dragon looked as it stretched its neck out and tilted its head. As if this was not enough, the dragon's lips started to twitch. Kade could take it no longer and started to laugh. The more he thought about it, the more he found this to be one of the most amusing things he had ever seen and started to laugh even harder. Pretty soon, he was sliding down the dragon's side and laughing so hard his sides ached. The dragon swung its head around, watching Kade, confused.

"I am sorry, my friend," Kade said with tears in his eyes, "but you do look funny doing that. I am glad I could help," he said, starting to get control of himself. "But, that nose thing you do and the way you stretch out your neck," he added and started to laugh again. His laughter came to an abrupt halt when a blast of rancid dragon's breath hit him full in the face. He coughed hard several times as he surged to his feet, struggling to breath while his stomach threatened to empty itself right there.

"Blood and ash! We should do something about that breath of yours," Kade said, breathing through his sleeve again. He chuckled and then calmed himself to relieve the pang in his side.

"I wasn't laughing at you. It's just that…" Kade said and then let it trail off, not wanting to start laughing again, almost failing. He turned to walk away and tripped over the knife that was stuck in the ground. He went down with arms flailing. As he lay there, he heard the dragon huff several times. When he looked up, he could have sworn that the dragon found it amusing. Its mouth was slightly open in what almost looked like a smile, but that just could not be.

"OK, I guess we are even," Kade said as he scrambled to his feet.

The dragon sniffed the air and licked its lips. It lifted its nose higher as if trying to orient on the scent it had caught. It got to its feet and searched the area. Kade watched with growing curiosity.

"What are you looking for?"

The dragon, after several more short sniffs, stopped as it appeared to be analyzing the air. After a few more short sniffs, it turned and headed in the direction of the well. Seeing what the dragon had its eye on, Kade smiled and plodded after, wanting a drink himself.

The dragon sniffed the edge of the well several times and then stuck its nose over the side. Finding no water immediately, it moved to the other side and tried from there. Frustrated at finding nothing, it huffed and clawed at the edge.

"Okay, okay, I got this," Kade said as he put his shoulder into the dragon's chest and pushed it back. He turned and cranked the handle to bring the bucket up, then dumped it into the trough. The dragon drank this before the bucket hit the water on the way back down. Kade cranked up four more buckets before he decided it was enough.

"Okay, we are not going to get into this habit," Kade said as he patted the dragon on the shoulder. "You will, most definitely, be finding your own water," he said as he took a long drink from the bucket.

"Dragon, I have more work to do," Kade said as he looked at the window to the den. He was apprehensive when he thought he should be excited. He shook his head slightly and turned to go but stopped as he glanced back at the dragon.

"I have to come up with a name for you. I can't keep calling you dragon. What would you like for a name? A beautiful silver dragon like you should have a beautiful name. Let's see. What can we name you? Dragon…dragon…hmmmm how about Draden? No, that does not have a good ring to it. Let's see. Dragon…hmmmm what sounds like a dragon name? How about…Rayden? Hey, now that has a good sound. You like that?" Kade asked as he looked into the huge, golden eyes. "Well, since you are not complaining, we will go with that. Okay, Rayden it is," Kade said as he patted the dragon on the shoulder.

Kade pointed to his chest and said his name. Then he pointed to the dragon and repeated "Rayden" several times. The dragon seemed confused so Kade repeated his actions. After ten minutes or so, he got the strange feeling that the dragon was starting to understand. It was as if there was some sort of connection being formed.

"Well, sooner or later you will get it. You are a smart one, so it will come," Kade said and turned for the cabin.

He walked in and made the sharp, right turn toward the den. After disarming the trap, he stopped in front of the precious hidden books. The bookshelf still hung open. He contemplated closing it after each use but decided it was not an issue at this time.

"Now, what should I learn?" Kade asked himself out loud. But, the Lightning Calling was already on his mind. "It would not hurt just to take a look at it," Kade said as he slid the book out. He set it on the table and sat. Making sure to disarm the trap first, he gingerly opened the book. After a few moments of consideration, he decided to put Zayle's insistence that he focus on the smaller callings ahead of his desire to learn the powerful callings. He decided he would come back to the Lightning Calling later.

"Now, what do we have here?" Kade asked as he read to himself. "Silence, eh? And, what is this?" he asked as he unfolded a small note that had been wedged in the crease of the book. There were just three words written on it in Zayle's hand. It read simply, Kade's next lesson. "Okay, I guess I know what I am going to work on now."

Kade glanced over the page and sighed, not really interested in working through another boring lesson. A stab of guilt made him grimace as he sat down and looked the calling over. Not understanding why Zayle chose this for his next lesson, he leaned forward, putting his fists under his chin and began to read.

When he finished, Kade stood and leaned over the book, trying to memorize the motions. He practiced the moves while referring to the book over and over again. Finding the calling more difficult than he expected, he considered dismissing it and moving on to something more exciting. After a moment, he leaned back over the book and continued.

Kade studied for hours, always working to add the next move of the calling to what he had already learned. Occasionally, the dragon would put its massive head up to the window, looking in, giving Kade an excuse to take a break from his lesson. But, no matter how many excuses he could come up with, he always knew he had to return to his study.

Kade worked on this calling well into the night before deciding to put it away until the next day. If one wrong move would not end up with him possibly losing his hearing permanently, then he would not hesitate to try, but he did not have that luxury. Without

Zayle there to save him, the first time he performed the calling had to be perfect.

Kade awoke to another dead animal at his doorstep. He was happy to prepare their meal and then return to his studies. After most of the day was spent practicing, he felt it was time to try. His heart started to pound just a little harder as the excitement of performing a calling for the first time hit home. He stood with his eyes closed as he practiced the moves in his head over and over. After visualizing the calling for several minutes, he felt he was ready.

Okay, here goes, Kade thought. He felt his stomach twist into a knot. He performed the steps perfectly and called on the Divine Power. And, with that, he felt the power fill him and then the whooshing feel as it left his body. He looked around, feeling odd. The sense of being alone washed over him.

"Okay, that should have…" Kade started to say but stopped, his eyes going wide. "Hello," he said, tapping his ears, not hearing his voice. At first, he tried to remain calm. Then, realization that the Master Chosen was no longer there to save him made him swallow hard. He felt panic. It was now up to him to correct his blunder. He shook his head and even opened his jaw wide, as if to pop his eardrums, but of course, nothing helped.

"NO," Kade felt himself say. He could sense the vibrations in his head as he spoke. He quickly returned to the book and read through all the steps. At the very end, he read where he was supposed to have intoned a word. He was so focused on getting the moves right, he forgot the easiest part of the calling. He hit himself in the head, frustrated with such a stupid mistake. Kade struggled to stay calm and think.

There has to be something that will fix this, he thought as he scanned over the page. He quickly flipped through the book but found it almost impossible to stay calm enough to focus. Kade stopped flipping pages when he read the top of one page with one single word. It was simply titled: DEAFNESS. Reading over the calling, he found it to be identical to the Silence Calling, but one had an incantation where the other had none. The discomfort of being completely deaf was making it difficult not to panic. He turned it sideways and read all the scribbles in the margins. As he started to stand, his eyes caught the number 57 scrawled at the very bottom, in the crease, where it was almost unreadable.

Kade sat down and forced himself to take deep breaths. *It had to mean something*, he thought to himself. He looked at the book only a moment more when it occurred to him to check and see what was on page 57. When he flipped open to that page, he found a one word title on the top of the page that simply read, HEAR.

A flood of relief poured through his body and he quickly read over the calling. There were just a few simple moves and the word, HEAR in the language of the Ancients. Knowing that it was difficult to get the moves of a calling correct on the first attempt, Kade studied for hours until he was sure he had it perfect.

He closed his eyes and went through the motions in his head. Feeling confident that he had the calling memorized, he opened his eyes and called on the Divine Power while performing the moves. As soon as he finished the last step, he intoned the word "hear" in the familiar language of the Ancients and felt the energy flow smoothly out of him. He held his breath, waiting for the results. Nothing happened. He could feel sweat forming on his brow.

I know something happened, he thought. *I felt the power leave me.*

Kade looked around the cabin for anything that may have changed but found nothing. He checked himself and was relieved to see he was all there. Shaking his head, he returned to the book. Reading over the calling again, he prepared to try once more.

It is almost impossible to get this wrong, he thought. He moved away from the book and then returned to lean over it, checking one last time. Moving to the middle of the room, he went through the motions, drawing in the energy as he intoned the word. He let the Divine Power flow once again.

"Okay, I know something must have happened. I felt it. I felt the calling work. It had to have worked. What did I do wrong?" Kade felt himself say in frustration.

Starting to wonder if this was even the calling he needed, Kade sat down at the table and forced himself to study the page. This time he noticed a small note at the bottom. The note simply read: Allow a small amount of time for the calling to take effect.

"So, maybe I did do it right," Kade heard himself say. He slumped in the chair, feeling immense relief. "It worked," he said just to hear his own voice.

The dragon came to the open window and looked in to see what Kade was doing. Rayden huffed a few times, trying to get Kade's attention. The Apprentice Chosen flinched at the first huff and smiled, happy he could hear it.

"What is it, Rayden?"

The dragon just stared at him. Quickly losing interest, Rayden laid down next to the window. It made Kade smile the way his dragon was always there, waiting for him to emerge from cabin. He sat down and looked at the window, seeing that most of the light was being blocked, but there was enough light to read by. There always was.

"Well, it looks like I got two callings right on the first try. Zayle would have been surprised to see that," Kade said with sarcasm.

Returning to the calling for silence once more, Kade readied himself to perform it. Seeing as the moves were identical to the Deafness Calling, he expected this to be flawless, but he was taking no chances. He was tempted to scrap the whole idea of this calling once more, but his eyes landed on the note he had previously read.

If the master wanted me to learn this, there had to be a good

91

reason for it, he thought.

While trying to focus on the calling, the sound of an insect interrupted his concentration. He tried to ignore it, but it was impossible since it seemed to be right there in the room. Kade put his hands on the table, preparing to stand when the sound stopped. He relaxed and returned to visualizing the steps needed for the calling. Just as he was starting to focus, the insect started up again.

"Blood and ash!" Kade said, swearing as he sat back hard in his chair. He stood up and stalked around the table, expecting to find the annoying insect right there. He scratched his head in confusion and then heard the sound again. "The kitchen?" he asked out loud and went in search of the bug. Several long seconds of standing still produced no insect. Just as he was turning to go back to the den, the noise started again. He narrowed his eyes, sure the sound was coming from outside, but how could that be? He walked out the back door, tracking the annoying bug.

The more Kade walked, the louder it got. Stopping to look back at the cabin, he marveled at the distance. Shaking his head, he turned and continued toward the sound. It was not long before he was standing over the insect, which was silent now that he was actually over it. Kade bent and grasped the bug in his fingers. He studied it closely.

"My you are an unusually loud bug. You are going to have to make that kind of noise somewhere else," Kade said as he prepared to walk it further from the cabin.

Kade had a code that he lived by. If it was not a threat or did not need to be killed for him to survive, it was wrong to take its life. Even something as small as this bug was not beneath his code. He paused as heavy breathing got his attention. His first thought was of the evil creature that should have been outside the barrier. He froze and listened closely.

"Is that my dragon I hear?"

Dropping the bug, Kade headed back toward the sound of breathing. The closer he got to the cabin, the louder it got. As he rounded the corner, the sound increased considerably. Rayden lifted his head quickly and stared at Kade.

"Was that you making all that noise?" Kade asked, again shocked that his own voice was so loud. The dragon looked at him, as usual, not understanding a thing that was being said. As Kade turned to go back into the cabin, Rayden lazily laid his head back down and was sleeping in seconds.

Making sure to remember to deactivate the trap at the door, Kade hurried into the den. He quickly walked over to the table and sat down, looking forward to finishing this lesson so he could move on to more powerful callings. He noticed the closed book and only hesitated a moment. He was starting to get used to how things worked. He deactivated the protection from around the book and opened it with more confidence now. Kade studied the calling just a little more and then moved to the center of the room. He rubbed his shoulders with his hands, trying to get the tension to release. As certain as he was that he could perform this calling perfectly, the memory of being deaf was still too fresh in his mind.

Kade squared his shoulders and planted his feet. He closed his eyes to allow his mind to slow as he visualized the moves for the calling. He took a deep breath and let it out slowly. He opened his eyes and moved smoothly through every step, remembering to add the word at the end. The Divine moved though him and then out to do his bidding. This calling might be similar to the other in the performing of it, but the way it felt once cast was immensely different. Kade could feel that he had control over the active calling. The power flowed through him continuously, keeping it in place. He smiled to himself and closed his eyes, feeling every part of the calling. He willed it to end, and just like that, it was gone.

Kade performed it again and it formed around him as it did

before, but this time, as an afterthought, he included the dragon. He could easily feel that the dragon was now under the Silence Calling also. They were both cloaked, keeping them from being heard.

Yes, this was a useful one, Kade thought. He nodded his head in appreciation of the new knowledge he now held. This would definitely come in handy.

"Now, let's see what else there is," Kade said as he returned to the book.

Zayle had a firm rule that no more than one calling was to be learned in a month. Callings that were learned in a short time were easily confused with each other. Unfortunately, Kade did not feel he had the luxury of this caution.

Turning the pages, Kade was looking for something that stood out. Something amazing. FAR SEEING was an interesting one that got his attention. *How exciting it would be to see things from far away*, he thought and smiled. He read through the steps and quickly decided that all those moves were way too much for him to master in one day, or even a week. He envisioned himself standing by the window with his eyes floating out of his head. *With my luck, that is exactly what would happen*, he thought. He chuckled lightly and moved on.

The next page was labeled TRANSPORT. He read the description for the calling and was almost tempted to learn it. Seeing far sounded like fun but being able to pop from place to place was even more tempting. There was a note at the bottom that he had to squint to read, but it was legible. It read: *Caution. This is extremely dangerous and should be used only in the event of an emergency! There have been cases noted of finding Chosen half teleported into trees, rocks...etc.* The note ended there. Kade looked at the wear on the page and took it as evidence that this calling had been practiced.

He shivered and decided that this was way too dangerous for him but not before tracing the symbol at the top of the page with his

94

finger. He followed its pattern with his eyes and found that he could almost read the name of this calling by focusing on the symbol. He looked at the number of moves needed and then over the warning one more time and quickly decided it was not for him. He shivered again and turned the page.

The next calling was title SUSTINENCE. He pushed the chair back from the table, surprised at the amount of noise it made. He did not recall it being so loud before but quickly put that off to just not paying attention.

This looks like something I can do, he thought as he read over the steps involved. It was actually pretty simple. There were only a few basic moves and then the word, FOOD in the ancient language. This had to be easy. He knew he could do this. *What could go wrong?* he asked himself. Just as he was focusing on the first step, Rayden gave a huff from the window that startled Kade.

"OK, what is going on? That was way too loud. I can hear a bug over a hundred feet away and you almost sound like you are roaring even though you are just breathing."

Looking down at the book, he reflected on the last few hours. *What was the first thing I heard that was too loud?* he wondered. *The insect. So, what happened just before that?* Then he hit on what had to be the answer. *So, that is where the Divine Power went. I did the Hear Calling twice and this is the consequence. Ahhhhh*, Kade thought to himself, pleased he had worked it out. "Well, being able to hear that much better may be to our advantage, Rayden," Kade said, grinning.

He flipped back through the book to page 57 and read the calling again to make sure he did not miss anything. He read to the bottom, studying each note but there was nothing that stood out. He saw some scribbling in the margin and turned the book to read it. It read: This calling is temporary and will wear off in hours.

"Well, I would most likely have just lost sleep with this

calling, anyway," Kade said. "But for now, I will enjoy it," he said with a smile.

The birds were chirping off in the distance, but Kade could hear them as clearly as if they were right outside his window. Closing his eyes, he could make out many sounds, even judging direction and distance accurately. The rustle of the grass along the edge of the forest was easily detectable. He smiled to himself, feeling like he had a special power.

"Incredible. Not everything turns out bad," Kade said as he opened his eyes.

He returned his attention to the book on the table. He flipped through, deciding to work on the calling for food another time and continued looking for something more useful. If Zayle were here, he would skin him alive. The Master Chosen was adamant that only one calling be learned and practiced at a time until it was mastered. But, his master was not here and he needed to learn as much as he could. He recalled the fear he saw briefly in his masters eyes and knew he needed more than food. It was also clear that he was not going to stay here forever, so the more prepared he was when he left, the better. There had to be something that was more relevant.

Scrutinizing each calling, he turned the pages slowly. His mind started to wander as thoughts of leaving drifted through his head. *Where would I go? Should I seek out another Chosen? Yes*, he thought. *Yes, that might be a good starting place. I just have to figure out whom, and more importantly, if I can trust them.*

Kade returned his gaze to the book and started flipping pages once more. After just a few pages, his mind started to wander again. *How will I defend myself? I need something for when I face that targoth*, he thought as he balled his hands into fists. *It was not just an excuse to learn it*, he said to himself, already knowing the calling that was luring him to it. His attempt to justify his decision might not be relevant right then, but he did not care. He cracked a smile and opened the book to the beginning and read the Lightning Calling. His heart started to pound at being able to command so much power. It was almost euphoric.

"Well, I did learn the next calling Zayle had set for me. I should be able to pick one that I feel is important. Besides, I have no idea what he wanted me to study next," Kade said to himself, afraid to look through the book for fear of finding another small note. He slouched in the chair and flipped through every page, hoping there was none. When he turned the last page, he sat up, feeling more justified in his decision. Turning back to the front of the book, he read through the Lightning Calling.

"Well, after those others, this one doesn't look so hard. Now, let's see how this goes," Kade said, feeling excitement growing in him as he visualized sending a searing bolt of lightning skyward. Or even better, at his fiercest enemy as he sent them crashing to the ground, easily defeated. Kade shook his head, realizing that he was daydreaming and refocused his mind back on his task.

This does not look so hard, he thought again, hoping he was not just trying to rationalize his decision. He ignored the twinge of doubt he felt. *Only thirteen movements*, he thought as his smile wavered just a little. Taking a deep breath, he continued.

The calling read: *Open yourself up to the Divine Power and then complete the first ten movements. After the tenth, draw fully on the Divine and empower the calling. At this point, you should start to feel the power build around you in the air. You must remain focused at all cost as there will be no turning back after completing step ten. It is critical that the energy be controlled and released accordingly. If released too soon, or too late, the consequences can be deadly. At the twelfth movement, intone the word lighting in the ancient's language. The thirteenth movement is simply thrusting your hand in the direction you want to cast the calling. You must release all of the energy on the final move or it will find its own way out, and this will cause severe injury, if not death.*

"Okay, maybe it is not easy," Kade said, considering closing all books for the day.

Staring at the calling for five long minutes, Kade struggled with the decision of whether to learn it or let it go. This was dangerous and anything could go wrong. It was very obvious this could end horribly, but Kade believed this calling would give him a better way to defend himself. The Fire Calling would serve in a pinch, but this calling was top of the line in stopping power.

Before today, Kade had never learned anything new without Zayle standing over his shoulder, watching every move closely. The Master Chosen had a way to cut him off from the power if things were not going correctly. He had done it a few times when the power seemed to twitch wildly every time Kade had tried to draw on it. He struggled desperately to get it to conform to his will. It was like trying to control an eel that would slip from his grasp constantly and then try to turn on him. Kade recalled how Zayle used to become frustrated with his lack of control. The apprentice always feared he would be sent back into the world as a failure. But, fortunately for him, he started to show real talent a year ago.

Pacing the room, he pondered what he was going to do. He stopped several times and focused on the calling only to shake his head and continue his pacing. Finally, he decided to leave the knowledge unlearned. Placing his hand on the book to close it, he hesitated.

If not now, when? he asked himself.

Kade slowly removed his hand from the book and returned to pacing around the room. He came back to the table and read over the calling again. His hands and arms twitched slightly as he read over the moves, envisioning every step in his head. Time slipped by as he stood focused on the book. The more he studied the calling, the more it did not appear so difficult. Soon, he was making the moves more deliberate. The Divine Power pulsed stronger in him each time he practiced.

"I know I can do this," Kade said with a smile, excited beyond words as visions of commanding such a powerful calling spurred him on. He completely lost track of time as he became determined to gain this new skill. He put his heart and mind into it with new-found confidence. Day turned to night, but Kade did not notice as his mind latched onto his studies.

Leaning over the book slightly, he subconsciously drew on the Divine Power. He did not notice that he was actually leaving trails of power. The drawing in the air was faint. He had stopped seeing the trails of power many years ago as now it was as common as breathing. But, there it hung in the air. The image never stayed more than a few seconds before fading away. He used to be impressed with the way Zayle could write in the air with the very faint flashes of power to the point of distraction. Now, it was nothing.

Kade practiced the moves over and over again, trying to imagine what it would feel like if he were to complete the calling to the end. A smile crept across his face as he started to believe he could actually summon this powerful bolt of lightning. To have a weapon like this at his command would be glorious. He would be formidable. He smiled again as the power called to him. He practiced the moves over and over in his mind while making slight movements. Time slipped by as his desire drove him on.

Kade only took small breaks to answer the call of nature or to dine with his dragon. But, no matter what he was doing, his head was whirling as he saw the page of the book in his mind, beckoning for him to return. He would give in to that call and quickly return to the den.

"This is not too difficult," Kade said to himself. He had the first six moves memorized.

He recalled how his master used to say, "When you can focus, you are the best learner I have ever had," but then in the next breath he would comment on how easily Kade could be distracted when he was not interested in the lesson. This was definitely one of those times when Kade felt he was focused. He quickly scanned the page again. Feeling much more confident, he continued to add the next step in the lesson. He would work over and over, picturing the move in his head, making gestures a bit more fluid and pronounced. The eighth move came easily.

Yes, that's it! That's it! Kade thought with more excitement. Continuing to block everything out, he focused more and more on the lesson. He leaned over the book, and just as quickly would stand back up again to practice the next move before it could slip from his mind. He would complete just the new step over and over until he was sure he had it and then perform all the moves learned thus far, adding the new one to the end.

I know I can do this, he thought with fierce determination. Another move learned, Kade leaned over the book for the next. Hours slipped by and he added the next three moves to his memory. *Eleven of the thirteen moves learned,* he thought in excitement. The thirteenth move was simply a throwing motion to symbolize directing the power. That meant the twelfth step was all he had left to learn. Kade felt excitement surge through is body. His heart was pounding with exhilaration as he read over the last step he would have to perform.

Steadying himself, he practiced the twelfth move over and over. This one was a bit more difficult. Several times he thought he had it only to find that when he got to the twelfth move in the sequence, he had forgotten a slight move here or had made too small a motion there. He went back to practicing just the twelfth step. When he felt confident that he had it learned, he would perform all the moves in sequence once more. As he closed in on the twelfth move, he would find that it slipped from his mind by the time he finished the eleventh. He ground his teeth in frustration.

Kade planted his feet firmly and focused harder on this moment than he had at any other time he could recall. *I am not going to get it wrong again*, he thought in fierce determination as he performed each move with exaggerated deliberateness to match the move as he saw it in his head. The first move was quick and easily flowed into the second. Now, only a slight pause, as the third and fourth came with no difficulty. The fifth and sixth were a bit more creative but gave him no trouble. He was so focused now that it would take a dragon's roar to get his attention. Sweat beaded on his forehead as he glided through the seventh, moving like the most elegant dancer. The eighth move was a quick twist of his wrist and a crossing motion with his arms. The ninth was a bit tedious, but nonetheless, was performed easily. The first nine moves completed flawlessly, he focused on the next part of the calling, while trying to remember the twelfth move as he closed in on it. *Now, I draw on the power*, he thought with force and slid by the tenth move easily. Excited at completing the first ten moves, he forgot about the warning. He continued into the eleventh move like a full-fledged master of the art. *Now, the twelfth move* he thought in confidence as the power thrummed in him, causing his heart to beat wildly. The familiar roar in his head should have warned him, but he was too focused to realize his disastrous mistake. The air was alive with power.

And, I channel the power out of my hand like this, Kade thought as his hand dramatically shot out toward the board with all the symbols drawn on it. He started to grin in triumph when a lightning bolt exploded from his hand with a deafening roar. It slammed into the front of the cabin, blowing the front wall to pieces and setting his home on fire.

The jolt from the power caused Kade to stumble back, slamming him into the bookshelf before he could catch his balance.

His jaw dropped as he gawked at the gaping hole in the wall. His ears rang furiously. Spots danced before his eyes from the brilliant flash, making it hard for him to see. He looked around the room in panic, as realization of what he had just done came crashing down on him. His chest constricted and his mind started racing.

"NO!" Kade wailed. "This can't be happening! Light in heaven!" he swore as he watched the fire start to spread.

His mind careening out of control with panic, he tried to force himself to think of a calling that he could use to fix this. *Water,* he thought desperately. *I need water and lots of it. Rain.* And then he remembered the calling that he had so easily dismissed as useless. The dragon roared, making his ears ring even more as his heightened panic caused his heart to pound.

Kade turned and grabbed the books of power from the cubby, making sure to keep them all closed. His eyes fell on the demon and his grip tightened even more. Deathly afraid of triggering any of the protections, he set the books on the table, putting the book with the demon on the bottom of the stack to make sure it did not flex open. He turned and looked back at the bookshelf. Rayden's panicked roar echoed through the cabin, making it almost impossible for Kade to organize his thoughts.

Seeing no other books that Kade felt needed saving, he moved back to the table. He did his best to steady his hands. He forced himself to calm as best as he could and carefully picked up the pile of books. He turned toward the door and the dragon roared again. His head rang from the increased ability to hear. For just a moment, he decided that his enhanced hearing was not such a good thing and then the thought was gone as the heat beat down on him.

Kade raced out of the cabin, running until he was sure that he was far enough from the fire and set the books down. He raced back into the blaze, and just as he went in the front door, the dragon rounded the corner. It had been running around the cabin, looking in each window in search of him.

Kade raced to his left and charged into his personal room. He quickly grabbed the largest sack he could find and proceeded to pack as many of his clothes as he could carry. He pulled the drawstring closed and raced back through the house to the front. He skidded to a stop and threw the bag out the door as far as he could. Seeing the bookshelf out of the corner of his eye, he turned and raced into the den to grab anything else that might be of importance. He took one step in and started to turn to his left when his legs gave out, sending him slamming into the table. His head hit with a jarring impact. The world started to slip away.

It took a moment for his head to clear enough for him to form thought. *No, I will not give in like this,* Kade thought as he fought to keep conscious. He forced his eyes to focus on the bookcase and the darkness slowly receded. His mind cleared and he realized he was lying across the table.

What in the land of the dead..., Kade thought, and then he realized that he had run through the door without deactivating the trap. Panic surged through him as the weight of his situation came crashing down on him. He was facing the front of the cabin and all he could see now was a wall of flames. Fear of burning to death hit him so hard that he would have screamed in sheer terror if he could have. The thought of being burned alive caused his mind to spiral out of control.

Master, where are you? Kade thought over and over as the heat caused him to want to blink.

If I get out of this, I promise I will never consider any calling unimportant, no matter how small it is, Kade vowed to himself as the ceiling started to creak. Dust drifted down onto his face and into his eyes, causing him to mentally wail. He found himself wishing this were over as despair racked his mind, but then in the next instant, was determined not to die such a painful death. His fear of dying by fire

103

was enough to force him to stop and think.

The dragon roared again, and at the same time, something brushed Kade's mind. Whatever it was, it did not go away. There was intense panic, and Kade was certain that it was not all his. He could hear Rayden running around the cabin, blasting every side with his panicked roar. Kade's mind came to a screeching halt.

There is one chance, he thought as a surge of hope hit him. *I know one use of the Divine Power that needs no motions. The Drift Calling. Just maybe*…he thought and started to draw on the power. He was relieved to feel the sweet sense of the Divine as it filled him.

Kade tried to clear his mind as much as possible. *Drift*, he thought in the ancient language. Nothing happened so he forced himself to focus again. The power was still surging in him so he concentrated again. *Drift*, he thought once more, but the panic started to consume him as he looked down at his body lying on the table. He looked around the room at the fire and almost lost control. It worked!

Now, if I can just get to the dragon!

Kade directed his awareness through the fire and out to the front of the cabin. The dragon came around the corner and roared. Kade tried to call out to Rayden but the dragon raced by him. He tried to catch Rayden but the dragon was moving too fast. Panic, again, started to take the place of hope until he saw the dragon pause at the front of the house where the lightning had blasted the wall. After several seconds, the dragon ran to the other sides of the house. It would pause at each side and then run back to the hole in the wall and roar his call.

I know what I have to do. This is my last chance, Kade thought as he forced his awareness over to the gaping hole as the home turned into a fiery inferno. He looked in and saw the roof sagging lower and lower. It would be moments, at best, before his body was buried beneath the blaze. He felt as though a hand had a tight grip on his heart and was squeezing.

Rayden raced around the corner at a full run. He leaned his body into the turn as his claws slid through the dirt, fighting to grip the ground for purchase. Kade drifted right to the dragon and merged. Rayden roared in desperation once again. Kade flinched, expecting his head to ring, but in this form, it was not like hearing with his real ears. The sound was muted considerably.

Rayden! Kade thought as strongly as he possible. *Rayden, help me!* The dragon flinched, breaking contact as it quickly swung its head around to the right and then to the left. Hearing nothing, it swung its head forward again to look for the voice. *Rayden, don't move!* Kade thought with force. The dragon froze. Kade saw its muscles twitching, desperately wanting to do something. *I am in the fire right in front of you! I am trapped and can't move! Save me*! he pleaded.

The dragon tensed, readying to tear the wall down to get to his friend. Kade sensed the dragon's intentions and thought as strong as possibly, *the roof is collapsing!* The dragon paused, attempting to puzzle out what Kade was trying to communicate. Just then, the roof creaked loudly and started to come down on the helpless man. The dragon broke contact with him and charged into the burning room. That was the last thing Kade saw as his panic took full control of his heart, mind and soul. Everything faded.

CH4

The smoky smell wafted over Kade, waking him slightly. He inhaled and coughed weakly as the pungent scent of ash and soot overwhelmed him. Trying to open his eyes, he flinched slightly at the excruciating ache he felt from his muscles as they protested greatly. He found it hard to think as he struggled to rise from the murky depth his mind was trapped in. His thoughts turned sluggish, and he slipped back into oblivion. For a brief moment, just before descending into nothingness, he heard rasping, as though something were struggling to breathe. The last thought he had, as he spun down into the chasm, was that it had to be something important.

As Kade started to awake, the strong memory of a fire caused his pulse to quicken. He was not sure why it was so familiar, but it was. He felt a stinging sensation creep over his body the more alert he became. Pain crept into his consciousness. A flash of a room on fire lit across his mind's eye momentarily and then was gone. He could see light through his eyelids as the pain continued to intensify. He ran his swollen tongue across lips that were cracked. His throat was torturously dry, but was there more? Breathing hot air possibly? He did not know why, but for some reason, that thought seemed to fit.

As he struggled to open his eyes, he heard an odd, rasping sound that had a slight gurgle to it. His adrenalin spiked, but his mind still struggled to understand why it should matter. The boost of adrenalin was all he needed to find the energy to pry open his crusted eyes. Straining through blurred vision, he tried to scan his surroundings. As his mind cleared more and more, his sense of dread and panic started to creep in, but why? That sound has something to do with it. He realized he was lying face down in the dirt and struggled to get to his hands and knees.

A huge mound several feet off to his side caught his attention as it heaved and fought for breath. He squinted, trying to bring the object into focus, knowing this was important. Visions of a wall of flames flashed through his mind and he flinched. As much as he tried to think, he could not quite grasp what was happening. The rasping sound followed by the slight gurgle, once again, drew his attention. The picture of a dragon blazed in his mind, and his heart skipped a beat before taking off at an alarming pace.

Kade squinted hard and forced his eyes to focus. Slowly, the blurred image of Rayden took shape and everything came rushing back. His painful eyes widened in horror. The dragon had been impaled with a large piece of wood from the roof. Rayden was coated with blood from the injury, turning the beautiful silver dragon a deep crimson. Kade struggled to his feet but stumbled and almost fell, catching his balance at the last second. Nausea threatened to overwhelm him as the taste of thick ash clung to the inside of his mouth and down his throat. He coughed hard several times, bringing up black phlegm.

Doing his best to ignore his own plight, Kade stumbled over to the dragon. Tears seeped out of the corner of his eyes from the pain that racked his body and the feeling of anguish that assaulted his mind. His dragon was hurt because of him. His carelessness caused this. Despair clung heavily to him. Wiping his eyes with the back of his hands, he leaned against Rayden's side. The dragon quivered slightly, breathed in raggedly and then out with a slight gurgle.

Kade ran his hand along the thick, wooden shaft and tried to get a grip on it. His hands felt as if he was wearing thick, leather gloves. As he grabbed the wood, the pain came, making him wince. He tried again, but his hands did not have the strength to grab a twig, much less this shaft of wood. Helplessness washed over him as his vision blurred from the tears. He stumbled to the head of the dragon and cringed at the sight. The dragon's tongue was lolling out, and its eyes were unfocused. There was a bloody froth coming from its mouth as it breathed. Rayden was suffering horribly. Every time he inhaled, he would quiver, struggling for each breath.

Rayden's eyes dilated slightly as he attempted to focus on his friend. He made a feeble attempt to raise his head, but he barely got off the ground before falling back down with a thud. Kade knew Rayden was not going to be getting up unless he could do something about it. He looked at his badly burned fingers in horror and felt the hand of fate demanding his dragon's life.

He shook his head in defiance and sheer determination. He ground his teeth hard and forced himself to think. While his dragon was alive, there was still a chance. He steeled his will to do battle with death, once again.

What can I do? he asked himself as his mind started to spin. *There has to be something. What can I do? There has to be*…and then he stopped and looked back toward the cabin for the books. He was expecting to see them burned up, but there they sat, just a short distance away. He had taken them far enough to keep the flames from consuming them.

With a small sense of relief, Kade limped over and slowly moved them one by one until he found what he was looking for. If any book was going to have something in it that could help, this was it, the book he had learned the Lightning Calling from. He dragged it out of the pile slowly and lifted it into his arms, holding it to his chest, careful not to let it open. He turned and worked his way back to the dragon.

Setting the book on the ground, Kade focused. The pain surging all over his skin was almost too distracting for him to think. If not for the dragon, Kade knew he would have been lying on the ground, praying for any release from the pain, even if it meant death. But, he did not have that luxury if he wanted the dragon to live, so he forced himself to continue.

The Healing Calling is not going to fix this, but it might give me some time, he thought desperately, as he cleared his mind and felt for the Divine Power. His swollen fingers and hands were going to make this difficult, but he was sure he could perform the moves. The sweet taste of the Divine helped numb the pain just enough for his mind to work.

Slowly and deliberately, Kade drew on the Divine, completing the motions with his hands. He gritted his teeth as he worked through the moves and then placed his hand on the area where the wood was protruding. The trickle of blood stopped its flow; at least for the moment, it stopped. This was temporary, at best. There was still lung damage and only the Divine knew what else. The wood needed to come out.

Kade gripped the shaft, but as hard as he tried, he was not strong enough to remove it. The pole was firmly embedded deep in the dragon's hide. He tried a few more times, causing his skin to break open and bleed. The blood was making this considerably more difficult by adding a bit of slickness to the wood.

"Blood and ashes!" Kade cursed as he threw his head back and roared in frustration at fate. "Why can't you just let something go right?" he screamed.

Kade forced himself to perform the Healing Calling one more time and then turned his attention back to the book. He dreaded having to perform a calling under these conditions. They were so simple before, but now with these hands and burns covering his body, it was torture. He glanced at Rayden, and with firm resolve, forged on.

As carefully as possible, he got down on his knees and performed the Disarm Calling. It only required him to hold his hands over the object. Not having to move his hands was a relief, but he knew it was short lived. He slowly reached out and turned the pages, hoping desperately to find a calling that would save his precious friend. He tried his best to keep from smearing blood on the pages, but it could not be helped.

Something to dissolve wood. Something to transport wood away. Anything at all, he thought desperately.

The calling for changing shape was no help. The calling for charming animals was no help. His mind flashed back to the clearing with the grimalkin and all the animals before continuing on. The Strength Calling was no help. The dragon needed healing not strength.

Maybe a Greater Healing Calling that might push the wood out, Kade thought hopefully as he turned the page. The next calling was the Illusion Calling. For a second, he wondered why he had not considered learning this one, but even before he finished asking himself the question, he already knew the answer.

I was too eager to learn the almighty Lightning Calling, he thought, chastising himself.

Kade fought despair as he found himself at the last page.

Nothing, he started to think and then paused as he remembered a calling that just might help. He quickly returned to the Strength Calling, reading it carefully. It was not a calling to enhance other's strength but a calling to enhance his strength.

I am such a fool for not realizing this right off, he thought. With the amount of pain he was in, it was a miracle that he was even able to read. But, he had no choice. At least, he had no choice if he wanted the dragon to live.

Kade looked at his hands and gave a slight whimper. *How am I going to complete such a complex calling with hands like these?* he asked himself as he clenched his jaw tightly against the pain. The blood on his hands had mostly dried now, but he knew all he needed to do was flex his fingers and the liquid would begin to seep out again. There were only nine moves, but they were not easy, and he feared his hands were far too damaged to work properly.

Kade shook in fear and agony as he slowly stood. He blinked away the tears as he searched the area for something to put the book on. He spied a barrel a little ways to his left, and with considerable effort, was able to retrieve it by pushed it with his elbows. He moved it closer to the dragon and set it upright. He laid the book on it and read through the first move. He gritted his teeth and ignored the lump in his throat.

Focus, he told himself fiercely. *Focus! You did this, now you need to fix it so FOCUS!* He thought fiercely.

He narrowed his eyes and forced his hands to move through the first step, ignoring the tears that were brought on by the pain from inflamed nerves. His clothes had saved most of his skin from being burned to the degree his hands and face were, but anything not covered had taken a lot of damage. Kade did not even want to see what he looked like. He reached for more of the Divine and was rewarded as it flowed through him like a torrent. To his amazement and relief, a good amount of the pain had faded. Not all, but enough that he felt he had a chance to perform the calling.

Kade returned to the book and read through the moves, occasionally glancing over his shoulder to make sure the dragon was still breathing. After focusing on the page and learning the first step, he returned to the dragon to perform the Healing Calling. The bleeding that had begun to flow again, stopped immediately. The healing was much more effective than normal, but Kade's mind was too focused on the Strength Calling to notice. He learned the second move and then it was back to the dragon. Although the bleeding had not started again, he performed the healing just to make sure. He moved back and forth between the book and the dragon in a rhythm, as his mind continually went over the steps of the calling. As long as the Divine flowed through his body, the pain was not overwhelming.

Kade was dimly aware of blood dripping from his finger as he finished practicing the third step. When he read over the forth move, he cringed, and again, felt a lump form in his throat. A simple move but... Kade held his hands out wide, then, through gritted teeth, made tight fists, lunged forward and brought his arms directly in front of himself. He finished with a motion that made it appear as if he were giving himself a hug.

The pain lanced up his arms, making him jerk and flinch. He ground his teeth and firmly planted his feet, getting ready to perform the move again. If he flinched like that during the calling, things could go disastrously wrong, and he knew it.

Again, he reached out, made his fists and lunged. And again, he could not help cringing from the pain. Not only were his hands sending crushing pulses of pain up his arms, but his legs and hips were threatening to give out each time he took a step. He recalled slamming into the table as he went through the door to the den and knew where the injury had come from. Or maybe it was from the roof...or maybe the dragon. All he knew was that it hurt, and it was impossible to ignore. Every time he thought he might not make it, all he needed to do was glance at his dragon, and he would firmly plant his feet, preparing to perform the move again.

The next step was open handed, making it more tolerable, but it started with feet together and then a sideways step. This was the first calling that he was aware of that required the movement of his legs and feet along with his hands and arms. He found new aches and pains as he struggled to add this next move. The next three steps were relatively easy to learn and memorize. Kade had the sixth, seventh and eighth practiced and memorized smoothly. The sun slid across the sky considerably as he closed in on the ninth move. The dragon was not getting any worse, but it was clear that it was not going to survive if this did not work. If this failed, he was out of ideas.

Kade planted his feet and readied himself for the final step. The last and final move posed no difficulty. He worked this over and over until he was sure he could do it in his sleep. Now, it was time to practice the moves without calling on the Divine that would be needed to activate the calling. He worked slowly through the first eight moves and then added the ninth, forcing himself to ignore the pain as much as possible. He completed the first run through of all nine steps without a mistake. Although a little of the Divine was drawn on during the calling, it was not until the very last move that one drew on the full power and completed the calling by intoning the word for strength. If he made a mistake during the calling, he may escape with a minor injury or setback. One never knew until it happened, but generally, the more Divine that was involved, the more disastrous the consequence.

Kade wiped the sweat from his forehead with his sleeve, leaving a streak of black. He calmed himself as much as possible and tuned out everything except the calling, just like Zayle had taught him. His beloved teacher had always told him that his focus was his greatest strength, yet at the same time, it was one of his greatest weaknesses. Kade paused, thinking on this. He shook his head, not seeing how it could be both good and bad. Chastising himself for letting his mind wander, he turned his attention completely on the calling.

Kade called on the small amount of Divine Power he would need to activate each move and let it flow through him gently. He swallowed hard and began the calling. The first couple of moves were not too difficult and the golden trails left through the air were flawless as the symbols took shape. He slowed slightly for the third move but performed it perfectly while dreading the next. Sliding into the forth step, he spread his arms, and then, in an act of defiance against the pain, clenched his hands so tightly that his nails dug into the burnt flesh of his palms. More blood dripped from his fingers. So much so, that the drips were on the verge of turning into a trickle. He ignored it and focused on the next. The Divine was paying close attention to his movements as it eager awaited the Chosen's command.

He opened his hand, and when he needed to step, he stepped hard, forcing his muscles to do what he wanted them to do instead of the slight cringe or the temptation to collapse that they preferred. The sixth step was a relief as the movement was fairly easy. Sliding into the seventh, he forced himself not to rush. Pivoting, he turned slightly and moved his hands in opposite directions as though he were stretching a band. The eighth move was smooth, but as he glided into the ninth move, sweat started to drip into his eyes, causing them to sting from the soot. His focus waivered slightly but he quickly recovered, called on the Divine Power fiercely and intoned the word strength...or attempted to intone the word, but instead, rasped the word out in a croak. He panicked, realizing his error. He had not practiced speaking. Was it enough? His throat was raw from the heat and the soot he had inhaled.

Kade felt the power pulsing slowly...at first. And then, within seconds, it increased dramatically, making Kade feel as if a hundred electric eels were shocking each and every muscle. He threw his head back and howled in pain. Every ache in his body felt like it was magnified tenfold. He clenched his jaw against the torment, praying desperately that the pain would either relent or kill him. His teeth clenched so tightly, he feared they would crack and fall from his mouth. His chest constricted, threatening to suffocate him. The world spun, and just when everything was starting to fade, the torture ended.

Kade fell to the ground on all fours with a gasp, panting hard with specks of blood spraying the ground. He felt at any second he was going to pass out from the exertion, but he knew he could not allow it. He forced his vision to clear. As he turned his head to look at the dragon, blood dripped from his mouth to splash the ground. He must have bit his tongue, but it just did not matter.

Just a little longer and then fate could do what she wants with me, Kade thought.

He forced one knee up, planting his foot flat on the ground. He leaned back, preparing to stand and almost toppled over backwards. He grabbed the edge of the barrel and pulled himself up, wavering slightly. He took several ragged breaths and waited until his vision cleared. When he felt more stable, he stumbled over to the dragon. Through the pain, a twinge of hope made its way to the surface; a ray of sun after weeks of thunderstorms. It was something to grab hold of.

Kade looked at the dragon, but something did not feel right. He listened for breathing and felt anguish for just a moment until the dragon took a shallow breath and then let it out again. He completed the calling for healing, and even though he winced at the pain, he was immensely grateful it was not as harsh as the last calling. The dragon breathed a little easier, but it was not much.

Kade worked his way over to the wooden shaft and gripped it with his blood soaked hands. When he pulled, his hands slid effortlessly along the shaft. *No!* he thought in despair, as he picked up a few splinters. *This has to work.* He bit down on one of the larger splinters and pulled it out with his teeth.

He grabbed the beam once more, but again, his hands just did not have the strength to grasp it tightly enough. He felt on the verge of weeping with exhaustion, frustration and desperation. He latched onto the desperation, ignoring the exhaustion completely, and grabbed the wood for all he was worth. Not noticing, his fingers sank into the wood with a crunch. Kade put his foot on the side of the dragon, and with all the might and will he could muster, sent a burst of strength, forcing his leg to straighten as he let out a yell.

Kade felt as though he were flying and then floating. He hit the ground hard and rolled, not putting any effort into stopping his tumble. The wind was knocked out of him as he landed with the piece of wood still in his grip. His ribs protested as he breathed. He spit blood and chuckled slightly, thinking, *what are a few broken ribs to add to the rest.* He felt a sense of giddiness as the world spun. The ground felt odd against his cheek as he sucked in dust.

Kade rolled onto his back to get his mouth out of the dirt and stared up at the sky. His mind cleared, and he smiled slightly as he thought to himself, *see fate, I can beat your odds.* He chuckled again and quickly stopped, overwhelmed with the pain in his chest. He turned his head and saw that he had landed at least thirty feet from the dragon. Rayden was bleeding freely from his wound now that the spear was removed.

"Oh no you don't," Kade croaked as he tried to get onto his knees. The first attempt caused him to roll onto his back, but his next attempt put him up on all fours. He tried to stand but pain lanced through his hips. He was afraid he may have broken his pelvic bone.

Kade put his head down and started to crawl, focusing on making sure to keep moving forward. The dry ground, mixed with his blood, caused mud to cake on his hands. Soon, he felt a bump on his head and looked up to see a flow of crimson liquid running down the dragon's side. He placed his hand on Rayden and slid up, putting most his weight on the leg that hurt the least. He stood and called on the Divine Power. He could not feel the dragon breathing, but he knew the spark of life was still there. It had to be. He let the healing flow, and it sank into the dragon's flesh. It seemed to take hold. He performed it again and could have sworn the blood had stopped flowing, but everything was a blur as the world began to spin. He called on the Divine Power over and over, fighting to keep from passing out. By now, he was performing almost blind, as blackness crept over him. Desperation threatened to overwhelm him as he called on the Divine Power....or tried to call on it as he hit the ground and was out.

Kade could hear muffled sounds, and surprisingly, his mind was just barely clear enough for him to remember some of what had transpired. He fought to drag himself out of the dream world and into the waking world. He wanted to leave the nightmares of monsters and burning buildings behind.

Kade forced his eyes to open just a sliver. The light helped fade the dreams, but exhaustion and pain throughout his body made it difficult to want to wake fully. Through blurred vision, he was able to barely make out a huge mound not more than ten feet away. It rocked slightly as it reached to scratch at its back. For some reason he could not quite put his finger on, seeing this caused immense satisfaction. His body was starting to let him know just how badly it was injured when blackness called out for him once again. He let it come, eager to escape the pain that was steadily building. A single tear leaked out of the corner of his eye and slid down his face to drop onto the dry, dusty ground. The nothingness took him away.

The sound of crickets chirping near his ear slowly dragged Kade from sleep. The air was cool and crisp with none of the feel of the heat that he remembered. His mind felt like it was wading through molasses, as it slowly fought to organize itself. A cool breeze blew across his face, and he welcomed it.

Forcing his eyes open just a crack, he could not see much as it was a very dark night without one of the two moons to light the sky. He tried to get his vision to clear, but it was a losing battle. His mind started to fall back into the abyss, but just before he crossed over into the world of dreams, he felt the ground thud, as though something large had dropped down almost right on top of him. His mouth quirked ever so slightly in what might have been the faintest of smiles, as he eagerly went with the darkness once again.

A slight nudging on his shoulder brought Kade back to the waking world once more. It was every few seconds and would be followed by rapid breathing, as though something large were trying to catch a scent. Every so often it would huff in frustration and the process would start again. The nudge would send pain shooting into his brain, dragging him further and further from that comforting abyss. Opening his eyes, he stared directly into a huge, golden disc that blinked back at him.

"My friend," Kade tried to say, but no sound came out. His mouth was as dry as a desert. He tried to swallow but his throat was not able to work up enough moisture. He did his best to wet his lips, but his swollen tongue felt like leather. His cracked lips were not much better.

Breathing in slowly and deeply, he refocused on the dragon and smiled the best he could. Unfortunately, it only served to show how much torment he had been through. The emaciated image did not instill comfort. The dragon let out a quiet whine as it continued to check over its friend. Kade slowly lifted his hand and brought it to the dragon's muzzle. He might not be able to talk, but he knew this would communicate what he needed. He felt an odd sensation on the lower half of his body. It was cool. He looked down at his legs, surprised to see that they were half submerged in a shallow stream.

With a considerable amount of effort, Kade turned so he was facing the water. He attempted to cup his hand and bring it to his mouth, but most of the life giving liquid ran out. Still, he was able to moisten his lips enough to soften the skin. He did this several times until his throat was not so dry and his tongue moved without sticking to the roof of his mouth. Wiping his face with water also helped him wake a little faster.

Kade put his lips into the water, drinking deeply. At that moment, the water was the sweetest thing he had ever tasted in his entire life and he could not resist gulping, but unfortunately, his stomach retched hard, rejecting most of what he had drank. He took a few seconds while staring at his reflection to compose himself. He wiped his mouth and drank again, but this time, more slowly. He fought the urge to gulp. As the liquid worked its way down his throat and into the pit of his stomach, he was able to trace its path every inch of the way. He closed his eyes and savored the clean, cool flavor. He could feel the life in him returning by the second.

Submerging his face completely in the water, he sat there for several long moments, allowing the cold to wash over him. The burns on his face and hands were not as bad as he remembered, but still, the cooling water felt good. He lifted his head, took a deep breath and then plunged it beneath the surface, swishing back and forth to clean the soot from his face and hair. Almost losing his balance, he decided he had had enough. Just as he was moving back from the water, he saw his reflection again and froze. If he did not know it was his image staring back at him, he would not have recognized the person in the water. The growth of hair, the shallow cheeks and the sunken eyes sent a chill through him. The burnt hair did not help the image either. He wondered how much soot and ash, along with blood, had been on his face before he had plunged it into the water. His eyebrows were just starting to grow back. His skin was pasty white from severe malnourishment. Not wanting to see the image any

119

longer, he splashed it away into ripples.

A grunt caught his attention, and he turned to see the dragon watching him anxiously. Getting to his knees slowly and carefully, he felt for any injuries on his body that he had not noticed already. His hips pulsed with pain, and the rest of his body protested against any movement, but it did not appear that anything was broken.

"You are the most beautiful sight I could ever hope to see," Kade said in a whisper while looking up at Rayden. Still on his hands and knees, his head slumped toward the ground once again. He pulled one foot up and leaned back slightly, testing his balance. He slowly rose but waivered dangerously. After taking a few seconds to get his balance, he shuffled forward, wrapping his arms around his quivering dragon. He let his head fall onto his friend's chest and heard a quiet rumbling that reminded him of a cat purring. It brought a smile to his face. He was grateful to be alive, and he had his dragon to thank for it.

Looking around to get his bearings, Kade recognized this as the stream that ran behind his cabin. He took just a few more seconds and then started in the direction of the burnt dwelling. His legs hurt furiously, and every step made him clench his teeth, but he kept moving, taking one small, shuffling step after the next. He looked over his arms and legs as he walked, seeing enough cuts and bruises to make him wonder why he was still alive.

Soon, the charred cabin came into view. It was almost burnt to the ground. Kade looked hard and saw not even a wisp of smoke. The fire appeared to have been out for days. A pang of sadness welled up in him as he recalled his incompetence that brought the home he loved to an end so quickly after becoming its owner. He chastised himself harshly. He closed his eyes and could see the bright bolt of lightning that had shot out of his outstretched hand. That image was burned into his memory, as was every step of the calling.

The pungent smell of smoke was still strong as he worked his way through the wreckage. Heavy of heart, he moved things with his foot in hopes that something of importance had survived. Everywhere he looked, he was reminded of his folly and it hurt. Despair overtook him as he stood where the den used to be. He cleared a spot where the chair previously sat and then slowly sank to the ground and wept. Tears dripped to the floor, making a small puddle. After a while, Kade stopped weeping and sat staring at the boards that made up the floor. His eyes traced the lines in the wood where his tears had landed. As the time passed, so did his sadness. He sat in the same spot for over an hour as he pictured the den as it had been.

As Kade prepared to stand, something caught his eye. *What do we have here?* he thought as he brushed away some of the soot. Rubbing his eyes with the palm of his hand, he focused on the floor. One of the boards was not the same as the rest. It was slightly raised and half the length as those surrounding it. Kade brushed away the rest of the ash, and gripping the edges, pulled it up easily. Beneath was a small enclosure. Kade sat there and stared at its contents, wondering what new thing was about to turn his world upside down. So far, nothing good had come of anything he had found here in the den.

Kade took a deep breath and reached for the scroll. When he held it, he could feel the Divine Power pulsing through it and almost dropped it as if he had grabbed ahold of a deadly viper. He unclenched his jaw and slowly set the parchment down on the floor. The simple looking scroll, tied with one very bright, red ribbon looked harmless as it lay there on the ground, but Kade knew better. He shook his head at his folly for even touching it before using his Divine sight to check for traps. Angry at himself, he got to his feet and stalked from the cabin.

"Am I going to constantly bungle everything?" he raged as he walked away from the charred remains of his home. "Again!" he screamed with his damaged voice. "I could be dead. What did you

121

see in me that I was worth putting up with?" Kade asked as he looked toward his master's grave. "I know better, and yet, here I am, making the same incompetent mistakes over and over again!"

Kade yelled several more times to the heavens with his dragon nudging him as if to ask, "What?"

"I should have known to check for the Divine Power," Kade said as he rounded on the dragon. "I am a buffoon. A complete and utter buffoon. If you knew what was good for you, you would run from me as fast as you can," Kade said. The dragon stood still, patiently waiting for Kade to do what it was he was doing. After several long moments to give the dragon its chance to flee, Kade stalked back into the cabin.

Making his way to where he left the scroll, he stood looking down at it. Everything looked the same, no thanks to him. He took a deep breath and forced his mind to think.

"Now, use your head. Think," Kade said out loud. "No more stupid mistakes."

He leaned down slowly and called on the Divine. He closed his eyes and let the power guide his sight. The scroll did not appear to have any traps. Looking very closely, he saw that the paper had some type of calling on it but nothing that looked deadly. He reached out with his eyes still closed and gripped the scroll. The power pulsing in the paper did not change. Kade let out the breath he had been holding but continued to keep his eyes closed, watching. Slowly, ever so slowly, he pulled the ribbon from the scroll. The paper unrolled slightly, but still, nothing.

Kade breathed a sigh of relief and opened his eyes. The scroll was not as old as he had first thought. The more he examined it, the more certain he was that it was actually very recently made. He handled it gently, feeling his nerves on edge again. He had had enough of this and would have loved nothing more than to throw the scroll away from himself, but he was absolutely certain that it was too important to ignore. He rolled his head around his shoulders to loosen some of the tension and refocused on the parchment. Carefully, he opened it and recognized it for what it was; a simple message of sorts. It had just one symbol on the page. Only Kade knew what it meant. It was Zayle's true name.

Kade saw a tear hit the paper and roll off the edge. He knew what this was, and at the same time, he was hesitant to proceed. He had had enough of sadness and danger for a lifetime, but something told him that it was just the beginning. Kade let his head sag against his chest as even more tears dropped onto the parchment. After several long moments, Kade took a deep breath, brought his head up and opened his eyes to take in the symbol again. This was one of the simplest callings to activate. It was a calling needing only the Divine Power to work. Kade had no doubt this was meant for him.

Closing his eyes again, he felt for the Divine. He beckoned to it, and it came to him with just a little effort. He directed it down to his hand and infused the paper with it. The symbol shifted and faded to be replaced with the image of his beloved teacher.

"I am sorry, Master. I am so sorry I failed you," Kade said to the face that floated in front of him. Sadness threatened to crush his heart as he looked into the eyes of his cherished teacher. It was only more torture for him, as he looked on through his blurred vision.

"If you have found this, then things have started sooner than I feared. I should have prepared you more adequately, but I believed I had time," Zayle said as he appeared to be looking Kade in the eyes. "For the sake of our kind, you must discover what hunts us. There is a danger far worse than I could have ever imagined. You must discover what it is. I wish I could have prepared you better but time was not on my side. You need to seek out your parents. Your path leads there. I do not know why or how it matters but you must return to them." Zayle said and then paused. He took a moment to compose what he wanted to say and then seemed to refocus on Kade. The apprentice waited with apprehension, sensing that his master was about to say something important. "I want you to know that I am very proud of you. What you should also know is, you are not just my apprentice, but you are my one and only grandson. We hid this from you because your life depended on it."

Kade's eyes widened in shock and awe. His mind was reeling out of control. It was too much. Too much was happening too fast. He was just a simple man who was barely out of boyhood.

Why me? he asked himself. *Why me?* Zayle's voice brought him back to the image of his master.

Kade did his best to take in everything his beloved teacher was saying, but his mind was assaulted with grief. He blinked the tears from his eyes as the figure continued to float in front of him. Kade knew he needed to hear everything his master was saying.

"Our bloodline is strong in the Divine Power. Your ability to control the Divine along with your gift makes you our best hope. I have placed a medallion with this letter. Wear it at all times. It should keep you hidden. The more Divine Power you use, the more you shine like a beacon for those who hunt you and the more difficult it will be for the medallion to hide you. I do not know if it has limits, but be careful not to push it. I love you, Kade, and I always will. It is now up to you, my Grandson. Find what hunts us before our kind is extinct," Zayle said as he started to fade, "I believe in you," he added, and then the image was gone.

Kade fought the tears and lost. He was tired of sadness and crying, but no matter how much he resisted, the tears came. He wanted to be done with the pain of loss. His sadness soon turned to fury and hatred. He needed to find something with which to focus his anger. He felt rage coursing through his veins and every part of his being. His fists were clenched so tightly that he could feel his nails digging into the palms of his hands. When he looked down, he saw that the page was now blank. He forced his hand open and the paper drifted to the floor, landing next to the medallion.

"I will avenge you, Grandfather. I will!" Kade vowed. He paused, sure he had heard a distant chuckle...or was it the wind? Either way, Kade knew where he was going to aim his fury and it felt good to have a goal. His revenge was going to taste sweet and he was eager to exact it.

No more careless mistakes, he told himself as he formed his plans.

Over the next few weeks, Kade studied the books while he continued to recover. Every day he would go to the edge of the barrier and pace, watching and sensing. After a while, he would nod his head in satisfaction and then return to his studies. He was driven and focused. He had a goal and nothing mattered more than that. Somewhere deep down, he knew that revenge should not be why he did what he did, but he did not care. He needed this.

Every day he would stop at his Grandfather's grave and sit in silence, meditating. When he felt sadness, he would turn it into hatred and focus on that. No more grieving for him until he had his revenge. None!

The days melted from one to the next with his routine changing very little. He would wake up early, eat what the dragon had caught and then study. He practiced his callings over and over, cementing them firmly in his mind. He perfected the Silence Calling and practiced the Transparency Calling until he was sure he could do it in his sleep.

Kade knew his faithful dragon was worried and confused, but he also knew that his friend would stay by his side for as long as he needed. He felt a bond form with this amazing companion. Rayden was the only thing that was able to disrupt Kade from his routine. There was a simple kind of communication that had developed. He could not say when it happened, or how, but he was able to sense Rayden, and the dragon could sense him. He was even able to

125

communicate simple thoughts to the dragon and it always seemed to understand. This was the only ray of light that shined through the gloom.

Several weeks passed with almost nothing but practice, study and more practice. Several weeks and a day, Kade awoke, but instead of his normal routine, he went out and sat by his master's grave as he formulated his plans. His heart turned cold, and a deadly seriousness descended on him. Rayden could sense the change and came to lay by him, waiting. The time had come.

After a while of sitting in silence, Kade stood, and with purpose, headed for the side of the barrier where Zayle had lost his life. He walked the boundary as he had done every day for the last two weeks, but this time, he stopped. He furrowed his brow in concern and listened closely. Something seemed wrong. Something was different. He could not put his finger on it but there was a change.

There was a different presence. He could feel its eyes on him. There was danger in the woods, and it had come for him. Kade clenched his fist, welcoming it, eager to have another target to feel his wrath. He turned and marched back to the cabin. On the way, he stopped by the grave for one last time.

"I will make you proud, Grandfather, but first, I must do this. I hope you can understand. I need this for me," Kade said as a way of an apology. He was certain his grandfather would not approve of revenge, but he would not be swayed from this path. He turned and headed for his makeshift lean-to. He looked around for what he knew was going to be the last time. He gathered his materials and packed his few meager supplies. He had found some sturdy straps with which to bind the books so he did not have to fear them opening. They also served as a harness, allowing him to attach the books to the dragon's back, leaving his hands free.

He moved around to Rayden's front and looked him in the eye

as he communicated his plans. Kade was not sure how much the dragon understood, but it had to be enough. The dragon sat very still while Kade did his best to explain. When he finished, Rayden became very eager to be on their way. Kade could feel a hunger building in his companion. It wanted to hunt and kill. No, not hunt...rend and devour. Kade could feel it growing through the link. To say it was contagious would be an understatement.

He looked around one last time as his pulse started to quicken. His breathing increased as he sent the dragon the signal to kneel. Rayden bent a front leg for him to climb. Kade slung the books over his shoulder and bounded up to sit on the dragon. He turned in his seat and strapped the tomes of knowledge to the dragons back, making sure they were secure. The mood turned deadly. Rayden spun and headed for the barrier. Kade's heart was pounding as he ran his callings through his mind. He practiced even when he was not practicing. He wanted to be ready to give death another life to carry away.

The sun glinted off the barrier as they approached. Kade steeled his will as they came to the edge. For a brief moment, he wondered if he had trained enough, but it was just that...a brief moment. They did not slow. He felt the hairs on his arms prickle as he and the dragon passed through the protective shield. A twinge of doubt caused a slight bit of hesitation, but he knew it was too late to turn back. He did not know how to deactivate the barrier to let Rayden back in, and he was never going to leave his dragon.

Kade listened for any sound, and soon, realized why something felt wrong. With a loud roar, his dragon leapt through the air, tossing him to the ground as it grappled with something monstrous. Kade was immensely grateful for his new strength, as it seemed to make it easier to be nimble. He landed smoothly and was up throwing a blazing blast of Divine Fire before he knew it. His training was enough. He paused momentarily as he took in what he was seeing.

Another grimalkin! This is what felt different, Kade thought in a rush. *I should have known. They know where I am. Why would they not send more?* he thought, chastising himself.

He hesitated only a moment and then renewed his assault. This time, the dragon had help, and Kade knew, as a team, they were going to destroy this foul creature. He only had one serious concern as he spared a glance every now and then, watching the forest.

They worked well together, alternating using fire and the dragon's deadly attack. Kade hit the creature in the face, blinding it, and when it turned on him, the dragon sank its teeth into the beast's ankle and tore furiously, snapping tendons, sending it to the ground. It howled in fury but nothing was going to help it now, and it knew it's time was up.

Kade and the dragon were too much for it, and soon, Rayden had his teeth sunk deep into its neck and tore for all it was worth. The grimalkin screamed and seemed to be calling for…something. It was a call that it had sent out several times already. The beast tried one last time as it attempted to claw the dragon free, but it was futile. The grimalkin lost its life for picking a fight that it could not win.

Kade was sweating and breathing heavily as he healed the wounds on the dragon. As soon as he was done, Rayden turned and charged into the woods, searching the area for more danger. Kade stood watching, waiting, and listening carefully. Nothing…yet. But, he was absolutely certain it would not stay that way.

Just when he was starting to doubt his suspicions, the ground shook ever so slightly. Kade could picture his master holding his hand above the ground, using a calling that detected the coming creature. He did not need to perform that calling to know what was going to happen next. It was a familiar shake that Kade remembered easily. The last time he felt this, his master had waved him to silence.

Kade ground his teeth and suppressed a moment of panic. He

felt for the anger that had been festering over the last few weeks and gripped it tightly, fanning it into an inferno. He felt himself shake with rage and anticipation. Again, a small doubt tried to work its way into his heart, but he flung it away violently and called to his dragon. It was time.

Rayden, Kade called with his mind, but the dragon was already coming at him at a full run. Kade could sense the dragon's intentions, and he turned just as the dragon slowed enough to scrape the ground with its head as it shot through his legs. Kade slid along Rayden's neck and bounced into the air several feet before he was able to reach down and grab its wing. He was laying the length of the dragon, barely hanging on as it exploded with speed.

The thudding on the ground was too loud and too close. He needed distance, and he feared he was not going to get it. Settling firmly into place, he spurred the dragon on with his mind. Rayden's muscles bunched and exploded with each burst of its powerful haunches, picking up just the slightest bit of speed. Kade smiled an evil smile, all doubt gone as the power and grace of the dragon made his pulse race. His heart pounded, keeping pace with the dragon's great stride. Kade turned to look over his shoulder and saw the trees parting as the creature came through them. They were not pulling away from the targoth, but it was not closing, either. Clearly, the dragon being at its full potential made the difference.

It would only be a matter of time before the targoth was able to wear the dragon out and catch them. But, for now, this was enough. The dragon ran, but it was the perfect pace. It was just enough to let the monster catch them slowly. Kade looked over his shoulder and saw the targoth closing in little by little. He called on the ancient power and started throwing the Divine Fire. The creature laughed as it batted it aside. For every three that Kade threw, one would hit its mark. The creature roared in frustration. After several successful hits, Kade smiled to himself.

Now, Kade thought to the dragon. Rayden made a sharp, right turn that almost sent Kade flying. He did not expect the dragon to react so precisely. He filed that information away for later.

Kade looked back and tossed the Divine Fire every so often, but his focus was on the terrain. *Now,* Kade thought again, and again, the dragon made a sharp, right turn. It took effort, but this time, Kade was able to stay on firmly. He returned to the throwing of Divine Fire. Surprisingly, he scored a hit on what looked like the jaw of the creature. It roared in anger and hate so intense that fear was able to penetrate Kade for just a moment. He forced himself to remember his master, and then his focus returned.

Now, Kade thought, and again, the dragon made a hard, right turn. Kade resumed throwing the fire, but it was not meant to cause any more damage than it had. It had done its job by showing Kade where the creature was.

Now, Kade thought, and with the next hard, right turn, they were back on the path they had originally started on. The dragon was starting to wear down. It ran as hard as it could, but the giant's stamina was helping it close the distance.

Was it enough? Kade thought and then stopped that line of thinking instantly. There was no room for doubt. His plan was going to succeed! It just was!

Kade commenced with the next part of his plan. He worked the next calling with intense focus and concentration. The dragon and rider disappeared from sight.

NOW! Kade thought. The dragon slammed to a stop, sending Kade sprawling. He landed with a jarring impact that made his head swim.

The dragon had stopped for only a moment, but even that was almost too much. As soon as Kade hit the ground and rolled to the side, the dragon put everything it had into racing for its life. The ground erupted next to Kade as the creature's claws dug a deep trench. He held his breath, waiting, not moving an inch or making a sound.

After just a moment, the heavy pounding continued after Rayden. As Kade hoped, the creature was focused on the dragon's scent. *So far so good*, he thought.

He was sure that without the boost of strength, he would not have fared well with how hard he had hit the ground. He ignored the pain in his side and leapt to his feet. He moved to the center of the path and grinned evilly, eager to kill. He turned to face the way he had just come. His heart was pounding wildly now. He forced his mind to focus as he reached out for the dragon. The time for his revenge was at hand. He did not want to think of how his master might disapprove of such a dark thing. Zayle had always said, "When one embarks on a journey of revenge, do not plan on returning."

Wait until you see what I have for you, Kade thought viciously as he watched the smoke trailing after the creature. His lust for revenge was strong, but he hesitated, almost hearing his masters disapproving voice. It was only a second, and then he hardened his heart. Blackness covered his soul as his lip curled in a sneer. A primeval urge to kill enveloped his very being as the Divine begged to fill him. And then, it was as if a dam had burst. The Divine rushed in, as if it were a raging storm eager to be used. His special gift was glorious and it made him one of the most powerful Chosen to ever walk the land. Kade was staggered momentarily, as the onslaught of raw power almost overcame him. He steadied himself as he forced his mind to return to his task.

He clenched his jaw, eager for what was to come. Again, he reached out with his mind for the dragon. Rayden was struggling to keep the speed. Kade's eyes widened in fear, as the possibility of this not working crept into his thoughts.

You can do this Rayden. Now run. Run for all your life is worth! RUN! Kade thought fiercely. The dragon responded, and

Kade could feel its renewed effort. It had to be enough. There was no more time for planning.

The dragon was coming, and it was coming fast. Kade could sense Rayden was about to turn the last corner. It was only moments away when the dragon would be coming directly at him. But, he did not need the sense from the dragon. The smoke coming off the targoth told Kade exactly where it was. Kade felt his heart pounding hard as his pulse raced wildly. The adrenaline mixed with the Divine Power was enough to burst his heart, but he did not care. He wanted this badly; needed this more than he ever needed anything ever in his life. His craving for the kill consumed him.

The dragon rounded the corner, and not more than a hairs breath behind was the giant. It was gaining. But, Kade was sure it was enough.

Now for the easy part, Kade thought as he straddled the path and squared his shoulders. He ground his teeth hard in fierce determination and started the moves.

Kade focused more on this moment than he had at any other time since starting his training. Unlike the first time he performed this calling, he knew it would come because he wanted it to come. There was no room for mistakes, and he was going to make sure it was perfect.

Eager to bring death, Kade spun through the first move. He was vaguely aware of the smoke from the creature in the distance, as he quickly flew through the next three moves in rapid succession. As much as he tried to keep his breathing relaxed and calm, it was almost impossible. His heart was racing, making it almost too difficult to focus, but he must if he was to have the revenge he so desperately craved. His concentration was slipping as the Divine pounded at him, eager to be used. He clenched his jaw in sheer determination as he forced himself to ignore the distraction. There was only the smoke, his dragon and the calling. He judged the distance of the creature momentarily, and for an instant, feared it might be coming too fast. His lip curled as he let out a growl and flowed through the next seven moves as fluid as water. He knew that even Zayle would be impressed with his skill, as he eagerly closed on the last move. He knew this calling as well as any Chosen Master.

Now, the twelfth move he thought in confidence as the power thrummed in him, causing his heart to pound as if it were trying to break free from his chest. The familiar roar in his head was like a drug to him now. He reveled in it. The amount of Divine Power he was channeling was seductive. It was addicting, and for a brief moment, he wanted to hold onto it, regardless of the consequences. With a flourish, he aimed directly at the creature and let the violent blast of Divine energy explode from his outstretched hand. The lightning sent a shockwave that flattened nearby bushes. The bolt sped toward its target with perfect aim. It slammed into the targoth's chest, causing it to scream in pain.

The dragon turned instantly and lunged. It drove its talons deep into the creature's thigh and tore with its deadly jaws. It leapt clear of the targoth's claws just in time. The next bolt of Divine Power struck home, destroying the monsters vision for good. Kade was learning quickly that monsters fell hard when they were plunged into darkness. It screamed in pain and agony, and probably for the first time in its life, it screamed in fear. The creature's hands came up as it covered its face in an attempt to protect its already destroyed eyes. Kade sent another quick command to the dragon. Rayden reacted in a flash. His claws tore at the ground as he raced to flank the creature. He lunged and sank his teeth deep into the targoth's heel, bringing his jaws together in a vice-like grip. He dug his claws into the leg for purchase and pulled with all his might. Before the creature could react, there was a sickening, loud snap and the tendon was done. The beast roared in pain and fell hard to the ground but not before raking the dragon and sending it sprawling. Rayden landed

133

like a cat and rebounded so quickly that Kade paused in shear awe. He hesitated only for a second and then was back to ending the miserable creature's life.

Kade went back and forth between lightning and fire, even though lightning was doing the most damage. The dragon flew in for a quick strike at critical points and was back out before the monster could react. The targoth was back up on its good leg as it struggled forward, desperate to find its target, but the dragon quickly tore at the other tendon, pulling the giant down onto all fours. Kade could feel the heat from the fire as the beast lit up like a pyre, but he was not moving back one inch. Never again would he run from this creature. He wanted it to suffer, needed to hear it cry in agony. He only wished he could look it in the eye.

The targoth inched closer and closer, trying to reach its goal. Kade continued his dance as he delivered death over and over, feeling drunk with power while the Divine raged in him. No matter how much closer this creature moved toward him, he would never again run from it. Retreat was not an option.

Rayden sensed Kade's refusal to move back and roared at him in frustration. Through his link with the dragon, along with the roar, it was clear that Rayden was chastising him hotly. The creature was struggling to breathe as it reached for Kade, yet again. The Apprentice Chosen opened himself up fully to the Divine and reached for the unlimited amount of power. Yes, his gift was powerful. Within arm's reach now, Kade let go a blast of lightning with such hatred and malevolence that the creature's head rocked back violently and then slammed down so hard Kade stumbled. The arm landed next to Kade, causing the ground to shake. The weight of that arm alone could have crushed him, but he did not care. He had to watch it die. At this close distance, Kade could just barely make out the creatures face. He smiled as he looked into its eyes…or what was left of them. He needed this. He needed this for himself. Its breath hissed out of its body, and it only twitched a few times before it lay still for good.

Kade walked up to the creature and reached into his pocket. As the tears started to flow, he unfolded the piece of paper and let it drift down to land in the targoth's open hand. It was only a blank piece of paper, but it once held the name of someone he loved dearly.

"You're next," Kade said to no one in particular. "You...are...next!" he said fiercely as he put emphasis on each word.

CH5

Feeling a bit of closure, Kade forced himself to clear his head and check his dragon for injuries. There were two deep gouges along the dragon's side where the giant had raked it viciously. Working the healing calling, Kade mended the wounds almost without thought and then felt a twinge of guilt.

"Seeing you hurt at my expense is almost normal now," Kade said with regret. He hung his head and pressed his lips together in a thin line as he looked at the ground. Shaking his head, he took a deep breath and let it out. Walking up and putting his hand affectionately on the dragon's strong, fierce jaw, he said, "I will never forget what you risk every time you help me. Nor will I forget the many times you have saved my life."

Rayden's mouth opened slightly in what probably passed for a smile amongst dragons. Kade blinked a few times, surprised at the feeling of pride that drifted through the link. The quiet rumble that came from deep within Rayden told Kade more than any words could ever say, and he smiled in return.

"You, my friend, are more precious than I could ever say,"

Kade said as he patted the dragon again as exhaustion washed over him. He walked to the side of the dragon, and with his back against the fearsome creature, he slid down to a sitting position. He knew he should keep moving, but he needed a few minutes rest. He could also feel himself crashing from his adrenaline high. His muscles ached more than he realized and his nerves were frayed.

"We cannot stay long, my friend. The longer we are in one place, the more chance there is that something else will show up," Kade said as much to himself as he did to Rayden.

As soon as his heart slowed to a normal pace, Kade dragged himself to his feet, ignoring his muscles as they protested strongly and walked to the head of his friend. He looked into Rayden's eyes, feeling a strong sense of understanding as the dragon fought to lift its head off the ground. It had run for its life and was exhausted beyond words. It desperately wanted to just let its muscles turn to water. Even though it was still breathing harder than normal, its half lidded eyes said loud and clear that sleep would have been a very welcomed friend right then. Unfortunately, that was a luxury he was not able to indulge in just yet.

Planting his feet firmly, he performed the Healing Calling and placed his hands on the dragon's head. Rayden's eyes cleared and it seemed to give him a boost of energy. Although it did help in the short run, Kade knew it was only temporary. The body needed rest and it was going to get it sooner or later.

"That's more like it," Kade said as he patted the dragon on the side, wishing for the hundredth time that he could cast a healing on himself. Unfortunately, it just did not work that way. There was a calling that helped with alertness and a calling that helped with fatigue, neither of which he knew. If there was a calling for self-healing, he was not aware of it.

Rayden was up and ready to go. Placing his foot on the dragon's knee, Kade reached up, grabbing Rayden's ridges and swung himself up, landing just in front of the wings. There was a natural divot between the wings that made for a comfortable seat, and Kade appreciated this as he settled in for the ride. Resting his arms on the slightly up-raised wings, Kade sent a mental message to the dragon, giving him a direction. He needed to head to his hometown of Arden to find out what part his parents played in discovering who or what was behind the attacks. He wished his message from Zayle was more specific. How they were involved in this was a mystery…for now.

His parents lived in a town eight days east on foot. Feeling the press of time start to work on him, he urged the dragon to go. He hoped his delay did not cause their demise, but if they were in danger, he was certain that Zayle would have warned him. He considered how long he took in preparing his revenge against the targoth and his mind started to work.

Was this another mistake? No, he thought firmly. *That thing was waiting and I had to be prepared. No. Getting to my parents alive just happened to coincide with exacting my revenge.* Kade did not want to focus too deeply on this.

It did not take much to make him feel guilt, even when it was unwarranted. He would question his decision and then rethink it again almost as if he expected to find a flaw in his logic. For most of his life, he would brazenly charge into any situation, acting first and thinking later. He knew, sooner or later, he must change this, but for now, it was who he was. He chastised himself for his dangerous ways and started to examine his decisions over the last month. Guilt slowly slid over him and he sank into a somber mood.

The dragon went from a gentle walk to a brisk, gliding gait, jolting Kade back to the present. He chastised himself for being so self-absorbed that he had lost touch with what was going on around him. Daydreaming was definitely something he was going to have to do less of.

This is how I met the dragon, he thought to himself.

Grateful for getting away from the torment of his own thoughts, he took in the view of his surroundings. Rayden increased his pace into a lope. The dragon went from a relaxed stretching of his body to a tensing of its muscles, ready for the next powerful lunge. It was more like the dragon was launching itself forward and then gliding through the air to land, ready for the next lunge. Not a far leap, but not a run either. Kade was not sure if he could take this kind of jolting for long. As if Rayden had read his mind, the dragon's gait changed yet again. It now stayed closer to the ground as the distance it covered shortened. It made for a much smoother ride. He smiled to himself in satisfaction and settled in for the journey.

Kade forced himself to stop criticizing his decisions and watched the woods for any sign of danger. He knew he would be a fool to think there would be no more fearsome creatures like the last. He tried to think back on the storybook and recall what other dangerous creatures he may find along the way.

Hours slid by as Kade's worry for his parents grew. His quest to find another Chosen had to wait until he knew his parents were safe. He was not about to let another loved one die at the hands of this evil; not if he could help it.

Everything was quiet with the exception of the dragon letting out a grunt here and there as it ran. There was not even a single animal in sight, but he was not going to let this lull him into a false sense of security. *I am not going to make that mistake again,* he told himself, trying to stay alert, but his mind would, inevitably, return to dissecting every decision he had recently made.

Patting the dragon's neck affectionately, his hand came away with a slight wet feel. *This is as good a time as any for a rest,* Kade thought as he directed Rayden deeper into the woods for cover. The almighty Divine knew he could use it and they had covered a lot of ground. It was not long before they entered a clearing under a large tree.

This looks like a good place to stop and rest, Kade sent to the dragon. Rayden eagerly came to a stop and bent down to one knee, trembling slightly until its front leg was down. Kade slid off, not using the dragon's knee for support, and landed on his feet, then his butt as his knees gave way. His legs tingled from the lack of circulation. He rubbed his thighs, trying to get some feeling back into them. After waited for the tingling to stop, he got to his feet, looking around for any signs of water. His throat was dry and he was certain that the dragon would appreciate a drink, also.

Thinking back on the stream, Kade turned to the dragon. *Can you find water?* Kade asked with his mind. The dragon eyed him without lifting its head off the ground. Its eyelids looked ready to close and the eyes themselves appeared to be losing focus.

Maybe later, Kade thought and considered just dropping to the ground himself when the dragon, with obvious effort, heaved itself up to stand unsteadily. It shook slightly and headed off at a slow meandering walk in a direction that left no doubt in Kade's minded as to where they were going.

For once, things seem to be going right. It was not more than a few minutes when Kade could hear the sound of babbling water. Suddenly, they stepped though a line of trees into one of the most beautiful lagoons Kade could have ever imagined. The water was a deep, clear blue with lush vegetation everywhere. There was a twenty foot waterfall that made him feel as if he had stepped into another land. To say it was majestic was an understatement.

The dragon seemed to pick up a bit of energy as it dropped down next to the edge of the water and took long draws of the cool, clean liquid, swallowing loudly. Kade did the same. Knowing that this must be a common watering hole for other animals, Kade stayed alert for anything that moved. The area stayed quiet, giving them the much needed break. After drinking their fill of water, Kade rose to his feet and beckoned for the dragon to follow. Lethargically, it rose and lumbered after him.

Kade worked his way through the woods, looking for a safe place to stop and rest. Several minutes later, he stopped next to a large tree that must have been close to a hundred feet tall and six feet wide at the base. He examined the ground for tracks or any other sign that would indicate animal life and found none that were recent. Believing this place to be safe, he removed the books from the dragon and plunked them down next to the tree.

As Kade was considering what to do next, his stomach grumbled loudly. The dragon dropped to the ground and its head started to slowly sink. Before Rayden could close his eyes, Kade's stomach protested again at the lack of food. As much as he wanted rest, remembering that tasty, hot, juicy meat made his mouth water. He was more famished than he realized.

Kade glanced at the dragon and gave a bark of laughter. Even though Rayden was quickly fading into a sleep state, he had just a little bit of drool coming out of his mouth. Kade knew exactly how the dragon felt. He watched for a few more seconds, waiting. Then…the dragon's eyes shot open as if it were stung. Its head rose up and it looked at Kade expectantly while licking its lips. Kade let out another laugh.

"So, food before sleep?" Kade asked. "You go get us something and I will start a fire," he prompted.

The dragon seemed to consider the proposition of food as it eyed the ground, tempted to lie back down. Kade gave a sly smile as he visualized the strong smell of cooking meat, and that was all Rayden needed. He was off on the hunt. Kade laughed again as he watched the dragon disappear into the woods.

He started to rub the soreness out of his muscles as he turned to look for wood to make a fire. He was certain he was going to suffer dearly in the morning as he tried to work the kinks out of his lower back. But that just could not be helped. It was either deal with the soreness or a walk that would take days.

There was plenty of firewood for the gathering. Kade had a pile of kindling ready to go and sat down with his back against the tree, waiting. The rough tree bark was not as comfortable as he would have liked, but he appreciated the chance to relax and regain much of his lost energy. He leaned his head against the tree and closed his eyes. His mind slowed considerably and his body relaxed more and more by the second. It felt amazing to finally be able to just let go for even just a short time.

It will only be a few moments, and then I will get back up to wait for Rayden, he told himself. At least…that was the plan, but he felt himself drifting, and he had no energy to fight it.

Kade jumped hard as something shoved him over, startling him awake. He rolled to the side and sprang to his feet, ready to face this threat. He tried to clear his head as a giant, golden eye glared at him. Well, he probably would not have realized it was a glare without the subtle mental connection. His face turned a few shades of color under the dragon's scrutiny.

"I did not mean to sleep. I was only resting till you got back," Kade said a bit sheepishly. "Okay, fine. You were out working and I was relaxing," he said as he shook his head. "What was I supposed to be doing?" That was the best apology the dragon was going to get, but it appeared to be enough.

Rayden turned and picked up something from the ground. He spun back toward Kade, and unceremoniously, dropped a boar heavily at his feet with a thud. The apprentice smiled and his stomach growled in anticipation. Turning his attention to the pile of wood, he called on the Blue Flame of the Divine and set the logs ablaze. Pleased with his work, he turned back to the boar and stopped. He glanced around for something to use to prop the boar up with. There was nothing. With no spit, this was going to be difficult.

"I have an idea," Kade said as he started to gather large stones.

142

Grinning to himself at his cleverness, he soon had the boar completely covered with large rocks. A good amount of confusion came from the dragon, making Kade chuckle. The dragon was mystified beyond words as to why Kade was burying their food and even attempted to dig the boar back up until Kade pushed it back.

"Just watch," Kade said and felt good about finding this simple solution to their problem.

He used several branches to move the wood around the pile of rocks. He heaped several more on top of the pile and gave the fire just a little help to increase the heat. He stood back and smiled.

"It's an oven. You will see. The rocks will cook it but not let it burn," Kade said proudly. Doubt came from Rayden as confusion drifted through the link. "Well, it's the best we have," Kade said defensively. "Okay, you just wait. When I have hot, steamy pork, you will see."

An hour passed as Kade tended the fire. It was not difficult to keep the fire burning hot, but Kade found it challenging to be patient as the smell of cooking meat wafted through their little camp. Kade looked at the dragon with an I-told-you-so expression, but Rayden seemed not to notice. Kade saw the drool starting and burst out laughing. *So you are going to keep being stubborn,* Kade thought in amusement. The thought drifted through the link. The dragon snapped at him but it only served to confirm what he suspected.

Recovering from his fits of laughter, Kade patted the dragon on the side. He chuckled to himself, wrapped his arms around Rayden's neck and hugged him tightly. Rayden relaxed ever so slightly.

"I would not trade you for anything," Kade said. This seemed to help even more. "I know what would make you happy," Kade said as he picked up a pole he had cut from a nearby tree. He shifted the rocks away from the boar to display their prize. Just then, Kade flinched as a big, wet splotch hit him on the head. Reaching up and

143

running his fingers through his hair, he pulled his hand away to display a massive amount of slimy wetness. He wiped his hands on the ground and glared at the dragon.

"Was that necessary?" Kade asked as he tried to clean more of the drool out of his hair. "Do you have to hover over me and do that?"

Kade used several large leaves to clean his head the best he could and then returned to their feast while looking forward to bathing in the lagoon. He could almost feel the water washing away the day's travel. He was wiping his hair with another handful of leaves when an odd sensation drifted through the link, causing his eyes to widen and his mouth to hang open. Kade looked at the dragon in shock.

"Oh, so now that's funny, eh? Okay, just remember you started this," Kade chided, feeling a friendly rivalry starting. He was good with this kind of challenge, even though he would have preferred not to have a head of slimy, wet hair. He refocused his attention on removing the boar from the makeshift oven. There were a few burnt spots, but for the most part, it had cooked nicely. Kade quickly forgot all about his hair as he licked his lips in anticipation of the juicy meal.

It took just a little work, but soon, Kade had one leg severed from the boar. He had to use leaves for pads or the meat would have burned his hands. With his portion in his hands, he motioned for Rayden to eat. The dragon's head dipped toward the boar and then shot back up to look intently at Kade.

"Yes, all of it is yours," Kade said, sensing the unasked question.

Rayden did not need to be told twice as he lunged at the boar as though it were trying to escape. Dragging the carcass away just a few feet, the dragon dropped down and tore hungrily into its prize. Using its front claws to hold the boar, it tore the meat apart easily and eagerly. Kade found himself staring at the dragon's ferocity.

Returning his attention back to his own food, he did his best to eat the steaming meat, but unfortunately, he did not have the dragon's tolerance for heat.

As soon as the food cooled, Kade stuffed himself full. Not able to eat even one more bite, he sat back against the tree and closed his eyes, enjoying the feeling of a full belly. After a moment, he noticed it was quiet, too quiet. He opened his eyes and turned to see Rayden staring at him. No, not just staring but locked onto him without blinking or even hardly breathing. It shot a glance at his left hand, which was holding the meat, and then returned to staring at him. Kade smiled and motioned with the boar's leg.

"It's yours," Kade said, allowing the thought to pass through their mental link. The dragon did not need any urging and snatched the meat up so fast that Kade flinched. "Easy boy, easy," Kade said, checking to see if he were missing any fingers.

Seeing that all appendages appeared to be intact, Kade smiled to himself and watched the dragon quickly engulf his leftovers. There were only a few bones left with just scraps of meat on them. He hoped the dragon had had enough, but he had his doubts. Kade knew it could eat a whole cow in one sitting, so this was probably more like a snack.

Leaning back against the tree, Kade enjoyed the calm of the woods. He looked around the clearing and for the first time really noticed the nature that was surrounding him. The air was clean and he felt good for the first time in a long time. He knew that having a full belly, plenty of water and the company of his dragon had a lot to do with it, but he was ok with that. He took in the sound of birds and smiled. He looked at his pile of books to make sure they were still secure and considered sliding them next to him in case he drifted off. He quickly discarded that idea, worried that he would inadvertently open one during his sleep.

He could feel his eyelids growing heavy, and welcomed it. He was almost out when the snoring dragon startled him. He smiled again, and then let go, enjoying the feeling of every muscle turning to jelly as his mind drifted in any direction it wanted. He felt himself take a deep, long breath, and as he was exhaling, the world faded.

The sound of insects chirping slowing worked its way into Kade's mind. His muscles protested as he tried to shift. The ground was not the most optimal place to sleep and his body was letting him know. His back hurt and his joints ached. Gritting his teeth, he pushed himself up on one elbow. He rolled onto all fours and then sat back on his legs. With the exception of the dragon taking long breaths that had a deep reverberation, the world was quiet. Wetting his lips, he looked around as his mind continued to wake. The sun was just starting to rise.

Something seems...off, Kade thought to himself as he scratched the sand out of his hair. Several small twigs and a good amount of dirt fell to the ground. He looked around but did not see anything that he felt should alarm him.

What could be giving me that feeling? he asked himself as he sat there staring at the ground, his mind still struggling to awaken. With a jolt, his eyes shot to where the books should have been.

"NO!" Kade yelled out, bounding to his feet. He ran around the giant tree several times but found no sign of the books. He was on the verge of full blown panic. His mind raced. He spun around and almost bounced off the dragon. Rayden sensed Kade's panic and was watching him intently, trying to find what was causing him to be so frantic. Worry flooded the link.

"The books are gone!" Kade said in a rush as he started to pace. He immediately suspected the unknown evil Zayle had warned him about as his heart started to pound. "I will get them back," he vowed, pounding his fist into the palm of his hand. For a moment, Kade looked at the tree as his fury started to boil over. He considered punching it to vent his anger, but his logical mind took over. If he were to damage his hands, the callings he could perform would be limited. A Chosen needed his hands.

"I need to think this through," Kade said out loud, trying to calm himself. He was partially successful. "Why steal the books without trying to kill me? That does not make sense," he said as he looked around suspiciously.

Kade definitely started to get the feeling there was more to this than he was seeing. He forced himself to calm considerably and looked around the area for any sign of what might have taken the books. Nothing presented itself. Turning to the dragon, he spread his hands, and with his mind, asked if the dragon sensed anything. He was not sure if Rayden could understand what he was asking, but it was worth a try. Surprisingly, the dragon sniffed the air several times but could offer no answers.

Kade felt frustration building and clenched his jaw in determination so as to not let it cloud his thinking. He closed his eyes and took several deep breaths, attempting to relax. On the second breath, he exhaled and ground his teeth hard enough to crack them, or at least it felt hard enough to crack them.

"What can I do?" Kade asked in desperation of Rayden. Unfortunately, all the dragon had by the way of help was a blank look as it swayed slightly.

"What callings do I know?" Kade asked as he started to slowly pace. "The Divine Fire will only burn the forest down. The Lightning Calling is useless. There is the Drift Calling. That is possible, but I will save that for last. What else?" he asked as he narrowed his eyes, thinking. "I wish I had learned a Locate Calling," Kade mumbled as exasperation started to set in. So much power at his fingertips, and yet, he felt as helpless as ever to solve this dilemma.

Kade stood next to the tree, trying to figure out what to do next. He was not about to give up, but things were not looking very promising. No matter how bleak, though, he always kept trying until he was absolutely certain beyond a shadow of a doubt that he had exhausted every possible option. It was one of the things that Zayle admired about him.

"What other callings do I know? The Disarm Calling. The Reveal Calling...THE REVEAL CALLING!" Kade said excitedly. "If the books are close, I may be able to see the protective Divine callings placed on them. With luck," Kade said, feeling a bit of excitement at having something to try. It was a slim chance but it was something.

Kade closed his eyes and started to concentrate. The slight trickle of Divine Power flowing through him felt good. The familiar tingling felt like an old friend that he could trust to always be there, but it was even more than that. The master had said that it has a slightly addictive quality and to be careful not to be seduced by it. He could see how someone could become addicted. It felt like power and it felt good.

Taking a deep breath, his eyes darted back and forth behind his closed lids, looking for any sign of glow that would indicate that the Divine Power was present. Turning slowly and peering as hard as he could, Kade held his breath, hoping. He had turned three quarters of the way around when he saw a faint, blue light. His eyes flew open only to find he was facing the tree.

Kade knelt down and studied the base of it closely. He examined the ground as his mind worked. *What am I missing?* he asked himself. Then, he saw it; faint scrape marks along the ground. He chastised himself for being so blind and refocused his mind. He studied the faint trail closely. Kneeling down slowly, not taking his eyes off the marks as though doing so would cause them to disappear, he ran his fingers over them.

Getting down on his hands and knees, he followed the scrape marks around to the back side of the tree. They disappeared in some moss and behind a sparse growth that was just enough to hide a small opening. Kade closed his eyes and was rewarded with a strong vision of the Divine Power directly in front of him. A sense of relief washed through him as certainty settled in that he had located his precious tomes of knowledge.

Calling up a small amount of Divine Power for light, Kade cast his hands toward the hole, preparing to reach in when he flinched back. His body reacted to a pair of eyes and a hiss even before his mind realized what was happening. His heart was pounding as he watched the hole intently, waiting for the owner of those eyes to come racing toward him. After several long seconds, he let out a breath that he was not aware he was holding and slowly crept back toward the hole.

Kade called on the Divine Power for light once again and cast the illumination over the entrance. Slowly, moving closer and closer, he peered in intently, expecting the creature to come bolting out. Closer and closer he crept, and yet, he was met with complete silence. Ever so slowly he reached in to light the darkness. Two feet into the tree, his light fell across the bundle of books, but unfortunately, they also lit up the two eyes that were watching him closely.

The eyes had an eerie white glow that made Kade stop and stare into them. The animal appeared to be as calm as if it was getting ready to lie down and go to sleep, but Kade knew better. It did not blink nor move and it did not even appear to be breathing. The animal shifted its gaze over Kade's shoulder and panicked as its eyes went wide. It took a deep breath and emitted an ear piercing shriek that seemed to go on forever. Kade leapt back and bounced off Rayden. If he had been a little more observant, he would have noticed that the dragon's muzzle was slowly creeping over his right shoulder.

"You scared him," Kade accused as he put his hand on the dragon's muzzle and gave him a gentle push backward. Rayden resisted to a point, then huffed and sat back. Laughing at being sneaked up on by this lumbering beast, Kade turned back to the tree.

Once again, lighting the small hole, Kade started to reach toward what he had hoped was a docile creature. He quickly changed his mind about the creature being docile. The closer he moved his hand, the more teeth it would bare. When Kade was just a mere six inches from the books, the small creature that could not weigh more than fifty pounds, had almost two inches of fang showing and was issuing a deadly hiss. It was not going to give up its prize very easily.

Kade considered lunging for the books, but he knew, from the way the creature was tensing its muscles, it was not going to go well for him if he tried. He pulled his hand back slowly and the creature retracted its fangs proportionately. He reached forward again, but for every bit he moved forward, the creature would bare more and more of its fangs, tensing its muscles as if readying for a strike. There was sickly green ooze dripping off its fangs, causing Kade to grimace. He was not sure if that was poison, but he was not ready to take that chance.

Running his callings through his mind, he was not able to find anything that would help. Again, he was at a loss, having so much power at his disposal, and yet, having nothing that would help retrieve the books. His eyes lingered on the books and then he sighed, thinking there was probably a calling in them that could have helped with this situation. The irony of it did not sit well with him.

He went to look over his shoulder at Rayden and almost smacked nose to nose with the dragon. He had not noticed the dragon creeping closer and closer due to the fact that he was so intently focused on the hole. Shaking his head at being sneaked up on so easily again, Kade moved back to consider his options. Rayden moved closer to the hole and took several quick sniffs.

"I think this is going to take a more delicate touch," Kade said as he shoved the dragon's head out of the way.

Moving forward toward the hole, Kade peered in cautiously. The creature had not moved one inch and was still watching him intently. Kade's heart jumped and his eyes widened as he saw the chew marks on the straps that were supposed to be securing the books. The straps were not in danger of breaking…yet. At least, from what he could see, they did not appear to be in danger of breaking.

"Come out," Kade coaxed. "If you don't come out, I am going to have to come in and there is definitely not enough room for both of us."

Kade sat staring at the hole and smiled as his master's favorite saying came to him. Zayle used to love saying, "For every problem, there is a solution."

Kade let his mind relax and then almost laughed out loud as the simplest solution possible came to mind. Still smiling, Kade got up and walked over to where the boar had been. Picking up a bone, he returned to the base of the tree.

Kade slowly reached in with the food and stopped when the creature's lip started to lift. He held still for several long moments. As he hoped, the creature's nose started to twitch more and more as it took in the scent of the meat. Its eyes shifted between Kade and the bone as it considered the temptation of food. The more Kade sat still, the more the creature's eyes would linger on the bone with its scarce pieces of meat still attached.

Kade could not help but to smile. The moments dragged on, but the creature was becoming more and more interested in the food. It focused on the bone, and with its nose twitching furiously, started to stretch its neck. Kade moved back ever so slightly as the creature extended its head out as far as it could. Any further and it was going to have to take a step. Kade held still, waiting. His patience paid off. There was the first step. The creature darted quick glances at Kade, but only for a moment, not wanting to take its eyes off the prize.

Kade glanced over his shoulder momentarily, making sure there was room for him to move backward. He was expecting to see his dragon crowding him, but surprisingly, it was out of the way. The last thing he wanted was for Rayden to mess this up by scaring the creature back into hiding. Kade retreated and the creature moved with him. Half of its body was out of the hole when it stopped and nervously looked around. Content that it was safe, it refocused on the food.

Kade moved back a couple more steps, trying to coax the creature the rest of the way out. It seemed to consider the bone but leaving the safety of the tree was something it was not accepting easily. Kade got the feeling that it was going to retreat and moved forward slightly to entice it again. Suddenly, there was a loud crashing of teeth that came together on the creature dragging it violently out of the hole in one swift movement.

Kade was lying on his back, looking skyward, gasping from having the wind knocked out of him as his heart raced wildly. He could not even recall being pushed over. All he knew was that he was now on his back, looking up at the sky. He glanced at the dragon that had bitten down hard on its victim, formerly known as the creature. The dragon sensed Kade's outrage through the link and froze, not understanding why Kade's anger was growing.

"No!" he yelled as he scrambled to his feet. "Drop it!" he commanded, feeling that he had betrayed the trust of this creature. Rayden sat there with it half dangling from his mouth. Kade could see that it was still alive and struggling to breathe, but it had taken serious injury from those long, sharp, dagger-like teeth.

"Now!" Kade demanded as he stepped toward the dragon. It did not sit well with him that this creature was going to die like this. In a way, he felt like he had been dishonest with it. Rayden opened his mouth to let the creature hit the ground with a thud. Kade felt sick to his stomach. It flipped over a few times, showing signs of having a broken back. Kade did not hesitate to bring the Healing Calling to life. Ignoring its teeth and claws, Kade placed his hands on the silky fur and felt the Divine Power take hold. He completed the calling over and over, willing the creature back to life.

"It was coming out," Kade said accusingly as he looked at Rayden. Kade could sense confusion along with something else. After a moment, the closest description he could find was something along the lines of demoralization for disappointing him.

"No, I am not mad at you," Kade lied. He sent the thought, also.

Kade turned his attention back to the creature and felt sad for it as it looked at him in fear. It tried to crawl away as it mewed pitifully. Kade stroked its fur in an attempt to calm it. It was going to live but it was not going to heal instantly. It lifted its head and looked longingly at its little hole in the tree.

"Not for you to eat," Kade said firmly to Rayden.

Calling on the healing once more, Kade placed his hand gently on the animal's head. It was hissing between its sad mews but it was recovering quickly. It attempted to stand but stumbled and fell over.

Kade glanced at the creature's hole and then raced for the books. He reached in and carefully retrieved them. He did not want to have to go through this all over again. He looked all the strappings over to make sure none of them had been chewed through and then relaxed, seeing none had been compromised. Satisfied, he moved out of the way of the opening to allow the creature to go into its little safe haven.

"Just hold on," Kade said as he scanned the area. "I think a little water will do you good, also."

Kade looked up and saw what he was looking for. He pulled one of the bowl shaped leaves off the tree. He worked his way back to the water and carefully carried as much of it as he could back to the tree. He leaned down and saw that the creature was back in its position, hissing violently.

"Gee, why would you not trust me?" Kade asked, his voice dripping with sarcasm. He forced himself to keep from chastising the dragon either mentally or verbally. He knew it had only done what it thought it should. Slowly, he put the leaf on the ground and pushed it as far forward as he dared. It tilted to the side, spilling some of the water, but there was still plenty left for the creature.

"You know your chance of surviving after being attacked by a dragon is virtually zero," Kade stated and then paused. "Hmmmmm," he said out loud as he considered the animal. "Chance. Yes. That is a good name for you. Okay, Chance. The water should help. No hard feelings, I hope," he said as he backed away from the hole.

Kade returned to the other side of the tree and sat down, plunking the books on the ground next to him. He sat staring at them for several long moments when he came to a decision. It had to be done sooner or later.

"I must continue to learn," Kade said as he slowly untied the straps. He grabbed the large book with the Lightning Calling and after performing the Disarm Calling, opened it and started to look for his next lesson. He was done looking for the awe inspiring callings and was now looking for something that would be more practical. Then he saw it; a Sustenance or Food Calling. He recalled finding this calling the other day and wished he had given it more attention then.

What could be more practical than being able to conjure food whenever it was needed?

Kade looked over the moves and was surprised at how simple they seemed. The only part that he thought might be tough was visualizing the food. The calling specifically said that the food was created from pure Divine energy, but it needed the person performing the calling to visualize it.

"So much for me calling up a seven course meal," Kade chuckled to himself.

He got to his feet and mentally prepared himself for his lesson. It was a simple three step calling. The only tricky part would be not going too fast. It clearly stated that each move should take three seconds and have a two second hesitation between each one.

"Well, it seemed easy at first," Kade said out loud. "Having to make sure I pay attention to the timing along with visualizing every aspect of the food, may be a bit tougher than I thought."

Kade practiced the moves and the timing for hours, completely losing track of time. It seemed simple, but completing the steps, keeping time and visualizing every aspect of the food was going to be more of a challenge than he expected. Finally, he decided it was time to try. He closed his eyes and calmed his mind. He cleared all thoughts except that of the calling. This was something that Zayle had preached over and over, and Kade was definitely seeing why it was important to follow this rule. Nothing could be allowed to break your concentration once you started or the outcome could be disastrous.

After several long moments, Kade opened his eyes, took a deep, slow breath and let it out as he spread his feet and squared his shoulders. He took another deep breath and opened himself up to the Divine Power. The sweet caress flowed through his body. Kade reveled in it momentarily before he brought himself back to the task at hand. He started the moves, focusing on timing it just right, and just before the end, he tried to visualize a piece of meat. Something materialized in his hands and he flinched. He had to force himself to keep from dropping the slimy, cold meat. Kade brought the food to his nose, and after one whiff, felt his stomach clench tightly. He gaged to the point of almost getting sick.

"What in the Great Divine!" Kade said out loud as he quickly tossed the meat aside with a scowl. The dragon had the unfortunate experience of believing it was food and caught it in its mouth, almost swallowing. It opened its mouth and shoved the food out without touching it with its lips. Rayden slid his tongue in and out of his mouth several times, scraping it against his teeth.

"Sorry," Kade said dismally, not wanting to see the look in the dragon's eye. "That was a huge failure."

"Well, I have a pretty good idea what I did wrong," Kade said, sneaking a glance at Rayden. The dragon actually looked like it was going to get sick. It even had small gouts of flames erupting from its mouth in quick succession as it attempted to remove the foul taste.

Kade shook his head and tried to visualize the food without doing the calling. He focused on how the meat should feel in his hands as best as he could. He thought how it should smell. He already knew how it was supposed to look as that was the only part of his calling that went right. After just a few moments of practiced visualizations, he decided to try again.

Kade cleared his mind, as before. He called on the sweet tasting power that always brought a gentle smile to him and performed the calling. He tried to keep count as he went through the motions while visualizing the food. He felt it materialize in his hands, and quickly dropped it. It felt too slimy. Frustration flooded through him as he realized he had to put thought into the texture, too. He gritted his teeth hard and pressed his lips together in anger.

"Come on Kade. This is not that hard!" he fumed, stopping just short of using some choice words on himself. "It's an easy one," he said, even though he knew better. "Okay, okay, focus. Picture everything," he chastised, not realizing he was sounding exactly like his mentor.

Kade spent several long moments trying his best to visualize the meat. Absolutely sure he had it fixed firmly in his mind, he decided to try again. He took several long, deep breaths to help clear out his frustration and calm himself. It took longer than he had hoped, but soon, he was ready to try again.

Kade squared his shoulders and called to the Divine Power. Focusing hard on the vision in his mind, he completed the moves to the calling and opened his eyes just as the power popped and fizzled, not producing anything. He closed his eyes tightly and clenched his teeth again. Through tight lips, he muttered, "Too fast." He had rushed the calling.

Kade could not help but to feel the exasperation building in him. He desperately hated to fail at something he considered simple. He was absolutely certain this was an easy calling and he knew he should have been able to complete it without so many failed attempts.

Failure was not an option; not with a calling this easy, he thought fiercely.

Kade realized he was clenching and unclenching his fists. He forced himself to relax, or tried to, but his mind kept returning to his failed attempts. He could feel his anger boiling like a volcano wanting to erupt. He sought something to take his frustration out on and turned to the tree as fury blinded his sense. Before he knew it, the moves to the Lightning Calling were forming in his mind and the sweet scent of the Divine Power was coursing through every part of his being. Kade let out a hard grunt of frustration that bordered on a yell. He flexed his muscles hard and relaxed them to keep from losing his very last shred of control. Some part deep in him knew it was wrong to be this angry, but he could not help feeling frustration at failure that should not have been. He had to wrestle control back. Realizing what he had almost done, he felt shame, knowing his master would deeply disapprove. The anger receded, but not completely. He recalled the creature and realized how close he had come to blowing it and the tree to pieces.

After pacing for several long minutes, Kade returned to his spot and worked at calming his mind and clearing it of any negative thoughts. It was not easy, but after some positive self-assurance, he was ready to try again. With his mind clear, he focused on the food while keeping an easy, steady pace. The feel of the food, the smell of the food, the salty taste of the food along with how it looked all came to him as he performed each step.

Kade focused on visualizing everything during the calling, not just at the end. Getting a perfect pace going and thinking of the food during the entire ritual was the key. He glided smoothly through the three moves and felt the meat materialize in his hands. His eyes popped open. Surprisingly, it smelled right. It smelled more than right, it smelled great. It was the perfect feel with the exception of being too light. It appeared that the sense of touch was going to be tougher than he thought, but this was serious progress. He smiled as he raised the meat to his lips and took a hesitant bite. His mouth puckered as he spat out the meat.

"Well, I definitely know how too much salt tastes. Wow, this is way more difficult than I expected," Kade said surprisingly without anger. The fact that he knew he was making progress with the calling, a calling that turned out not to be as simple as he originally thought, helped keep him focused and calm.

Kade could imagine how his master would be lecturing him now. "You have to be the smart one here. The Divine Power is just a tool waiting for you to mold it. If there is a mistake to be made, it will not be because of the power. It will be due to your unskilled use of it."

Kade paced as he considered the deeper meaning to his masters wise words. He needed to visualize each sense individually, but he needed to bring them together to visualize them at the same time. He was eager to have the ability to feed his dragon, and he wanted it to be sooner than later.

Touch had to have the right weight, feel and even temperature, Kade thought as he recalled the lack of heat in a previous calling. Smell was not as difficult and the way it looked was not proving to be a challenge, either. Taste was another task that needed more focus put into it. Not only was there a slight bit of salt needed, but there were also other flavors. *The tangy taste of the juice from the meat along with the slight, and I mean slight, taste of salt,* Kade thought to himself sarcastically. He considered how the texture of the meat was supposed to feel when bitten into. He smiled to himself as he closed his eyes and relived the experience. His smile widened and he knew he had found the solution to this dilemma. He did not need to visualize it per-se. He only needed to remember every aspect of it as he performed the calling. Or, more accurately, relive it.

Kade moved back to his spot with excitement, eager to try his new approach. He cleared his mind and did his relaxation exercises, the smile never leaving his lips. He glanced at the dragon, certain Rayden was about to enjoy this calling very much.

Kade called on the Divine Power and started the three simple moves. With barely a conscious thought to the timing, he relived the memory of his last meal. When he finished, he almost dropped the steaming piece of meat that materialized solid and heavy in his hands. It smelled amazing. Kade could feel his mouth watering and was eager to taste his creation.

Before Kade could even lift the food to his lips, he heard a grunt to his right and saw Rayden eagerly eyeing the newest conjuring. The dragon looked intently at the Divine creation and then cast a quick glance at Kade in anticipation, fidgeting slightly. Kade recognized a begging animal when he saw one and laughed a deep victorious laugh. This could not be more perfect if it were straight from the boar itself.

"Oh no. I am not going to take the chance of giving you something that might not be right," Kade said with a grin as he brought the steaming, hot meat to his lips and took a huge bite. He burned his mouth but he did not care. He closed his eyes, experiencing every nuance of the taste and could not help but revel in this small victory.

After tearing off a good size chunk with his teeth, Kade tossed the food in the air and was not surprised in the least as the dragon lashed out with lightning quick speed to snatch the food in midair. A sense of pride filled Kade, but before he could enjoy the sensation too much, his master's voice came into his head, saying, "Too much pride is not good, my young student. Be careful that pride does not turn to arrogance. Hubris has no positive aspects to it. Pride alone has brought down many a powerful Chosen. You must learn to temper pride with just the right amount of humility."

"I understand," Kade said out loud, as if he were actually answering his master.

Ignoring the twinge of sadness, he glanced at the dragon and chuckled, sensing its craving for the meat. "You will never again go hungry from this point on," Kade said as he prepared to conjure more food for his endless eating machine. It took virtually no thought when reliving a memory. As a matter of fact, he suspected he was imagining it better than it was the first time. A moment later, he was tossing Rayden another piece of meat and the dragon was happy to snatch that one from the air as well.

"I know another creature that might appreciate some," Kade said as he conjured more of the juicy meat. Rayden danced eagerly but this was not to be his next bite. Kade moved over to the tree and knelt down while craning his neck to look in at those eerie, white, glowing eyes. The silky, black creature was sniffing the air as Kade stretched out his hand to offer the food. He knew there was no way it was going to trust him enough to come out, but this was about making up for how it had been treated. Kade smiled and set the meat down on the ground just inside the entrance. He stepped back, and in the blink of an eye, the meat disappeared. In that instant, he noticed that the animal had a bent ear now, whereas before, it was straight. His healing was clearly not perfect but it was enough to save this beautiful animal's life.

"That should help," Kade said, pleased with himself.

Kade could hear the creature sniffing furiously as it checked over this delicacy. It did not take long for it to start tearing into the meat. Feeling incredibly satisfied, Kade went back to the dragon.

He made another piece of meat and tossed it to Rayden. Before he could swallow, his head came up sharply and swung around to the right. Kade paused, shocked, certain he could tell what the dragon was sensing. This surprised him because he was sure he was not using his own senses, but instead, using the dragon's. This went further than being able to communicate simple thoughts with Rayden. This was using the dragon's senses as if they were his own.

Rayden seemed to go into a silent hunting mode as it stalked in the direction of whatever had gotten its attention. It swallowed the food and focused on the woods. Kade listened closely, trying to make out what had put the dragon on edge, but it was not quite clear, yet.

There was a hint of a lightly traveled path where the dragon had stopped. It had a sharp bend a short distance from Rayden that wound around a large tree. He froze like a statue as he straddled the path, waiting, ready to pounce. Kade watched, impressed, certain it had used this technique in the past to ambush unsuspecting prey.

Kade cocked his head as he listened. For a moment, he thought he could sense what had gotten Rayden's attention. He was not sure if it was the wind he was hearing or…possibly…a woman's voice. Yes, he was sure of it. It was a woman's voice. He felt the urge to run out and meet another human but sensed danger from the dragon. The voices continued to move closer and he could almost make out what was being said. He could even swear that he heard the voice of a child.

"Torvod, try to be quiet," Kade heard a woman hiss. "There are probably bad men in these woods," she added. Kade could feel the fear as her voice broke at the end. She gave a quiet sob and then

Kade heard a child.

"I am trying mom. Why are we running from our home?" the boy asked in a pleading voice.

"Because, there are men trying to hurt us. I am sorry, but we must. We have to leave for at least a little while," the mother said as she fought back the sadness that threatened to send her into more sobs.

Kade stood rock still as they continued to approach. He could see flashes of movement through the shrubbery on their left as something moved along the path toward them. His eyes slowly drifted down to the path to where he was standing and then back up to where he heard the voices. After a moment of consideration, he decided to wait. He was betting his life that they were what they appeared to be, but the dragon was not. At any moment, he would know, and hopefully, they could answer some questions.

Kade watched as the family rounded the corner. There was a man who appeared to be lost in his own thoughts. He ducked under a branch, stepped over a root and then offered his hand to his wife to help her. The child eagerly scampered over the root and then froze as his eyes grew as wide as saucers. The parents were still too focused on their woes to see what was right before their eyes. Kade smiled to himself as the awe took hold of the child, who appeared to be around the age of nine.

The dragon held completely still, not even blinking. Kade took the dragon's lead and waited for the man and woman to notice. He felt a twinge of guilt for waiting to see their reaction but it was only a twinge. The woman had a boy about the age of six on her back. As soon as the man turned to continue, his eyes landed on the leg of the dragon and froze. Slowly, his eyes traveled up until he was looking directly into the dragon's eyes. His face turned white, and he crumpled to the ground.

"Dran, what is it?" his wife asked in alarm, looking at him in surprise and worry. She turned to see what had him speechless and froze. The boy on her back yelped.

The man stood up very slowly, as if to move too fast would send the dragon into action. He and the woman stared in shock, frozen, unable to even breathe. *What a sight it must be,* Kade thought as he pondered how he wanted to approach the family. He could step out and introduce himself, but that would mean someone would know who he is and where he is. *Or, maybe I should retreat, but they might have information I can use.* Kade went back and forth with his thoughts while the family stood completely still, as if moving might cause the dragon to pounce. *The less people that know of me, the less danger I will be in.* The boy's next words changed his mind and he smiled a broad, wide grin.

"WOW! A real live dragon!" the nine year old said as he raced up to Rayden. The parents both turned white as a sheet.

Kade sensed the dragon's intention to swat the boy aside and quickly sent it the mental thought to be patient and leave the boy alone. The dragon looked askance at Kade. Patting Rayden affectionately, he just smiled. The boy wrapped his arms around the dragon's legs. The mom and dad both gave a squeak but neither was able to move.

"Easy, Rayden," Kade said as he stepped out from behind the massive bulk of his friend. This seemed to break the mother out of her trance and she screamed.

"No, Torvod! Get away from that beast!"

The man came to what senses he could muster and grabbed his wife while hissing in her ear, "No Tracella. Do not move. It may attack if you make any sudden movements!"

Kade held up his hands as if to placate the parents. He smiled and then looked down on the boy who was still clamped tightly to the dragon's leg. The child was absolutely beaming like he had just found the most wondrous thing in the land. He knew how the child felt and instantly liked him.

"It's okay. Rayden will not hurt the boy. He is my dragon," Kade said, still sensing the dragon's strong urge to shake the child from his leg. The parents focused on Kade and were back to being speechless. This was way too much for them. The boy, on the other hand, was far from speechless and proceeded to babble excitedly.

"Is this really your dragon? WOW! How do I get a dragon? Where did you find him? How many are there?"

"You can't just get a dragon," Kade said as he slowly unwrapped Torvod's arms from Rayden's leg. Kade chucked at his friend as a flood of relief came rushing through the connection. "As a matter of fact, you should never do what you just did. Any other dragon would have eaten you. He is the only one that is tame," Kade said to the parents as much as he did to the kid. "If I was not here, it may have hurt the boy."

Tracella and Dran looked at him in awe. They still seemed to be frozen, so Kade tried once more. He did not hold out hope that he was going to be able to calm them anytime soon, as they were still ashen, but he had to try. He thought back on his first encounter with this fearsome creature and knew how they felt.

"It is alright," Kade said, trying to make eye contact and get them to understand. "You are not in danger. Rayden will not hurt you," he said slowly.

The man blinked. His gaze shifted back and forth between the dragon and Kade as he tried to comprehend what was happening. After a moment, his eyes seemed to focus on Kade and stay there. He relaxed slightly as he took a deep breath and let it out slowly.

"This is your dragon?" Dran asked incredulously, waving a hand toward Rayden.

"Yes. Well...he is not really mine," Kade said, emphasizing the last word. "But, he does listen to me and mostly does what I say."

The woman seemed to break out of her trance and see Kade

for the first time. She flinched as her eyes focused on him. After a moment, she broke into a run and wrapped her arms around the boy, and not too gently, dragged him away.

"Dran!" Tracella exclaimed as she took a step back, ready to turn and flee.

"Tracella," Dran said in as soothing a voice as possible. "I believe this man and his dragon," he said, darting a cautious glance at Rayden and then back to his wife, "mean us no harm," he finished. After a moment's consideration, she seemed to calm and then her mood went dark as she locked an accusing eye on Kade.

"Then you are not more of the evil men who have come to our town, taking what they want and killing our men?" she asked, snapping from too much stress and fear over the last few days.

"What evil men?" Kade asked as his sense of danger grew. He tried to keep calm, afraid that he would lose the progress he had already made, but the hairs on the back of his neck went up. "What evil men?" he asked again with force as he spoke each word slowly. He needed to know. Dran stiffened, and the smile slowly faded from his face, his keen sense of danger kicking in. Kade was, after all, one of the Chosen, and if Dran learned of this, he was certain to mistrust the Divine user.

The man and woman looked at each other and something passed between them. The woman whispered something and the man seemed to agree, relaxing again. They both turned back to Kade, appearing to ease a little more, but not dropping their guard completely.

"You did not come from town?" Dran asked, casually dropping his hand to land on the knife at his side. Kade, feeling overly confident that he was in no danger, did not see the move.

"No. I came from the west," Kade said.

The man looked to the west as he tightened his grip on the hilt. He looked at the ground as if he were thinking and slowly shuffled

165

forward. Kade took the move as one of trust and relaxed.

"So you say you came from the west, eh? Where from in the west? I don't recall any towns in that direction," Dran said calmly. His hand tightened and his muscles flexed slightly. Kade was oblivious to the move. Unfortunately for Dran, the dragon was more alert. Rayden, sensing danger, slowly moved forward as his lips parted and his mouth came open to display his deadly fangs. The dragon continued moving toward Dran until its mouth was mere inches from the side of Dran's head.

Before Kade could ask what in the great Divine had gotten into Rayden, he sensed danger through the link and froze. His eyes narrowing, he saw what had the dragon on edge. Locking eyes with Dran, he held his hand out as if he knew the entire time what was happening.

"You were about to show me your dagger?" Kade asked casually, cocking an eyebrow, as he had seen his master do so many times. Dran gripped the dagger and his muscles flexed. The smile left Kade's lips and any hint of kindness faded from his eyes. He gave Dran a hard stare that promised death if he did anything other than what was asked of him. Dran exhaled shakily as he slowly changed his grip on the dagger to one of just finger and thumb and drew it out, handing it to Kade.

"It is okay, my friend," Kade said as he patted the dragon on the neck. "He just wanted to show me this fine weapon?" he said to the dragon as much as asking the question to Dran. The man muttered something that was supposed to be assurance and took a step back with his hands raised.

"I know of no town to the west," Dran said meekly but with a tone that indicated he still did not believe.

Kade sighed and took a step forward. He put his hand on the man's shoulders while looking over at his wife who was starting to sob, and then he glanced at the boy. With a smile, he held out the dagger to the man.

"He was only trying to defend his family," Kade said to Rayden.

Dran stood in stunned disbelief, looking at the proffered blade. He glanced at his wife, who wilted and gave a shrug as if surrendering. He slowly accepted the weapon and sheathed it. He opened his mouth to speak, but before he could get one word out, Kade held up a hand.

"I did not come from a town. I was in training with a man named Zayle," Kade said before he could stop himself. He held his breath, knowing he had said too much.

The man's eyes opened wide. He glanced at his wife and then back the way they had come as if watching for someone. He narrowed his eye, his mind working furiously as if he were trying to come to a decision. His wife grabbed him firmly by the arm, making the decision for him and whispered, "Tell him."

"The men that came to town mentioned that name," Dran said in resignation. "Said he was one of the Chosen, but no one knew what he was talking about. That would be you?" he asked apprehensively.

"Where did you say you came from?" Kade asked with a growing suspicion.

"From a town further to the east," Dran said cautiously.

Kade, suspicious of this man, decided it would be in his best interest to check and see if the Divine was being used. Warning the man not to move and indicating the dragon, he closed his eyes while preforming the Reveal Calling. If this man was tethered to anyone, Kade would see the connection. There was nothing.

"Uh, sir?" Dran stammered. "Could you please call off your dragon," he pleaded. Rayden had moved close again.

Kade clenched his jaw in exasperation. Dran had, once again, put his hand on his knife. It was most likely a habit for him to just rest it there, but nevertheless, it was foolish. "If you do not want to lose that hand," Kade said, trying to keep the anger from his voice and failing, "then I suggest you keep it off your knife!"

Dran's hand moved so fast it was virtually a blur. Kade gave him a hard stare and it was all that was needed. Dran reddened slightly at the mistake and smiled sheepishly. He did everything with his hand but let it get close to his side again.

"He meant nothing by it," Tracella offered by way of an apology, ignoring the boy on her back who was starting to fidget. Kade waved away her apology.

"Sorry. He does not trust as easily as I do," Kade said as he, once again, pushed the dragon back. Rayden shuffled backward only a few feet, but then no matter the amount of pressure from Kade, he was not going any further.

"Thank you," the man said in relief.

"Now, tell me all you know. What is happening in this town, and what do you know of these men?"

"Late last night about fifty men dressed all in black came to town and started attacking everyone." Dran paused, expecting Kade to ask a question. After a moment, he continued. "When we asked them what they wanted, all they would say is they were looking for someone coming from the west. No one knew what they were talking about. We tried to fight, but it was useless. They had these two…," the man said as he waved his arms wide and high, "huge beasts," he finished and then crossed his arms over his chest to keep his hand away from his weapon. He spared a quick glance at the dragon. Kade stayed silent, waiting for the rest of the information.

"Most of the people that tried to fight were killed. I got my family together and hid all night until we were able to sneak out of town. We were heading to a refuge where we would be safe when we ran into you. There is a cave," the man said as his wife hit him in the ribs. "Oh come now, Dear. If this man was going to hurt us, he would have already done so already," Dran said as much to Kade as to his wife. He was hoping that Kade would give him the assurance he was hinting for, but the apprentice was busy processing the information. "I say we trust him," Dran said and he meant it.

Kade seemed to be lost in thought as Dran and Tracella waited for him to speak. The moments dragged on and the man and his wife started to become restless. Dran edged forward while eyeing the dragon.

"You should join us," Dran said, making sure not to get too close, fearing that the dragon would attack. "The evil ones cannot find our hiding place, and your dragon would be excellent protection."

"I can't," Kade said with regret. "I have much that I must do. If I do not continue on my journey, you will never be safe."

The man gave Kade a questioning look. The Apprentice Chosen shook his head as though to say, "It is too much to tell." He glanced at the family and for the first time, noticed that they were dirty and appeared to be hungry. The more he looked at them, the more he realized that they must have fled town quickly. They had nothing except the clothes on their backs and a sack with precious little in it.

"You look tired," Kade said, changing the subject. "Sit down and relax for a while. I will explain as much as I dare," he said, leading the way back to his clearing.

"We should keep going. We are cold and tired and we haven't eaten since the men came to town," Tracella said.

"I will take care of getting food and warming your family. Rayden will provide excellent protection while you are here. I am no easy mark myself," Kade said as he thought about the giant that he and his winged friend had killed. Rayden seemed to understand and grunted an agreement as his eyes showed a glint of malice. It was a look that was truly fearsome.

The man looked around the area, attempting to find the food that Kade was offering. Seeing none, he turned to his wife and told her with a look, "Something was out of place." She shrugged and turned back to Kade, waiting.

"May I pet your dragon? Please, please, please," Torvod pleaded, dissipating any tension that might have still remained. Kade laughed, completely understanding the child's excitement.

"Of course, but make it short as he can be a grumpy one," Kade said as he sent the thought to Rayden to be patient. The dragon grunted and thudded down on the ground to put up with the pawing. "He is also welcome to touch the dragon," he added, pointing to the younger boy, peaking over his mother's head.

"Adalm is afraid of his own shadow," Dran chided.

"Oh you hush," Tracella said. "He is still young. Give him time."

"If I may ask you to gather some wood," Kade said to Dran, interrupting the dialog. "I will prepare some food."

Dran looked at his wife, but she waved for him to continue. He let out a quick breath and gave in to the request. Turning to leave, he glanced over his shoulder and said as much to his wife as to Kade "I won't be far," then moved off to look for wood.

Tracella removed the boy from her back and the pack from her shoulder. The boy clung to her with a death grip as he eyed the dragon. She ignored him the best she could and pulled out a thin blanket from the sack to spread on the ground.

"Torvod, Adalm, sit and behave," Tracella said to the two children. She offered a spot for Kade, but he politely declined with a wave of his hand and a smile. He grinned to himself, looking forward to the reactions he would get when he conjured food from thin air. He even chuckled at his private joke.

"It looks like you and your family could use some hot, fresh food," Kade said with a grin. The woman did not take her eyes off him but sat quietly, clearly perplexed. "If you and your family are hungry, please, allow me to feed you. It is the least I can do." Kade said reassuringly. After a moment, she glanced around the area and looked questioningly at him.

"You don't appear to have enough food for yourself much less any to share with us," Tracella said.

"Here is my food," Kade said with a grin. He was eager to awe them with his great power. The dragon tensed slightly, sensing that Kade was starting to draw on the Divine. It sat up quickly, hoping for a tasty morsel, knowing that Kade was preparing to call on food.

Kade forced his mind to clear and calmed his heart. Vanity had no part in the actual calling. Zayle had preached that vanity only led to the wrong uses of the Divine Power.

Momentarily fearing failing in front of this small audience, he redoubled his focus and performed the calling perfectly. The meat was almost hot enough to burn his hands. The smell was amazing.

Kade opened his eyes and saw a look of terror in Tracella's eyes mixed with concern and confusion. She was on her feet instantly, glancing behind herself without thinking, as if preparing to flee for her life. Kade quickly held out the food for her so she could see it was, indeed, just food.

"This is for you," Kade said, surprised and a bit disappointed that this was the reaction he was to get. After a moment, he shrugged as he continued to talk, still holding the meat out.

"I must confess. I am the one the men are looking for. I will explain when your husband returns," Kade said as he extended the food a little further, urging her to take it. She did not move so he took a step closer. If not for the children, Kade was sure she would have run like the wind. "Go on. It's safe, and I can tell by the rumbling of your stomach that you have not eaten in some time. Take it," he urged again. She reached out with great hesitation, ready to jump back as though the meat itself were going to attack. When nothing happened, as she gripped the meat, she exhaled loudly and appeared on the verge of collapsing.

"You are safe. You are in no danger from me," Kade said, doing his best to reassure her.

"Please forgive me," Tracella said, her hand shaking slightly.

"The mistake was mine. I should have prepared you," Kade said.

She relaxed considerably as her eyes returned to the food. After just a moment more of hesitation, she took it eagerly, handed some to her children with a firm order to share and took a large bite. Kade smiled.

Dran returned and froze, seeing his wife eating what appeared to be freshly cooked meat. The wood fell from his hands as he looked around to find from whence the food had come and the fire it must have been cooked on. He was hungry but caution had a firm hold on him.

"Where did that come from?" Dran asked as his wife offered him a bite. Slowly, he took the hot meat and held it up to his nose. It smelled perfect, of course. Kade could see that it was not going to be long before he threw caution to the wind and devoured it. "It's hot. How did you cook the food with no fire?" Dran asked with a fair share of suspicion, but still eyeing the steaming, juicy meat.

"Step back from the wood, and I will show you," Kade said as he prepared the Fire Calling. He let the Divine Power envelop the wood, causing the logs to burst into flame.

Dran stopped chewing and the food fell from his lips. Tracella and Adalm also stopped chewing and stared in awe. Torvod, was of course, impressed. Adalm was clinging to his mother in mortal fear. Tracella slowly turned, looked up at her husband and said, "He says he is the one the evil men were seeking."

Dran stood, frozen, looking at Kade, his face going white.

The Apprentice Chosen feared that Dran had stopped breathing and was going to pass out if he did not inhale soon. Kade waited for the moment to pass and started to feel impatient. This was not the glorious moment he was expecting. He found it confusing that after displaying his amazing powers, he was not enjoying this as much as he thought he might.

"You can do that, too," Dran barely whispered. Every sense in Kade came alive as he replayed the last words spoken.

"What do you mean…too?" Kade asked more forcefully than he intended. He was afraid he already knew the answer to his question.

"There was this man that could do things like that," Dran stammered.

"He says he is one of the Chosen that the men were looking for," Tracella said again while indicating Kade, her voice full of fear.

Dran just stared at Kade as he worked through this. He was dealing with an internal struggle as indecision gripped him. After several seconds, he squared his shoulders, and in a confident voice, said, "If those men are looking for you, then obviously you are not with them. If you are against them, then I stand with you."

Tracella's head whipped around so fast Kade would have thought she had whiplash. Her mouth went tight as her eyes started to smolder in anger. Dran feigned not to notice. Kade mentally cringed, knowing she was going to really let him have it when they were alone.

"I mean what I say," Dran said, holding his head high.

Kade was touched by the man's conviction. He looked from face to face as he considered Dran's pledge. He thought about it only for a moment and then quickly came to the realization that he had to decline the offer. He shook his head slightly and stepped up to him. He placed both hands on his shoulders and looked him in the eye. Dran tensed.

173

"Thank you," Kade said with deep compassion in his voice. "But you have a family to take care of, and I would never ask you to risk your life when they need you."

He nodded once but Kade was not convinced. There was a fire that had been kindled in the man's heart and it was growing into a blaze. Kade feared that he was going to cost this family their father and husband. He recognized that blaze. He had the same fire in his heart for weeks until the giant lay dead.

Tracella grabbed her husband's arm and squeezed. He hesitated for a moment and then looked into his wife's eyes. She glared hard at him but he glared just as hard back. She gasped in exasperation and dug her nails in but he still held his ground. If they meant this to be between them, they were failing miserably. Kade did his best not to notice.

Settling down on the blanket, Kade spent the next hour telling the family all that had happened to him. Torvod sat in complete rapture as he soaked up every word that Kade spoke. Adalm sat close to his mother, never leaving her side. When Kade mentioned the grimalkin, he noticed Dran stiffen.

"What town did you say you were from?" Kade asked, seeing the man's reaction to the creature.

"We have come from Arden," Dran answered. Kade's eyes came open wide and he leapt to his feet, startling the couple.

"I am sorry but I must leave now! My mother and father live in that town and I need to get to them as soon as possible!" Kade said and sent a strong mental command to Rayden to prepare to leave immediately, causing him to jump. Kade grabbed his books and turned to run for the dragon when Dran grabbed him by the arm, holding him firmly. Kade spun around so fast the man let go and jumped back with his hands up.

"Your parents are probably gone already. I am sure the men own the town by now," Dran said, trying to placate him. "Who was your…," Dran started to ask when he grunted from the impact of Tracella's elbow in his ribs. "I am sorry," Dran said sheepishly. "Who are your parents? Maybe we know if they got out of town," he continued, his gaze shifting between his wife and Kade.

"Garig and Judeen Stone. You might know my father. He is the town peace keeper," Kade said while watching the couple's expressions closely. They exchanged a knowing look. Kade felt a knot in his stomach and it was tightening by the second.

"My father would not have left unless everyone was out safely or the men were turned aside. Am I correct? What is it that you know?" Kade demanded. "What has happened to my parents? Tell me!" Kade said as he felt a lump develop in his throat. He fought the panic and swallowed.

"You are correct. They never left," Dran said, compassion in his voice. His eyes held such a fierce look that Kade almost took a step back. "I will come with you!" Dran pledged, almost demanding to be allowed to join the fight. For one fleeting moment, Kade, once again, considered letting him come and then shook his head.

"I cannot. It will be too dangerous!" he said, matching Dran's fierceness. "You have your family to take care of. Once they are safe, then…maybe. I have to go now."

"Then at least take this sack for your books. You are bound to drop them if you continue to carry them like that," Tracella said as she thrust the bag at Kade. He hesitated as he looked at Tracella, not wanting to take what meager belongings they had left. She put the sack to his chest and he quickly took it, shoving in the books. It was a relief.

"This may also come in handy," Dran said as he pulled the well-honed weapon from its sheath and handed it to him. Before the apprentice could refuse, Dran held up his hand and said, "I have another identical to that one. Take it." Kade took the knife and slid it into his boot.

He ran to the dragon, and with a much practiced acrobatic move, quickly bounded up the side of the dragon, landing squarely on its back. Rayden let out a fierce roar, causing the family to cringe. The young boy covered his ears and cowered behind his mother's skirts. Torvod smiled and clapped his hands excitedly. Kade tied the sack in place and spurred the dragon.

Dran watched as rider and mount disappeared into the woods. He was focusing so hard that he did not hear his wife say his name until she shook him by the shoulders. She grabbed him by the arm and turned him, or tried to turn him, but Dran was too focused as his mind worked.

"Dran!" Tracella said as a warning. "No!" He glanced at her, and for several long moments, they locked eyes. "Husband, what fool thing are you considering?" she asked as her voice broke. She was on the verge of crying.

Without answering his wife, Dran quickly packed up their possessions and headed toward sanctuary at a much quicker pace than they had been previously moving. Stopping after just a few steps, Dran looked around for the eyes he felt on him. There, in the weeds, almost invisible, was a black, silky creature with one bent ear. After just a few moments of studying each other, they both moved off in different directions.

Tracella watched after her husband, feeling exasperation growing, knowing that he would not share his thoughts with her until it was too late. She also knew that once his mind was made up, whether logical or not, he could not and would not be swayed. She was afraid to press him more. When he kept something from her, it usually meant she was not going to like it. She started down the path after her husband. A flash of something black moving through the brush caught her attention. When she stopped to look for it, there was nothing. With a shrug of her shoulders, she turned and followed after Dran.

CH6

Kade hunched over Rayden's back to keep the wind out of his face. The only thing that mattered was that his mother and father were in grave danger because of him, and he had to get to them in all haste. Kade did his best to be positive by telling himself that his parents were safe, but in his heart, he feared the worst.

If you hurt my parents, Kade thought to the unknown evil as his lips curled. He knew his father was very clever and extremely capable of handling almost any situation, but this had to be too much for him to deal with. If Zayle, the most powerful Chosen could fall, then clearly an ordinary man would have no chance.

Kade fought to keep his mind from torturing him with all the horrors that his parents could be experiencing, but failed miserably. The thought his parent's lives might be in peril at that very moment was twisting his gut in knots.

The dragon, sensing Kade's panic, surged constantly. As

much as he tried to shield his mind from the dragon so it would pace itself, his thoughts would, inevitably, return to visualizing all the suffering that his parents may be experiencing. He had to find a way to keep his mind from visualizing the worst.

"Pace yourself, my friend. You must not push yourself this hard or you will wear out too fast," Kade pleaded.

Rayden slowed considerably but Kade could tell that it was as if the dragon were pulling against unseen chains as it fought to maintain a consistent pace. It was torture for both the rider and dragon. He knew he had to content himself with this, as it was the best he was going to get. Hopefully, the dragon would find a speed it could keep, but he feared the worst.

Maybe they won't know who my mother and father are. Maybe they are just looking for me, Kade thought, but still, he was unable to remove the knot in his stomach. *Well, if they did find out who they are, I am sure they would keep them alive for leverage, if nothing else,* he considered, seeing just a small ray of hope slip through the clouds of doom. *Of course, they would most likely resort to some form of torture first to get what information they could,* he thought as his heart constricted.

The dragon surged again and Kade quickly chastised himself once more for broadcasting his thoughts of dread. His hands started to feel slippery against the dragon's hide. He wiped them on his pants to dry them, but it only helped temporarily.

The trees and land were a blur as they raced along, but even at that pace, they would not get to Arden fast enough. He forced his mind to stop thinking and made himself look around at the landscape. None of the area looked familiar, yet.

Kade needed something to distract his mind or he was going to howl in frustration. He considered his recent lessons in the Divine and started running the moves over and over in his head. After a while, his mind drifted back to the first and simplest calling he had ever performed. It was the calling for light. The only requirement was to channel the Divine into his body, urge it into his hand and hold it there while shaping his hand as if he were holding a bowl. Then, he just needed to let it build. The more of the Divine he let fill the calling, the more it would glow and turn to light. He was thoroughly amazed at this easy calling when he first learned it. He recalled how his master even forbade him from making light because of how much he used the calling. For a brief moment, he almost laughed as he recalled his master's sarcasm.

"You would never know night ever came with how much you use that calling," Zayle had quipped.

In the blink of an eye, Kade felt sadness threaten to slip into his mind at thoughts of his master and he quickly changed his focus to that of another calling, the calling to look for Divine Power. Thinking back on his exercises, Kade smiled. Zayle would make a game out of his lessons which made learning fun and easy. The Master Chosen would cast the Divine on something in the cabin and Kade was to find that object. Again, thoughts of his beloved master made his heart hurt. With regret, he realized that any calling he thought about was going to remind him of Zayle, which was only going to depress him, so he cleared his head and focused on his surroundings for the second time.

As his eyes took in the landscape, he realized that it was a little familiar. He was making great time as more of what he saw looked recognizable, but still, he guessed that he had a good solid day of riding ahead of him. In an attempt to stay positive, he reminded himself that this should have been an eight day journey. That was something.

The dragon's head came up sharply, causing Kade to flinch. As he was about to ask the dragon what it sensed, he saw what had gotten Rayden's attention. Off in the distance, Kade could see a large winged creature flying in circles while spitting something from its mouth. It looked odd, even from this distance. At first, Kade thought it could be a dragon but quickly discarded that thought as it had none of the grace of Rayden, and it was shaped all wrong.

"What is it?" Kade asked, forgetting his family for the moment, alert for danger. He opened his mind up to Rayden as much as possible. He found that when he consciously tried to connect with the dragon, he was able to get a stronger sense of what it was trying to communicate. It was almost as good as if the dragon had spoken. Almost. Rayden was as confused as Kade about the flying creature.

His parents flashed through his mind, reminding him of his current course, but his intuition told him he should not ignore this. Indecision had him in its grip. He quickly glanced in the direction of his hometown and then back to the creature off in the distance. It had dipped below the tree line momentarily as it swooped down on something only to rise unsteadily back into the air again. Clearly there was something wrong here, but he did not have time to waste looking into this. He clenched his jaw tightly as he brought Rayden to a stop, watching for just a moment more as his mind worked, trying to decide if he should continue on or investigate. His parents flashed through his mind again and the decision was made.

"Come on Rayden. This is not for us. We have other important things we must attend," Kade said and urged his mount forward. The dragon launched with a powerful burst of its legs when Kade heard…something. "Stop!" Kade commanded.

The dragon stopped so fast that Kade slid from his seat and almost came off completely. After moving back into position, he turned to look in the direction of the creature. He was not sure what he heard, but he knew it was something important. He listened hard. He sifted through the sounds that were coming to him, but there was nothing that he thought was important enough to interrupt his race for Arden. And then he heard it. It was a woman's scream. And not just a scream, but a scream of terror. Kade felt anger in him start to grow as he watched the creature, envisioning it attacking a helpless woman.

"Rayden, head for that vile beast. Its time has come to an end," Kade said as his heart started to pump at the thought of battle again. Rayden roared his eagerness to enter the fight. Kade sensed the dragon's thoughts and grinned. Rayden felt no fear because he believed in Kade and trusted him.

The dragon had good reason to believe in me, he thought as he felt the Divine swirl within him. He was going to save this unknown woman, and rip the life out of whatever that thing was.

Rayden sensed Kade's blood lust and shared in it as he set off at a break neck speed, almost unseating his rider. The dragon lowered its head and tore at the ground with fury as he locked onto the creature. Kade's heals came up as he rocked backwards. He reached for the dragon's ridges and barely got a grip. Pulling himself forward and settling into place, his eyes scanned the sky for the beast. Kade directed Rayden to stay under the cover of the trees so as to not be detected as they approached. Rayden protested momentarily, wanting to attack the creature but then complied.

The closer they got, the more they could see of the flying creature. It was nothing like a dragon at all. It had none of the agility or grace and it was bulky instead of streamlined. This creature appeared to have claws on the ends of its wings that worked as hands when it was on the ground. It was the color of gray ash like the ash from a day old fire. It had deep, shiny, black talons that seemed to glisten in the sun. It was not as big as the dragon, but it was a solid block of muscle. When it screeched, it sounded as though it had something lodged in its throat. Its shrieks were not nearly as loud as the dragons, but then it was not the shrieks that were of concern. Its head almost looked like a horse with pure black eyes but the nose was far too short. Its ears were small and pressed flat against the sides of its head.

Kade could see the muscles rippled along its body as it made a turn in flight and prepared to make another pass. It was clumsier than Kade would have expected as it wheeled in the air as if trying to get its balance. It even appeared that the creature could not get itself organized enough to stay in flight, as though at any moment it should just give up and fall to the ground. Just when it seemed hopeless, it would stabilize and be on its way for another pass. Kade was certain it would more than make up for its lack of prowess in the air with its ground abilities.

The cabin was just coming into view as they moved through the trees. To Kade's horror, he could hear the sound of a boy crying. So far, he had not been discovered, but he was on the verge of not caring and charging in. He untied the sack of books and slid down off the dragon, moving quickly up to the last remaining trees. Rayden followed Kade's lead, staying low to the ground and keeping as quiet as possible. Surprisingly, the dragon was making only slight sounds as it slid past trees and brush alike.

There is a boy in there. We must help at all cost, he thought, letting the books settle to the ground as he started to call up the Divine Power for the Fire Calling. Just as he was on the verge of pushing through the last of the foliage, he caught sight of something as tall as the dragon. It was raising its massive club-like hands and bringing them down with such force that Kade was sure its target would be crushed. He could feel the impact from where he stood. The creature was made for crushing. Its clumsy fists closed to form the shape of boulders. It was humanoid in shape with what looked like a bulls head with horns. Its bare chest heaved with muscles from using its massive arms. It had a loincloth held up with a simple rope. It was a bronze color as if it were in the sun all the time. It had massive feet that could stomp a man into the ground easily. It would slowly lift its hands up as if they were too much weight, even for itself, and then clench them tightly, bringing them down with all its might.

Kade saw the intended target and his breath caught in his throat. A woman was holding her shaking arms above her head as though she were holding up an immense amount of weight. There was a shield surrounding her that glowed a soft green until it was hit, and then it would shimmer and fade. Her arms were shaking badly and her legs were wobbling dangerously. When the ground creature brought its massive fist down again, the woman let out a shriek as her legs gave way. She fell to her knees and it was all she could do to keep her hands raised over her head.

Rayden, we must help her, Kade thought to his companion as terror flooded through him. If she could survive this next hit, she had no chance to survive the one that was sure to follow. Kade could feel the dragon straining to keep from charging in with its fierce battle cry. It wanted to rend and tear those creatures to pieces as nature intended for dragons to do.

If the flying creature had taken the time to look around, it would have seen the dragon approaching, but it was too focused on its victim. Kade knew he had to come up with a plan fast or the dragon was going to decide for him. He forced his mind to ignore his racing heart as he decided to let the Fire Calling go for a more prudent one.

I am going to use the Transparency Calling to keep us unseen. You take care of the flying creature and I will deal with the other. Be as quiet as possible so you can take them by surprise. Our timing has to be perfect, Kade thought as he watched the giant swing its massive club-like fists again.

Kade forced himself to ignore the woman's pitiful cry and completed the Transparency Calling. They faded from view. He turned his attention on the hunters who were soon to be the hunted…he hoped. Kade looked up, seeing the flying creature make another pass as it spit out a blast of heat that appeared to be a black flame. He quickly sent a reminder to Rayden that he was not to fly but to grab the creature from the air when it made a pass. There was no response. Rayden was too focused to take the brief moment he would need to respond.

The bushes showed the dragon moving toward its prey. Kade felt his heart pounding hard as he prepared to call on the Divine and strike. He took just a fraction of a second before deciding which calling to use. There were really only two callings he could use to attack with. He could use the Fire Calling and maybe he would not be sensed by those who were tracking him, or he could use the Lightning Calling, which would be the obvious choice as it was most lethal.

Kade glanced past the woman as something on the ground drew his eyes to it. There was an old woman lying in the clearing that no longer appeared to be alive. Kade felt anger start to grow as his lip curled ever so slightly. The Divine was flowing through him like a river raging out of control.

The young woman had a faint, green light coming from her hands that was starting to fade. She tried to stand but fell to her knees. She was gritting her teeth hard as sweat beaded on her forehead. Her face was reddening from the exertion as she struggled with her last remaining strength. It was only going to be seconds until her shield would give way and she would collapse from exhaustion.

Kade decided on the more powerful Lightning Calling. He quickly opened himself up to the Divine Power, but before he could start the moves, a young toddler came stumbling out the front door, arms raised to the young woman as if asking to be held. Tears were streaming down his face as he walked toward the woman.

That was the very last straw for Kade. He completed each move of the calling faster and with more anger than he had ever done. Just as he finished, the woman collapsed under the onslaught and fell on her back with an explosive gasp. Kade let out a yell of fury and anger as he let the lightning bolt rip through the air to slam into the monster. The full force of the bolt crashed into the creature, causing its head to snap back violently. It stumbled and fell forward, landing just feet from the woman. She raised her head slightly as she looked at the beast, and then she fell unconscious.

Kade knew they were far from done as he watched the clumsy horse-headed beast in the air turn and start to make another pass. It opened its mouth to spit out its black flame of death. Kade panicked as he started to conjure the Lightning Calling but realized with horror that he was not going to finish in time. He saw the faint black fire start to emerge from its mouth when something collided with it, dragging it to the ground. Its beady eyes bulged as Rayden clamped down hard on its neck. Kade stopped on the twelfth move of the calling, afraid that he might hit the dragon.

The ground creature stirred and struggled to rise. Kade felt the power from the completed Lightning Calling start to swirl through his body, trying to find a way out. His heart raced as he remembered the warning about the calling. Fear flooded through him as he started to lose control of the Divine Power. Now, as the warning had said, the power was trying to find its own way out, no matter what that way was.

To Kade's dismay, the large bull-faced ground creature was still alive and looking to complete its mission. It glanced up to see the woman lying on the ground just within reach. It grinned as it raised its massive fists to complete its task. In an instant, Kade knew he was her only chance for survival. He felt the power raging through his body, knowing that he only had seconds before it exploded from him, killing him and the woman at the same time. He clenched his jaw hard and struggled to straighten his arm as he attempted to complete the last move. His head started to pound dangerously, but he ignored it. Panic threatened to take over, but he refocused his will as every muscle in his body convulsed. With all his strength and sheer determination, he brought his arm forward, ever so slowly, as he fought to keep the Divine under control. To say it was agony would be an understatement. He ground his teeth hard as he struggled against the forces waging war within him. His arm was shaking furiously as every muscle in his body pulsed from the power.

Kade let out a wail as he fought furiously to force the Divine Power to do as he commanded. Bull-face started to bring its club-like fist down for its crushing blow. *NO!* Kade screamed with his mind as he held his breath and put every bit of his being into controlling, no, commanding the power out through his open hand. It hesitated slightly and then exploded from him with a deafening blast that sent out a shockwave that could be felt for hundreds of feet. The monster never completed its swing as the bolt tore into it, throwing it head over heels like a leaf caught in the wind. It was dead before it hit the ground.

Kade fell back and screamed in agony. He looked down to see his arm smoking as red, angry blisters started to form instantly from his hand up to just past his elbow. All the hair had been singed off. His fingers started to swell and he knew it was only moments before his hand was going to be useless. The pain was almost too much to bear. He hugged his arm to himself as he rose and stumbled into the clearing toward the woman.

Kade gritted his teeth to keep from passing out as he focused on the boy, who was trying to climb into his mother's lap. She never moved. Kade let the Transparency Calling fade from himself while keeping the dragon cloaked. The boy looked up in surprise as tears streamed down from his big, brown eyes. Kade felt the urge to reach down with his good arm and pick the boy up while telling him that it was all going to be ok. He knelt down, and to his surprise, the boy started toward him, eager to be held. Kade hesitated only a moment. He let go of his burned arm and carefully scooped the boy up. The child wrapped his arms around Kade's neck and held on as tightly as he could. Kade stood, trying to keep his injured hand from being touched. As soon as he was standing, the boy loosened his grip and turned to point at the woman.

Kade paused, realizing that the clearing had gone quiet. It was too quiet. He started to turn when something hit the ground heavily just behind him, causing him to stumble. He used both hands to hold the boy and winced hard as pain shot up his arm from his injury. He clenched his jaw hard as a tear seeped out of the corner of his eye, waiting for the agony to lessen. He removed the Transparency Calling from the dragon to check it over for injuries. As soon as Rayden popped into view, the boy started to scream in fear. Kade tried to calm the child, but he was too frightened of the dragon.

There was blood coming from Rayden's underside. Kade ducked down to inspect the dragon's injuries. He inhaled sharply when he saw how much Rayden was bleeding. It looked like there was blood coming from everywhere. Rayden seemed to be moving well enough, but with this much blood there was a danger of the dragon bleeding out.

"Lie down and turn over on your side," Kade said. At first, Rayden only looked on as he struggled to understand. Kade closed his eyes and envisioned the dragon lying down. When he opened his eyes, the dragon was on its side. Kade set the boy down, having to pry his arms from around his neck. The child stood looking between Kade and the dragon. He held his arms out for Kade, his eyes pleading, terrified of the deadly creature. As much as Kade wished he could help the boy, right now the dragon was the priority.

He turned to Rayden and started to perform the calling. He stopped as the pain from his hand shot up his arm, causing tears to well up in his eyes again. He squinted through his blurred vision and looked at his hand. It was already so swollen he was afraid it was going to be useless. It did not matter. It was going to work. He was going to make it work.

Closing his eyes, Kade concentrated on breathing slow and easy. He had to block the pain or at least ignore it for just a few moments until he completed the calling. After a few seconds, he gritted his teeth hard and started the calling, forcing his swollen fingers to do his bidding. Fortunately, it was just a simple gesture but even this put him on the verge of screaming as he completed it. He placed his hands on the bloody chest of the dragon and let the healing power flow. To his immense satisfaction, he felt it immediately go to work.

Kade squeezed his eyes shut tightly as he held his breath, waiting for the throbbing pain from his hands to subside. This one healing had to be good enough. It felt like it took forever, but the pain finally lessened.

The sound of the boy's crying broke through Kade's haze of pain, getting his attention. He opened his eyes and saw the child standing over his mother, his shoulders slumped slightly. He was losing his breath as he was crying in sobs now. It was a cry of hopelessness. It was heart wrenching to see the boy reach down and shake his mother, trying to wake her but to no avail. The child looked up at him and Kade could see that the child's eyes were rimmed with red. The tears were running freely down his cheeks.

Kade walked over to him and held his good hand out. The boy eagerly walked over to Kade with his arms up, desperately wanting to be held. Kade picked him up and felt the small arms of this precious human wrap tightly around his neck once again. He could not explain why, but he felt a strong sense that somehow this was right. The boy took comfort in those strong arms as he laid his head against Kade's shoulder and the sobbing slowly came to an end. Every few seconds, the boy would take a deep, shaky breath and let it out again.

Kade heard a slight shuffling sound just behind him. Turning, he found the dragon on its feet, watching curiously. To his relief, Kade saw that the bleeding had stopped.

He looked back at Horse-face as the dragon grabbed one of its legs in a bone crunching grip with its teeth and started dragging it off to feed. One of the creature's wings was lying on the ground, completely torn away from the body. Kade saw the odd angle its neck was in and knew how it had died.

Kade shifted the boy slightly to keep his injured arm from being touched. As he was situating the child, he moved over to look upon the old woman lying in a pool of blood. There was a deep gash in her chest. Kade knew, without a doubt, that this was what had caused her life to come to a cruel end. Because of how mangled the body was, he knew checking for vital signs would be futile.

Kade turned and walked back to the young woman still lying on the ground, unconscious. He considered putting the boy down but knew the child would only start crying again. He shifted him as he considered what to do next.

Rayden left his meal and moved over to Kade to sniff the boy. With blood all over his muzzle, he tilted his head from side to side, trying to understand what manner of creature Kade was holding. The apprentice went to shoo the dragon away for fear of scaring the boy when he noticed the child was taking slow, even breaths. He was relieved to see that the child was fast asleep.

"It's just a kid," Kade said as he moved away from Rayden.

The dragon turned and lumbered back to Horse-face. Rayden took a deep bite from the creature as he lay down to enjoy the half burnt meal. At least half of it was edible and the dragon was not going to let good food go to waste.

Kade pondered what to do about the young woman. She was out of danger and still alive, so that was not a concern. But, moving her was out of the question. Looking at the cabin, he decided to find a place for the boy so he could better attend to her. Cringing, as pain shot up his arm at every move, he quickly found the room that was the child's and proceeded to lay him down. Well…at least that was the plan until the boy latched on reflexively every time Kade tried to unwind his arms. He even got as close as laying the child down flat, but before he could retract his arm, the child would start to whimper. Kade sighed to himself and clutched the boy to his chest as he headed for the door.

He returned to the young woman and looked upon her once more. He considered moving her, but after checking his useless arm and then the sleeping boy, he quickly discarded the thought. It was hopeless and his pain was not getting any better.

"Hello," Kade said as he knelt down and gently shook the young woman. She did not respond. "I will be right back," he said as he carefully stood and went into the cabin.

Kade found a pail of water and a square piece of fabric. After wetting the cloth, he returned to the young woman and knelt next to her. He gently wiped the blood off a small cut on her forehead and removed a smudge from her cheek. Just as he finished cleaning her face, she stirred. Kade watched as her eyes fluttered open. He was amazed at the beautiful, deep, blue eyes, and for the first time, noticed the clear, soft skin, the silky, blond hair and the sensuous, full lips. Kade felt an odd sensation build in his chest that he had never experienced. He had seen women before, but he had never felt like this.

The young woman raised her head and looked directly into Kade's eyes. For a split second, the pain had lessened, and he began to feel a bit lightheaded. It took him a moment to realize that she had asked him a question and was asking for the second time. He forced his eyes away from her so he could concentrate on what she was saying. He felt like a complete idiot and he could not even say why. The pain returned and he winced.

"Are you daft?" she asked in irritation. "I said, who…are…you?"

"Me? Oh. My name is Kade," he said, unable to shake the feeling of being a bumbling fool.

"You helped me?" she asked, indicating Bull-face as she

struggled to a sitting position.

"Yes. I did not think it was fair for those monsters to pick on a girl," Kade said with as much of a smile as he could muster while looked into her deep, blue eyes. He felt his thoughts quickly begin to scramble and looked away. He started to open his mouth to say something but could not figure out what he was going to say. He closed his mouth quickly to avoid doing a fish imitation.

She looked about twenty years old. Her hair was light blonde and barely came to her shoulders. Kade watched how her mouth moved as she spoke. He realized that she was asking him another question and forced himself to concentrate on her words.

"I'm sorry. What did you say?" Kade asked, doing his best to regain his composure. He wanted to be seen as her hero, and so far, she was only seeing a buffoon.

"I said, how did you come by my cabin?" she asked, obviously becoming impatient. She rolled onto her hands and knees, getting ready to stand.

"We were on our way east when we saw the flying beast making passes at your cabin," Kade said as he looked back at her and noticed a puzzled expression.

"We?" she asked and jumped as the dragon lumbered back into the clearing. She inhaled sharply as her eyes went wide. She let out a scream as she quickly rocked back and raised her hands in an attempt to bring up her shield. Kade mentally chastised himself for being a fool.

"The dragon is my friend," Kade said in a rush to the woman, who failed in her efforts to raise her defenses. He had to force her to look him in the eye and hold her by the wrist to keep her from fleeing. She was on the verge of full panic but he persisted, holding her firmly, calling to her over and over. She slowly stopped struggling as his words started to make sense. Breathing heavy, as if she had run several miles without stopping, she looked back and forth between the two of them as if not believing what she was seeing.

"He…is your friend?" she asked incredulously. Kade could feel the pulse in her wrist pounding hard and fast. He ground his teeth as he tried to ignore the pain that lanced through his mind. "A dragon? Since when do dragons make friends with humans?" she asked as she tried to regain much of her lost composer. There was a fair amount of suspicion in her voice, also. Kade could see she was still not fully recovered. It was almost as if she were still waking from a dream. He blamed it on the large lump on the back of her head. She must have taken a fall at some point.

"It was an accident. I will explain later. Right now, we need to get you inside and get you cleaned up," Kade said as he continued to feel her pulse with his one hand while still struggling to keep a grip on the boy with the other. She started to reach for the boy and froze when her eyes took in his injury. Kade turned slightly as if to hide it. She forced her wobbly legs to work and reached for his damaged arm.

"Let me see it," she said as she gave her head a light shake in an attempt to clear her mind. It was obvious she was not going to accept no for an answer as she pushed his hand off her wrist. He resisted because he did not want her to see him as a cripple or maybe a charity case. And pity was never anything he would accept. It would only mean that he was weak. Kade hesitated and then, reluctantly, turned for her to get a good look. She continued to cast several quick glances at the dragon, never turning her back to it, but soon her focus was completely on his arm.

Has she not even seen me holding the boy? Kade started to wonder when he saw her glance at the child as she moved around to his arm. It was very slight, and had he not been watching her closely, he would have missed that glance.

Why in the Great Divine would she not take this child? It is hers, he thought as he shook his head.

"Why…" Kade started to ask when she cut him off, clearly

knowing the unfinished question.

"Because, he is asleep," she said absentmindedly as she examined the damage. "Because, if you put him down, even into my arms, he will wake and cry. And," she said as she hesitated and looked him straight in the eye, "because he is a good judge of character. You can't be all that bad if he likes you. Normally, he does not like anyone but me. You get to be my sitter while we get that taken care of," she added while indicating his hand and arm. Any suspicion she had was now gone.

Kade felt his heart leap when she looked at him. He could not help but smile. Right then, he knew he would do anything she asked. Kade shook his head hard in an attempt to stop these uncontrollable thoughts. He felt drawn to her, even though he had just met her.

Was she using the Divine? he considered when he realized that she was talking again. Taking a deep breath in an attempt to regain control, he focused on what she was saying.

"I said, what happened to your hand? Did you hit your head?" she asked with concern as she looked for injuries. She gently felt the bump on the back of her own head and pulled her hand away to see if there was any blood. There was none.

"Yes," Kade was saying as he looked into those beautiful, mesmerizing eyes. It was the best way to cover for his strange behavior. Angry for looking like a buffoon, he furiously chastised himself and forced these odd feelings to go away.

She must think me a fool, he thought, regretting that his chance to impress her with his prowess was slipping away.

"Well?" she asked.

"Well what?"

"Well, what…happened…to…your…hand?" she asked with forced patience.

It had to do with her voice. It had to, he thought. Her voice was musical as it rang in his ears.

"My hand?" Kade asked as if just remembering. "Oh, it happened when I almost lost control of the Lightning Calling," he said and immediately regretted it. *She does not need any more reason to see me as incompetent,* Kade thought harshly. Anger cleared his head and he, once again, forced this strange influence from his mind and body.

"A what?" she asked in awe.

"It was a Lightning Calling. I was using it when I lost control of it. I lost my concentration," he said, giving up trying to hide his incompetence. "I had to force the power up and out my hand, but by the time I did, it had built to a level beyond my abilities," Kade said matter-of-factly.

"You can control the Divine?" she asked as her eyes widened. Are you...are you ...a Chosen?" she whispered.

Kade felt himself start to swell with pride, and then just as quickly, he felt a sinking feeling in his stomach. He dreaded having to tell her he was only an apprentice. He wished he could tell her he was, indeed, a great Master of the Divine Power, but it was not his style to lie. He took a breath, ready to confess to being a lowly apprentice, but before he could answer her question, she refocused her attention on his hand.

"If you are one of the Chosen, then why don't you use the Divine Power to heal your hand?"

"Well, if it was possible, I would need my hand to perform the calling. As it is," Kade said with a sigh," I cannot use the Divine Power to heal myself. At least, I don't know a calling that allows me to heal myself."

"Oh," she said as she gently slid her hand down his arm to his palm. Kade felt himself melt at the soft touch and soaked up the sensation. She was caressing the burned palm with the fingers from her right hand while supporting his with her left. Kade felt his eyes close slightly. He became angry that he was, once again, losing what sense of mental balance he had and jerked his hand away from her. She tried to grasp it before he could pull it away but was not quick enough. The flood of pain flowed through him like a dam breaking. Kade sucked air in violently through clenched teeth, making a sound like a hiss. She quickly reached for his hand and started her gentle caress once more.

"It takes time for this to work," she said as she looked at him apologetically. "You did not notice the pain was almost gone?" she asked as she looked at him with a sidelong glance.

Kade did not answer as he gritted his teeth and waited for the torture to end. She stroked his arm and he could feel her working…something, but he could not put it into words. It was almost as if she were soothing the pain with the Divine Power, but there was no sign of the Divine being used. He would have sensed it, or seen the trails of it as she moved her hands. There was nothing.

"Come inside and I will put something on that. We have some herbs that will help the healing. It will take the swelling down," she said as she turned toward the cabin. She wavered slightly from exhaustion. Kade prepared to catch her when she steadied. He could see that she was doing her best to hide her plight, but it was obvious that she was completely drained.

"You may have a head injury," Kade said as he looked at where he had dabbed blood from her forehead. The bump that was already swelling confirmed his suspicion.

"I am not physically hurt," she said, trying to dismiss his concern. "I just passed out from the exertion. I am a little sore is all," she said as her grip on his hand loosened slightly. Kade winced at the pain that he knew she was keeping at bay. Her grip became steady again and Kade got the strong feeling that she was very focused on whatever it was she was doing. It almost appeared as if she were taking very deliberate steps as though she was being careful of where to put her feet.

"Good," he said, as he studied her. By the way, what is your name? I can't just call you girl," Kade said as he walked up the steps and went into the cabin.

"Darcienna," she said. Her voice wavered ever so slightly.

Kade smiled. The name sounded musical to his ears. He said the name in his mind several times, waiting for her to continue.

"Thank you," she said over her shoulder. Kade found himself leaning to the side to see her eyes and quickly forced himself to stand up straight. She had turned forward too quickly, regardless. "Come inside," she said as she tugged at him.

Kade followed her and was surprised when she led him straight to a room with a bed and chest for clothes. By the clothes hanging in the corner and the hairbrush sitting on a table in front of the mirror, he knew this was her bedroom.

"You can lay the boy here," she said as she indicated a small bed just inside the door to his right. "Do you feel okay?" she asked. She had to focus on her words as though she were under a strain.

"Yes. I am fine. I don't think it would be a good idea to put him down. He will just start crying again," he said as he narrowed his vision suspiciously, sensing something was wrong.

"I doubt he will cry even one little squeak," Darcienna said as she held onto the bed for support.

Kade looked at her hand on the bed for just a moment and then turned his attention to the boy. He was, indeed, breathing deeply and rhythmically. Kade noticed, for the first time, that the boy had loosened his grip on his neck and was hanging limp at his side. He leaned the child back to get a good look at his face. Content that the boy was sound asleep, and as gently as possible, he laid the child down on the bed. To his immense relief, the child did not utter the slightest sound other than the deep breathing. Kade flexed his arm, working out the cramps. The boy was heavier than he realized.

"Are you okay?" Kade asked.

"Come in here," Darcienna said as she pulled him toward the kitchen. She stumbled and fell against the wall. Kade quickly put an arm around her waist for support. He did his best to ignore how she felt as she stood this close. "I'll put something on your hand," she said with just a hint of slurring to her words. "You should notice most of the pain fade," she continued, dismissing his questioning look.

She pushed him into a chair and fell heavily into the other one that was facing him. She could no longer hold his hand and let go. Kade gripped the armrest hard with his good hand and the wood crushed beneath his grasp. He did not see that she was breathing heavier, his mind still reeling from the pain. The crease in her forehead gave away that she was under immense strain, but he could not see it through his eyelids that were slammed shut.

"Hold still," Darcienna said.

Reaching into a jar, Darcienna pulled out a large amount of a green, slimy substance. She reached for his arm to spread the gel and missed. On her second attempt, she was able to grab his hand and spread the salve thickly from his wrist up to his elbow. Next, she wrapped both her hands around his arm and clenched her jaw as her head rocked backward, straining. After a moment, she took a ragged, gasping breath. She wobbled slightly in the chair and would have fallen had Kade not reached forward to steady her.

"You are not well," he said, concern heavy in his voice. He flinched from what felt like pulsating pressure being applied to his injured arm. When he looked down, he saw that the gel writhed along his arm as if it were alive. He had to fight the urge to scrape it off as if it were a deadly snake. It was surging all around his arm and even appeared to be melting into his skin. It was not necessarily painful, but it was incredibly uncomfortable and very unsettling to watch. Kade looked on in awe as the swelling went down, and the pain dwindled to a dull thrumming.

Darcienna was sitting back with her hands open, palms up. She was breathing in deep as if pulling air as far into her lungs as possible. There were beads of sweat on her forehead. Kade flexed his hand, testing his muscles in hopes of using the Healing Calling on her. Still not good enough, he pressed his lips together in frustration. He felt helpless with so much power at his fingertips, and yet, he was not able to use any of it. But, even if his hand had been healed enough, he could not have used the Divine. His hand was jumping and flexing as though something were squeezing and letting go, only to squeeze again.

Kade looked over at Darcienna and found her looking back. Her color was returning. She was doing her best to appear normal, but Kade could see it was an act. He chose to pretend not to see the strain on her face. He looked at his hand and then back to her as if to ask for an explanation.

"The Divine is very powerful. You are lucky it did not kill you," she said, ignoring his unspoken question.

"Yes, I am lucky that this is all that happened. I could have easily been blown to pieces," Kade said as he mentally shivered. He recalled how hard it was to get control of the Lightning Calling and visibly shook.

Darcienna took several more steadying breaths and then reached for the clean cloth on the table. She motioned for him to give her his hand. Kade complied with just a little of hesitation.

Wrapping the cloth around his hand several times, she gently tied a knot to keep it secure. Carefully, she set his hand down on the table. When Kade went to pull it back, she gently laid her fingers on his arm, indicating he was not to move. When he ceased his pulling, she closed her eyes and then tilted her head as if listening to something. After a moment, she smiled slightly and opened her eyes. She looked down, as though she could see through the cloth, and a slight quirk at the corners of her mouth indicated she was pleased with the results.

"There. That should do. It will heal in good time," Darcienna said and sat back heavily. She resumed her pose of palms up and deep breathing for several long minutes. Kade watched her closely without moving a muscle, afraid that any sound or movement might disturb whatever it was she was doing. After what felt like an hour passed, she slowly opened her eyes. Kade was amazed at the improvement. She looked better than he expected. The slightly dazed look she had had since he woke her was gone.

"OK, what was that?" Kade asked, tilting his head toward his hand without breaking eye contact. He was watching her closely as he analyzed her reaction. "Divine Calling?" he asked, already suspecting it was not. She took a breath in to answer and Kade's eyes narrowed. He could not say why but there were times when he could sense when someone was about to lie and this was one of those times. She saw the look of suspicion in his eyes and stopped. Her shoulders slumped in resignation and she let out her breath.

"We call it Nature's Gift," Darcienna said as if she were giving away a sacred secret. She glanced at Kade but he sat silently, letting her continue. "I had to take the energy from within myself and apply it to your wounds. Every little thing I do with my gift drains me. If I was not already so exhausted from using my deflection casting, I could have healed you without any help," she said, indicating the salve, "but I was almost completely drained. The best I could do was to energize the gel and let it do the healing."

"What do you mean the energy from within?" Kade asked, confused. This Nature's Gift was new to him. Kade had a suspicion that this was another thing that Zayle had conveniently forgotten to tell him.

"The ability comes from within me. If I use too much, I can deplete the energy, and I have to replenish it to use it again." Darcienna saw that Kade was trying to work this out and continued.

"It is like having the strength to lift a log. I can do it the first time easily but using it over and over I get weaker and weaker until the log is too heavy. I have to rest and replenish. Jorell's abilities are much more impressive than mine," Darcienna said and then stopped. Her eyes lost focus as she narrowed her vision, trying to recall something.

"That explains why your Deflection Casting failed," Kade said.

"Yes," she said as she slowly looked back over her shoulder, searching for what was missing. "My strength was exhausted," she said as she slowly rose from her chair, her eyes moving around the room as she listened. "I am lucky I held out as long as I did," she said almost absentmindedly. A look of concern flashed in her eyes and she quickly glanced back at Kade.

CH7

Darcienna left the table and Kade got a very sick feeling in his gut. He found it hard to look up from his hands as Darcienna ran from room to room. He took a breath several times to tell of the old woman he had seen at the edge of the clearing but could not bring himself to cause her the same crushing sadness he had felt at losing his precious master. He swallowed several times, trying to remove the lump from his throat.

"Jorell," Darcienna called out. "Where are you?" she yelled, trying to stay calm.

Kade felt as though he was going to be sick. His stomach twisted into a knot. He could feel the blood drain from his face as he tried to figure out how he was going to break such devastating news to her. Darcienna came to a stop directly in front of him and he cringed.

"Do you know where she is?" Darcienna asked. "Well?" she

asked impatiently.

Kade's eyes slowly rose to look into Darcienna's soft, beautiful, blue eyes, knowing the pain he would see as soon as she learned of her teacher's demise. He swallowed hard and tried to find the best way to say what needed to be said. He took a breath to speak when she spoke first.

"The last thing she told me was I need to keep the shield up as long as possible, no matter what. I am sure…," she started to say when she saw the look on his face. "Are you okay? You look pale." Kade, still unable to speak, sat silent. "She has to be around here somewhere." Darcienna said. But, even in her own ears, it sounded more like she was trying to convince herself of something she knew was not true. She paused, watching him while he was looking down at his hands again. "Kade," she said, her voice a bit shaky. "What is it?" she asked, her voice already filling with pain. "What's wrong?"

Darcienna looked away, not wanting to hear what he was about to tell her. Kade heard the ever so soft intake of breath, as if she were starting to cry but trying hard not to. He would have taken any amount of physical pain to save her from the hurt he knew she was about to feel. He was all too familiar with the crushing sadness felt when losing a cherished soul to the land of the dead.

"Do you know?" she asked, and then her throat closed up. Darcienna swallowed hard and squeezed her eyes shut momentarily as she ground her teeth. After a few seconds, she tried again, but the words just would not come. Kade's eyes started at her boots and slowly traveled up until he was looking into the windows of her soul. He could feel the pain already. It cut him deep. Her voice broke slightly and all she could utter was, "Show me," as a single tear worked its way down her cheek to catch the edge of her soft, pale, pink lips.

Kade desperately wished he could be doing anything other than leading Darcienna to the old woman laying at the edge of the clearing. If he could, he would have been wringing his hands together in discomfort. A habit he had picked up from his mother. Taking a deep breath, he slowly stood, and with just a slight glance into those sad, blue eyes, he turned and headed out of the cabin. As he walked across the clearing, he cast a quick glance back at her. She was trying so hard to be brave.

Kade led her to the broken body and stopped several feet away. He expected her to fall to her knees but she just stood, staring. She shook her head several times and then looked around the clearing as if trying to figure something out.

"But how? She killed them."

"We killed two," Kade said, looking around to see if there were more and found none. He reached out to comfort her. He could not recall ever feeling such a burning desire to hold and comfort someone as he did right then, but as he reached out a hand toward her, she pulled away.

"You…killed them?"

"Yes," Kade said, feeling a slight bit put off by the tone that hinted at doubt. He quickly dismissed it, feeling ashamed.

He felt incredibly helpless. Never in all his life did he feel so much at a loss as to what he should do. He watched as Darcienna turned her attention back to the broken body. She slowly knelt down and placed her hands on the old woman. Kade was not sure if she was crying or praying until he saw the slight shake of her shoulders. Then, he saw the tears start to fall from her face and land in the dirt, making little puffs of dust. She slumped forward, letting her hair fall over Jorell's face. Darcienna picked up her mentor's hand and stroked it affectionately, as though it were a small pet.

Kade felt his heart break for this precious young woman. He did not know if he should put his arm around her or just leave her alone. He looked around as if to find the answer elsewhere but found only his dragon looking askance at him. He turned his attention back to Darcienna. He ached to hold her and tell her it was ok, but fear of doing the wrong thing at such a painful moment froze him to the spot. It occurred to him that whatever had killed his master might be behind this slaying, also. His blood started to boil by the moment.

"I will find you and destroy you!" Kade vowed with every fiber of his being. "By the time I am through with you, you will regret ever knowing life!" Kade hissed with such fury that he shook. His nails bit into the palms of his hands. He was so focused on his curse, he almost missed that he was drawing on the Divine. With one last burst of hate, he let the ancient power evaporate.

Kade took a deep breath to steady himself, and as he let it out, he looked down to see Darcienna looking up at him. Afraid she had seen his outburst and thinking him a crazed man, he recovered as best he could. He decided to follow his heart and do what he knew to be right. He sat next to her and gathered her in his arms. She resisted and even tried to push him away but she needed this and he wanted her to know she was not alone. She gave up and let her walls come crashing down. She fell into his arms and laid her head against his chest as she cried. He held her tightly and whispered into her ear, "I will avenge her death! I swear it!"

Darcienna slumped and the sobs came freely. Kade stroked her hair, not knowing what else to do. He held her for so long he could feel his muscles cramping in his legs. He shifted as little as possible to ease the discomfort, but he never took his arms from around her. Slowly but surely, she calmed. He glanced down and looked right into her eyes.

"Thank you," Darcienna said.

"I didn't do anything."

"You shared my pain and grief," she said as she reached up and kissed him lightly on the cheek. Her lips lingered briefly. "Will you help me bury her?" Darcienna asked, not wanting to look at the body.

"Of course," Kade said as he went to put his hand on her cheek, but before he could, she pulled away. He thought he could feel her close off a little, but he was not sure. "You do not need to help. I will do this," Kade said, trying to save her from any more grief.

"No. I have to help. I want to see her off to the land of the dead. It is the last time I will be able to say…" and then she stopped, her lips trembling, unable to say the word goodbye. She tried to keep the tears from coming but failed miserably. She slumped into his arms once again. After several more minutes, she was able to bring herself under control but her red-rimmed eyes told of the pain she was still feeling. She tilted her head back and looked into his eyes, staring for several long moments. Kade could see her mind working. He waited.

"Who would do this?"

He stiffened instantly as his mouth went tight, causing her to flinch. Doing his best to relax, he looked past her as he gathered his thoughts. He forced his hatred to a slow ebb and looked at her.

"I don't know who caused all this destruction," Kade said as he looked around the clearing. "Something is hunting those with power."

"When you spoke that vow, I sensed a lot of anger and hate. Is it because of this?" she asked as she nodded her head in the direction of Jorell, "or is there more?"

Kade opened his mouth to give any of the many answers that came to mind but paused. He thought of his master and his own hardships. He thought of the family that he had met in the woods. He thought of his parents. He looked deep in her eyes and saw the pain there.

"I have my reason," was all Kade said, not feeling this was the right time for a full explanation. She nodded weakly.

"We can bury her over here," Darcienna said as she indicated a spot next to a large, silvery tree. "She used to love this tree. I think she would like that."

Kade did not speak, nor did he look at Darcienna. He moved over to Jorell, lifting her into his arms and turned to take her to the spot she indicated. Kade sent a mental request to the dragon to dig a hole next to the tree. The dragon eagerly bounded over and turned, looking at Kade as if asking, "Here?" Kade nodded and Rayden began digging by using his front claws to throw the dirt through his hind legs. It was not more than a few minutes when there was a crudely dug hole in the ground.

"Thank you my friend," Kade said.

He knelt by the edge of the grave and started to lean over, but he was not going to be able to lay Jorell in the hole without dropping her or falling in himself. He gently laid her on the ground and then jumped in. He turned, picked her up and then laid her gently in the bottom.

Kade climbed back out of the hole and paused, looking Darcienna in the eyes. She was doing her best to be strong but Kade could see the slight quiver to her chin. He did not need to see her to sense the sadness starting to pour out of those rivers of blue.

"I am going to have Rayden bury her now. If you have anything you want to say, or if there is anything you want her to have, now is the time."

Darcienna did not speak nor did she move. She just kept staring at her cherished teacher. Kade asked Rayden to fill the hole. Confusion flooded the link as Rayden looked between Kade and the body. Kade asked again, and this time the, dragon did as Kade bid. He cringed as the dragon let the dirt fly. Most of it went in the hole but much of it flew past. It was far from the solemn event Kade was hoping for, but it was what they had to work with. There was an indent in the ground where the hole was when the dragon finished.

"Are there any last rights you want to perform?" Kade asked.

"No," she said in a whisper so low he barely heard.

Kade looked down while scratching the back of his head. He just did not feel right leaving without saying something…anything. He wanted to make a suggestion but feared he might offend her. In the end, he just could not leave it like it was without at least trying.

"Darcienna," Kade said softly.

"What?" she responded just as quietly.

"Would you like me to perform the Divine last rights for Jorell?"

Darcienna seemed to be deep in her own thoughts. Kade was starting to think she had not heard his question. He was about to ask again when she shifted. He waited.

"She does not use the Divine," Darcienna responded.

"I know, but if I am right, then it won't matter," Kade said, still not looking at her.

Darcienna stood for a long time without answering. Kade let the silence continue without speaking a word. He decided he was not going to ask again, and he was not going to distract her as she spent her last remaining moments saying goodbye. She took a deep breath and then sighed.

"I guess it will not hurt. Go ahead."

Kade nodded slightly and stepped up to the grave. He placed his right hand over his left hand, palms down and held them over the ground. Since he did not need the movement of his fingers, this was easy. He called up the Divine Power and directed it out his hands and into the ground. He spoke the word in the ancient language that translated simply as, "What is yours is yours." And just like that, it was done.

He could not say why, but he was sure he had done the right thing. It was not just a feeling but more like knowing, even though he could not explain it. Kade dismissed the odd thoughts and prepared to go back to the cabin.

"We will not be able to stay here," Kade said gently. "We are both still in great danger." He felt her looking at him and started to fidget. He slowly turned and looked at her, surprised to see her smiling. All his discomfort melted away.

"Thank you, Kade. I wouldn't be alive if it were not for you. You have been a big help with everything," Darcienna said as she glanced at the grave. As Darcienna stood watching, Kade saw a hardness enter her eyes. Where there should have been sadness, there was now a wall. He moved to stand in front of her to study her, wanting to offer her comfort but she stepped away. It was almost as if she were denying needing the compassion as if nothing had happened. Kade felt his heart sadden for her. If she did not feel it now, she was going to feel it later, but one way or the other, this was going to hurt sometime. But, each person needed to deal with loss in their own due time. With one last look into those hard eyes, he stepped back as an image of his parents flashed through his mind.

Kade's anxiety started to grow. He felt a stab of guilt for being so casual when he should be racing to his parent's aid. Every minute might make the difference. He fought to remain calm. He was trying to figure out a way to encourage Darcienna to hurry, but didn't for fear of offending her since she had just buried her teacher.

"Kade, what is it?" Darcienna asked, seeing the discomfort on his face.

"I fear for my parent's lives. I was on my way to Arden when I stopped at your cabin. There are evil men taking over the town where my mother and father live."

"How do you know?"

"I met a family that left Arden and they told me everything," Kade said, feeling the strong urge to jump on the dragon's back and compel it to run like the wind.

"It will take us a few days to get there from here," Darcienna said as she turned to go into the cabin.

"It will take less than a day by dragon. We will ride Rayden,"

Kade said as he looked at his friend. Darcienna turned to stare at the magnificent silver creature with dried blood on its muzzle.

"You ride the dragon?" Darcienna asked in astonishment.

"Yes," he said, feeling pride swell in him, a sly smile lifting the corner of his mouth. "He is a much faster way of getting around," Kade said as he patted the dragon's lean, strong neck. Rayden swung his head down to look Kade in the eye.

Darcienna approached Rayden slowly and stopped ten feet from him. The dragon flopped down and laid its head on its front legs. As she approached, Rayden followed her with his eyes. It occurred to Kade that Darcienna had not been up close to the dragon until this moment. She got to within one stride of the magnificent creature when it lifted its head to watch her. She turned slowly, not wanting to take her eyes off it and then glanced at Kade for reassurance. He nodded once. Darcienna took a deep breath and then glided up to the dragon. She slowly raised her hand and lightly touched Rayden on the neck. The dragon huffed slightly and then settled back down on its legs.

"He is…beautiful," Darcienna said in deep appreciation as she walked around the dragon, marveling at its magnificence. Kade smiled, immensely enjoying showing off this wondrous creature. If she saw the blood on its muzzle and body, she chose not to show it.

I don't know what I would do without you, Kade thought with affection as he had so many times already. The dragon responded with a grunt and Kade laughed. Obviously, impressing others was of very little importance to the dragon.

Kade smiled and walked over to give Rayden an affectionate pat on the neck. Darcienna stopped next to Kade. She put her hand next to Kade's and felt the muscles ripple beneath the skin as Rayden raised his head and swung it around. Darcienna pulled her hand back and retreated a step while looking at Kade for reassurance once more.

"I think we are irritating him," Kade said with a chuckle. The dragon proved Kade right when he quickly jumped up, took four steps away and then fell heavily back to the ground with a thud. With a lazy look at his friend, Rayden dropped his head down onto his legs and started to close his eyes.

"It just occurred to me that the dragon did all the digging. How did it know what to do?" Darcienna asked.

Kade noticed the way her eyebrows went up when she was puzzled about something and smiled. He found himself looking into her eyes again and marveled at her beauty. His eyes lingered on her mouth as she talked, and he found himself wetting his lips. He shook his head to clear his thoughts, feeling like a letch for thinking like that at a time like this. He also realized he was staring again.

"That's okay. You don't have to tell me if you don't want. I guess I am being nosey, huh?" Darcienna asked, misunderstanding his silence.

"No, that's okay. I don't mind answering," Kade said as he noticed the alluring way she tilted her head. "The dragon seems to be able to understand my thoughts. That is about the best way to put it."

Darcienna studied Kade, trying to decide if he was pulling a fast one on her. Her eyes narrowed as she watched him, waiting for him to confess his jest. Kade saw the doubt in her eyes and quickly continued.

"Honestly. He can seem to hear my thoughts when I want. He did dig the hole," he said as he indicated the grave. Darcienna glanced at the ground by the silver tree and the suspicion melted from her eyes.

"You really can talk to dragons with your mind?" Darcienna asked rhetorically. "That's incredible. I have never heard of anyone able to do that. As a matter of fact, I have never even seen a dragon before. I was wondering if they were extinct."

"Well, I don't know about talking to all dragons," Kade said while looking at Rayden. "I suspect it is just this one," he said, pointing to his companion. "And I thought dragons were extinct also until this one tried to kill me," he added with a grin. Darcienna looked at him with raised eyebrows once again. "Well, I stumbled upon him by accident. He was injured when I found him. If he wasn't already hurt, I am sure he would have made a meal out of me. I had the chance to attack him but I decided against it, and I think Rayden realized that I showed mercy when I could have done differently. After that, I healed him of some very serious wounds. We even fought a grimalkin together and he has been with me ever since," Kade said with a smile.

"Wow! That is truly incredible! You two must have been together for quite some time to work so well with each other. The fact that you both killed those creatures is amazing."

"Actually, I've only had him for less than a month."

"Only a month?" Darcienna asked with disbelief in her voice.

"Yes," Kade said. He realized that it really was a very short time, even though he felt like he had known the dragon all his life. He looked at Rayden and couldn't imagine being without him. "Forgive me for pushing, Darcienna, but we really should hurry," Kade said, irritated at being distracted so easily. "Darcienna, we do have to go," he said, emphasizing each word, trying to impress upon her the importance of what he was saying.

"First, you are going to get cleaned up. The dragon can use some cleaning, also," Darcienna said, leaving no room for argument as she noticed the dried blood still on Rayden. Kade started to open his mouth to argue when she planted her hands firmly on her hips and glared at him. Exasperated, Kade gave up on the argument. He knew if it had been anyone else, he would have left without even giving them a chance to convince him, but with her….

Something about her caused his will to bend to her wishes. He was not sure if she was using this Nature's Gift on him, but he would do her bidding, regardless. Any contest of wills was going to leave

211

him in second place, and he knew it with more certainty than he knew his own name.

"Besides, you need to give that," she said, pointing to his hand, "at least a little time to heal. If you run into more of these creatures, you are going to need it working," Darcienna finished confidently. Kade looked at his injury and realized she was right. Holding onto the dragon during their run would be difficult at best. This made it easier to stomach the delay

Kade ran his hands through his hair and pulled it away with bits of dirt and leaves. He looked down at his clothes, seeing how mangy they were. If he was hoping to impress her with his appearance, he knew he could just forget it now as he realized how disheveled he was.

"Where will I be taking a bath? I don't recall seeing a tub," Kade said, blushing slightly. Darcienna smiled to herself at his discomfort.

"We don't have any use for tubs here," she said with a sly look in her eyes.

Kade paused, feeling bats flapping around in his belly at the tone in her voice. He was trying to analyze her to see if she was having some sort of fun at his expense, but for the life of him, could not see what it might be. The mischievous look in her eye was impossible to miss, though.

"We…I have a hot spring in the back of the cabin," Darcienna said. The wall she had put up around her heart faltered for just a moment and then was back in place as firm as ever.

Kade closed his mouth. He was not going to let her see his embarrassment. The more he thought about it, the more he was starting to look forward to a hot bath to wash away the filth. Previously, a bath would have meant a trip down to the freezing, cold stream. It was so frigid he would go as long as possible to avoid a cleaning until Zayle forced him into the river.

Come on Rayden. Time for us to get cleaned up, Kade thought to his friend. Rayden stirred slightly but did not wake. Kade looked over his shoulder and noticed that Rayden was still sleeping soundly. He stopped and focused on the dragon. Again, he sent the command to the dragon but this time more forcefully. Rayden's head popped up, scanning the area for what had demanded his attention. Kade, once more, communicated that they were going to enjoy a bath in a hot spring. Before he could finish the thought, the dragon was on its feet. Kade got the strong impression that Rayden was more than eager to enjoy the hot water.

Darcienna led the way into the cabin. She indicated he was to wait in the kitchen by the door that led out back while she went into her bedroom. When she emerged, she was carrying several large towels, some kind of yellow substance that Kade took for soap and a large scrub brush. Kade looked at the brush and started to redden. Darcienna took one glance at Kade and gave a sweet, lighthearted laugh.

She is enjoying this a touch too much, Kade thought.

"It's for the dragon," Darcienna said with a grin. Yes, she was clearly enjoying this.

"Of course," Kade said, embarrassed. He took the towel and headed out the door.

"The hot spring is just a short walk. Follow me," Darcienna said as she pushed by him.

They traveled a well-worn path and Kade could smell the moisture in the air as they approached the spring. The area was very plush with many different types of vegetation due to the abundance of water. He noticed several small springs about five feet wide and then the path opened up into one huge one that must have been two hundred feet across. Kade could see the steam rising off the water and smiled at the thought of the relaxing bath. He couldn't wait to step into the hot spring and let himself melt. He was suddenly conscious of his sore muscles.

Kade started to take off his shirt when he noticed Darcienna was watching him with great amusement. He stopped and tried to keep from blushing but failed miserably. Before he could decide what to do, she spoke.

"I am waiting for your clothes. They are filthy," Darcienna said, feigning innocence. Kade could not miss the mischievous look in her eye, even if he were blind. She was grinning as she turned her back to him.

Kade gave a huff as he quickly undressed, leaving the medallion on, and then, slid into the water. He tossed his clothes back to land at Darcienna's feet. She bent down, picked them up and headed back the way she had come. He heard her laugh to herself as she disappeared around a bush with leaves as big as his head.

He lowered himself into a sitting position and immediately felt the heat start to undo the knots in his shoulders. He laid his head back on a rock that was just under the surface and started to close his eyes when he remembered the dragon. He looked back toward the cabin but didn't see Rayden anywhere.

"Rayden, where are you?" Kade yelled out. There was no answer so Kade focused his mind on his dragon and sent the question again. He was answered with a roar from the front of the cabin. Kade chuckled lightly as he realized his mistake. Of course the dragon was still out front. How would it know to go behind the cabin?

Come around to the back. I am already in the water, Kade mentally called to his friend.

To Kade, it sounded like there was a stampede as the dragon charged around the home and raced for the water. Kade was just lifting his head to look behind him when all sound of the dragon vanished. He caught something in his peripheral and flinched hard as the dragon launched itself into the air, passing directly over him by mere feet. Because of his reflexive action, he smacked his head on

214

the rock that was just under the water's surface. A second later, the dragon landed, causing water to splash Kade just as he was taking a breath. He sat up coughing and sputtering.

Rubbing the water from his eyes, Kade struggled to catch his breath. As soon as his vision cleared, he could see the dragon not more than fifteen feet away with a strange look on its face. It was a look that Kade had not seen yet and it puzzled him. Its mouth was open slightly as it watched him. Kade could not believe it, but he could swear the dragon was grinning at him. It just stood there, staring at him as it panted.

"What are you doing?" Kade asked as he shook his hair and rubbed the bump on the back of his head. The dragon answered by way of splashing a torrent of water at Kade with its tail and then bounding away. Kade stared, not believing what he was seeing and then laughed like he had not laughed in a very long time.

He stood and waded to the deeper part of the pool. He stared at the dragon as it bounded along the edge with its head held high, as if to keep it out of the water. Its eyes were open wide and it had its neck stretched out as it ran, giving it a comical look that caused even more laughter from Kade. After a moment, the dragon returned to stand just in front of Kade, again, with that same odd look on its face. He smiled widely as he realized what was about to come. He formulated his own plan.

"So, you want to play, eh? Okay, I'll play," Kade said just as the dragon sent another torrential downpour at him. Kade ducked under the water and held his breath, waiting, as Rayden made his circuit around the pool. Kade watched for Rayden to return and laughed out an air bubble as he pictured what the dragon's reaction would be when he played his own prank. It was not long before he saw the splashing racing directly for him. For just a moment, he thought he might be making a mistake as he visualized the dragon flattening him to the bottom. To his relief, it stopped very close to where it had the first time. Kade grinned deviously as he swam forward. He almost laughed as he closed in on his victim. Rayden shifted his balance as he looked around. Kade let out a bubble of laughter and almost lost it completely before forcing himself to get control. He stopped just in front of Rayden and looked up just as the dragon was looking down at the water. Before the dragon could reason out what it was seeing, Kade sank to the bottom, planted his feet firmly and then sprang out of the water with a loud "RRRRAAAAA," showering the dragon with a spray of water. The dragon was completely taken by surprise as it retreated frantically. Rayden lost his balance and fell over backward. Kade laughed so hard he was sure if he did not work his way to more shallow water, he would drown.

The game of who could splash who the most was on. The dragon raced around the spring, bounding and leaping only to return to splash Kade with its massive tail. Before Kade had a chance to make his minor splash back, Rayden would bound away again. They played this game for several more minutes until Kade finally fell over, exhausted. He was listening to his heart pound from the exertion when he heard a muffled laugh. He turned quickly to see Darcienna standing on the bank, watching him. He tried to sink deeper into the water, embarrassed at what she might have seen.

"How long have you been standing there?" Kade asked as he felt the blood, once again, rush to his face.

"You know, your face is going to stay red one of these times," Darcienna said, deepening Kade's embarrassment.

"Well?"

"As soon as you two started making all that noise, I had to see what was going on. I couldn't help watching. You two looked like you were having so much fun I almost jumped in myself," Darcienna said with a sly look.

"You obviously have too much fun at my expense," Kade

said, exasperated as he turned back to his dragon. Darcienna gave a squeak of laughter. She tried to stifle it with the back of her hand but failed. Kade's head whipped around and she quickly looked away.

Kade scoured his memory for any moment he might have been out of the water too much. With chagrin, he came to the conclusion that he was more out of the water than in the water. He grunted his frustration as he sat lower in the pool.

"What have you done with my clothes?" Kade asked while pretending to watch the dragon.

"They are soaking in one of the other springs. I am going to scrub them clean in just a moment. I don't want to travel with someone that smells like an animal," Darcienna said with complete innocence. Kade caught a look in her eyes and then it disappeared as quickly as it had come. The corner of her mouth twitched and Kade rolled his eyes, knowing his torture was not over yet. "I'll take care of the dragon now," she said as she hefted the large scrub brush and proceeded to wade into the water directly at him.

"That's okay," Kade said a little too quickly. "I will take care of Rayden myself."

"Okay. If you are sure," Darcienna said as she tossed the brush just a little too high over his head. He reflexively went to jump for it but stopped and glared hard at her. The brush made a splash behind him. With a grin, she turned and casually strolled off, disappearing from sight.

Kade could hear the soft sound of a bristles running back and forth on cloth. He considered grabbing the scrub brush but decided it could wait just a few minutes longer. He laid down in the water and let his muscles relax again. The dragon splashed over and dropped down next to him. Kade listened to the rhythmic scrubbing of the clothes as he stared up at the sky. His heart slowed to a more relaxed beat as the rhythm of her cleaning lulled him.

"That's a cute boy you have. What's his name?" Kade called

out.

"Thank you. His name is Marcole."

It dawned on Kade that he had not seen a man around. He considered asking about the father of her child but was afraid he might not like the answer. He cursed himself for a fool for not realizing that she must have a man in her life. With such a young boy, it would only make sense. With a sigh, he let it go.

"I only met his father once. It was in a town two days journey to the south by the name of Corbin."

"Yes, I know the town. I was there once," Kade said, feeling his head spin slightly at the good news.

Darcienna didn't respond. The silence stretched on for so long he started to wonder if she were upset. Kade looked in the direction of the scrubbing sound as he waited for any response. None came.

"Is something wrong?"

"No," she said in a hesitant voice. "I was just remembering the night I met Marcole's father. I fell in love with him and have been in love with him ever since. I returned to Corbin several times, but I never saw him again. I was such a fool."

Kade's heart shattered. He closed his eyes and shook his head. He hated the sick feeling in his stomach and could not even explain why it was there.

"Kade?" Darcienna asked, the sound of scrubbing stopping.

Kade lost all interest in talking and sat silently. The minutes dragged on. He closed his eyes and saw the image of Darcienna. Her beautiful, blue eyes drifted toward him from the darkness of his mind. The sensuous way her mouth moved as she spoke haunted him. He opened his eyes and shook his head to dispatch the image. This feeling of hurt was ridiculous, but no matter how he tried to reason that it made no sense, he could not dispel it.

"You must think badly of me," Darcienna said, misunderstanding his silence.

"So, what abilities do you have?" Kade asked weakly, not wanting to talk at all.

Darcienna did not answer right away. Kade chastised himself for having these foreign feelings. He vowed to ignore them and force them from his heart.

"You have seen two of them. The last one is the ability to sense when there is danger."

"So, are those the only abilities you have?"

"Yes, for now."

"For now?" Kade asked, feeling a semblance of control returning.

"We normally gain more abilities the longer we are alive. Unlike you, I cannot just learn something new when I want. We have to wait until Nature decides to awaken the ability inside of us. I am still very young. Jorell...," Darcienna said and then paused. After a moment, she took a deep breath, let it out slowly and continued. "Jorell told me that I was lucky to have the abilities I have at my age. She says every one of my kind develops their abilities differently. Some may be able to do similar things, but rarely do two people have the exact same skill. For example, Jorell couldn't make a shield but she could repel things," she said as she wrung the water out of the clothes.

Darcienna picked up the outfit and worked her way back to the large pond. With a smile, she dropped a pink robe onto the grass next to the water. She spared a quick glance at Kade, and with a smile, said as innocently as possible," You will have to wear this until your clothes dry." Kade was not in the mood for this anymore, but he let it go.

"Did Jorell have a lot of abilities?"

"Oh yes," Darcienna said with pride.

Kade paused as he thought about the one monster that had killed his teacher. He reminded himself that the invisible giant was a

219

lot more dangerous than all the monsters he saw today. He instantly felt ashamed of himself for his thoughts.

Darcienna's eyes lingered on the medallion that hung around his neck not more than ten feet from her. If not for the steep grade of the sand beneath his feet, he would not be this close and still be hidden by water. Kade slowly looked down to see what she was studying. He looked up and saw the question in her beautiful eyes but said nothing. He was not going to offer the information, but not surprisingly, she pretended not to notice his reluctance to answer and asked anyway.

"What's hanging around your neck?" Darcienna asked. She leaned forward to get a better look. It was an image of a man sitting with his legs crossed and his hands together in a prayer. There were three concentric circles around the man representing a barrier. There were three symbols on the back, representing the callings active on this ancient artifact. It looked like it was made of silver, except, it was almost too bright. He reached up, gripping the medallion tightly.

"Would you mind," Kade said as he indicated he wanted to exit the water. She feigned confusion as she smiled sweetly. Kade glared and she turned her back with a light laugh.

Kade walked almost right up to Darcienna, as she was standing not more than a foot from the robe, and bent to retrieve it. He was sure, at any moment, she would turn just to embarrass him even more, but to his relief, she stood still. He took a breath as he quickly swung the robe around himself, as though he were a performer flourishing his cape, and quickly tied the fuzzy belt.

"It's supposed to keep me from being tracked," Kade finally offered.

"Are your abilities difficult to use?" Kade asked, bringing the topic back to her.

"Difficult? No. I just need to concentrate on doing it and then it happens."

"You don't have to perform any moves?" Kade asked, recalling how she put her hands on his when she used her healing abilities.

"Are your powers difficult to use?" Darcienna asked, ignoring his question.

"Divine Powers," he corrected.

"Divine Powers," she repeated as she turned to face him.

"Unfortunately, yes," Kade said with a sigh. "It is very dangerous if done wrong," he said as he looked at the soaked bandage hanging from his hand.

"I guess both our ways have their advantages and disadvantages."

Darcienna glanced one last time at the medallion and then headed for the cabin. Kade turned to see the dragon panting as it lay in the hot water. He decided to leave it to its own and followed after her.

Walking through the back door, Kade could hear Darcienna in her bedroom. She called out for him to dress in the adjacent room. Kade found his clothes laid out on the bed and picked them up, marveling at how much better they looked. The smell was much improved, also. They were still damp, of course. Kade looked at the pink robe and made the obvious choice between the two sets of clothes. It was not comfortable wearing the wet outfit, but it was much better for his pride.

"You sure are full of surprises," Darcienna called from the front of the cabin. "What a beautiful animal you have. This is your animal with the books?" Darcienna asked as she knelt down in an attempt to get close.

Kade panicked as he remembered the sack he had left in the woods. He mentally cursed himself for being so careless with something so important. He quickly pulled on one boot, jammed his foot in the other one and hopped out of the room while struggling to get his heel in all the way.

"How come he won't let me touch your books?" Darcienna asked while studying the silky, black animal. It was lying on the floor, panting hard. "He looks like he has been running for days, the poor thing," she said as she bent down to stroke its shiny fur. She thought better of it when she saw the razor sharp teeth start to show. "He is…your animal, isn't he?" Darcienna asked as she looked at him from her crouched position. Her eyes widened slightly and her hand went to her mouth. Her face even seemed to lighten a few shades.

"What is it?" he asked as he looked behind himself.

"Nothing. It's just that you look like someone I know," Darcienna said, looking away. "It's just the light. You…look much better cleaned up," she said as she regained a little of her composure.

"No, it's not my animal," Kade said as he shrugged his shoulders at her odd behavior.

"He is not yours?" Darcienna asked as she quickly stood and took a step back with her hands raised as if to fend off an attack. She was ready to call on her shield.

"Not like Rayden. I healed him and fed him last night. He seems to have this fascination with my books," Kade said while smiling at the animal. He noticed how hard Chance was panting and looked around the kitchen.

"Water?" Kade asked.

Darcienna quickly walked into the kitchen and came back with a small bowl of water. Kade took the bowl and placed it on the ground just in front of the creature. It eyed the life giving liquid thirstily, and yet, did not let go of the books. Kade reached out slowly toward the sack and was surprised to see Chance let it go without hesitation. The creature quickly buried its nose into the bowel and drank deeply. After a moment, it sat back and looked at Kade expectantly.

"What?" Kade asked, confused.

222

The creature gave a slight huff. Kade raised his hands up as if to say, "What" when Chance jumped up and became excited. He leapt onto the chair and put his paws on the arm as it stared at him expectantly. Kade looked at his hands and then laughed.

"So, you want something to eat? Okay, just a moment," Kade said as he closed his eyes. He prepared to do the Food Calling, but before he could start, he felt the wrapping still on his hand. He opened his eyes and pulled the bandage off, amazed to see that his injuries had healed completely. Kade looked closely and could not see any signs that he had ever been injured.

"Impressive," he said as he flexed his hand.

Closing his eyes again, Kade immersed himself in the memory of the steamy, hot food. Within seconds, he was holding a perfectly cooked, mouthwatering, juicy piece of meat. He opened his eyes to see the animal fidgeting as it licked its lips hungrily. Kade tossed the tasty morsel to Chance, who easily caught it with its front paws that worked very much like human hands. It lay down and started chewing eagerly, unconcerned with the greasy mess it was making.

Darcienna took several deep breaths as she inhaled the aroma of the cooked food. Her eyes were locked on the animal as it devoured its precious meal. She swallowed while trying to appear casual, but Kade could easily see the hunger in her eyes.

"Where did that come from?" Darcienna asked in awe.

"I made it for the animal," Kade said passively as he looked upon the silky creature.

"Can you do it again?" Darcienna asked. Kade found himself watching the way her tongue ran along her lips and the way her mouth parted just slightly as she imagined the taste of the food. He mentally told himself to stop and focus but fond he was powerless to follow his own command. He took a deep breath as casually as he could and looked her in the eye. Fortunately, she did not see him staring, as she was focused on the food.

"Yes," Kade said nonchalantly. "Would you like some?"

Darcienna looked at Kade and nodded her head. He closed his eyes and easily produced a hot piece of meat just like the one that was being devoured by Chance. The silky creature dropped its food and sat up, waiting for the new one.

"Not for you, you greedy little imp," Kade said as he handed the meat to Darcienna. She immediately took a big bite and let the hot juice slide down her throat. She closed her eyes as she savored the taste of fresh meat. Some dripped down her chin but she did not seem to care. Kade found himself watching the way she would take a bit and then chew. Even this, he found enticing.

"You can make as much of this as you want?" Darcienna asked around the food in her mouth. She had her wrist over her mouth in an attempt to hide her bad manners of talking while eating.

"Yes," Kade said, surprised at how easily she was impressed.

He had always eaten well and didn't know what it was like to go without food. Master Zayle could conjure a four course meal with virtually no effort, and yet, most of their food was prepared by hand. Kade recalled not understanding why his master would go to such pains to do things the hard way when he could just call for the food. Zayle always preached that they should not be too dependent on the Divine for life.

"What I would give not to worry about where my food is going to come from," Darcienna said with her mouth still full. She paused as she chewed absentmindedly. Soon, she was standing completely still. As he watched, her eyes changed from her normal blue to a milky, bluish glow, and then to a look of bright blue lightning as if she were in some sort of trance.

"Your eyes!" Kade said in awe.

"Danger!" Darcienna said in a tight voice.

"What is it?" Kade asked.

"I am sensing that there is danger!"

"Your eyes look like that with danger?"

"Yes," Darcienna said, still trying to control her fear.

"Where? How long until it is here? Can you tell me what the danger is?" Kade asked in a rush, feeling his own heart start to pound. Darcienna seemed almost petrified with fear.

Rayden, danger. Come to the cabin right away! Kade thought quickly. Immediately, the dragon let out a fierce roar and raced to the front of the home.

"What am I going to do? Jorell is not here to fight them!" Darcienna said as panic seized her. Kade grabbed her roughly by the shoulders and forced her to face him.

"Darcienna!" Kade said, almost yelling, demanding her attention. "How long until the danger is here?"

"A few minutes, maybe. I am not sure. I never get much of a warning."

"Can you tell me what the danger is?" Kade asked, speaking slowly, but in a commanding voice. This was not the time to fall apart. He knew it was up to him if they were to survive. He needed to decide if they could stand and fight or if it was best to flee.

"No. I can only tell that it is danger, but I have never sensed it this strongly. It's overwhelming!" Darcienna said as if she were on the verge of hyperventilating.

That was all Kade needed to hear for him to decide. He forced Darcienna to look him in the eyes. With effort, those glowing eyes focused on him.

"Gather your things! We are leaving now!"

"But…," Darcienna started to say when Kade cut her off as he raised his voice.

"NOW!" Kade demanded, making it clear he meant it and pushed her toward her room where the boy was still sleeping.

Rayden, be ready to leave immediately! Meet us out front! Kade thought as he picked up the sack of books. Rayden roared again, causing the house to shake.

Darcienna was back almost as soon as she had left. She had the boy strapped to her back and a small cloth sack full of clothes. The boy started to cry, causing Kade's heart to pound even faster.

Great, Kade thought. *Just what we need; a crying boy to make things worse. I can't take any more distractions.*

Ignoring the wailing noise, Kade grabbed Darcienna by the arm and led her toward the door. He looked around one last time, making sure he had not forgotten anything. Darcienna jerked to a stop as he quickly scanned the room.

"What about the animal?" Darcienna asked.

The chair was empty except for the half eaten piece of meat. The animal was nowhere to be found. Kade paused only a moment to consider what would make this hungry, little creature leave its precious food and then decided it was definitely time for them to leave. He turned and pulled Darcienna through the door a little rougher than he had intended. He would apologize later.

Rayden was waiting just as Kade had instructed. The dragon knelt down and prepared to let his passengers mount. Kade boosted Darcienna up easily. He forced himself to be careful with how much strength he used as he was sure he could throw her clear over the dragon. Next, he swung up to sit in front of her just as the ground was starting to shake.

GO! Kade thought fiercely to the dragon. Rayden took off in a burst of power that nearly unseated Darcienna. Even Kade, who was ready for it, almost came off. He grabbed Darcienna's arm as her legs shot up and yanked her back into place. It was close, but they were on the dragon.

Darcienna locked her arms around Kade in a death-grip that he was not sure he could undo, even with his increased strength. Fear was a powering thing. For just a brief moment, Kade could feel the contours of her body as she pressed up against his back and then

226

quickly forced himself to ignore the distraction. He cleared his head and focused on what was important. He sent the dragon instructions to head east.

Kade looked over his shoulder just in time to see the cabin explode as though something hit it from beneath. He watched in awe as a rock-like head emerged from the roof, sending wood in all directions. The irony of seeing another home taken from another student was not lost on him. He considered turning back for just a moment as his rage built to a dangerous level. Then, he saw a speck on the horizon winging its way toward the cabin. Kade did not need to see it up close to know it was another flying creature like the one they had killed earlier. As much as he wanted to vent his fury on these creatures, he had other lives to consider.

Getting his rage under control, Kade held his breath, hoping not to be spotted. He looked over his shoulder as the trees raced by and felt relief. The rock creature never stopped pounding on the cabin until it was unrecognizable as a home. The flying beast circled the cabin, spitting its black flame, setting ablaze anything that would burn. Kade faced forward to settle in for the ride as he tried to organize his thoughts. He reached down, against his better judgment, and put his hands on hers. She intertwined her fingers with his and held on tightly. He hated feeling this way when her heart belonged to another, but he was powerless to change the affect she had on him.

They raced at the break-neck speed until they could no longer see the monsters. Kade felt the tension start to flow out of his body as the distance increased. Darcienna responded to Kade's more relaxed posture and withdrew her hand. Kade regretted that release and vowed to get his feeling under control. He knew it was clouding his judgment and it could easy get them killed. He feared that this internal battle was going to be fiercer than any physical battle he had ever fought, and he was afraid he was not strong enough to prevail. Not even close.

Kade cleared his head as he forced his mind on what was to come. Guilt at the delay worked at him. He looked down at his hand and flexed it, checking to make sure it was healed enough for battle. He closed his eyes and thought to himself with all his heart, *Mother, Father, please forgive me if I am not in time.*

CH8

"Are you ok?" Kade asked.

"Yes, I guess. What happened back there?"

"More creatures showed up to finish the job." Kade felt Darcienna stiffen. "It is a good thing."

"What?" Darcienna asked.

"He must think we are a threat to him. As long as he believes that to be the case, then we must do what we can to prove his fears well founded," Kade growled. He was still angry and she could hear it in his voice. "We just need to learn why he fears us. Whatever it is has been trying to kill me for several weeks now and has yet to succeed," Kade said, stating the obvious. "I regret to say that they will be after you, also, if they know of your existence."

Kade turned and looked at Darcienna, waiting for her to say anything. At a loss for words, she just stared straight ahead without uttering a thing. He felt his heart melt as he watched her blink her eyes several times while trying to work through this. Kade knew he would do anything for this vulnerable person. All he could see was a helpless, scared, young woman looking to him for protection and safety. He turned forward and scanned the woods for danger as Rayden continued to run.

"His ride is smooth," Darcienna said, trying to lighten the mood by changing the subject.

"He is incredible, isn't he?"

"Yes," she said and paused for several long moments. Kade sat silently, hearing the intake of air, indicating she was going to continue talking. "Kade?" she asked meekly.

"Yes?" he responded, wondering what she was working up the courage to say.

"I…I just wanted to say thanks. You saved my life twice now. I don't know if I'll ever be able to repay you for your kindness and willingness to risk your life for me," Darcienna said, sounding small and scared. Kade did not answer. The one thing he would ask for, she wasn't willing to give. She had already pledged her love to someone else and that person didn't even seem to want it. The feelings in his heart started to come to the surface again. He clenched his jaw, hating himself for being so weak.

"Kade?" Darcienna asked hesitantly.

"What?" Kade responded, trying not to listen to the melody of her voice, and hating himself for hanging on her every word.

"What is going to happen to us?"

Kade's heart leapt when he heard her refer to them as "us." He felt a struggle raging inside of him. One part of him wanted to touch her and be with her all the time, wanted to hear her voice and watch the way she moved her lips when she spoke. He recalled how soft her hands had been when she had laid them on his arm, and he felt himself craving that feeling again. He put his hand to his cheek where her kiss still seemed to linger. The other part of him wanted to throw her off the dragon before she clouded every last bit of his senses. He shook his head, forcing himself to answer her question.

"Well, first, we are going to Arden. I need to see if my parents made it out safely. If you want me to drop you off somewhere, I can do that," Kade said.

The voices inside his heart started to argue again. One side hoped that she would leave as soon as possible before he was affected too much, and the other side that was making him hold his breath, wanted her to say that she would stay with him. It was only logical that she would tell him someplace that she wanted to be dropped off, especially since she had a young child to consider.

Darcienna looked at the strong muscular back of this man as she considered his words. She was certain that he was going to try to get rid of her. He seemed the type to be over protective. She also feared that he may think of her as a burden. She did not hold out much hope that he was not going to send her away, but he had to let her come. He just had to.

"Kade, please let me come with you. I will make sure the boy is safe," Darcienna pleaded.

She looked at him, knowing that she was already becoming dependent upon him. She felt safe with him and the thought of being on her own with this unknown evil after her scared her more than anything. She feared that if a third time came, she would not fare well at all.

And, how would I keep Marcole safe without Kade there to protect us? she asked herself. She believed, with all her heart, that he could fight off any danger that presented itself. She just knew he could take care of them.

Kade turned and studied her for several long moments. Not only was she going to stay with him, but she was actually begging him to let her come. The only thing that would explain her pleading was her desire for revenge. He dearly wished her motivation for

231

staying were for other reasons, but as long as she was staying, that was good enough for him. At least…for now.

"You can stay under a few conditions. First, you will leave if I tell you," Kade said firmly. He felt Darcienna stiffen and he was sure she was preparing to argue. When it came to her safety, there was no compromising. If it had to do with anything else, he was afraid that she could maneuver him into doing what she wanted. She saw the look on his face and quickly closed her mouth. She would fight it later if she had to, but for now, she knew to keep quiet.

"You can be tough," Darcienna said as she looked into those deadly serious eyes.

"Next," he said, ignoring her comment, "you will follow my instructions without arguing no matter what," he said just as firmly. Remembering how Zayle talked to him helped him put a tone in his voice that allowed no room for argument. He put every bit of firmness into his words because he knew that this was where she could affect him and manipulate him if he showed her weakness. She just nodded. "And lastly, you do not ever leave me unless I say it is okay. You are to let me know where you are at all times. No exceptions!" Kade said. She opened her mouth, preparing to argue. "No exceptions!" He emphasized again in as firmly a voice as he could muster. He put a little heat into his words to make his point and even managed a glare.

"Everywhere?" Darcienna asked, thinking about the few times a female would want privacy. Her face reddened slightly. Kade found it very satisfying to see the tables turned where embarrassment was concerned. He almost smiled, but he did not want her to think he was softening. "Everywhere," he said with finality.

"Okay," Darcienna said with just the slightest hint of a smile. The corner of her mouth quirked just barely.

Kade hesitated momentarily, seeing a look of satisfaction in her eyes. It seemed as if she had agreed too quickly to that last part.

For that matter, he thought, *she had agreed to it all pretty easily.* He got the odd feeling that even though he felt he was in control, he was not. He thought back hard on how the conversation had gone and could not pinpoint where he did not make it clear that he was in charge. Seeing nothing, he shook his head and dismissed it as just a crazy passing thought.

"How is Marcole?" Kade asked.

"He seems to like riding the dragon," Darcienna said in a cheerful voice as though there was never any tension between them. Kade looked over his shoulder and studied her.

"He has been pretty quiet," Kade said as he narrowed his eyes while watching her closely, his suspicions tugging at him. Darcienna was smiling sweetly now; almost too sweetly. Kade sighed and let it go. "Is he always this good?"

"Most of the time," Darcienna said and then hesitated. He waited patiently as he heard her take a breath. The more time that went by, the more curious he became. "Kade?" she finally asked, almost too quiet for him to hear.

"What?" he asked, sensing her trepidation.

"Did you mean what you said back there?"

"I meant everything I have said to you."

Darcienna sat quietly, trying to formulate her thoughts. Kade could tell that she was thinking hard and sat patiently. As he waited, he found himself enjoying the way she was pressed up against him. He took in a deep breath and reprimanded himself for not keeping his thoughts under control.

"What's his name?" Kade asked to give his thoughts a different direction. A part of him could not help but want to know.

"He…never told me," Darcienna said in a whisper.

Kade was not sure if she was ashamed or if it was regret he was sensing. After a bit, he thought that she might even be sad. He could feel it, even though he could not see her. But, why would she be sad?

"Was he your first?" Kade asked, and for the second time, realized he was prying into things he did not want to know. Was this jealousy he was feeling? *Why am I so bothered?* He asked himself. He vowed to stop walking so clumsily through this conversation and put just a little more effort into not being such an oaf. "I am sorry. You don't have to answer that."

"Yes," Darcienna said, ignoring his apology. She needed to answer his questions. She wanted him to know her and get the judgmental part out of the way before it was too late.

Kade found he was at a loss for words. He made it a point not to ask any more questions that he did not want answered. The more he thought on it, the more he realized that having that answer helped nothing. If her heart belonged to the stranger, even if it was just once, then once was too many times.

"What are we going to do when we get to Arden?" Darcienna asked, changing the subject. Kade was grateful for the shift in topic.

"I am not sure, yet. It all depends on the situation when we get there. If my parents are safe, then I am going to find another Chosen and get some help," Kade said as he thought about the information in the small, black book.

"What if they are still there?"

"I don't know. I do know if they are there, I will do everything in my power to free them."

Darcienna smiled at Kade's back. His bravery and dedication were strong traits that made her feel secure and safe. She leaned forward and lightly put her head on his back. Kade did his best to keep still, enjoying the feeling of her being so close.

"Kade?" Darcienna asked.

"What?"

"How did you get so good at using the Divine Power?"

Kade almost laughed out loud at such an absurd question.

Me? Good at using the Divine Power? Zayle would have had a good laugh at that one, Kade thought. He took a deep breath to confess his status as an apprentice and hesitated. How would she see him once she knew he was no more than a mere apprentice? Would it cause her to lose confidence and want to leave? Would she not feel as safe? Darcienna sensed his hesitation and felt like they had stumbled into, yet, another conversation that was causing discomfort.

"I learned from my Master, Zayle. He was my teacher for most of my life."

"Was?" Darcienna asked as gently as possible, hearing the sadness in his voice, even though he was trying to be strong. Kade sat silently, trying to decide how much he would tell and how much was just too painful to relive. He did not want to let his emotions get the better of him. He wanted to be done with sadness and this topic was going to make that difficult.

"Would you like to talk about it? You don't have to if you don't want," Darcienna said gently.

Kade took in a breath and held it as he considered how much he was ok with telling her. He felt the pain in his heart and resented her for asking the question that brought back these unwanted feelings. After a few moments, the resentment evaporated and he decided it was best that she know, but before he could answer, his heart told him to think twice about opening up to her. Sharing was only inviting pain. Sighing, he decided to confide in her.

"A month ago, several creatures came to kill us. They were able to get Zayle but Rayden and I escaped. I wouldn't have survived without Rayden," Kade said as he patted the dragon on the neck. Rayden's head came up in response. "He got me away from the danger."

"You...weren't able to kill them?" Darcienna asked in surprise.

"Not until later," Kade said firmly. "But we did end their

235

miserable lives." Kade's lip curled in a slight growl as he recalled the memories. "One of his monsters made the mistake of coming back. It was a giant cloaked in the Divine. A targoth," Kade said while looking over his shoulder. Darcienna's eyes widened in shock and she inhaled sharply. "You know of this creature?" he asked, easily seeing her reaction.

"I do. They are abominations. I was taught that there are evil creatures that love nothing more than to torment and kill. They revel in causing misery," Darcienna said but did not offer anything more. After a moment, he continued.

"Well, this one will enjoy no more misery," Kade said, remembering how the giant had fallen at his hand. She felt him stiffen and gave him a squeeze for support. He instantly relaxed and even smiled ever so slightly. He found it easier to talk to her than he expected. "I believe whoever or whatever knew I was Zayle's apprentice, tried to have me killed. With the help of Rayden, I was able to bring their lives to an end."

"I was right about you. You are strong and powerful," Darcienna stated resolutely.

Kade wished he could bask in the praise and even would have loved to let it go to his head, but he just did not feel he deserved it. He thought about the many times that he could have died in the last few days and laughed sarcastically. He recalled how the giant had just barely missed killing him and shook his head.

"Luck," was all Kade said.

Before they could continue with the conversation, the dragon's head came up, indicating that it sensed something. Kade looked around and noticed smoke in the distance. His heart started to pound as he recognized where he was.

Rayden, be alert for danger, Kade sent to the dragon. *Let me know as soon as you sense anything,* he thought and then turned to Darcienna.

"Be ready to use your shield and let me know as soon as you sense danger," Kade said over his shoulder. She did not answer. "Darcienna?" Kade questioned as he twisted around to look at her. He saw fear in her eyes that brought a knot to his stomach. "Darcienna," Kade said more forceful as her eyes began to glow.

"I can already sense danger; a danger more evil than what we faced back at the cabin. It's like there is more than just the monsters. Kade, they are going to know we are coming," Darcienna said, the fear heavy in her voice. He started to regret his decision to allow her to come. He knew if anything happened to her or her boy, it was on his shoulders.

Kade sat staring at the town off in the distance. He turned to face Darcienna and pulled the medallion out from under his shirt. "We won't be sensed as long as I have this," he said as he held it up for her to see.

Darcienna seemed to take small comfort as she stared hard at the medallion. After a moment, she looked into his eyes as though she were looking for something more. He was not sure what she saw but she calmed down immediately.

"What do you plan to do?" Darcienna asked.

"I have a few ideas," Kade said. He looked into her eyes and saw her confidence in him was complete. He desperately hoped he could live up to her expectations. "I can make us invisible so they can't see us, and I can make it so we can't be heard, but I am not sure that will be enough. The last time I did, they were able to track our scent. But it's a start. Let me think for a moment to see if there is something we can do about our scent."

"Kade?"

"Give me a minute while I think," Kade said as he started going through callings in his head.

"I have an idea," Darcienna said, trying to get his attention. Kade was too focused on the town and his own thoughts. "Kade!"

237

Darcienna said forcefully.

"Darcienna, I need you to let me think. Please," Kade said a bit rougher than he intended. She wilted. He regretted his words instantly, realizing that she was trying to offer a solution. "I am sorry, Darcienna. What was your idea?" he asked softly.

"I was just going to say, if we can find a stream or river with a lot of mud on the bottom, we could use it to hide our scent."

Kade brought the dragon to a stop and turned in his seat to look at her. She smiled but it was not her normal smile. It was more timid. He hated himself for causing this change in her.

"That is a good idea," Kade said and meant it. "That is a good idea," he repeated, smiling as he thought more on it. "I am sorry I was short with you. I am just worried about my parents," he said, seeing some of her real smile return.

Suddenly, the dragon tensed. Kade felt as though he were sitting on a rock as the dragon's muscles hardened. He closed his eyes and opened his mind to the dragon's thoughts. It was the strongest connection he had made with the dragon, yet. It was almost as if he were the dragon. Then it hit him. The familiar scent of a grimalkin came to him. Not just one but two. And, they were on the edge of town, waiting.

"They have laid a trap for us. That's good."

"Why is that good?" Darcienna asked incredulously, thinking that he was losing his mind.

"Because it means they are still searching for me, otherwise, they would not have set a trap."

"But, what about your parents? What if they find out who they are?"

"I expect they found out. If my stubborn parents would not leave town, which I know they won't, then the invaders only hope in catching me is to keep them alive to use as leverage," Kade whispered as he scanned the area. "That's why it is good that they have set a trap."

"Well, that does have a twisted sort of logic," Darcienna said, doubt heavy in her voice.

"Yes," Kade said as he turned toward her. "It might be their only chance of surviving; otherwise, whoever it is has no reason to keep them alive. As long as I am free, they would be a fool to throw away their only leverage against me. They will keep my parents alive until they have me, and then, they will kill us all. I have no doubt about that."

Darcienna nodded slowly. She looked off in the distance as she studied the town. She was conscious of Kade still watching her so she did the only thing she could. She gave him hope.

"Your logic is sound. So, let's get on with our plan to make sure we are not caught," Darcienna said with a smile she dearly hoped conveyed trust. Her heart feared otherwise, but for now, she was going to force herself to believe. "Imagine their reaction when we get your parents out right from under their noses," she said with a grin.

A slow smile crept across Kade's face. He nodded slightly as he looked toward town. It was time to make this happen. He ignored the trepidation he felt and scanned the area for the river he remembered from his childhood.

"Rayden, there is a river that runs through here. Can you find it?" Kade asked, allowing the question to pass through the mental link, also. The dragon took several deep breaths and then swung its head around to look off to the north. Kade sent the thought to keep quiet and Rayden grunted his acknowledgement. "Okay Rayden, take us to it and prepare to get dirty." The dragon was confused by the thought, but regardless, it headed north.

Rayden took off and ran for several minutes as he followed the scent of water. They came out of the woods and stopped on the bank of a slow moving river that was not much wider than the length of the dragon. Kade recalled it being much larger. It was drying up, but he

239

was sure it would have what they needed.

"This should do," Kade said.

He slid off the dragon while holding onto the ridges, making sure his legs didn't buckle from the long ride. He flexed his muscles and pounded on them to get the circulation flowing again. Content that he could feel his legs once more, he turned and held his arms out to catch Darcienna as she dismounted. Her legs buckled slightly, causing him to stumble under the awkward weight of her and the child, almost falling into the river. He stood up, and for a brief moment, stared into her eyes. The world seemed to fade. Kade steadied her and took a step backward.

Turning toward the river, Kade stood looking at the passing water for several long moments without saying a word. He forced his mind back to their plan instead of the beautiful, blue eyes that stared back at him in his mind.

Darcienna studied his back, noticing the way his muscles tensed and relaxed several times. As she started to slide around him to get a better look at his face, he turned toward her. He had a hard look in his eyes. She got the uncomfortable feeling that he was preparing to say something that he knew she would not like. She feared he would try to send her away to safety once again. She smiled at him in an attempt to soften his resolve, certain she was not going to like what he was about to say. She knew her smile had some effect on him and she was willing to use it for all it was worth.

"You have a choice," Kade said firmly, shocking her into the realization that he was much less affected by her smile than she thought. But…if he was offering her a choice, one of the choices had to include staying with him. What she did not know was that he was struggling to keep his resolve. "You can either go south with my parents when we free them," he said as she hung on every word, "or you can let my parents take the boy with them."

"I think that would be best," Darcienna responded as he turned his back. His heart was pounding, certain she was leaving. He hated pushing her away, but he knew it was for the best. "Do you think they will take him?" she asked as she removed the boy from his sling and looked lovingly into his eyes. Kade's head whipped around to study her face as her words struck home. He nodded and let out his breath. She looked over the boy's head to catch his eye. "I don't want him in any danger, either. If your parents are willing to take him, then I think that is the right decision."

"Are you sure? This is no easy decision," Kade said as he studied her closely.

"Of course! I will miss him dearly," Darcienna said as she looked upon the boy with deep fondness, "I have a debt to settle, also, and I think you are going to need me," she said as she looked at the river. He nodded once and relaxed.

"Okay," Kade said, relieved she was staying with him but disappointed he was correct about her motive. Revenge. It was selfish on his part to let her come and he knew it, but he had given her the chance to go, and if her reason for staying was revenge, then so be it. He still knew that if she came to harm, he would remember this moment and know that he should have made a different decision. He paused momentarily as he considered changing his mind. He turned toward her and she glared hard at him.

"I…am…going," Darcienna said so firmly that he flinched. "You gave me the option and I have chosen. This conversation is over," she said as she put a hand defiantly on her hip. And just like that, it was done.

Kade nodded just once. It was final. Besides, he knew she had talents that might make the difference between success and failure. That shield was not to be taken lightly.

Darcienna turned and looked at the horizon, judging the position of the sun. Two hours of light left at best. She turned back to Kade to warn him when she noticed his eyes a little lower than she expected. She was considering teasing him when he spoke.

"You okay with getting mud all over those clothes," Kade said as he indicated her outfit. She laughed at herself for thinking this oaf would notice anything other than a dragon.

"I can always get more if I need."

He nodded and turned toward the river, grateful for being quick with his wit. *Why does she have to be so incredibly alluring?* he asked himself, picturing those shapely hips. *I must keep my eyes in my head,* he thought as he stole a quick glance over his shoulder. He found her calmly watching him.

"When the sun goes down, we are going to coat ourselves with mud and sneak into town," Kade said. "I want to scout first before we decide how to proceed."

"Do you know what you are looking for? What traps might be set?" Darcienna asked.

Kade took a few precious moments, making sure to sound like he knew what he was doing. He turned to look her in the eyes and smiled. With a confident, calm voice, he said, "It will be as if we are ghosts. We will be in and out without them even knowing we were there. Have faith," he said, not feeling the confidence he was pretending.

Darcienna smiled, relieved and walked down to the river. She bent, scooped up a handful of water and drank deeply several times. Kade and the dragon followed her lead.

"I think it would be a good idea if we had something to eat while we wait," Kade said as he called on the Divine food.

"Is this all you can make?"

Kade paused, trying to digest her tone. Was it disappointment or just plain curiosity? He noticed the way she was looking at the meat, on the verge of salivating, and grinned as he handed it to her. She accepted it eagerly.

"I can make anything, I guess, but I must know the food

extremely well. You can't just ask for something."

Kade heard a low growl and felt a strong puff of air as Rayden huffed at him, eagerly waiting for his share of the food. Kade chuckled at his eating machine that had stealthily crept up on him. He performed the Food Calling, tossing the meat to Rayden, who caught it and swallowed without chewing. Kade conjured and tossed as fast as he could, trying to see if he could get ahead of the dragon. He grinned at his little game. After cooking ten times, and feeling as though he were on the verge of sweating, he looked up to see the dragon eagerly waiting for the next toss.

"Okay, I give," Kade said, holding his hands up in surrender. "I cannot make enough to even get close to filling up that stomach of yours," he said with a grin. "You are always hungry."

Rayden sensed that his feeding was over and stepped up to the water. He took a long drink to wash down the food and then collapsed, clearly content for the moment. His eyelids began to close almost immediately.

Kade stood next to the dragon and considered trying his hand at calling on anything other than meat. After some consideration, he decided on something simple. Closing his eyes, he pictured a small piece of cheese. He found it easy to submerge himself in the memory as his craving for the food grew. He completed the calling and was pleasantly surprised when he felt it materialize in his hands. He took a bite and found it was better than he could have hoped for. He started to suspect that his vision of the food might actually be better than the real thing.

"Perfect," Kade said with a smile.

"Are you going to share some of that, or are you going to keep it all to yourself?" Darcienna teased playfully.

"Sorry," Kade said as he handed her the cheese.

"Can you make some bread for the boy?"

"I think so," Kade said, looking at the child that had fallen asleep. He closed his eyes and completed the calling. After tasting the bread to make sure it was made right, he handed it to Darcienna. Within minutes, the child was awake and eating hungrily.

The time seemed to pass slowly as Kade and Darcienna both checked the position of the sun constantly, eagerly waiting for it to disappear over the horizon, and at the same time, dreading it. As much as he wanted daylight to end and the dark to surround them, the lower the sun went, the larger the knot in his stomach grew. Before he knew it, the darkness spread and night reigned across the land.

"It's time," Kade said, feeling like bats were fluttering wildly in his stomach. "Rayden, into the river and roll in the mud."

The dragon eagerly obliged, enjoying the romp in the slippery substance from the river bottom. It returned after a good deal of splashing mud in all directions. Kade and Darcienna both held their hands up in an attempt to shield their eyes from the spray. Kade wondered if he was coated with enough mud already from the dragon's enthusiastic pursuit of the wet, sloppy material. He had the sneaking suspicion that it was no accident, but he could not prove it. Regardless, he was not in the mood for play. Darcienna and Kade both coated themselves without saying a word. Darcienna smeared Marcole with the earthy smelling substance. The boy grinned, enjoying the warm mud.

"Darcienna," Kade said as he turned toward her, all serious.

"We are not going to have this talk again," Darcienna said, turning her back on him and walking out of the water. "You need me, you sheep brained oaf. Stop trying to get rid of me. You gave me a choice and I chose. It is decided. Now, what next?" she asked with fire in her eyes. She was furious.

Kade was surprised at how much he admired her resolve. He smiled to himself, knowing she was right. He needed her in more ways than he cared to admit.

"Now, we go," Kade said as he headed for the dragon.

He jumped up easily and turned to offer her his hand. He quickly swung her up to sit behind him and recalled how much he enjoyed feeling her closeness. He immediately cleared his head and soon had the dragon moving stealthily through the woods. Rayden could move as smooth as a snake if he wanted and right now, he wanted.

"Darcienna?"

"Yes?"

"If you are able to sense danger, are you able to sense when you are closer to the danger or do you sense it all at once? What I am asking is…does the sense get stronger the closer you get?"

"I think the feeling gets stronger the closer I get. It's still a new ability for me, but I am sure it works that way. I did get to put it to use recently," Darcienna said with a grimace.

"Okay. You are going to help guide us through the traps. There are several set to capture us. Rayden should be able to find them, but you can make sure he does not miss anything. It is going to be dangerous," Kade said, half looking over his shoulder.

"I will box your ears if you are bringing that up again," Darcienna said, sure he was trying to scare her into staying back. "Now keep going," she said.

Kade looked up at the larger of the two moons as it started to rise in the north. The night was cool, almost to the point of being cold. He was grateful for it.

Closing his eyes, Kade drew on the sweet tasting Divine Power. It felt like a familiar friend comforting him in his time of need. He smiled as he molded it to his will. For anyone watching, they would have seen the large dragon and its riders fade from sight as the Transparency Calling took effect. Darcienna wrapped her arms around Kade in a death grip.

"It's ok. Sorry, I should have warned you," Kade said as he loosened her arms so he could breathe. All he got in response was an exasperated gasp.   He could not help but to let a laugh slip.   She smacked him in the head so hard his ears rang. *It was worth it,* he thought with a grin, careful not to laugh again.   This small amount of levity helped settle his nerves.

Next, he drew on the Divine Power once more as he prepared the Silence Calling. For a moment, he hesitated as he ran the moves through his mind. The second move was not as familiar as it should be. He considered checking the book but decided against it. He completed the calling and let the Divine Power flow. He realized he was clenching his jaw so tightly it hurt. He let his breath out and relaxed.

Kade stayed focused on the town as they approached. He reached out with his mind to tap into the dragon's senses and found nothing that stood out. He started to wonder if he was being a fool, all covered in mud, when Darcienna grabbed his arm and clenched so tightly that she dug in her nails. It did not take Kade long to realize what she was trying to convey, but she added a hissed warning.

"I sense something," Darcienna whispered as quietly as possible. Kade could easily hear the fear in her voice.

"Be ready with your shield," Kade responded.

He sent a mental warning to Rayden. The dragon tensed as it slid closer to the ground.   After several more steps, the dragon froze and appeared to stop breathing. Kade strained his eyes, and then, he saw it. A massive shadow slid through the dark, barely the length of the dragon away. Rayden did not need a warning from Kade to stay still.

"Do not move or make a sound," Kade whispered to Darcienna, even though he was sure they could not be detected.

Rayden, do you sense anything more? Kade ask the dragon mentally. He could feel his friend expanding and knew it was either tasting the air or smelling it. It did this three times in a row and on the third time, Kade got the distinct impression that the dragon was sensing something further down and to the right. *When it is safe to move, take us to the left,* Kade sent.

Out of habit, Kade turned to look at Darcienna and chastised himself for being a fool. He missed seeing those blue eyes staring back at him. He was looking forward to letting the calling go so he could see her again. With a sigh, he turned forward again.

The dragon started to move. Kade found he was focusing on the way Darcienna's legs rubbed against his with every step the dragon took. He forcefully made his mind focus on the town ahead. He chastised himself for not considering how distracting it would be to have her come with him. It was too late to do anything about it now.

They were three hundred yards from town when Darcienna squeezed his arm. He was sure he was going to feel blood anytime now. He clenched his teeth against the pain.

"Can you tell where it is?"

"I am not sure, but there is definitely something close."

Once again, between the dragon and Darcienna, they were able to spot the danger and avoid it. They circled to their left and continued on at the slow pace. Kade made sure to keep clear of any bushes as he directed the dragon though the woods. He had to fight his urge to find cover and force himself to accept that they needed to be in as open an area as possible so as to not move any brush or trees.

They were within two hundred yards of the town when Darcienna squeezed his arm again. He could feel the sweat from her hands as she gripped him. Kade wished he could take her to safety, but that thought was gone as soon as it came. He knew he needed her and her abilities.

"I sense danger," Darcienna said. Her voice sounded unsure. "It feels like it gets stronger and then weaker again. I think we should wait here for a minute. I don't know if we can avoid this one,"

Darcienna said, hesitantly.

Suddenly, the child started to make small sounds. Kade got a sick feeling in his stomach as he considered the boy on her back. The more he thought about it, the more he wished he would have made her stay by the river where it was safe. Yes, he felt much more secure with her abilities to back him up, but he had no right putting her child in this type of danger. In the blink of an eye, he knew this could not be avoided. Darcienna was not going to leave his side. She believed he was their best chance for survival and that meant staying close to him in the event that he would need her shield or any of her other abilities. Seeing that this kind of thinking was going to help nothing, he dismissed it completely.

Kade had the dragon wait, once again, and asked if it could see anything. Rayden seemed to sense something but was not able to give any more information. Kade urged the dragon ahead another twenty yards, and again, had it search the area.

"What are you getting?" Kade asked Darcienna.

"It's like before. It gets stronger, and then it gets weaker. It makes no sense."

Kade listened intently and then he heard it; the sound of a twig snapping. Now it made sense.

"There is something patrolling," Kade whispered. "I am a fool. They know I am coming from the west. We need to circle around and come into town from the east."

Kade signaled the dragon to turn north. They worked their way around that end of town, making sure to check frequently for any stray creatures. After almost an hour, Darcienna relaxed her grip on his arm.

"Kade, I am getting a feeling of danger, but I think it's coming from town. There is something there that is very strong," Darcienna said and emphasized this by squeezing his arm. "Maybe this is not such a good idea. How can we hope to defeat them?" Darcienna asked. Kade could hear the despair creeping into her voice.

"Are you saying you want me to take you back?" Kade asked, a little angry that she had pushed so hard to come and now was having second thoughts.

"No," she said after just a slight hesitation.

"After I find out what happened to my parents, we can leave."

Darcienna never responded. If Kade could have seen her face, he would have seen the shame she felt for suggesting that they leave before learning of his parents. They had already come too far to just turn back.

"I am certain my parents are here. If they weren't, whatever or whomever wouldn't have gone to all the trouble of setting so many traps. I am expected," Kade said, but Darcienna was sure she could sense his doubt. She came to the realization that he was trying to convince himself more than anything else.

Kade was met by silence. He turned his attention back to the surrounding area, searching for any more signs of danger. He knew if the dragon or Darcienna did not sense any threat, he was not going to find anything either, but he had to keep his mind busy with something.

They traveled slowly as they crept through the woods. It felt like hours when they finally crossed the north end of town. It was slow going as the dragon slinked stealthily, making sure not to snap even the smallest of twigs. Surprisingly, the area was clear. Kade directed the dragon to the east end of town and stopped. His heart started to pound. This was to be his entry point. He was certain this was his last chance to turn back. Darcienna also knew this was the point of no return and sat silently, waiting for Kade to decide what to do next. He was about to signal the dragon to move forward when Darcienna squeezed his arm so hard that he almost yelped.

"What?" Kade hissed.

"I sense something very close."

Kade studied the town, but nothing moved. He strained his ears but again…nothing. He was getting ready to signal the dragon to proceed when he changed his mind, getting a feeling that something was out of place. Something was not quite right. Kade scanned the shadows and found himself staring at one spot by a building. When he would start to look away, his attention would be drawn right back to it. It just did not feel right, but nothing appeared to be out of the ordinary. Darcienna squeezed his arm again. Kade made a mental note to purchase leather arm bands for their next trip.

Okay Rayden, move forward slowly. Very slowly, Kade thought.

As they slinked forward, Kade kept returning his eyes to the shadow alongside the building. The dragon smelled something just ahead and Darcienna squeezed his arm again. Kade was sure he was going to have bruises for weeks but, he continued to focus on the shadow. And then, he saw it. A slight movement caused the outline of a man to come into focus. Kade stopped the dragon in mid step.

"It's a man," Kade whispered so quietly that he was not sure she heard.

Darcienna released her grip. Kade was sure she was freeing her hands, preparing to use her Gift of Nature if needed. He could feel his heart pound a little harder.

Now things get very dangerous, he thought.

Kade watched as the man slowly leaned around the corner, looking up the street. After several long seconds, the man returned back to the cover of the shadow. It was obvious he was waiting for something and that something was most definitely Kade. Just as the Apprentice Chosen was formulating what he wanted to do for his next move, the boy started to wake and fuss. Kade held his breath, hoping Darcienna could get the child under control. She didn't. The child burst out into a loud cry. Kade felt panic seize him and he held his breath, watching the man closely as he prepared to use the Fire

250

Calling. The seconds ticked by and the man did nothing more than look around the corner again. Kade let out his breath, cutting off the Divine Power.

"Well, I am pretty sure they can't hear us," Kade whispered. He still could not bring himself to talk normally.

"Good. I don't think I could have shut Marcole up if I wanted."

"I could have," Kade said under his breath.

"What?" Darcienna asked as she jabbed him in the ribs and none too gently.

"I didn't say a thing," Kade said.

Darcienna didn't answer. If Kade could have seen the glare in her eyes, he would have cringed. She did not say another word. Kade was relieved that she let it go.

He was about ready to signal the dragon to move when the man in the shadow stood up and stared in their direction. After a moment, he started moving toward them, silent as a ghost. Kade felt the dragon tense, ready to strike. The man stopped just short of Rayden and studied the ground. Kade felt his heart start to pound, and forced himself to stay calm. And then, Kade realized with panic, that the man was seeing the claw prints left by the dragon.

"Blood and ash!" Kade hissed. "Darcienna, prepare to use your shield on my word," Kade said, doing his best to sound in control. *Rayden, when I say, eat him,* Kade thought.

Kade held his breath, waiting for the man to move back to his hiding spot. The longer he could avoid killing, the longer he would go undetected. Sooner or later the man would be missed, if he was not at his post. Kade got an idea and quickly drew on the Divine Power and casted his calling. Now, time would only tell if it worked...or was even needed.

The man bent down to look closely at the ground in the dim light of the moon. He turned and looked over his shoulder at the street he was assigned to watch and then returned his attention back to the ground. Kade watched in horror as the man stood up slowly and raised his eyes to look directly at them. Kade could see him squint, as though trying to focus. Rayden swung his head around and stopped not more than two feet from the man's head.

"No," Kade started to say, but it was too late. He watched the man flinch as the dragon breathed directly into his face.

CH9

The man's eyes flew open wide. He knew they were there. In an instant, he leapt back faster than Kade would have expected just as the apprentice gave the dragon the order to attack. The man opened his mouth and screamed as he grabbed a spear leaning against the wall and then spun to face them. Kade felt every muscle in his body turn hard as stone. Had the man realized his cry for help had gone unheard, he might have retreated, but believing reinforcement were just moments away, he attacked.

It did not take more than a second before Rayden had the man in his jaws and was tearing limbs off as though they were made of paper. Kade felt nauseous as he watched the carnage. He clenched his jaw tightly and ignored his stomach. He felt a sickly, wet splash on his arm and his stomach heaved once. The man vanished as the dragon finished him off.

"Kade," Darcienna said in a panicked voice, turning as if to watch for attack from every direction at once.

"It's okay," he said firmly as he raised his voice slightly. He turned as far as he could and grabbed Darcienna by the shoulders, ignoring the screaming child. It was chaos and he knew he had to get things back under control. He squeezed as he hissed into her face, "Settle down! We are undetected. I cast the Silence Calling on the man before he could raise the alarm. Now, please, quiet Marcole so I can think."

Darcienna didn't move, nor did she speak for several long moments. Kade was starting to wonder if she was okay when she responded by putting her hands on his arms again. He was relieved by this simple gesture.

"I am sorry. I thought…there is so much danger here, Kade. I am more scared than I have ever been in my entire life," she said as her voice waivered. "If they find us, we won't have a chance."

Kade wished he could hold her in his arms to let her know that everything was okay. Half turned in his seat, he did the best to hold Darcienna in an attempt to calm her. She responded by wrapping her arms around him and hugging him tightly. It seemed to help, but the boy's crying was starting to grate to him.

"It's okay. I would have told you what I was planning, but I didn't have time. Now, please settle him down," Kade said through tight lips.

"I shouldn't have panicked. I should have trusted you," Darcienna said in as calm a voice as she could muster.

"The boy," Kade said firmly.

"Yes," she said as she pulled the child to her front and tried to sooth him. No matter what she did, he continued to wail.

"Cover his eyes," Kade said, hitting on what he thought was the problem.

"Kade…"

"Just do it."

"Okay," Darcienna said. She whispered in Marcole's ear as she held him tightly. To her surprise, the boy calmed almost instantly. "Very clever," she said, realizing why this was working.

"Just do what it takes to keep him calm, please," Kade said, attempting to control his agitation.

The dragon was completely still as if it were stalking prey…which it was. Kade turned his attention back to the town. He urged Rayden forward at a slow pace as he took a deep breath and let it out to settle his nerves.

There had to be eyes all over the place, Kade thought as he looked deep into the shadows. Every alley had the potential to be a call-to-arms against him. The dragon moved to the edge of the building just before stepping into the street and stopped at Kade's command. He scanned the road and saw a wooden tower that had been constructed in the middle of the town. There was not much light, but it was enough to see the tower and what sat at the top. His chest constricted as his eyes fell on the figure that was strapped to a beam.

In an instant, Kade felt rage build in him to a dangerous level. His lips pulled back as his anger soared. Hate filled him quickly. Kade realized he was clenching and unclenching his fists as the Divine Power coursed through him. He was not even aware he had been drawing on it, but it was there, waiting. It was begging to be molded and used. For the first time ever, Kade understood the warnings from his master. Be aware of the seductive power of the Divine. He fought to release the power but his rage and anger kept the power building in him, whispering for him to use it. He could not tear his eyes from the suffering form. The more he looked, the more his fury built. The Divine was a promise of raw power that could not be stopped. He squeezed his eyes shut as he struggled. It was like a slow rain that had built in to a hurricane. Kade felt himself giving way to his rage. He wanted a target with which to aim his fury. He desperately needed to vent his anger as he shook and then…something…touched his very soul. A sweet sound whispered gently through the hurricane. He felt the soft touch and the power hesitated. Then, ever so slowly, it started to withdraw. The hurricane lessened until it was a gentle rain and then…nothing. Kade felt the power fade until it was gone. There was an emptiness that left him longing. He had to fight to keep from calling it back.

"Kade? Kade, are you ok?" Darcienna asked for the third time as she squeezed his shoulder.

He found he was breathing heavily. His throat was raw and his chest burned. He closed his eyes as he forced himself to calm, doing his best to return his breathing to normal. He unclenched his hands and relaxed the muscles in his jaw.

"Darcienna, I am not positive, but I believe that is my father on top of that tower," Kade rasped as he pointed with his unseen arm.

"Kade," Darcienna said, her voice full of concern. She pulled him back to lean against her as she hugged him. He was not sure if it was her or her Nature's Gift, but something reached right to the core of his being to calm him. "We will free him. I swear on the most sacred Nature's Gift that we will do everything in our power to save your parents." Letting out a long breath, Kade relaxed and leaned forward.

"Do you see?" he asked, regaining control.

"Kade, I see your father, but what about your mother?"

He squinted in the dim light, and sure enough, he could only see one person. He took a deep breath as he felt his anger start to boil in him again. It was almost too difficult for him to think clearly while he looked on as his parent suffered.

"Maybe she is on the other tower," Darcienna said as she looked down the street.

"What?" Kade asked in shock as he looked from one end of

the town to the other. Then, he saw the tower fifty yards beyond the first. "They have split them up so I won't be able to get them without being seen. As soon as I free either of them, they will have me before I can get to the other one," Kade said as he clenched his fist again. For just a moment, he could taste the Divine Power, and he quickly shut it off before it was able to overwhelm him.

Kade briefly recalled the beginning of his training. It had taken him years to sense the power, much less channel it, and now he was so attuned to it that it flowed to him with barely a thought. He took a deep breath, and once again, cleared his head. He reached back for his teacher's lessons on staying calm. It never made sense to him why Zayle had preached over and over that it was imperative that emotions not be allowed to control the power. That never made sense until this very moment.

Kade felt sweat break out on his forehead. He closed his eyes and visualized his breathing. The more he pondered his teacher's words, the more it was starting to make sense. He could command the full force of the Divine Power...and not just the normal amount like other Chosen. To be called a Chosen was to command awe and deep respect, but each Chosen had only so much of the Divine Power they could channel. But, he was different and he knew it. It was at that very moment that Kade finally understood what Zayle meant when he said, "You are one of the most powerful users of the Divine." Kade put aside his thinking and returned to the present.

"They will have many eyes on those towers. If the Divine is being used here, there will be traps all over the place."

Rayden, take us forward, and stay close to the right side of the road so we can keep to the shadows. We don't need anyone seeing us disturb the ground as we pass, Kade thought to the dragon. *Be alert for danger.*

Rayden started forward at a pace that was slower than a man's walk. Kade tried his best to calm his impatience and almost failed.

He was not able to relax completely, but it was enough for him to clear his head so he could think.

Kade felt his heart pounding the closer he got to the other tower. As he closed the distance, he became more certain that it was his father on top. He forced his breathing to stay calm in an attempt to keep from lunging for the Divine and killing anything that would present a challenge. The only thing that kept him from doing just that was his certainty that it would cause his parents death.

The south end of town was smoking with several small buildings on fire. A smoky haze drifted through the streets as the breeze carried the occasional soot toward the towers. The north end still appeared to be virtually untouched. There were three oil lamps along the road, giving just enough light for anyone walking to be seen. Kade was sure it was no accident that the towers were right next to two of them.

They were within fifty feet of the closest structure when Darcienna grabbed Kade's arm again. He jumped, chastising himself for not being used to her doing this by now. He exhaled as he turned slightly, waiting for her to explain.

"There is danger all around us. I also believe you are correct about there being traps set up around the towers. The closer we get, the stronger the danger is."

"Do you see anything that looks like a trap?" Kade asked.

"No."

Rayden, do you sense anything between us and the tower? Kade thought to the dragon. Rayden took several deep breaths, tasting the air. He could sense a lot of different smells in all directions but nothing directly in their path that would indicate danger. Kade signaled the dragon to stop, forcing himself to be methodical and logical in his approach. As he sat there, he saw several shadows duck out of alleys to survey the street only to move back out of sight again. Something about being right under their noses gave him a euphoric feeling.

"Kade," Darcienna said firmly, "the closer we get to the tower, the more the danger threatens to overwhelm me. I am sensing it so strongly that it feels like we are standing right on top of it."

Kade closed his eyes and performed the Reveal Calling, feeling like a fool for not thinking of this sooner. He gasped when he saw all the pulsing patterns just ahead and to their left. There were many callings just waiting for him to blunder into. There was barely enough room for the dragon to get by the traps, if they stayed close to the buildings.

"Kade, what is it?" Darcienna asked, hearing his gasp.

"There are several callings placed around the tower. If we had taken two more steps, we would have been caught, or most likely, killed."

"What are you going to do?" Darcienna asked much calmer than he expected. By the tone in her voice, Kade could see that she put a lot of trust in him to keep them safe. This was not lost on him. He only hoped he did not disappoint her...for their sake and his parents.

He was about to tell her that he was unsure when he thought better of it. Once again, he decided it was important for her to have faith in him so she would not panic. *Well...at least, keep the panicking down as much as possible,* he thought as he recalled her recent reaction in the alley.

"I think we should work our way to the next tower," Kade said as he looked up at the slumped form of his father. He took a deep breath and let it out, controlling the anger before it started. *So close, and yet, so far,* Kade thought as he tore his eyes away from the broken body of this parent. Even from this distance and this poor light, Kade could see that his father was in dire shape.

Darcienna sat silently, seeming to accept this. Kade looked at the tortured man, wishing there was some way of telling him that he was there. It broke his heart. *Just a little longer, Father,* he thought and then instructed the dragon to start moving forward again. Kade closed his eyes and performed the Reveal Calling once more, opening his mind up to the dragon in hopes that it could see or sense the traps. Rayden moved a little bit more to the side. They slid past the tower, clear of the traps. Kade looked back at his father, watching very closely, desperately wanting to see him move just a little. He never did. Kade turned and focused on the next tower.

The dragon moved forward, keeping to the shadows as much as possible. Kade closed his eyes again and used the calling once more to check for traps. He was not surprised by what he found. Kade brought the dragon to a stop just outside the furthest trap. Looking up, he was certain beyond any doubt that he was seeing his mother. He cringed. She was bound to a beam by her wrists, as she dangled just inches off the platform. Kade was also certain that he was meant to see her. The limp form stirred as it raised its head momentarily only to collapse a second later.

At least she is alive, Kade thought, feeling a sense of relief.

He felt the strong urge to jump down from the dragon and climb the tower as fast as he could. He paused as he looked at her, sure he was seeing a slight hint of a smile while she looked down. He got the strange feeling that she was looking right at him. He quickly glanced at the dragon to make sure he had not released the Transparency Calling, even though he knew he had not. It was, indeed, still intact. When he looked up again, her head had fallen back to her chest.

"Kade?" Darcienna asked, pained for him.

"Yes, that is my mother," Kade said through clenched teeth. Darcienna sat completely still, feeling pity she was sure Kade would not want. She looked up at the battered woman, desperately wanted to rescue her and end her suffering. Even though it was difficult to see in the dark, it was obvious that the woman had been tortured.

Darcienna felt her heart break for the man that was trying so hard to be brave and save his parents in the face of so much danger. She did not know where he got all his strength from, but her level of respect for him grew. She marveled at his ability to think under such duress.

"Darcienna, we have to leave the town so you and the boy will be safe."

"Kade, what are you planning?" she asked with suspicion, knowing she was not going to like the answer.

"All you need to know is that I need to get you and the boy out of here," Kade said.

Darcienna started to worry, fearing Kade was going to do something rash. She firmed her resolve and waited for him to try to dismiss her. She was not about to let him send her away that easily. If he wanted her gone, he was going to have to be a lot more convincing than that, or at least assure her he had a plan that sounded like it would work.

"You are planning to use the Divine to free your parents without being discovered?" Darcienna asked hesitantly, prodding him for any hint of what he was planning. "You are not going to try to take them by force, are you? There are too many of them. It will only end in disaster."

"You are right," Kade said, sidestepping her question completely.

"Good," Darcienna said, not realizing that he had not really answered any of her questions.

"Did you want to make a suggestion?" he asked, hoping she would not see that he had no plan of his own.

"No," Darcienna said hesitantly. "You do what you think is best. I trust you."

Kade felt frustration and helplessness descend upon him as he looked up at his mother, just out of reach. As he continued to

261

consider the callings he knew, he hit on a simple one. It was so basic and yet...

Kade closed his eyes and drew on the Divine, molding it into the Disarm Calling. The power flowed through him and out just as quickly. He opened his eyes and looked to see if the use of the Power was noticed by anyone or anything. Reaching up and gripping the medallion, he hoped and prayed that it worked. He felt it vibrate as though it had a life of its own. It also felt cool to the touch. After a moment, the vibration subsided and then there was only the feel of the medallion again.

Kade closed his eyes and studied the patterns surrounding the tower. He felt failure start to come crashing down on him when he noticed that at least one of the callings on the far side might have been disarmed. Hope flared.

It seems there is a chance this might work after all, he thought.

"Kade, what are you doing?"

"I tried to disarm the traps," Kade said quietly as he continued to study the patterns.

"Did it work?" Darcienna asked with optimism in her voice.

"Maybe," Kade said cautiously. He directed Rayden to move around the tower. *There is, indeed, a path about two feet wide where a calling had been disarmed,* Kade thought excitedly. He smiled in triumph. "I was able to disable at least one of the traps, but," he said and then paused, as he studied the ground, "I am not sure it is good enough," he added, losing some of the excitement. "I need to watch the traps and see if I can spot anything else." He closed his eyes.

"Then, there is a chance we can get her down?" Darcienna asked.

"A chance," he said. "But, even if I get her down, I am certain they will notice she is gone. I won't make it to my father before we are discovered."

Darcienna looked up at the woman and then back to where Kade was sitting. She wanted dearly to come up with a way to help. She sat for several long moments, giving Kade time to study the traps when an idea came to her.

"What if we create a distraction?" Darcienna asked.

"If we cause a distraction, it will only give away that we are here." Kade said.

"I am not talking about blasting a building or anything like that. I mean something simple. Something to throw them off so they won't be watching so closely," Darcienna said. What she was thinking was causing a commotion in the woods away from town. But, it was enough to get Kade's mind working. And then...it hit him.

"Yes!" Kade said, excitedly. "You are amazing!"

"Excellent!" Darcienna exclaimed. "So...what did I do?"

"The Transparency Calling," Kade said as hope grew in him.

"Like the one you used on us?" Darcienna asked, confused.

"Yes," Kade said. "Don't you see?"

"I am not quite sure," Darcienna said hesitantly.

"What if I just make it look like they are gone?" Kade asked in a rush. Darcienna sat silently, trying to piece together how this was going to work. "Okay," he said, sensing her confusion. "If I can make them both disappear, then they will think that my parents are gone, right? They will go searching for them, believing that we are escaping. They will, most likely, expect us to be fleeing from town, right?"

"Seems to make sense. But, wouldn't you need to make them both disappear at the same instant? Is that possible?" Darcienna asked, causing Kade's new found hope to fade slightly. "Do you have to be next to them?"

"I have only done this while being very close to the object. I don't need to be touching them, but as for how close I have to be...I am not sure," Kade said as he turned and mentally measured the distance between the two towers. "If I can make it up to my mother, then maybe I can try to cast the Transparency Calling on my father, first. If it works, I can then cast it on my mother right away."

Darcienna took a deep breath and let it out, knowing that things were about to get deadly. This was the moment that was going to decide everything. It was one thing to consider a course of action but entirely something else to put it into motion. She was glancing around nervously, trying to search for anything he may be missing as her heart started to race. And then, she felt Kade shift and slide down from the dragon.

"Kade, what are you doing?" she asked urgently.

"I am going to find a way up there," Kade said as he closed his eyes and performed the Reveal Calling. "Hold onto this," he said as he swung the sack of books off his back and up to where he believed her to be. It thudded against her leg.

"Kade, I thought you said you were just going to look around and then come back later. Are you sure this is the best idea?" Darcienna asked, ignoring the jolt from the books that she did not see coming.

"We are here. What good is it going to do for us to go, only to come back and get to this point all over again? And besides, when they find their man gone, they are going to suspect something. We may not even be able to sneak into town again. Yes, this is best," he said, resolutely.

Kade closed his eyes and used the Reveal Calling to guide him. He moved to the edge and studied the pattern as it pulsed. This small path was all he had. Walking it with his eyes closed was not going to be comfortable. He was not sure if he had to touch the ground to trigger the calling, or if simply passing his hand through the space above the ground could spring the trap. Regardless, he was not going to take a chance. Kade walked heel to toe and found himself wobbling dangerously. He had to fight from throwing his arms out to the side to keep his balance. After just three steps, he turned sideways and started to edge his way along the path with his hands pressed firmly against his legs.

Rayden, do not let anything find you. If you must move, then move, but avoid contact with anything, at all costs. We must remain undetected until I get my father from the other tower, Kade thought to the dragon. He sensed a response from Rayden that he took for acknowledgement.

With his eyes closed, the ground felt like it was starting to rock, causing Kade to go up onto his toes and then back to his heels. He even opened his eyes once to get his balance just as he was about to take a step. A knot grew in his stomach as he breathed a sigh of relief. He fought to keep his arms at his side and succeeded…just barely. Kade looked and saw that he had moved considerable closer to the tower. He measured the distance and realized he could almost jump the rest of the way.

Just a few more steps, Kade thought. He took a deep breath to steady his nerves and closed his eyes, performing the Reveal Calling once more. He was able to take four more steps before having to open his eyes again. This was more nerve wracking than he expected. He closed his eyes and continued edging his way along the narrow path. This time, he made it without issue. Kade saw directly under the structure was clear of any traps, so he ducked under a board to stand in the middle.

He looked up and studied the build of the tower. Reaching up as carefully as possible, he grabbed ahold of one of the boards that looked the strongest and slowly pulled himself onto it. Tearing one of the boards off would be a great way to give away their position, and he was not about to do that. The tower was solid and did not move but the board groaned quietly. In the dead of the night, without another sound anywhere, the creak must have been heard for miles…or so Kade thought. He froze. He held his breath as he scanned the area. Nothing moved. Why would they?

The tower might creak from mother's movements, right? he asked himself, trying to relieve his trepidation. He continued his climb, moving as slowly as possible. It was exhausting, and after what felt like forever, his head hit the underside of the platform. He climbed through the slats to stand on the ladder and then pulled himself up to stand next to his mother.

Kade turned to look at Judeen and froze. She was looking at him as though she could see him. Kade moved forward slowly, watching the look on her face. He stopped directly in front of her and wondered if this was another trap. He considered turning and going back down, suspecting that he was being deceived, but decided he had come too far to just leave before knowing for sure. And besides, if she was a trap, he would have already been caught.

Closing his eyes, Kade used the Reveal Calling to check for anything that did not look right. Nothing seemed out of the ordinary. There was only his mother. He reached out and put his hand on her arm. It was taut with tension as she hung from the beam, but she still managed a weak smile.

"Mother?" Kade whispered, but she did not answer. "Mother," he repeated and then remembered the Silence Calling. He dismissed the calling from just himself while keeping it intact for the dragon and its riders.

Kade moved close to his mother and whispered in her ear, "Mother." Before she could respond, he whispered, almost too quietly for her to hear, even though she was just inches from his mouth. "Shhhhh. Don't talk yet." With that, Kade performed the Silence Calling for him and his mother. As soon as he felt the calling take hold, he relaxed and breathed a deep sigh. "Hello Mother."

"Hello Son. I knew you would come," she barely croaked, but there was something in her voice. Hope? Maybe even a touch of amusement, and of course, a fair share of defiance. It made his heart feel good to hear this much life still in her.

"We cannot be heard, Mother. You may speak without fear of discovery."

"My son," she said, still staying quiet. There was deep affection in her voice.

"I've come to get you out of here," Kade said as he studied the ropes binding her wrists.

"You can't. There is a very evil man by the name of Morg that is waiting for you to try. He has men all over town, watching like hawks." She made a sound that most likely was a chuckle and then continued on. "It sounds like you have stirred things up," she said with a lisp through a split lip. Kade gasped, recalling his grandfather's note.

"Morg? That is who is behind this?" Kade asked, feeling his heart pound like mad. "Don't worry mother. I am going to do more than stir things up when I am done," Kade said as he performed the Healing Calling. He let it flow and she sighed.

"You have been busy learning I see," she said in approval. Kade smiled despite the situation.

"I have a plan," Kade said, excited to have a name to put to the evil.

"There is no room for mistakes, Kade. I fear what he will do if he catches you."

"Then we shall make no mistakes," Kade said with confidence. There was a growl in his voice.

"Morg has been here for a day, waiting for you. You have him…worried is best how to put it. He even has a healthy fear of you, if that makes any sense. But I do not think he wants you dead. He needs you for something."

"He has good reason to fear me, Mother. He killed Zayle and I am going to make him pay for that. She gasped and Kade could feel the sadness come off her in waves. He chastised himself for being such a fool. This was not the right time for that kind of information. "I am sorry Mother, but we must focus. Please," he said, feeling her pain. The last part of what she said had his mind whirling.

Need me for what? he asked himself. He dismissed the thought completely and refocused on their situation.

"He told us that he killed Zayle, but we did not believe him. It did not make sense to us that he would kill Zayle and not be able to handle an apprentice. We believed he was just trying to scare us, but now I see that he spoke the truth," she said, sounding on the verge of tears. "He kept asking us where you were, but we would not tell him. We could not tell him, even if we wanted," Judeen said and paused. After a moment's hesitation, she continued. "Zayle made it very clear that it was imperative that no one know where you were," she said, her voice gaining a small amount of control. She swallowed the tears and forced herself to be strong. There would be time enough for grieving later. That was the mother he knew. Her personality was one like a mountain. When she needed to be strong, there was no moving her.

Kade could tell she was trying to hide her fear and the sadness, but he could see it in her eyes. He was always able to see the truth in those windows to her soul no matter what she said. He smiled a reassuring smile, forgetting that she couldn't see him.

"Here is the plan. I am going to use a Transparency Calling to hide you from sight. No one will be able to see or hear you. It will look like you are gone. I have to be able to make both you and Father disappear at the same moment, or they will know I am here. When they start to search for you, I will free you and Father."

Kade looked up at the ropes and desperately wanted to remove them. She was just inches off the platform but inches or feet did not matter. The ropes were cutting into her wrist, causing her to bleed. After a few seconds of consideration, he decided a few more moments of discomfort were worth the price of her freedom.

"Mother, how did you know I was here?" Kade asked, trying to keep the suspicion out of his voice.

"That was easy," she said with a slight smile. "Look down there."

At first, Kade did not know what he was supposed to see, and then it made sense. He was able to see right where the dragon was standing, even in the dark. There were tracks in the street where the dragon's claws had scraped the ground, making them visible, especially from up on the tower.

"That does not explain how you knew it was me," Kade asked, watching her closely.

"Morg thought we knew about your dragon. When he asked where you were, he always asked where you and your dragon were. Of course we didn't know you had a dragon until he told us," she said with a sly smile. "We are good at listening. And besides, you are my son. I could feel it was you," she said with such fondness that Kade felt a rush of emotions.

He felt himself relax. It made enough sense that he let his suspicions go. He stepped forward and lightly put his arms around her and whispered, "I will get you out shortly. You will have to stay here just a little longer," Kade said as he performed the Healing Calling again. "Once Morg has left town looking for us, I will come back and get you down," he reassured her as he scanned the area. His mother did not respond. Kade turned to go and gave her one last look before grabbing the edge of the platform and lowering himself down to the ladder. He made sure to be as cautious going down as he was going up the ladder. Once on the ground, he performed the Reveal Calling and worked his way past the traps and back to the dragon.

Kade decided to go to his father and explain the plan to him first, before putting it into motion. From his father's platform, he would then try to use the Transparency Calling on his mother. He only hoped that Morg was not clever enough to alter the callings he used on each tower.

"I'm back," Kade said as he walked into the dragon. Rayden flinched hard and swung his head around to take several quick sniffs before relaxing. "Darcienna?" Kade called and then realized what was happening. He quickly dismissed both Silence Callings and then performed it again so they were all under the same one. "Darcienna?"

"Kade? You had us worried when you did not answer," Darcienna said, breathing hard.

"I had to recast the Silence Calling but enough about that. We need to get to my Father, now."

"I am just happy you are okay. I was starting to worry," Darcienna said, concern in her voice.

Kade mounted the dragon and directed it to the other tower. It felt like it took forever as Rayden carefully picked up each foot and put it down again very slowly. Kade explained the plan to Darcienna as they worked their way to his father. He stopped well clear of the traps and dismounted.

After studying the callings surrounding the second structure, Kade readied himself to disarm them as he had done at his mother's tower. He sent the Divine to do his bidding and quickly scanned the ground. To his dismay, there was no gap. All callings were still intact. Kade felt his pulse start to quicken. Taking a deep breath to help himself focus, he closed his eyes and performed the Disarm Calling once more. To his horror, there was no change. Kade slowly looked up to his father, yearning desperately to get to him.

He fought down the panic and studied the traps once more, hoping to find that he had missed something. Everything still looked the same. There had to be something.

Why would Morg place two different sets of traps? He wouldn't, Kade thought. *He would use the best he has.*

Kade closed his eyes, performed the Reveal Calling and started to work his way around the tower. As he rounded the far side, he saw it. There was a narrow path to the tower where one of the traps had disarmed.

Breathing a sigh of relief, Kade made it past the callings easily. This time, he was able to slide right up to the tower without opening his eyes. He relaxed slightly as he slid through the slats and stood in the middle.

Kade was worried as he still had not seen his father move. He gripped the lowest board and pulled himself up. The wood creaked so loudly that Kade was sure someone was going to come running to investigate. If his father was not alive, this was definitely going to bring them for there would be no reason for the tower to creak so loudly. It was a small bit of comfort when nothing stirred in the darkness. After letting out his breath, he continued. It took much longer this time as Kade put extra effort in not causing any more sounds. By the time he reached the underside of the platform, his lungs were burning from the effort. He reached for the ladder and swung himself up, still trying to be quiet. He carefully stepped on each rung as he inched his way higher, eager to put his plan into motion.

Kade pulled himself onto the platform and found himself face to face with the limp figure bound to a beam. Just like his mother, Garig's feet were just inches from the platform. There was a lot of dried blood, making his face almost unrecognizable. Kade could see the bruising on his ribs through the tattered shirt, indicating broken ribs. Kade felt his heart fill with sadness as he regarded the face of the one man that he had always looked up to and respected more than almost any other man alive. Zayle was the only other man that had gained Kade's respect to the level his father had.

He let the Silence Calling dissipate from himself and then recast it around him and his father. He quickly called on the Divine and used the Healing Calling on his father. The power sank into the flesh and faded. Still, there was no movement from the man. Kade

271

leaned closer to listen for breathing and thought he could hear just a wisp of breath. He performed the calling again and placed his hands on his father for the second time. He felt him move ever so slightly.

"Father, can you hear me?" Kade asked the still figure. "Father!" Kade said more insistently.

Garig slowly opened his right eye. His left was completely swollen shut. He struggled to focus as if he were coming out of a daze. He raised his head with some difficulty, trying to search for the source of the voice. Kade could see the pain in his eyes as he tried to turn his head, looking left and right. Anger was there waiting to take over but Kade took a deep breath and let it out. It was not enough to calm his rage. It started to build. The best Kade could hope for was to keep it in check, but as he looked at his father's face, he knew the anger was not going away anytime soon. The Divine was like a raging river pounding on a dam, trying to break through. Kade focused to keep what logical sense he had left.

"Son, is that you?" Garig asked through swollen lips. His voice was strained as he struggled through a coughing fit. Kade performed the healing again and placed his hands on his father's head. The swelling visibly melted and Garig's eyes seemed to become sharper. There was even fire in that look.

"Yes Father, I am here," Kade said as he placed his hand on the bruised arm, careful not to put any real weight on it.

"You must keep your voice down, Son," Garig hissed, barely audible. "Kade, you have to get out of here. They have traps set up all over the place to catch you. There are men in every store, waiting. You have to leave now! Morg is expecting you to come. We are bait, Son. Don't let him win. You must leave now!" Garig pleaded.

He was frantic, trying his best to persuade his son to leave before another second passed. Kade felt the anger and it engulfed his heart. He wanted desperately to call on the Divine Power and unleash its full fury. The dam started to break as the Divine called to him. He

272

took a deep breath, and steeled his will, forcing the Divine to do as he commanded before its temptation took too strong a hold. It was too late. It refused to go. Kade wrestled with it but it came rushing at him as the dam broke. Kade felt it calling to him to use it, to wield its might, to bend it to his will, or was it him bending to its will? He held it in check as he forced it to do as he commanded. For now, he was in control.

"Yes, I am aware, Father. Mother told me much of this," Kade said in a growl. "Don't worry about them hearing us. I have cast a calling that hides all sound. Morg is not the only one who can control the Divine Power," Kade said as he flexed and relaxed his fists, fighting desperately to keep from allowing the Divine to consume him completely. The amount of power racing through him was staggering. His special gift was causing the Divine to rage through him, making it almost impossible to think.

He heard his father inhale sharply. Kade ground his teeth hard in sheer determination in an effort to keep control. He wanted desperately to dance the moves to a calling and send the Divine out to destroy, but it was not the right time. His muscles twitched and convulsed as he fought to keep his arms at his sides. Callings flashed through his mind in rapid succession.

"You…can call on the Great Divine Power? Kade…," Garig started to say but was at a loss for words. Was that fear or something else underneath his father's words? Without skipping a beat, Garig changed the subject. "Your mother? You talked with her? Is she ok?" he asked in a rush.

Kade could not ignore the way his father reacted to his use of the Divine. He thought about Garig's reaction and was not sure if it was good or bad. *Was it fear or respect? Or, was it something else?* He decided to return to this topic at a later time.

"Yes, Father. She is on the other tower." Kade felt frustration, but he knew he had to keep thinking as best as he was able or everything he was working for could fall apart. He tried to sound calm and confident for his father.

"What do you plan to do?" Garig asked. It was obvious he was still hurting considerably as his head sagged forward to rest on his chest while he struggled to breath.

"Just hold on a little while longer, Father," Kade said. He eagerly sent more Divine Healing into the suffering man. Garig gasped hard as the calling raced through his body. Giving the Divine release helped Kade get a firmer hold on it. "I'm going to make you and Mother vanish at the same time. It will look like you have already escaped," he said, feeling more in control again.

"Ahhhhh. I see. So you are trying to fool him into thinking we have escaped while we are still here?"

"Yes, and when that happens, he will go looking for you. Then, we will go free Mother and I will get you both out of here," Kade said.

"Dangerous, Kade. Very dangerous, but I am ready when you are." Garig said with confidence. He even seemed eager to see this put into motion.

"Be ready," Kade said.

"Son, what have you been doing to me? I am almost completely healed," Garig said in awe. Kade grinned ever so slightly. The Divine slowed a little more.

"I have been using the Power to heal you. It should take away most of the damage and help with the pain, but it won't fix everything. Your body has to do the rest, but it will keep you alive," Kade said as he worked his way to the edge of the platform. "I have to finish with the rest of my plan. My dragon is down there, waiting for me," Kade said.

"So it's true?" Garig said, incredulously. "You really do have a dragon? But...how? Wait. Save that for later. What now?" he asked, gaining strength by the moment.

Kade looked down where the dragon was and cringed. *How could we have not been discovered?* he thought. If Morg had put men on the towers, they would have been done. Seeing the tracks easily, he was far from confident that they would go undiscovered.

"Now, I send the dragon away. Darcienna is not going to like this, but it is for the best. I will weather her wrath later," Kade said and almost flinched at the onslaught he was sure to get.

"Darcienna?"

"Another long story, Father. I have much to tell. Now, we focus on this. I need a moment to send the dragon away."

Rayden, Kade thought, as he reached out for the mind of his faithful companion. *You must go back the way we came. Go into the woods and work your way north until you reach the river. Enter the river and follow it. That should hide your scent and keep you from being tracked. The river will lead around to the southeast. Follow it until it bends to the left and wait for me there.*

Kade sensed Rayden's apprehension. He was expecting this. The Apprentice Chosen would have resisted also, so he was ready with his response.

At any moment, there are going to be many people overrunning the town, and they are going to find you. You need to be gone. You must trust me, my friend. It is very important, or we may be caught. The dragon was reluctant, and Kade could feel its intense worry, but he knew Rayden was going to do his best to follow the instructions.

Darcienna was going to skin him alive when she saw him again, but he knew if he told her of his plan, she would have fought tooth-and-nail to stay. He grinned despite himself. Kade returned to his father and looked him over once more for any critical wounds that needed immediate attention. He was completely shocked to see none at all. He turned to survey the town.

"Okay Father, it's going to be a little while before I can free you. Be ready," Kade said as he scanned the area. "Is there anything you can tell me about Morg while we wait?"

"Just that he wanted to find you at all cost. He is dangerous, Kade. You must be careful."

"He fears me, Father. He fears me and there has to be a reason."

"Kade, stay away from him. I have seen what he can do." Kade did not respond. "Son, it's not that I think you can't handle yourself. This man is evil and he will not hesitate to kill. The amount of power he wields is indescribable."

"I know, Father. I know," Kade said as the Divine slowed to a manageable level.

He knelt down on the platform as he continued to scan the town. Every so often, he would see a black shape step out of a shadow, and then, just as quickly, disappear. He could not help but to grin, knowing he was right under their noses.

Kade knew he might not be as powerful as Morg, but he believed he was more than a challenge as long as he continued to think his way through this. He looked up at the sky to see the position of the moon, trying to calculate how much time had passed, but could not even fathom a guess.

Rayden, let me know when you are in position, Kade thought. There was nothing. Kade took a deep breath, focused his attention hard and sent the thought again. He was about to give up when, very faintly, he got a response. He was not sure if he was really hearing the dragon, or if it was just wishful thinking, but he had to believe it was Rayden. He held his breath and reached out for the dragon's mind, again. It was so faint he would not have connected if he was not so focused, but it was there. *Let me know when you are in position,* Kade sent.

"Kade?" Garig started to ask but Kade quickly cut him off.

"I am sorry Father, but I must focus. This is critical," Kade

276

said as he listened intently for the dragon's response. It seemed to take forever, but Rayden finally made contact. "It's time. Are you ready?" Kade asked as his heart started to pound.

"I am," Garig said, his voice a mix of excitement and fear.

Kade moved to the edge of the platform and focused on the other tower. He took a deep breath and performed the Transparency Calling, sending the Divine Power to his mother. He looked closely and was shocked to see she was still visible. Kade shook his head, took another deep breath and performed the calling once more. Again, it failed. Kade felt a knot grow in his stomach. Fear worked its way into his heart. Fear of failure and no back-up plan was causing him to doubt. It had to work.

I am too close to freeing my parents to fail, Kade thought angrily. He curled his lips as he fumed. He cast the calling again, but it made no difference. She was still in plain sight.

Kade clenched his fist as he turned to look at his father. Anger exploded in him. He was not going to allow this evil man to lay one more hand on his parents. Kade felt the Divine Power growing as his anger increased. He clenched his fist, and when he was on the verge of losing his last sense, a vague hint of an idea worked its way into his mind. Kade grabbed ahold of the Divine with a vengeance. He completed the calling and directed it at his mother. She faded out of sight. Stunned, Kade felt the power snap into place and it was his. He spun quickly and performed the calling on his father. He, too, disappeared.

Retrieving the knife from his boot, Kade turned and lunged for his father's ropes. He gave a mental thanks to Dran for the knife. He ran his hands up his father's right arm to find the rope and frantically sawed through it. Garig's feet hit the floor with a thud but thanks to the calling, none heard the sound. As Kade was reaching for the next arm, he saw a figure slide out from an alley, cautiously moving toward his mother's tower.

"What next, Son?" Garig whispered.

"We work our way to the bottom and we stay under the tower," Kade said as he watched the man drift closer and closer to the tower. The man then turned and ran to the tower they were on, stopping just at the edge of the traps. Kade felt as if the man were looking directly at him. The apprentice froze. The man edged a little closer as he peered up at the empty beam. Kade felt his father work his way across the tower to the ladder, but before Garig could start down, Kade hissed, "Wait!"

Several more shadows drifted out into the open and it was not long before an alarm was sounded. Kade felt his pulse pound so hard he could hear it in his ears. He reached for his father, found his arm and pulled him away from the ladder.

"We can't go down, yet," Kade hissed as he recalled the way the tower squeaked. That would, most definitely, call attention to themselves with the number of people filling the streets. "And, if that man is able to come up, he would meet us on the way down." There were more than twenty men and the numbers were growing by the moment.

Kade felt the structure shift slightly and inhaled sharply as he pulled his father to the back of the tower. So close to succeeding, and yet, even closer to failing. Kade embraced the Divine Power and prepared to use it. The tower shifted rhythmically as someone climbed the steps. A head appeared at the edge of the platform. The man stopped and looked closely at the beam that had previously held a prisoner. He eased himself onto the platform and moved over to where his father had hung, running his hand over the wood. The man spun and ran to the edge, staring intently at the other tower.

"They are gone!" he screamed frantically. "They are gone!"

Kade could sense fear coming off the man in waves. A figured stepped out of the shadow, slowly, and all the other men gave him a wide birth. The man on the platform shifted nervously.

"You let them escape?" the man asked quietly but his voice carried throughout the town. He looked up at the man on the tower and pointed at him. Kade could see the one just a few feet away start to shake. His bladder let loose as he wet himself. Kade wrinkled his nose in disgust.

"They just disappeared. I was watching the whole time, but they just vanished," he said in desperation. His voice broke and the last word came out as a squeak. Kade did not need to see the man to know he swallowed hard as he tried to speak. The man in the street took two steps toward the tower and aimed something. The other men nearby scattered. The one on the tower gasped and reached for his neck. He backed across the tower, turning red in the face, clearly unable to breath. Kade tried to slip by him but was not quick enough. Man and apprentice collided. He spun around still scratching at his neck. There was blood where his nails had raked his skin. The man's eyes widened as his hand shot out and touched Kade in the chest. Kade could see the man's eyes go wide as realization hit him. He stumbled to the edge of the tower and then fell over, hitting the ground with a thud, taking his discovery with him.

"Morg," Garig said so quietly that Kade barely heard.

Kade watched as the figure walked to the tower where his mother was and stood, studying the ground. He tensed, hoping with all his heart that Morg would not climb the tower. The man slowly walked around the structure while his small army stood by, nervously fidgeting. He stopped at the narrow pathway where the one calling had been neutralized and followed it with his eyes.

Kade could still feel the Divine Power swirling in him like a calm stream…waiting ominously. He closed his eyes and completed the Reveal Calling. He watched as the traps surrounding the tower faded out completely. Morg circled the structure and put a hand on the ladder.

"Stay still, Father. Do not move until I say," Kade said as he walked to the edge of the platform. He planted his feet firmly and prepared to cast his most powerful calling. He watched intently as Morg started up the ladder. Kade began the moves for the calling. He was at the seventh move when a man yelled out.

"Here," the man yelled as he studied the ground. "Here," he said again with excitement.

Morg stopped just short of the platform and looked at the man. Instead of going back down, he turned, studying the platform just above him. He moved up another step, his head barely above the edge. Kade moved onto the eighth move. Two more moves and there was no turning back.

"I found something!" the man said urgently.

Morg paused for a moment more and then quickly started down the ladder. Kade almost let out a cry of relief as he froze at the end of the ninth move. His arms shaking, he dropped them to his side.

Morg stopped in front of the man who was down with one knee on the ground. He was looking up at Morg like a child who looks up at a parent, waiting for approval. Morg slowly knelt down to study the ground. After several long moments, he stood and turned to look at all the men. A few of them started to plead for their lives and backed away with their hands up protectively. Kade felt sorry for them, but he would not help them if he could. They deserved this.

Morg was shaking with rage as he glared hard at the men. Kade could feel the fury from where he stood and cringed, grateful he was not at the end of that glare. He took an involuntary step back. Kade could feel Morg drawing on the power and it scared him. There was something different about it. He could not explain it, but he knew his father had been telling the truth. This man was more than deadly.

"Find them!" Morg screamed like a mad man. "They went that way," he raged as he pointed the way Rayden had gone. "They got away right under your noses, you fools!" he yelled as he aimed something at them. The small army of men raced in the direction the dragon had gone, frantically trying to push past each other. The two buildings on either side of the alley exploded. The few men not fast enough to make it through the alley never had to fear Morg again. They died with the explosion, and Kade was sure that many of them welcomed their deaths.

Morg held something out in front of himself, gripping it in both hands. Kade felt the Divine flow and then he hissed harshly as the amulet turned into a scalding piece of metal. He leaned forward to let the protective necklace hang away from his skin. After a moment, Morg dropped his arms and the amulet cooled. Morg let out a yell of rage.

Morg stood with his feet apart, his left arm at his side, while his right hand clenched something but Kade could not quite make it out. Debris was still raining down, but Morg did not appear to notice. Several large pieces bounced off him but he never flinched. The evil Chosen started forward when a grimalkin raced into town from the west. It ran up to Morg and put its head against the ground in an act of submission. Morg yelled for it to follow after the men, but as it stood, it whipped its head around to stare at the tower where Judeen was still held captive. It sniffed the air several times and then took a step in her direction.

Kade's gut twisted into a knot. He had no doubt that it had caught the scent of his mother. He hoped and prayed that it did not have the ability to communicate with Morg the way he and the dragon did. If so, this was going to turn into a disaster when it was on the brink of success. Morg started down the path after his men and yelled for the cat-like creature again, but it ignored him, and instead, took another step toward the tower.

Kade felt as though his nerves could not take any more. He focused on the beast as it moved forward another step. Morg

281

screamed in rage as he spun on the creature. Within moments, he had unleashed the Divine. The grimalkin writhed violently. Kade realized, in shock, that Morg could cast a calling that could crush the air out of anyone, or anything, and that was exactly what he was doing to this beast. It kicked out furiously, catching one of the support legs for the tower, causing it to explode in a shower of wood. The tower teetered dangerously. Kade gasped, expecting it to fall at any moment.

"Come," Morg commanded as he let the beast breath again.

"Father!" Kade hissed.

"I know. We have to get to her!" Garig said as he moved forward.

"Stay with me," Kade said as he reached for the ladder.

"What about the traps?"

"They are gone. Morg must have dismissed them for the man who came up," Kade said as he grabbed ahold of the ladder and started down as fast as he dared.

The tower creaked as they descended. Kade stepped around the still form of the man that had fallen from the tower and moved back, giving his father room. He waited until he felt his father hit the ground. As they turned for the other tower, the structure let out another creak, causing Kade to cringe as he held his breath.

"Run, Son! We have to hurry!" Garig said in a panic. Kade's heart pumped wildly at the urging from his father. They broke into a run and then slid to a stop at the tower. Fortunately, the support leg that was missing was opposite the ladder. Kade quickly grabbed ahold, climbed a few rungs and stopped, hoping his extra weight would keep the tower from toppling.

"I have this, Son," Garig said as he grabbed ahold of the ladder, urging his son to climb. Kade scrambled up, still fearing it would fall at any moment. He could feel the sweat run down his back as he reached the platform. Before climbing the rest of the way, he glanced over his shoulder to the other end of town and saw a movement. He froze as he watched. Kade felt his muscles go taut as he recognized the man by the way he moved. It was arrogance and power. There was only one man it could be. Kade could feel his heart pounding like mad. He was in no position to defend himself. He was at the mercy of fate now, and he knew it.

Kade felt his grip on the edge of the platform slip. He wiped his sweaty hands on his pants and reached back up for a firmer grip. He pulled himself up slowly, afraid the wood might creak, and also, afraid his weight might take them crashing to the ground.

"Mother, are you okay?" Kade asked. There was no response. Kade realized instantly why she had not answered, or at least hoped he knew why. He prepared to dismiss the Silence Calling but at the last moment, decided against it. Even though the medallion seemed to be working, he was not sure that Morg would not see the use of the Divine Power or sense it, since he was this close.

Kade moved forward and reached out for his mother. He found her arms and gave a gentle squeeze of reassurance. He was relieved when she responded to his touch. He reached down, retrieved his knife from his boot, and then followed her arms up to the ropes. He stood on his toes as he grabbed ahold of the bindings, trying not to injure his mother's already raw wrists. He carefully sawed through, making sure not to cut her. As he sliced through the last of the rope, she slipped from his grasp and dropped to the platform. Kade flinched, waiting to hear his mother land with a thud, but it never came. The Silence Calling he had cast previously was still in place. He breathed a sigh of relief until he felt the tower shift ever so slightly.

Judeen weakly reached up to find Kade's searching hand and struggled to stand. He looked back in the direction where he had last seen Morg but found nothing. He decided he had to take the chance. He dismissed the Silence Calling, and then quickly reformed it. The tower creaked again. Kade felt the medallion on his chest turn ice cold. He reached up and gripped it tightly. After a moment, he let it fall back to his chest as his mother's voice popped into his ears.

"I don't think I have the strength to climb down," Judeen said, out of breath, obviously struggling.

"Easy, Mother. I am not going to leave you. I have come too far to give up now. Either we all get out, or none of us do, but we stay together. This should help," Kade said as he performed the Healing Calling. He found her head and let the power melt into her. Her hand came up to his hand and she held it briefly.

"Yes, Zayle was able to teach you a few things," she said with a little more strength. Kade felt relief at the improvement in her voice.

"Mother, I know he is my grandfather," Kade said, dispelling any further need to deceive him. She gasped and for just a moment, Kade feared she may start to cry.

Once again, Kade felt the medallion go cold, but this time, it was colder than before. He was afraid he might be pushing its limits and decided not to press his luck. So far, it appeared to be keeping them safe.

A loud creak emanated from the other tower. Kade's head whipped around to see a black, cloaked figure climbing the ladder. Time was running out. If that figure came to this tower next, everything they had worked for was done.

Kade felt his mother move, and at the same moment, the tower leaned a little further. He quickly pulled her toward the ladder to shift the weight of the structure. For the moment, it stopped its fall. That was the best they were going to get. The tower was coming down, but the question was, would they get off in time.

"We must hurry! Hurry, Mother, hurry!"

"Kade, I am not sure if I have the strength, but I will try."

"Now! We must climb down, now! Father is trying to keep

the tower from falling, but he can't hold it for long" Kade said as he climbed over the edge onto the ladder. "I will go first, in case I need to catch you, but we must hurry. I know I am asking a lot, but it is important to try to be careful. Morg cannot hear us but he can hear if the tower makes a sound, so be careful."

"Then we need to go," she said, trying to sound confident. Kade could hear the doubt in her voice.

He moved slowly as he worked his way down each rung. Even with his extra strength, he still found it strenuous to move carefully. He could not imagine why his mother did not just collapse and fall but she kept pace and kept her footing. At one point, the tower gave a slight creak, threatening to topple, but it was not enough to get Morg's attention...yet.

Kade was almost at the bottom when he stepped on something that squirmed under his foot. He flinched slightly, realizing it must have been his father's hand. He could feel movement below him and guessed his father was going down. He tentatively put his foot back on the rung and found it clear as was every rung until he was touching solid ground. He reached up to feel for his mother and found her leg. As she stepped down, he put his hand on her back to give her support just as she collapsed.

A loud groan made Kade look up as the tower leaned dangerously. He quickly turned, searching frantically for his father. Since he and his mother were not under the same Silence Calling as his father, finding the man was going to be difficult. Kade desperately wanted to recast the Silence Calling to include his father, but with Morg so close, it would be foolish at best.

"Mother, stay with me!" Kade said, his voice thick with panic. "We must find Father!"

He turned toward a side alley, praying his father went in that direction. As he started toward the narrow path between the buildings, the fifty-foot structure creaked loudly and continued to

285

moan as it picked up speed in its fall. It was coming down. He turned in time to see it topple and hit the ground with a loud crash. Kade's head turned so quickly toward the other tower, you would have thought he had been slapped. As he feared, Morg had moved to the edge of the platform to stare at the fallen structure. Kade knew, without a doubt, that it was only moments until Morg would be there. He watched in alarm as Morg quickly swung over the platform and descended the ladder so fast it almost looked like he was falling.

"Morg is coming!" Judeen screamed. Kade felt his heart racing and panic threatened to overwhelm him.

With a firm grip on his mother's hand, he turned to run for the alley, but before taking two steps, he bounced off an unseen, solid object, sending it sprawling. Kade knew instantly that it was his father and quickly scrambled forward. Just as Morg hit the ground, Kade's hand closed on a leg. Morg was moving toward them at a run. Kade found his father's arm, and with more strength than he had intended, jerked him to his feet. With an iron grip on both his mother and father's wrist, he raced for the alley. Just as he was leaving the main road, Morg let out a yell. Kade glanced over his shoulder and saw Morg pull something from under his cloak. The street was instantly a dust storm. Buildings started to rattle dangerously, and signs flew by impaling walls and trees. If the small party had been in the street, they would have been sent flying. Buildings started to give way as the wind increased considerably.

The ground started to erupt randomly, sending dirt flying in all directions. Kade was amazed at the amount of callings that Morg was able to cast so quickly. This just had to be impossible. Callings this powerful had to require too many moves. The more powerful the calling, the more difficult it was to perform, and the more complex the steps involved. This calling that Morg was using had to be immensely powerful and very intricate, but they were coming so fast it was impossible, and yet…they were happening.

Kade raced out of the alley and into an open area with very little cover. He stopped just behind one of the trees and quickly released the Silence Calling he was under, also releasing the one his father was under. His heart was pounding so hard from fear he thought it would burst.

"Father," Kade whispered frantically. For just a moment, he wanted to be the kid again who counted on the parent for safety and then it passed. It was up to him and he knew it.

"Blood and ash, Son!" Garig swore loudly. Kade quickly shook his parents free, and as fast as possible, performed the Silence Calling to include them all. "What happened back there? I tried to talk to you but you were not answering!"

"Father, I can't explain right now, but I need you to stay calm while I work on getting us out of here," Kade pleaded, trying to keep his own fears in check.

Before they could take one step, the ground exploded just behind them, sending Kade and his parents sprawling. Kade looked over his shoulder in time to see Morg exit the alley and aim something at them, as he spoke in the ancient language. Another blast struck the ground just past his head and set off an explosion so loud that Kade's ears range violently. It was impossible for him to focus as his eyes rolled back in his head from the concussion. There was dust and dirt showering the area, blurring his vision. Kade shook his head and then his anger and hate erupted. The Divine Power crashed into him, filling every part of his being. He let it consume him. He welcomed it. The more hate he felt, the more of the Divine coursed through his veins, matching his fury. It was a raging torrent of power that demanded to be used and Kade was not going to deny it any longer. If Morg wanted a fight, then so be it.

He is soon to find out that he is not the only one who can command the Divine! Kade thought vehemently.

Kade launched into a move that would have left the most

practiced dancer in awe. Lightning burst forth from his hands in an explosion that could be heard for miles. It raced toward its intended target with blinding speed. The concussion shook the ground and Morg's eyes flew wide. At the very last possible moment, the evil Chosen waved something in front of himself. The bolt slammed violently into the man, sending him through the wall of the building behind him. Garig felt hope as he watched his son deal his share of justice. His ears rang furiously, but he was more than ok with it. But, to Kade's complete horror, the evil Chosen emerged from the wreckage of the building.

Kade felt the anger and hate grow even more, and he welcomed it. He let the blackness take him completely and the power consumed him. He spun into his next calling and Divine Fire shot forth. Kade felt the adrenaline coursing through his body and felt invincible. At that moment, he felt power beyond his wildest dreams. His gift was alive, firing rapidly. The flash from the lightning had him seeing stars, but he never slowed. He wished with all his being that he had another devastating calling to use, but it was not to be. He returned to the Lightning Calling, and just as he let loose, something tore into his shoulder, sending him reeling. He hit the ground hard and rolled, coming to one knee with his right foot planted firmly. He tried to raise his arm but it was dangling uselessly at his side. Kade looked up through pain filled eyes to see that Morg had staggered from the impact of the lightning.

At least some of it had an effect, Kade thought. Something shimmered around Morg and then winked out. The evil man's cloak was smoking and his hair was singed. The Master Chosen struggled to stand and was soon on his feet.

"Son!" Judeen screamed in horror. "Son, where are you?"

Kade looked on as the feeling of euphoria was replaced with horror. *How could Morg have survived that?* he thought with despair. *No! NO!* Kade thought as he slowly stood. He still had his strength, and if he had to die while strangling Morg with his one good arm, then so be it.

"You almost got away with it," Morg said as he pointed at them with his right hand and brushed his badly torn cloak with his other. "I could have found you sooner, you know. But, better later than never, I say. You can drop the calling," Morg said with arrogance enough for ten men. "It was that tower falling that got my attention. My pet wanting to get to it made me think. It all made sense," he said as he barked a laugh.

Kade squinted to see through the dust but he could not make out what it was he was seeing. Was Morg holding something or were his eyes playing tricks on him? He could not get his vision to clear, but it did not matter. With his increased strength came an increase in speed. He judged the distance and prepared to charge.

"Kade," Garig said.

"Mother, Father, you must stay silent. No matter what, when I make my next move, you need to run for all you're worth. Run or all I have done will be for nothing. Find Darcienna," Kade said, leaving no room for argument.

"Kade," Garig said, as he found his son's good shoulder.

If it had been the other one, that touch would have sent him to the ground in agony. There may be no physical pain in that touch, but the feel of his father's hand made his failure hurt. He wished his parents didn't trust him as much as they did. Now, he knew he was going to let them down, and they were all dead because of him. Kade felt his rage return, and his determination to rip the life right out of Morg redoubled. The pain in his shoulder dulled considerably as the Divine Power returned in full. It might not be useful as a weapon right then, but it did dull the pain. Kade flexed his legs, ready to charge no matter the consequences.

"No, Father! Right now, I am in charge and it is my plan. If you do not do as I say, then Mother will die," Kade said, playing on his father's protective role as a husband. He knew he was putting his father in a position he could not refuse, but it had to be done. Judeen sobbed Kade's name once but he ignored it and refocused on Morg.

"Give up young one. You have no chance," Morg said with a sneer.

Kade was certain that Morg only wanted him to drop the calling so the evil Chosen could look him in the eye as his life was violently torn from him. At that moment, Kade would have given anything to rip the life from this man, but he knew it would take a miracle for that to happen. He crouched, ready to spring, hoping he would give his parents the much needed diversion to escape. It was all he had left and he was going to make the best of it.

"Have it your way," Morg said boldly.

As the evil Chosen raised his arm and started to speak the ancient language, Kade launched. Something black flew from the dark, landing on Morg and raked his face with its razor sharp claws. It sank its teeth viciously into his shoulder and tore. Kade had only taken two steps when he skidded to a stop. In the next instant, he realized the creature was a fraction of a second too late as the blast raced directly for him. He only had time to grit his teeth, hoping to survive the impact.

CH10

A bright, blue explosion blinded Kade and sent him sprawling to the ground. He gasped as he lay on his back, half blinded from the flash. He was clenching his jaw and every muscle in his body so tightly that he trembled. His mind raced through his arms and legs, checking for pain and injuries. There was nothing more than the throbbing in his shoulder. He quickly ran his good hand over his chest, and feeling nothing, leapt to his feet. But that would mean…something had intercepted the calling. Something unseen had come to his aid. And then…his eyes focus on the familiar, green barrier directly in front of him.

Kade recognized Darcienna's shield. He turned to see the green light coming from a spot thirty feet behind him. An image of her holding out her hands popped into his head. It was short lived as the pain from his shoulder drew his attention.

Kade struggled to his feet and quickly ran to where he had left his parents. He looked back and saw Morg swing at something that was no longer there. The shiny, black animal was already gone. Kade decided the next time he saw that beautiful creature he was going to feed it until its stomach burst.

"Mother, Father, follow the green light. Hurry," Kade said through clenched teeth as he drew on the Divine Power. If nothing else, it was good for numbing the pain.

Rayden, be ready, Kade thought as he stopped next to the green light that appeared to be coming out of thin air. He lifted the Silence Calling and heard a roar that he was sure was going to make his head throb for hours. He considered keeping the Transparency Calling but it was going to be virtually impossible to get his parents on the dragon, much less get Rayden to understand what was going on if he kept it intact. Regretfully, he let the calling go and everyone shimmered into view. Darcienna had her hands up with the green energy radiating from them. Her son was looking over her shoulder, wide-eyed. Kade looked upon Darcienna's face and thought it was the most beautiful thing he had ever seen. He needed her and she was there.

"Rayden, I know I am asking a lot, but I have two more that need to go with us. These are my parents. Please allow them to ride," Kade said. He was relieved to see Rayden kneel quickly. Kade turned to see both Garig and Judeen standing there, speechless, as they looked on in awe.

"Kade!" Darcienna exclaimed as she saw his shoulder. He waived away her concern, but he had to do it with his left hand.

"Mother, Father, get on!" Kade yelled. "Now!" he commanded as he propelled them forcefully toward the dragon. "You will sit in front of the wings and we shall sit behind," he added.

Kade looked over his shoulder, waiting for the ground to explode around them at any second. The man was nowhere to be seen. Kade closed his eyes and used the Reveal Calling. He was shocked to find nothing.

Why would he just leave? Kade thought, and then he recalled the dripping, green ooze he had seen coming from Chance's fangs when they had first met.

"He is poisoned!" Kade said with hope. "Let's get out of here."

Kade went to help lift his father up and stopped, clenching his teeth hard as the pain racked his shoulder. Although the Divine Power did a great job of numbing the pain, it did not keep it away. Pain or no pain, he was not using that shoulder. Kade sagged to the ground, waiting for the agony to lessen.

"What would you do without me?" Darcienna asked, her voice dripping with sarcasm. "And yes, we are going to have a very long talk about that stunt. If you think this was bad, wait until I get done with you," she said as she laid her hands on his shoulder.

That familiar, uncomfortable squeezing that happened as his muscles pulsed and writhed, spread all through his shoulder. He winced as the damage mended itself right before his eyes. Kade smiled weakly at her as she glared furiously at him. He was sure she meant everything she had said and wondered if giving up to Morg might have been a better choice.

After several long moments, Darcienna took her hands away and staggered over to the dragon, panting hard. Kade flexed his shoulder and found it tender but it was usable. He quickly moved back to his father and lifted him easily onto the dragon to sit in front of the wings. He then lifted his mother up to sit in front of Garig.

"Darcienna, are you okay?" Kade asked. She turned and glared at him so hard he hesitated to get within striking distance. She was every bit of fire and ice all rolled into one. Her hands were balled into fists and Kade was sure she was considering delivering a clubbing he would not forget. "I will take that as a yes," Kade said, keeping his distance.

"You could have died if I were not here to save you, you empty-headed flea brain," Darcienna scolded hotly.

"But, I needed you and the dragon to get out of town. There is no chance they would not have found the dragon," Kade pleaded as he glanced back where Morg had been.

"Yes, fine then. Send the dragon away, but I could have stayed," Darcienna said adamantly.

Kade sighed, desperately wanting to be away from here as fast as possible. He shook his head and held his hand up to Darcienna before she could continue to speak. She clenched her jaw in anger as she glared daggers at him.

"Enough of this talk," he said firmly.

He vaulted onto Rayden's back and held his hand out for her. He was not sure if she was going to bite it or take it. She reluctantly passed on biting and took his hand. Kade easily swung her up to sit behind him, relieved and eager to be away.

"Rayden, head to the east," Kade said as he worked the Transparency Calling. He followed with the Silence Calling. The tree next to them exploded, sending shards of bark in all directions. *Obviously the poison was not going to solve our problems,* Kade thought. "Run Rayden, Run!"

The dragon launched as the ground erupted where they had just been standing. Kade was ready for the bolt of speed. He had quickly reached behind him and grabbed Darcienna's arms and wrapped them tightly around himself, knowing what was coming. Just as his father fell back against him with the added weight of his mother, he latched onto the boney wing-joint. Kade's muscles bulged hard as he strained to hold the weight of his parents along with Darcienna and the boy's. A vein bulged in his neck as he held on tightly. The dragon's back sloped dangerously behind the wings, making it more difficult to hold on. His sweating fingers were starting to slip but he had come too far to fail, especially with escape

294

this close. He pressed his lips together in sheer determination and closed his fingers around the bone. They reached their top speed rapidly, allowing him to relax his grip.

The blasts continued, but the more they ran, the less of the explosions he saw. Kade heard a scream of fury so intense that the hairs on the back of his neck stood up. He took a deep breath, looked where his parents sat and smiled to himself. He looked over his shoulder and knew he could not have done this alone.

Kade tuned out Darcienna's torrent of words as she hotly chastised him. Knowing that he had saved his parents right out from under Morg's nose was an intense satisfaction that allowed him to weather Darcienna's rage, for the time being. Sooner or later, she had to let up.

Kade marveled at Rayden's ability to carry so many people with hardly any effort. The dragon showed no sign of slowing, even with four people on its back. Well, five if the boy was to be counted. The ride behind the wings was a little bumpier for Kade because he was sitting right over the hind legs, but he wasn't complaining, considering the alternative. After an hour into their travel, Kade let the Transparency Calling go. That seemed to help everyone relax. Almost everyone. Darcienna was still angry as she glared daggers at him. She may no longer be yelling, but she was far from done talking.

"Kade, can you hear me? I will not let this go. Why didn't you tell me what you were planning? If I had known you were going to do something so foolish, I would not have let you go alone. Can you hear me?" Darcienna asked, barely taking a moment to breathe.

Kade considered not answering, but if he let her continue on like this, his parents were sure to think she was a tyrant. Of course it might be too late, but this constant verbal attack needed to end. He sighed and rolled his eyes, preparing to attempt to disarm the situation.

"Yes, I can hear you," Kade said, trying to assert that he was in charge.

"Well?" Darcienna asked.

"Well what?" Kade asked, feigning ignorance.

"Well, why did you do that?" Darcienna asked, exasperated that she had to explain when she was sure he knew very well what she was asking.

Before he could answer, he heard his name whispered while his parents talked. He was going to ignore them when he heard his mother say just a few words that got his attention. "Couples fight" and "work it out" and something like, "her side" but he could not make out much more. He narrowed his eyes as he studied the back of his parents' heads.

"Because I didn't want you to be in danger," Kade said as he returned his attention to Darcienna. "I needed you to be away so I wouldn't have to worry about your safety and my parents. And yes, I did know you would try to come with me. That's why I didn't tell you," Kade said roughly, angry at the fact that he felt like he had to defend himself. He was supposed to be the one in charge. She was supposed to do as he said. That was the rule. He considered making that clear when he noticed for the first time in a while she was not talking. Kade was going to continue on about how his word was law and that she was not to question his judgment when he heard a sound from her he hoped never to hear again. She was crying a cry that comes from deep within the heart. It was one of pain and loss. He immediately hated himself for causing it.

"I was worried you were going to be killed. I needed to be there to protect you," Darcienna said through her quiet sobs. "And, I could not get this stupid dragon of yours to do anything I said. When I tried to get off, he would growl at me. I even hit him with my fists, but he just ignored me. That's when I realized it was probably your idea to have the dragon leave like that. I thought we were going to be separated again, and it scared me," she said. She slumped in her seat as though her will had been broken. Kade felt a lump in his throat.

He wanted to tell her that he was wrong, and that he should have kept her with him just to make her feel better, but he knew it would be a lie. He knew his decision was right and she had to know, also. She had to.

What is she talking about? Is there more to this than I can see? he asked himself. The phrase, "I thought we were going to be separated again, and it scared me" kept going through his head. He couldn't remember leaving her anytime in the last few days no matter how hard he tried.

"I am sorry. I really am. I thought it was best. I needed you safe so I would not have to worry about you, and there was no way you and the dragon would remain undiscovered once the streets started to fill. As it was, Morg was able to find me, somehow," Kade said as he put his hand on her knee in an attempt to sooth her. "And, besides, it worked didn't it?" Kade asked and then stopped. His hand was still on her knee. He was about to remove it to avoid any awkwardness when he felt her hand cover his.

"With my help," Darcienna said so quietly that he almost missed it.

Kade soaked up the feel of her hand on his. His heart pumped with the thrill. For a brief moment, he considered moving his hand away but then quickly discarded the thought. *Besides,* he said to himself, *she might see it as a form of rejection and that just would not do.* And then, he hit on the perfect solution that would solve all this. He leaned back as he looked into her eyes and smiled.

"Thank you for saving my parent's lives. If you hadn't been there, they would have been killed. We all would have. Thank you, Darcienna," Kade said as he watched her closely for any mood change. She lifted her head and tilted it sideways as she studied him. A smile spread across her face.

"So...," she started to say, with a look in her eye that made Kade feel as if he had fallen into a trap. He could not say why, but the look in her eye was that of a hunter who had trapped its prey. He shrunk in his seat, waiting. "Since we clearly need each other," she said. Kade felt the snare spring. "We should discuss our plans together from now on so we can come up with what works best," she said triumphantly. Kade firmed his resolve and was about to let her know who was boss when he caught the, ever so slight, quiver at the corners of her mouth. Before he could speak one word, he saw it as clearly as the moon over his head. She was pretending. The real truth was, she was afraid to lose him and wanted to be there for him. She needed him and needed to be there for him. He shrank inside at the thought of almost berating her and showing her who was in charge.

"We do make a good team," Kade said. He was not sure what he did wrong, but a single tear slid down her cheek. He chastised himself for being such an empty-headed ox. *Why do I have to always hurt her?* he asked himself, frustrated that interacting with her was always full of pitfalls. Before he could apologize for this latest mistake that had her in tears again, she spoke.

"Good. Now at least I will know when you are going to kill yourself," Darcienna said half playful but full of relief. Kade was completely off balance. If he had made her sad, why was she teasing him and smiling? Exasperated, he took a deep breath, held it, and let it out slowly. And then...closed his mouth. This was way past his ability to understand.

Okay, now, how did I go from being in charge to this being a partnership? he thought as he examined the conversation. *Was it her tears that did it to me? Was it really the right thing? Next I'll tell her she can make all the decisions,* Kade thought sarcastically in a huff. He shook his head and decided it was best to just not think about it. His head was starting to hurt, trying to solve this mystery. He needed to change the subject to something easier.

"By the way, how far can you extend that shield of yours? We were at least thirty feet from you."

"I'd say about thirty feet," Darcienna said with a smile. "I've never tried to use it any further than that. As it turned out, I was just barely able to get it around you. If it weren't for your animal, you would have been dead," Darcienna said as she moved her hand to brush a hair out of her face. Kade took that moment to remove his hand from her knee. "After the first blast, the shield almost failed. One more hit, and I would have lost it," she said.

"Well, you did great. It did not matter when it failed. You saved my life," Kade said with a smile.

"I did, didn't I?" Darcienna said, brightening considerably.

"Yes," Kade said as he turned to look into her eyes. He wanted her to see that he meant every word he spoke. He looked deep into those rivers of blue and felt as if he could lose himself in her loving eyes forever. "Yes, you really did," he repeated as she beamed at him.

"Kade," Judeen said, breaking up the interaction.

Kade colored slightly as he realized his parents had been watching the entire interaction. Sitting directly in front of him and he missed that they were completely quiet, taking in everything that was going on. Or, was it that they were just giving him the courtesy of being quiet while he and Darcienna worked out this issue?

"Are you going to introduce us to your girl?" Garig questioned while making a point of chastising him for ill manners.

Kade paused, completely caught off guard by his father's query. His mind tried to grasp the implication. He opened his mouth to say something, anything, but his mind was blank.

Why in the Great Divine would they assume she is my girl? he wondered, shaking his head to himself. He considered his father's words and smiled slightly at the idea. Before he could fully enjoy the thought, he remembered how she said she was in love with a guy she had met only once, the father of her son. Darcienna stiffened at the question. *Was she repulsed by the idea?* he asked himself. Kade turned cold, feeling as if his heart were being choked. Jealousy made men do stupid things, and Kade was definitely a man through and through.

"She is not my girl, Father. She has another man in her heart, a man she has not seen in over a year and a half," he said bluntly, wanting to hurt her the same way he was hurting. In the next instant, he regretted striking out at her and wilted. He cursed himself for being a fool ten times over. If there ever was a chance to be with her, it was sure not going to happen now.

Darcienna's head came up with a snap, as she inhaled sharply. Kade had a sick feeling in his stomach and wanted to throw himself from the dragon. Nothing was ever going to go right where she was concerned, and now he had just destroyed any chance he had. It just wasn't, and he chastised himself for the fool he was. She dropped her head and Kade got the feeling she was going to cry again. He tried to ignore it, and even tried to tell himself he really had not said anything that was not true. *It is what she told me,* he reminded himself. But, even he knew it was a weak argument and gave up trying to convince himself.

After a moment more, he conceded no matter what he thought, he had blundered horribly. He took a breath to tell her he was wrong and how sorry he was but could not find the right words and closed his mouth. He wanted to tell her he only said it because he was hurt and he did not mean it, but when he opened his mouth to try again, he could not get the words to come.

Why can't I be this other guy? Kade thought desperately.

"I'm sorry, Son. With the way you and she were going on, it sounded like you two were already a...," Garig was saying when Judeen hit him in the ribs. He grunted and turned to glare at his wife. She was not fazed even a little by that glare.

"You have said enough, dear," Judeen said easily.

Kade had caught the odd tone in his father's voice, as though there were more to his words. If he could have seen the look on his parents' faces, he would have seen the smiles that slowly grew. He wallowed in his misery.

"You can still introduce us," Judeen said.

"You're right, Kade," Darcienna said. There was hurt mixed with fire in her words. "I did fall in love with a man over a year and a half ago, and I didn't even know his name. Is there anything else you want to say?" She fought to keep from crying. "How about the fact that the man never even took the time to come back to see me? How about the fact that the man does not even know about his child?" Darcienna asked, anger now the dominant emotion.

Kade could not even bring himself to respond. The hurt in her voice took all the fight out of him. He had humiliated her. He had embarrassed her in front of his parents. Kade hesitated, afraid of how they may now judge her, and it was entirely his fault. He hated himself for not thinking before he spoke. He wished he would have just sat without speaking a word until they had reached their destination. All he had managed to do was upset her and make her cry.

Not only did I hurt her again, he reminded himself painfully, *but I have crushed any chance I had to get close to her,* he concluded as he recalled how her hand felt on his just minutes ago.

Kade's mind struggled to figure out a way to fix this disaster. How could he make her look better in his parent's eyes? It had been only one guy, one time. That had to be something. He considered making this point to his parents but something in him knew that he should just stop. Defeated, he slumped in his seat.

"My name is Darcienna," she said.

"How long have you two been…," Judeen started to ask and paused in midsentence, as though she was choosing her words

301

carefully. "...been traveling together?"

"Just one day. Kade saved me from some of Morg's monsters," Darcienna said. "They killed my teacher and were trying to kill me when he showed up with his dragon. If it were not for him, I wouldn't be here right now."

Kade thought he heard a slight tone of admiration and respect in her voice. He dismissed it and continued to listen. He was glad to hear her speaking again. Judeen always did have the gift of talk. Darcienna appeared to find conversing with his mother very easy. Kade wished he had his mother's talent.

"What were you studying?" Judeen asked.

"I was being taught to use powers gifted to me by Nature. Those of us with the Gift are connected to nature. It takes many years of practice and patience, but the rewards are well worth it," Darcienna said with pride, starting to let the tension in her voice fade.

Kade smiled, despite himself. He felt proud of her without even knowing why. After a moment, he realized that she had worked as hard toward her studies as he had with his. He admired her for her efforts and found himself wanting to tell her, but he did not want to interrupt the conversation. Darcienna was sounding better and better by the moment. He was not going to take the chance and bumble into a good thing, messing it all up as he was so good at doing lately. Suddenly, Kade realized what his mother was doing and smiled. She was trying to get Darcienna's mind off what had just happened, and it was working. He took a deep breath and let it out, grateful for his mother's own special gift.

"Wouldn't you say, Kade?" Judeen asked, waking Kade up from his thoughts.

"What? I am sorry. I wasn't listening."

"I was saying that all the work Darcienna has done is impressive, don't you think?" Judeen said, drawing Kade into the conversation.

Kade was surprised and impressed with his mother's tactics. Never the less, it was working. He decided to thank her later.

"Yes, she has put a lot of work into her studies. You should see all she had to go through to become..." Kade paused as he searched for the word.

"An Essence Guardian," Darcienna added.

"An Essence Guardian," Kade repeated. "She can make things happen by just wanting them to happen," Kade said excitedly.

"Yes, but you should see Kade! What he can do is much more impressive than my few abilities. The way he used lightning to kill the creature that attacked me was amazing. He destroyed it easily," Darcienna said with enthusiasm.

"Yes, but it was your shield that saved your life and your boys life, not to mention mine and my parents," Kade said, enjoying the exchange.

"Yes, but without you, I would have been killed," Darcienna said, truly trying to give him the credit.

"But, without you, I would have been killed by that blast from Morg."

There was a moment of silence as Kade realized he was turned, facing her. She looked down at her hands and a small smile quirked at the edges of her mouth, happy that most of the tension between her and Kade had evaporated. Darcienna and Kade paused as they realized that Garig and Judeen were deep into a conversation of their own.

"They are a lot further along than I would have guessed for just meeting each other," Judeen whispered.

"They fight like they are a couple and they don't even know it," Garig said as he chuckled. "Were we like that when we first met?"

"I don't remember. I do remember that you were pretty feisty in those days," Judeen said with a sly look in her eyes.

"Me? I think it was you that was the feisty one," Garig said as he laughed.

"You are the one who used to follow me around like a puppy dog, every time I would come to town," Judeen said teasingly.

"Don't flatter yourself. You always wanted me to follow you," Garig said and grinned at her. "Well, you can't blame me with the way you swung those hips every time you walked by."

"No, of course not," Judeen said with a little laugh. "But then, I did know we were destined to get married after our first night alone," she said as she blushed furiously.

Garig and Judeen stopped talking at the same moment, both noticing the silence. They looked at each other and then quickly turned to see Kade and Darcienna hanging on their every word. Kade grinned widely at them.

"Oh, don't stop on our account," Kade said as he laughed loudly.

"Yes. I was rather enjoying this," Darcienna said as she gave out a musical laugh of her own.

Garig smiled a genuine smile as he looked upon the face of his son. It always made his heart sing to see Kade happy. He joined in with the laughter, and pretty soon, all the passengers on the dragon were laughing to the point of tears. After several long, sidesplitting moments, the group finally fell silent, each lost in their own thoughts. It was almost an hour later before anyone spoke.

"Kade, I would really appreciate it if we could stop. My back and legs are killing me, and I am hungry. Would you mind?" Darcienna asked. The boy started to fidget and whine a little to support her request.

"I would agree. I think my parents would like a chance to stretch their legs."

"Yes," Garig said.

"Please," Judeen added.

Rayden was more than happy to stop. He was breathing heavily but not to the point of exhaustion. Kade smiled as he knew what would make this worth it for the dragon. He turned to watch his parents from the corner of his eye as he addressed his oversized companion.

"Would you be hungry, by any chance?" Kade asked. The dragon perked up instantly and Kade started to laugh. He worked the Food Calling and tossed the chunk of meat to his friend. Kade was ready for the dragon's lightning quick reflexes as it launched itself at the food. His parents were not. Kade grinned to himself. Garig flinched hard and almost fell on his butt as he scrambled back, while his mother gave a squeak and did fall on her backside. The loud clash of teeth as it snapped up the meat made him smile. Garig glared at Kade, knowing his son knew what to expect but conveniently forgetting to inform them. Kade chuckled despite himself but tried to give them an innocent look.

"Kade, those are your parents. That was not nice," Darcienna scolded.

"You never change, Son," Judeen said as she shook her head, but there was a glint in her eye. Kade knew she may not say it, but his sense of humor kept things interesting, if not fun. It was never boring with him around.

Darcienna looked back and forth between Kade and his parents, trying to figure out the mood. It did not take her long to see that this was something Kade's parents were used to. After seeing no real harm had come from this, and seeing that his parents were truly not angry, she grinned despite herself.

"Now, what was that?" Garig asked in awe as he pointed between Kade and the dragon.

"The food?" Kade asked casually.

"Yes. What was that?" Judeen asked a little wide-eyed, also.

Darcienna seemed confused as she glanced from the

apprentice to his parents. Kade saw the look on her face and took a long breath and let it out, considering how much he should tell her. She glanced questioningly at him and raised an eyebrow.

"It's a long story. I will explain later," Kade said.

"Well, how about you sum it up for me right now? If you don't, I am sure you will conveniently forget to tell me," Darcienna said.

"Okay, okay," Kade said as he held his hands up in surrender.

"The short story of it is that I was taken from my home at around the age of ten and I have not seen my parents since." He turned back to Judeen and Garig, who were waiting for him to answer. Darcienna's eyes widened at this news, and she realized that there was, indeed, too much story for him to tell right then.

"You were about to explain that to us," Judeen coaxed as she indicated the food the dragon had just inhaled.

"Actually," Kade said, very much enjoying drawing this out. "It is something I just recently learned." He hesitated for dramatic effect. His dad gave him that look that dads give their sons when they are starting to get out of line. Kade continued. "It is simple, really," Kade said, dropping all pretenses. "The most difficult part should have been calling the Divine Power to do my bidding, but lately, it has been increasingly easy," he said as a stray thought drifted through his mind. "It's almost as if it seeks me out," he said absentmindedly. Kade shook it off and continued with his explanation. "Basically, I call on the Divine and mold it to what I am trying to create. I make certain movements with my hands and speak the language. If I have done it right, the food appears."

"Oh, don't let him convince you it is that easy. He makes it look easy," Darcienna said. "Just making food could kill him," she said as she looked at him accusingly. It was almost a glare. Almost. Kade sensed there was a, "Be careful with that power" in her tone. He shrugged his shoulders casually, as if to downplay the seriousness of the issue and grinned sidelong at her. She threw up her hands and huffed in exasperation as she turned away and stomped over to a log, sitting down heavily. Kade turned his back and his grin spread from ear to ear. He had no doubt when she had her chance to repay him, she would and then some.

"Okay, yes, there is some danger, but we train constantly to keep safe. There is always danger, but Zayle taught me well. As for the Food Calling, it was a little work to get everything right, but I have a good handle on it now. It just takes focus," Kade said as he smiled genuinely at his parents. Judeen returned the smile but Garig was not looking at him. Kade's mother seemed pleased and at ease but Kade noticed that his father was not. Garig was trying to look everywhere but at him. Kade sensed that they were about to have one of those talks; a talk that a father has with a son who he believes is making a questionable decision or is showing poor judgment. Kade resigned himself to address what it was after everyone had a chance to eat and relax.

"I am sure you are hungry?" Kade asked his parents.

"Yes," Darcienna said quickly.

"We could all use some food and rest," Judeen put in smoothly. Garig said nothing. Kade studied his father, concerned about what could be troubling him. He sighed and then prepared to feed the group.

"Okay. Some meat, cheese and bread coming up," Kade said as he moved into an open space for the calling. The dragon was right there with him as it eagerly licked its lips. Kade put his hands on the dragon's chest and pushed. Rayden resisted, not wanting to move. Something hit Kade in the head, and he jumped back as he ran his hand through his hair. "Again?" Kade asked with frustration. "Would you please drool on someone else next time?" he asked as he wiped his hands on the grass. "Uggg," was all he said as he wiped his hair with leaves until he was satisfied he had removed as much of the slime as possible.

Kade shook his head and returned to stand in the middle when he caught a look on Darcienna's face. He turned to look directly at her while she tried to hide her mouth with the back of her hand. Her shoulders were shaking slightly. Kade glared at her but that only served to make it considerably worse as she broke out into laughter.

So, it's going to be like that is it? he thought. But, seeing her happy caused the edges of his mouth to twitch just slightly.

"Someone is not going to get any food if they keep distracting me," Kade said as he pretended to scold her.

"Well, at this rate, no one is going to get any, regardless," Darcienna quipped back.

"Hush," Kade said.

"Okay, okay. Sorry," Darcienna responded, smiling sweetly.

Kade was about to start again when he saw a knowing look pass between his mother and father. They grinned and looked back at him. Kade glared at them as if to say, "Stop," clearly getting the meaning that had passed between them. They both held their hands up as if to say okay, but the smile never left their faces.

Kade took an exasperated breath and let it out forcefully, readying himself. He prepared to start the calling, and for just a second, felt fear at the possibility of failing in front of his parents. He chastised himself for even thinking the thought as he had just performed the calling flawlessly moments before. Again, he shook his head and closed his eyes, focusing on the meat in his memory. Even though he was a bit more nervous under the watchful gaze of his parents, the food materialized perfectly. Kade let out a relieved breath. The dragon danced eagerly, waiting.

"I will give you some shortly. Rayden, you will have to wait your turn," Kade said to the dragon while it looked from the meat to Kade's eyes then back to the meat again. "Shortly," Kade repeated, allowing the thought to travel through the mental link they shared.

The dragon seemed to be pained by this as it emitted a pathetic whine. He shook it off and turned to hand the meat to his mother but Judeen waived it over to Darcienna.

"You take it," Judeen said politely as she stared at the food, clearly eager to have a piece of the juicy meat. Darcienna saw the look in Judeen's eyes and held her hand up, refusing the offer.

"It would be rude of me and I would take offence if you were to think I would be so uncivilized to eat before the elder female that is present," Darcienna said smoothly and elegantly. Kade was stunned at what appeared to be much practiced etiquette. He got the image of someone sitting proper and straight backed while they adjusted their dress to ensure an appropriate appearance. Judeen was caught off guard, not expecting such a perfectly worded response. Kade grinned as Judeen reached out for the food.

"If you insist," Judeen said evenly.

"I do," Darcienna responded with a glint in her eye. It was all Kade could do to keep from laughing out loud. It was rare that anyone every outmaneuvered his mother in conversation.

Kade closed his eyes and performed the calling again. Shortly, he had another piece of steaming meat almost too hot for his hands. Kade went to hand it to Darcienna who again held up her hand to refuse. Kade glanced at his father and saw him cock his head, ready for what was to come.

"Your father is clearly next," Darcienna said, expecting nothing less than for Garig to take the food.

"Oh no," Garig said as he fixed her with a stare. "It would be rude of me and I would take offence if you were to think I would be so uncivilized as if to eat before any female that is present," Garig said, tossing her words back at her. She tried to find an argument but did the best imitation of a fish gaping that Kade had ever seen. Garig raised his brows as if to challenge her and the contest was over instantly. Darcienna smiled a warm smile and there was an instant connection of affection between the two.   Kade grinned as he prepared to return to what he mentally called his kitchen. He almost laughed at his own joke and then created another piece of meat. He handed it to his father and then created bread for the boy.

Rayden danced every time the Apprentice Chosen performed the calling, but Kade kept him at bay with mental reassurances that he would get his share. He made sure never to promise to fill the dragon until it was stuffed as he was not sure if that was even possible. Kade created cheese and handed it around to everyone in the proper order, since that was now established and then created bread. He moved over toward his dragon to feed the endless eating machine and glanced back at Darcienna as she let out a musical laugh. He looked on proudly as his parents and Darcienna were engaged in animated conversation while they ate. Darcienna was describing something she found exciting and would gesture grandly with her arms as she spoke. His parents would then look at him briefly during the story and laugh. It was a good laugh. Obviously, he was the main character in the story. He made a mental note to ask her about it later. He could not be happier at that moment, and he soaked up every bit of it.

Seeing that everyone was content, Kade turned to his beautiful, silver dragon, with the huge golden eyes, and smiled widely. Rayden huffed and danced from side to side, eager for what was to come. Kade created chunks of meat over and over until he felt sweat start to form on his shirt. He had lost count but the dragon was always ready for the next piece. When Kade felt his breathing start to pick up considerably, he held his hands up in surrender and patted the dragon on the neck as if to say, "You are done." Rayden moved to the edge of the clearing, and after making several circles, dropped to the ground and curled up.

"Kade, you need to eat," Darcienna said

Garig and Judeen had finished their food and were wiping the grease off their hands onto the grass, but Darcienna still had a good amount of food left. He smiled and felt such a fondness for her because she was waiting to eat with him so he would not have to eat alone. That little act of consideration made such a difference to him that he could not even begin to put it into words. He decided, at that moment, no matter what it took, or who this guy was that she had fallen in love with, he would do what it took to win her heart. With this, failure was not an option. This stranger had had his chance and blew it.

"We only have a little way to go," Garig said.

"To where?" Kade asked as he sat on the log next to Darcienna.

"Your mother and I bought a piece of land that is so secluded only the previous owner knows where it is. We built a cabin there. It took us years, but it's perfect."

"We bought the land two years ago when your father decided to quit being peace keeper. He would have quit sooner, but we could not decide where we wanted to live. It had to be somewhere safe and somewhere secluded," Judeen said.

"What happened to your land up north?" Kade asked around a mouth full of food. Judeen gave him a look that Kade instantly recognized, even though it had been so long since he saw it last. He definitely still felt like a kid in his parent's presence.

"Sorry," Kade said, hiding his mouth with his hands. He swallowed before speaking again.

"We decided we did not like the weather there. It is too cold," Garig said.

"I guess Morg helped move those plans along," Kade said, wanting it to be a joke but no one laughed.

Both parents gave a disgusted grunt at the name. Kade dropped the subject immediately. He took a huge bite of bread and chewed hungrily. He followed that with a large bite of juicy meat and used the juice to help the bread go down. He sat in silence while he pondered what he wanted to do next. Darcienna, Garig and Judeen were talking but much calmer now. Kade half listened but his mind was far away. As he finished his food and stood, so did his father. Kade stopped and looked at him, waiting for him to speak. It was no coincidence that his father had stood with him. Garig had a grave look in his eyes that put a knot in Kade's stomach. He started to worry about what was on his father's mind.

"Son, I would like a word with you," Garig said as he headed across the clearing to the other side. Kade looked at his mother for a hint of what was troubling his father, but she just smiled at him while she sat straight and proper. Darcienna looked at Kade and cocked her head as if to ask, "What is happening." Kade shrugged his shoulders slightly and turned to follow his father.

She could have been a queen with her mannerisms and posture, Kade thought as he glanced at his mother. Judeen sat with her hands in her lap and her back straight. Her facial expressions were always calm and easy, but she could convey anything with just a look in her eye. Kade turned his attention back to his father and continued to follow him.

"Kade," Garig said and hesitated, trying to find the words. "Kade…I was against you going away with Zayle," he said as he turned to look out over the land. Kade stood still, waiting for his father to continue. Garig was thinking as he searched the horizon, as if what he was looking for might be there. After a moment, he sighed and turned to look his son in the eyes. "I was against this because I knew it was too dangerous. We rarely ever saw Zayle. He used to tell us it was for the best. He used to say if he was around, he would only bring danger." Garig took a deep breath and forged on, working his way toward what was bothering him. "He visited us one day and said you had a very dangerous path to walk in life, and for the sake of the world, you had to walk it."

Kade got a sinking feeling in his stomach. His parents

312

obviously knew things that he did not. He stood quietly, waiting, knowing that his father had much more to say. Garig gave Kade a chance to respond, but seeing that his son was content to stay quiet, he continued.

"He told us he would need to take you away and train you in the use of the Divine Power, when you were old enough. He said the Chosen had discovered that you had the potential to call on immense amounts of power but it could destroy who you are," Garig said as a grim look crossed his face. "He told us the chance of you actually developing the ability was so slim he considered not even trying. It was the only reason I agreed. But, when he actually held you and looked into your eyes while you were still just a babe, he decided it was worth trying. I expected that since the chances of you developing this ability were so slim, you would just be returned. But, as he held you, I watched him, Kade. I saw the way he looked at you that day."

Garig looked away and Kade got the feeling that his father was trying to decide how much he should tell. He got a sick feeling in his gut but still said nothing. Garig took another deep breath and continued.

"I did not see hope in his eyes, Kade," Garig said and then paused as if he might stop there. After several long seconds of contemplation, he continued. "I saw fear," Garig said as he looked his son in the eyes. "Fear," he repeated.

Kade felt like everything was moving too fast. His head was starting to spin. He felt a pain begin to grow in his chest as a profound sadness descended on him.

Why would he say that? Kade thought. *Why fear? Who looks at a baby and sees fear? I thought I was supposed to be a savior.* Kade found he was looking at the ground and lifted his eyes to find his father watching him.

"Why would there be fear in Zayle's eyes, Son? For someone as powerful as Zayle to show fear...," Garig said and then left it unfinished.

"I don't know," Kade said and broke eye contact with his father. "Is that why you reacted the way you did when we were on the tower?" he asked, as he kicked a rock around with his foot. Kade looked up, and for just a brief moment, he thought he saw an accusation in those eyes. It was gone instantly as if it had never been. Kade saw nothing but a loving man looking back at his son. Garig looked off into the distance again.

There is more? Kade thought to himself incredulously. He waited.

"I don't know everything," Garig said, still studying the horizon. "Zayle and your mother talked about it. Your mother was reluctant to tell me, and I did not want to hear any more so I did not push."

"What else?" Kade asked quietly, afraid to know. Garig continued staring off into the distance for a long time. Kade did not look at his father, but instead, stood looking off into the same horizon. Garig could have stood there for hours, and still, Kade would not have moved one inch. "What else?" Kade asked and then added one word almost too soft for Garig to hear. "Father?"

Garig sighed and his shoulders slumped, as if in resignation. Kade could feel…something from his father, but he could not quite figure out what it was. It was not fear. What was it? And then Kade realized what it was. It was uncertainty.

"He stood holding you for so long, Kade. He looked at you as if he were holding the fate of the world in his hands. He stood for so long," Garig said as he relived the memory. "He did not know I was watching from the hall. I stood completely still, afraid, hardly breathing. Zayle scared me. He still scares me," he said as he swallowed hard.

Kade knew there was more, and he felt his father trying to work up the courage to say what it was. The suspense combined with

314

the dread of what his father was trying to say was making his head spin faster. Kade was not sure if he wanted to hear it or not.

His mind wandered back to a lesson Zayle had given him about knowledge. At the time, it was just babble, but now it hit home hard. "Knowledge is power, Kade," Zayle used to assert. "Just one single thought can change the world. Just one small piece of information could change the course of history. An idea can save lives or take them," Zayle would preach, but to Kade, it was always just talk. It was the next part that Kade thought was nothing more than the ranting of an old man, but now, it made more sense than ever. "Sometimes not knowing something can make more of a difference in a positive way than knowing something," Zayle would say. Kade recognized that this was one of those moments and stepped forward, turned his father toward him and hugged him tightly. When he stepped back he looked his father in the eye and said, "I love you, Father. I always will. I think it's time to get back to the women."

Kade could see all the tension and stress melt out of the man he had not seen for ten years, as relief flooded out of him. Kade smiled at his father and Garig saw only his son standing before him once more. He reached up with his hands, squeezed Kade's arms in affection and then turned to go.

"I take it you two had a good talk?" Judeen asked, as she barely gave Kade a look, her eyes locking with Garig's. He hesitated for just a moment as he glanced at his son. Kade smiled at his father with admiration, respect and love. Garig eased a bit more. That seemed to quell any concerns Garig was having…for the time being.

"Yes," Garig said as he clapped his son on the shoulder. "We talked," he said with a smile. He nodded once while looking at Kade.

"Good," Judeen said, but she did not take her eyes off her husband. She did not even blink. He sighed as he sat next to his wife and patted her hands. Kade could swear he heard him whisper, "It's ok," but was not sure.

He smiled warmly at his mother and was only able to keep that smile until he turned away. He walked over to his dragon with a heavy heart. He felt his head swimming as he tried to grasp what had just happened. He felt lost and more confused than he had ever felt at any other time in his life. He put his hand on the top of Rayden's head and stroked his ridges absentmindedly. Rayden lazily looked up at Kade and then settled back down to sleep.

Why do I feel like I am a piece in some game that others are playing? Kade thought to himself. *And, what could terrify my father so much that it scared him to death to tell me? What is all this?* The world was spinning out of control and he had no way to stop it.

Kade was deep in thought when he heard a commotion behind him. It took a moment for him to realize that Darcienna was calling his name. He turned around, and froze, staring at the silky, black creature that was lying in the clearing, panting heavily with its tongue lolling out in the dirt. He shook his head as he came completely out of his thoughts, and his eyes widened at what he was seeing.

"Chance!" Kade exclaimed in surprise.

"He needs water," Darcienna said, her voice thick with concern.

"He just barely made it right there and then collapsed," Judeen said.

The animal must have been running hard to catch up. Its eyes were rolling back in its head from exhaustion as its chest heaved hard, trying to catch its breath. Kade knelt down and ran his hand over its head. Chance did not respond. Kade looked up to see Rayden watching with curiosity.

"Rayden, water. Can you find water?" Kade asked in a rush. Rayden tilted his head back and forth, and then he lifted his nose to the air, inhaling. Kade closed his eyes and merged his mind with the dragon. He found he was so strongly linked he could have been the dragon. There was water. It was close. "Rayden, take me to it,"

316

Kade said as he scooped up the silky creature and quickly climbed onto the dragon's back.

"I will return soon," Kade said as he gave the dragon the signal to go.

Rayden whipped around to the north, almost dislodging his rider. Kade would not have had it any other way. He owed his life to this little, black creature and he was not going to let it die. The dragon was moving so quickly that when they burst into the opening at the edge of the river, they splashed right in. The water came up to Kade's legs. The dragon turned, trudged back to shore and knelt down, already sensing Kade's intent.

Kade leapt down and laid Chance at the edge of the water. He cupped his hands in the life saving liquid and let it drizzle over the creature's nose. Chance's tongue came out weakly to lap up the water. Kade scooped up as much as his hand would hold and to let it drizzle over the creature's tongue. He performed the Healing Calling, which seemed to help revive it. Its eyes cleared and soon, its nose was working furiously. Kade leaned back and sat on his haunches as he watched the creature roll over to get its legs under itself. It shuffled forward to the water and dropped down, drinking deeply. Kade smiled and breathed a huge sigh of relief.

Kade reached out and ran his hand down the silky, black creature's back. He performed the Healing Calling again and Chance appeared to respond quickly. He looked at Kade and then went back to his drink.

Kade stood as he watched the strength return quickly to this magnificent creature. It did not take Chance long to get his fill. Kade reached for Chance, expecting to take him back the way they had come but the creature moved away.

"Someday, my little friend," Kade said as he let his hands fall to his sides. "Okay then, you will need to walk, but I would have thought that you would have appreciated a ride," he said as he looked over his shoulder at the dragon. Kade froze as he noticed that Rayden was locked onto his little friend. Rayden moved forward slowly as he approached the creature. Chance turned toward the dragon and the two were nose to nose. Kade was on the verge of yelling at Rayden when he stopped with the words still in his throat. They were learning each other's scent. After just a few moments, they separated and Kade breathed a sigh of relief as the tension melted from his body. The dragon moved back a ways and slumped to the ground.

"I bet you would like a little of this," Kade said as he molded the Divine into a hot, steaming, juicy piece of meat. The creature's whiskers twitched furiously as it locked its eyes on the food. Kade tossed the meat to Chance and watched as he laid down to his meal. It used its paws like hands as it twisted and turned the meat over and over as it ate. "You will never get that anywhere else my little friend," Kade said as he smiled. "I bet that is why you keep following me, eh?"

Kade stooped and took a long drink of the fresh, clean water. He closed his eyes and enjoyed the taste of it as it slid down his throat. It helped to clear his head.

He sat down as close to the creature as it would allow. He did not blame it for still being cautious, since it was his dragon that almost ate it. But, sooner or later, it was going to trust him. He stayed right there until it had finished its meal. Kade looked up at the sky and decided it was time to get back to the group. He was sure they would be worrying. He walked over to the dragon that was still lying down and vaulted onto its back. He looked at the creature and marveled at how fast it seemed to recover. It showed no signs of ever being anything other than a healthy animal. Kade could not help but to ask himself if there were such things as creatures with powers, with how fast it seemed to recover.

"You sure you don't want a ride?" Kade asked. The creature just kept its distance as it watched. "Have it your way," he said as he urged the dragon to stand.

Rayden heaved himself up lazily and turned back toward the they had come. He started at a slow, lazy lope. Kade looked over to see Chance attempting to keep pace with them.

Those healings must have really done the job, Kade thought. The dragon sniffed the air several times and then turned to look at the creature. Rayden increased his speed to a smoother gait and casually swung his head forward again. Kade looked over, surprised to see that Chance was now actually keeping pace. Rayden lazily swung his head around toward the creature and added yet more speed. Kade felt the wind in his hair with the increase of their pace. Smiling, he looked over to see the creature gracefully running along as it stretched out to keep up with the dragon, yet again. It flowed as it covered ground easily. The dragon swung its head around, again, to look at the creature. Kade grinned furiously, leaning close to the dragon's neck and grabbed hold of the ridges tightly, knowing what was coming. And, it did. The dragon's muscles turned rock hard and it launched.

Kade felt the exhilaration race through him and turned to see how far behind the creature was. He flinched hard as his eyes landed on Chance, right next to them. He watched in astonishment as the animal raced along next to them at the breakneck speed. The cat-like grace and agility of the animal left Kade speechless. Chance's claws raked the ground, giving him the traction needed to propel his slender body forward and keep pace with the mighty Rayden. Kade laughed hard at the game and knew he would never have to worry about the dragon eating his silky, little friend ever again. Although the creature was most definitely fast, Kade was sure, sooner or later, it would have to back off, and he was correct. Looking off to his right, he was surprised to see that Chance was no longer beside them.

He urged Rayden to slow and give the creature a chance to catch them. The dragon continued to reduce its speed in stages, and still, there was no sign of the black creature.   They were almost at a walk when they entered the clearing.

"I think it is about time we continue," Kade said, giving up on finding his fast, little friend.

"I think you are right," Judeen agreed.

It was not long before they were on the dragon, moving along smoothly once more. Kade was quiet as his mind kept replaying the conversation with his father. Nothing made sense.

It was almost as if my own father believes that I..., Kade started to think, but he could not continue the thought. It would have hurt too much to know his own father looked at him as an aberration. It just could not be. He did not feel like a bad person. He was good. He was. He had to be.

They all sat quietly, lost in their own thoughts. Darcienna laid her head against Kade's back. He started to wonder if she had fallen asleep but then she would shift. The boy was sleeping again. He was sure it was the rolling motion of the dragon that soothed the child, and he thanked the Divine for it. Because of his chat with his father, his nerves were on edge and a crying boy would have definitely made things tense.

Garig continued to give directions as they moved through the countryside. Kade felt his mind start to relax as the beauty of his surroundings made him feel more at peace. It was not long before they could see a cabin in the distance. Garig leaned back and pointed to it.   Kade nodded his head, and before he knew it, they were stopping in front of the home.

"Would you like to go in?" Garig asked, seeing the impressed look on his son's face.

Kade marveled at the intricate woodwork as he studied the front of the cabin. This was no simple cabin but much more like a small mansion that could house two families. Massive amber-colored logs spanned the front of the house, breaking for the windows and door. The windows were of the finest glass but also thick enough to withstand the elements. The door was made from exotic woods. It was intricately carved by a master woodworker. Kade admired the craftsmanship as his eyes traced the patterns in the wood. It swung heavily on ornate hinges with a solid brass handle as Judeen opened it and stood, waiting for Garig to follow.

Before Kade could enter, Judeen put up a hand to his chest and pointed toward a shallow hot spring just inside the edge of the woods. Kade looked at her, not understanding. She scrutinized him up and down and then smiled. Kade had completely forgotten that he was coated with mud. It was dry, but nonetheless, he could understand why his mother did not want him in the house just yet. He and Darcienna took their turns washing up. After changing into fresh, clean clothes provided by his mother, they both returned to find Judeen waiting on the porch.

"This place is amazing," Kade said as he smiled. A part of him recalled the meager cabin he had lived in with Zayle and he quickly dismissed the thought.

"Let's go in," Judeen said, prompting them to follow.

Kade started to head for the door when he heard a roar off in the distance. He swung around and could have sworn it sounded just like a dragon. He quickly looked at Rayden but the dragon did not appear to be concerned. Its head was raised high as it tilted it from side to side as if to get a better fix on what it was hearing. The roar came again and Rayden perked up considerably. Garig and Judeen both looked at their son with concern. Kade watched the dragon, and seeing nothing that indicated danger, reassured his parents it was safe.

The roar came again and Rayden swung his head around to stare at Kade only to turn and stare off into the distance again. Rayden was obviously excited about something. The roar came again and with that, Kade understood. There was another of his kind out there.

"Go, have fun," Kade said. It took no more than that for the dragon race off. With a mental reminder not to fly, Kade turned back to the home.

He walked in the front door and looked at the marble that was used to make the floor. He walked from room to room with Darcienna close behind, impressed with how beautifully crafted everything was. As soon as he walked into the bedroom, he felt himself drawn to the large bed with the thick, fluffy blankets. It looked inviting and made him feel like he wanted to sleep for a week. He shook it off, deciding it was best to stay awake and chat with his parents before considering any rest.

"Go ahead," Garig said, noticing the longing look in Kade's eyes. "That is where you are sleeping tonight," he said with a smile.

"I will wait until later tonight or I won't get up for days," Kade said as he looked at the bed longingly. "Where is Darcienna going to sleep?"

"Her room is down the hall to the right. She will have a bed just like this," Garig said as he ran his hand over the plush blanket. "Follow me," he said as he led them out into the hall.

Kade continued through the cabin until he had seen everything. Garig led him out back to a river that ran just behind the property. Kade found himself wishing he could forget the world and live here with his parents. He desperately wanted to forget the name Morg ever existed.

Garig led Kade down to the river where they sat on a makeshift dock. Kade enjoyed the peace and quiet. He knew that his life was not going to afford many chances like this. For the first time in days, Kade felt his mind actually start to relax. It was as though everything had been blazing along and now things slowed to a crawl. The silence was deafening. He closed his eyes and soaked up every bit of the nothingness.

Kade felt his father looking at him, waiting for him to talk. He had a lot to talk about, as it had been ten long years since being taken away from his family. He started the story from when he met the dragon and explained everything up to the present. It took several hours to tell it all. Garig hung on every word, not asking even one question. As Kade told of the events, he felt the anger and hurt well up in him all over again. Frustration filled him.

"Father, is there anything that you can tell me that will help me fight Morg?" Kade asked with deadly seriousness.

"I can't think of…wait. Wait a minute," Garig said, perking up. "He mentioned something about a doorway to the land of the dead. He needs to find it for some reason. I think you are involved with the doorway, somehow," he said as he gave his son a questioning look.

"He didn't say where it was, did he?" Kade asked, listening intently.

"No. I don't think he knows where it is," Garig replied as he studied Kade's expression.

"That may be to our advantage," Kade said thoughtfully.

The two men sat in silence for several long moments, each one in his own mind. Garig was trying his best to recall anything else from the last few days that might be helpful, and Kade was trying to recall ever hearing Zayle talk about a doorway of any kind. Neither was able to find any memory that was useful.

"You know you can stay here if you want," Garig said as he looked out over the river. He did not need to see his son, or even hear his response, to know what it would be.

"I can't," Kade said, not looking at his father. "Right now, I may be the only Chosen alive. I have heard stories of others, but that is the best I have…for now. I have to try and stop Morg. Anyway, I don't believe Morg will stop searching for anyone who can use the Divine Power, or any special abilities, so that means I'll never be safe until I stop him," Kade said as he shrugged lightly.

"I knew you would say that," Garig said with a sigh.

"I would like to come back and stay with you when this is all over," Kade said, leaving out "If I survive."

"You are welcome to stay with us as long as you want, whenever you want," Garig said as he put his hand on Kade's shoulder.

"Thanks, Father." Kade paused before continuing.

Kade glanced at the cabin and wondered what she might be talking about with his mother. Or, more to the point, what embarrassing things his mother may be saying about him. Regardless, he wanted to see her.

"Let's go back and see what the girls are doing," Garig said, seeing the look on his son's face. There was a knowing look in the older man's eye.

Kade looked at his father, and for just an instant, was sure the man could read his mind. He narrowed his eyes suspiciously and Garig laughed. Kade reddened slightly and grinned, despite himself. After a moment of feeling sheepish, he let out a sigh.

"Is it that obvious?" Kade asked, exasperated.

"Very," Garig said with a laugh.

"Does Mother know?"

"She knew before I did. It's your mother. What did you expect?" Garig asked as he let out another sincere laugh. He was definitely enjoying seeing his son squirm.

Without another word, they got to their feet and returned to the cabin. They met up with the girls in Darcienna's bedroom as they prepared a place for Marcole to sleep. Darcienna stopped for a moment and gave him a smile. Kade felt his heart light up and then glanced at his father, who was grinning widely at him.

"Father," Kade hissed and walked out of the room. The only response he heard was a good hearted laugh as he walked down the hall. He could not help but to smile to himself.

"Kade," Judeen called as he was walking away. He stopped, hearing something in her voice that slowly melted the smile from his face. He slowly turned to see his mother reach into a pocket and pull out an envelope that had been folded in two. Garig exited the room and froze when his eyes saw what his wife was holding. The happiness that had been there just moments before was nowhere to be seen.

"Mother?" Kade asked, recognizing his grandfather's writing.

"He said you were to have this," she said as she extended the envelope to him. Her hand was shaking as she tried to keep her emotions from showing. Kade stared at the envelope without moving. He closed his eyes as he fought to keep the pain from returning. "He said it was important for you to have this."

Kade felt a tear slide down his cheek and opened his eyes to see his mother sharing his pain. His feet felt heavy as he forced them to move forward. Darcienna watched, wishing she could be at his side. Kade looked his mother in the eyes and she swallowed hard while urging him to take the letter. He took a deep breath to help calm his nerves and reached for the envelope. Garig turned to stone. He was tempted to lunge for the letter and tear it to pieces.

Kade gently held the letter and slowly tore the end open. His heart started to pound as it did anytime he dealt with anything his grandfather was involved with. Before sliding the sheet of neatly folded paper out, he performed the Reveal Calling. There was nothing but a sheet of paper. He focused on keeping his hand steady as he slid the note clear of the envelope. No one said a word as they waited.

Steeling his will, he unfolded the note. It read:

If everything has gone as expected, you should know what hunts our kind. The calling on this page will allow you to communicate that knowledge to any Chosen still alive. Learn it quickly.

Kade closed his eyes and images of his grandfather danced through his mind's eye. He wished with all his heart that he could have known Zayle as other than a Master Chosen. He opened his eyes and studied the steps for the calling. His eyes drifted to the bottom of the page where he continued to read.

Tell my daughter that I wish I could have been a better father. Tell her family means everything to me and it is for this reason I have lived as I have. Tell her I love her.

I love you, Grandson. You must still be careful of the path you walk in life. Your future is far from decided. You must be very careful with the decisions you make.

Zayle

Darcienna slowly approached Kade and put a gentle hand on his arm. She glanced at the note and then gave Kade a gentle squeeze for support. He held the note out for his mother, who took it as reluctantly as he had. She could not help the tears that came. Kade could not miss his father's anger. She handed the note back and Kade turned without saying a word, walking alone back to the dock to memorize the calling.

Several hours later, the sun was starting to set. It was time. Kade called on the Divine and activated the calling. His eyes lost focus. He felt several minds connect with his.

It is Morg who hunts all Chosen, Kade thought. Shock assailed him through the link.

So you know. It changes nothing, came Morg's scathing thoughts.

You have done well, Apprentice, came another voice in his head. *We will deal with it from here.*

Kade stopped the flow of the Divine Power and the calling ended. The presences' in his mind faded. He should have been relieved that this mystery was now unraveled, but for reasons he could not explain, he was not.

For the rest of the day, Kade, Darcienna and his parents sat around talking about anything other than Morg. It was obvious that the evil Chosen was always in the backs of their minds, but it was understood that no one was to even speak his name. It was the best they could do to pretend he did not exist, and they were grateful for that much.

Unfortunately, the night was not to be without tears. Judeen asked about her father and Kade would tell all he knew. She broke down and cried many times. She continued to ask questions, laughing occasionally, agreeing that she could easily see her father doing what Kade accused him of doing. After several hours, Judeen seemed to recover a fair amount from her grief, but Kade knew it was only temporary.

After dinner, they moved outside to a deck built on the back of the house and chatted about the little things in life. Garig was more than content to sit quietly, allowing Judeen and Darcienna to talk excitedly amongst themselves. Kade was fine with just listening as he watched the sun set. The lower the bright, glowing orb sank, the more he could feel the exhaustion crashing down on him. After nodding off several times, Judeen tapped him on the arm and pointed down the hall to his room. Kade eagerly excused himself, walked to his bedroom and fell onto the bed, enjoying the way it fluffed out under him. He wanted to lie there, soaking up the relaxation for just a moment before undressing and climbing under the blanket. At least, that was the plan before he was fast asleep.

Kade was barely awakened by the soft touch of a hand on his chest. His mind felt like it was wading through molasses as it struggled to formulate thoughts. He tried to clear his head enough to get up when he felt moist, warm, wet lips against his, making his arms feel weak. He didn't know if he was asleep or not, but he did not care. He went with the dream. He allowed it to completely take him as he imagined it was Darcienna pressing against him. The thought of her caused feelings to awaken in his body, driving any sense from his mind. He felt like he was on fire as a desire slowly built within him. His hands started to follow the contours of the finely shaped flesh that was pressing its weight onto him. His pulse started to quicken as the warm, soft lips moved to his neck, sending waves of pure pleasure throughout his entire body.

Kade let himself go completely. He could not stop if he wanted. Every bit of his willpower was gone. He felt as if a tornado was building in him, crying for release, and he was willing to give it that release; was willing to beg for it, craved it more than he craved anything in his life. The sweet, seductive pleasure was so powerful that he could not stop it even if he were to call on every bit of Divine Power he could muster. The promise of such intense pleasure was more than he could take. A moan of deep pleasure slipped from him as he arched his back. Those sweet lips covered his, quelling the sound.

Kade felt a warm, moist feeling in other parts of his body and gasped. Then, the body on his started to move to the same rhythm as his. His sense of touch was heightened as a burning feeling started to course though his body. The movement became faster and faster, causing Kade to fall deep into this pleasure, craving it more than he ever craved anything in his life. At this moment, there was no such thing as Morg. For that matter, there was no such thing as Kade, or any other name. There was just pleasure beyond his wildest imagination. Just when the feeling was as intense as he could possibly imagine, he felt an explosion within himself. Every muscle in his body clenched tighter than granite as the feeling ripped through his brain. He held his breath, the sensation so intense he was sure he would lose his mind. Moments that felt like eons passed, and then slowly, ever so slowly, his muscles unknotted as he sank back into his pillow. All tension, along with any remaining anger and pain flowed from him.

Kade felt peace wash over himself, and he welcomed it. He savored the feeling of the warm mouth that had just moments before, caressed his eager lips. It was there again, and then it slowly withdrew. He lay there with his eyes closed, enjoying the feeling of relaxation that was spreading throughout his body. He felt happiness as he let himself drift where his dreams would take him. He enjoyed the most peaceful sleep he had experienced in a long time. This night he would dream about nothing but Darcienna.

THE DIVINE SERIES CONTINUES

LOOK FOR

THE DIVINE PATH

PLANNED RELEASE IN

DECEMBER 2013

and

THE DIVINE UNLEASHED

PLANNED RELEASE IN

JANUARY 2014

ABOUT THE AUTHOR

Allen Johnston is a resident in Lansing, MI. His wife, Amber, keeps life fun and interesting for him. They share four children. He loves aviation and works as an Air Traffic Controller at the Capital City of Michigan. He lives by the motto that anything is possible. When considering learning to fly, he was told that it is not possible to achieve a pilot's license in less than a month by his supervisor, who was also an instructor pilot. Needless to say, he proved that the impossible was, indeed, possible.

Allen loves to interact with his readers. He encourages everyone to send him a message from his website, www.AllenJJohnston.com or go to his Facebook page and comment there.

Made in the USA
Charleston, SC
19 June 2014